Nether Isle

By

Nicoline Evans

Author: Nicoline Evans – www.nicolineevans.com
Editing: Andrew Wetzel – www.stumptowneditorial.com
Cover Design: The Filigree – www.thefiligree.com

And a big thank you to everyone who has offered me support (in all ways, shapes, and sizes) during this entire process.

Dedicated to the lonely.

Chapter 1

The bay was calm as dawn approached. Theodore considered the water might be *too* calm. The sky shifted from black to dark purple as he waited for sunrise. An eerie silence emanated around him; it fascinated him how the quiet could be so loud. The lack of noise was overwhelming and granted him the tranquility he so desperately yearned. Nothing soothed his loneliness like the vast and serene ocean beyond. His sailboat sat in its waters, rocking slightly as the fierceness it held outside the bay trickled toward him with tenderness. The harbor kept him safe from the dangerous waters of the open sea, as did the natural landscape which created the Gulf of Maine.

Nether Isle was his home and it sat in the middle of the gulf, right between Machias, Maine and Yarmouth, Nova Scotia. This little island was an ageless sailor town, home to ancient trade, hardened people, and years of resentment. Life was tough, dirty, and unreliable. Everyone did what they had to in order to survive, no matter the means. Taking cheap shots and sneaking about was common and looked upon as clever. If a person could get away with a devious deed without hurting anyone else, then they were all the smarter for it. These deceitful types of adventures were laughed about amongst the adults as they drowned themselves in alcohol each night.

Every evening, after a day at the docks schlepping dead fish to and from the market, a crew of men gathered in Theodore's living room to commiserate with his father. They often got belligerent, shouting and partaking in rough horseplay. Theodore cringed when they joked about the scams they proudly pulled off and the innocent bystanders who suffered from their behavior. Violence wasn't tolerated among the masses, but stealing and emotional damage were not considered foul play. Theodore didn't like it, not one bit. His heart felt trapped in this lawless town and he longed for a way out.

But he lived at his father's mercy, relocating every time he got fired from a job for drunkenness. Always moving to a new place, with new faces who didn't care to know him at all. This town was just like the others. Everyone worked tirelessly, until they were sour to the world around them. They were devoid of compassion, unless showing it benefited them in some way. Theodore was still in school, but he knew his future held no more than what this town had to offer: fishing, trade, and unruliness. Nothing more, nothing less. It scared him to tears every time he imagined growing into this life.

He did his best not to think about it. He was fifteen and managed to get to this point without succumbing to this fate. Maybe, if he stayed strong, he could escape it. Maybe he'd turn out different. He wasn't sure. The only solace he found lay in the water, so he placed his troubles there where no one else would find them.

Theodore patiently waited for the sun to rise. It was the start of a new week and he had to absorb this moment of solitary peace before he faced it. He quieted his mind and let the sound of nothing caress his thoughts.

A burnt-orange sky lined the horizon, indicating the sun would soon arrive. His wooden dinghy sailboat began to rock violently despite the lack of wind. Theodore sat upright, confused. The air felt still and the waves were minimal. There was no indication of a storm brewing. Then a cool breeze whipped across his skin from the east. Theodore's eyes widened at this new foreboding sign. Still, there were no clouds above and he was desperate to see the sunrise.

The orange turned to pink. Soon he'd be able to head back to the docks. Eagerly hoping the sun would stop playing games and hurry up, Theodore's knee began to shake. The sudden anticipation to get off the water was immense; he did not want to get caught in a rainstorm. If he capsized, no one would know.

His focus was on the skyline ahead, but his intuition caused his mind to wander toward the west. He shifted his gaze toward Maudit Cove in the distance. The waves lapped aggressively against the jagged rocks surrounding it. Hitting the cove repeatedly with great force, as if punishing it for crimes unknown. Then a scream echoed into the sky. An icy chill shot through Theodore's entire body.

The cry happened a second time. It was a girl. The terrorized shriek resonated through the bitter dawn sky, carried and prolonged by the breeze that now filtered in without remorse. It knocked Theodore's boat around like a toy in a bathtub and he held on tight to prevent going over. As his heart raced thinking about the cry from the young girl in the distance, the first roll of thunder cracked, booming so loud it made him forget about the scream and refocus on his own precarious situation. He reefed the mainsail and turned his boat back toward the town. Lightning flashed, filling the entire sky with momentary brightness before returning the world to its original darkness. While it was only a second of light, it was enough to make him wish he had the sun to guide him home. Instead he remained in the middle of the cold bay with only a flashlight and the dim sunrise to help him navigate the choppy waves. Clouds covered overhead as the wind picked up and without warning, the rain came down like a blanket of frozen daggers. The raindrops stung as they hit his face. He took out his telescoping paddle and tried to steer his boat home.

Through the onslaught of rain and frequent roars of thunder, Theodore swore he heard a girl's cry again. But with all the commotion, he couldn't be sure. He looked toward Maudit Cove, squinting through the downpour, but he saw only the dark shadows of storm clouds.

He hoped it was only his imagination. *It had to be.* In any case, he had to save himself now. He was still one nautical mile from the docks and he had to get there before his small sailboat filled up with water and sunk. The sail was rolled halfway up to prevent it from capsizing. Using it to get back would have been too dangerous. Luckily, the wind was at his back, so he used his paddle to help steer the boat in the right direction. The airstream was harsh and unpredictable. It smacked the back of his skull viciously as he kept his head bowed and did his best not to let the storm take him down.

As the dock grew near, Theodore stuck his paddle straight into the water as a brake, hoping to slow down. But the wind pushed him forward at a speed he could not contain. With great effort, he managed to turn his boat by use of paddle and rudder and avoid a head-on impact. The starboard made contact with the splintered wooden dock, scratching chunks of blue paint off. Theodore cursed as he held tight his grasp and embraced the initial thud. After the collision, he hastily tethered the line of his small sailboat to the cleat as fast as he could. Then he stood with wavering balance and tried to grab hold of the dock ladder. When he finally felt secure in his upright position, a gust of wind came from the north, hitting him square in the chest. He lost his balance and fell backward into the water.

Waves smacked his face as he failed to stay afloat in the tumultuous water. He was a skilled swimmer, so he did not let his fright control his thoughts. As rationally as he could, he calmed his nerves and focused on grabbing onto the side of his boat to prevent being carried out to sea. His young muscles fought nature and eventually found purchase. Grabbing hold of the gunwale, he was able to work his way around the outer edge and back to the ladder.

The surrounding boats slammed against each other and into the beams of the high-risen dock. Theodore had to submerge beneath the water once to prevent another small boat from crushing his body against his sailboat. The scene was unbridled chaos; in most other towns, this type of destruction to one's property would cause a person great grief, but not here. On Nether Isle, everyone's vessels were beat up and worn down. No one took care of their property as they almost expected such casualties to occur to their beloved belongings. It was thought the more dings and scratches your boat had, the truer a sailor you were. Theodore didn't agree. He cringed as he watched his precious sailboat get beaten and marked by the clutter of boats below. Eyes forward, he climbed the creaky ladder away from the raging storm. Once at the port, he could focus on breathing normally again.

His body ached but he managed to reach the top of the ladder and collapse on the splintered wood of the pier as he caught his breath. The rain continued to pour down on him, but it wasn't nearly as threatening now. He let it fall on his face as he regained his composure.

Looking out to the sea, he could see a bright spot of light on the horizon. Sunrise had come and it fought to be seen through the rain clouds. He could not see it, but he knew it was there. Theodore smiled.

He stood up as the sky fell down around him. Eager to feel morning's light, he raced through the rain toward the spot of sun that battled to be seen. Dodging the missing planks and uneven boards with nails that didn't lay flat, he reached the end of the pier and found a smooth piece of wood to sit on. His feet dangled over the edge as he silently cheered the sun on, willing it to succeed. Eyes wide, he watched eagerly, waiting for the moment its warmth would hit his face.

Twenty minutes passed before the rain slowed and Theodore's patience was rewarded. The downpour trickled into a drizzle and the clouds ahead began to part ways. Between the cracks, a powerful source beamed through, lighting up the world around him. Its rays were splintered but it shone across the landscape regardless, proving, as always, that no amount of darkness could defeat light.

Theodore resigned from his morning adventure and headed home. He walked along the rickety boards that connected the entire bayside of the town together. Rejuvenated from the sun's

perseverance, he was ready to face the day.

Chapter 2

He hurried. A second wave of early morning storm clouds were passing over head and he did not want to get caught in the worst of it again.

He ran along the crooked planks that were hastily nailed together years ago. These wooden stretches made up the maze of docks that formed this side of Nether Isle. They were lined with lopsided houses that sat upon stilts and a few gaps where ladders descended to the water below.

Theodore followed his memorized route home. It was easy to get lost or confused while navigating the labyrinth of piers along the harbor. But Theodore knew the only paths he needed: home, school, the market, and the bay; all other routes were unnecessary to learn since those were the only places he ever went. The endless web of footpaths with unknown ends only enhanced his view of the town's messy and mysterious nature. He wondered, but never explored.

There was a formidable distance left to travel when the rain returned, pelting his exposed skin. The wood beneath the rubber soles of his topsiders was slick, so he ceased running and resorted to a cautious jog.

A holler echoed through the wind. Theodore was reminded of the girl's cry near Maudit Cove. Though he knew it was harsh to brush something so serious aside, Theodore was fairly certain the noise had been a figment of his imagination. *It had to be a hallucination.* His heart raced as a small space in the back of his mind wondered if it wasn't.

The shout came again. This time, Theodore saw the source: Adelaide McClaine was standing on her porch, staring at Theodore with exasperation.

"Are you crazy, boy? Get over here before you catch a bug." She waved her old and withered arms wildly, indicating he ought to obey.

Without much thought, he shifted his course and headed toward Adelaide's home. Dry as a summer's day, she shook her head in disbelief at his current state before hurrying him inside.

The fireplace was alive with flames and Theodore instinctively went to its warmth.

"Take off your shirt and give it here," she motioned with her hand, "then take the wool blanket off the sofa and sit by the fire. I can't believe you kids these days. When I was your age, we actually feared getting sick cause it meant you could die." She continued to bustle about the house with Theodore's wet shirt in hand. He sat by the fire, bundled up in the blanket, and heard her mumble something about antibiotics and modern medicine.

He still wasn't used to the accents here. Six months in and their weird blend of French and American dialects remained foreign to his ears. Smooth and choppy simultaneously. It was due to their

10

location directly between Nova Scotia, where many people spoke fluent French or English with Canadian Maritime accents, and Maine. From where he came in Alaska, this was a big adjustment. He was used to a blend of American accents and the traditional Inuit of the Eskimos. The sound produced between his last home and this one were drastically different. It was just another peculiarity to get used to, or not, depending how long his dad would be able to keep his new job here.

Adelaide returned with a large flannel button down and a mug of hot cocoa.

"Now tell me, what you were doing out of bed at 5 a.m. during a terrible storm?" Theodore took the warm drink and savored its aroma before speaking.

"I like to take my boat out on Mondays before sunrise. It helps me get through the week."

"You were on the water?" Adelaide was outraged.

"Yeah, but I saw the storm rolling in and got out in time." Theodore lied. Adelaide gave him a knowing look.

"Is that so? I suppose it was just the rain that drenched you head to toe?"

"It was coming down in buckets."

Adelaide shook her head, aware that he lied to spare her a heart attack.

"Didn't anyone warn you there was a storm coming this morning?" Adelaide continued.

"No, I had no clue. We don't have a TV in my house."

"Well, ask me next time. I see you every weeknight at work. I own a TV. I'm a pretty reliable source. Not to mention, I've lived on this island since the day I was born. I can practically smell a storm coming."

Theodore laughed and took a sip of the hot chocolate. He hadn't realized how cold he was until he felt warmth again. After a long gulp, he peered over the edge of the mug and saw Eustice standing in the shadows of the kitchen. He was Adelaide's husband, so Theodore showed him respect, but the man was very creepy. Theodore had seen him a million times but couldn't recall a single instance where the man said anything to him.

"Hi, Eustice," Theodore said kindly, hoping to coax him into a chat. Eustice, caught off guard, grunted in acknowledgement then slithered further into the shadows. Still there, but less visible. Adelaide saw her husband lurking about, watching them.

"Go away, Eustice. You're not wanted here. I told you to leave weeks ago, but you don't listen."

Theodore looked at Adelaide in shock. She was always brash with her husband, but this was new. He had never heard her sound authentically repulsed by him. Annoyed, but never hatred.

Eustice continued to linger; his facial expression did not change. He was persistent, standing there and watching Adelaide intently. Theodore noticed for the first time that he appeared to be waiting for her, patiently biding his time as she went back to ignoring him.

"Is he okay?" Theodore whispered, not wanting the old man to hear him.

"Yeah, he's just a stubborn old fart. Won't leave until I go with him. So goddamned selfish."

"Where does he want you to go with him?"

"The lighthouse."

"Apres Monde? The standalone lighthouse a few nautical miles south of Maudit Cove?"

"Of course, that one. What other lighthouse would he be speaking of?"

Theodore didn't like to see two people who once loved each other fight, especially over something so trivial.

"Well, my sailboat can hold two people. It's dark out now," Theodore said, unsure why Eustice would want to go this instant, "but you can borrow it anytime you like for a day trip."

"Are you out of your mind, boy? Do I look like I want to go to that hellish lighthouse?" Adelaide pursed her lips together, tightening some of the wrinkles along her face. "Do I seem *ready* for a trip like that?" A look of pain crossed her face, but she reminded herself Theodore was still new to Nether Isle. Her old eyes gleamed with youthfulness as they shifted from hurt back to anger at her husband. She stormed into the kitchen.

"If you don't stop harassing me about this damned issue, I will conjure up a way to be rid of you for good. I know people, I can talk to the Ouijans on Salamander Pier. They'd be happy to oblige my request."

"But my dear Adie," Eustice said, his voice barely a whisper, "I only wait because I love you. I cannot bear this journey alone."

"You have two choices: wait patiently, without pestering me, until I'm ready, or go alone. I will not have you determining my fate. It's not my fault you loved the sea more than me."

Eustice, so pale he sometimes looked like he was disappearing, nodded and shifted further into the darkness of the unlit room.

Adelaide returned to Theodore's side, "I'm sorry about that. He has become very difficult as of late. I'm trying my best to be patient, but these things are hard enough to begin with. Then having to deal with it all over again after you've already dealt with it once? It's a lot of pain for the heart to hold." She shook her head. "One of the drawbacks to living here, I suppose."

Theodore had no clue what she was talking about. Completely bewildered, he resigned from trying to help her solve her elusive problem. He assumed the elderly had their own set of dramas to deal with that he was too young to comprehend yet.

14

"Anyway," Adelaide said, "tell me about school while we wait for the rain to stop. We don't get much time to chat at the market. You've been here half a year, how is it going?"

Theodore shrugged his shoulders. He didn't like to talk about it.

"Oh, c'mon, a handsome young fellow like you must be having no problems fitting in."

"I haven't made one single friend since I moved here. They look right through me, like I'm a ghost."

A pan dropped in the kitchen, clanging against the linoleum floor loudly. Eustice remained there; his gray eyes seemed bothered.

Adelaide sighed and ignored the interruption. "Theodore, you must make more of an effort. You can't expect the lot to come flocking to you. You're new here, take the initiative."

"I have, but the only time I get is recess and lunch. I've tried to join in on the pick-up games of baseball and basketball in the yard, but they often pick me last, and then don't let me play at all." Theodore took a deep breath. "The whole thing is stupid. None of it matters. I'll probably have to move again soon anyhow, so it's better not to have friends when that happens."

"Stop being a martyr. Make the best of what's happening now. You can't control the future, but I bet you could make the time in between now and whatever happens next a lot more bearable if you found a way to be happy. I'm an old lady, and your boss, so I can't be your buddy forever."

"This is all irrelevant. I am happy. I am perfectly content by myself."

Adelaide clicked her tongue. "You are an old man in a boy's body. I hope you learn to enjoy your youth before it's gone."

Theodore shrugged. This was old news to him. He always had to be the man of his house because he couldn't count on his father to be it. His mom abandoned them years ago and he was left to hold the pieces of his crumbling family together. If his father had his way, he would have found some relative to take Theodore off his hands as a baby. Since there were no relatives that would answer his phone calls, he was stuck with an infant to raise. Time changed everything and now he relied heavily upon Theodore's smarts and work ethic to make their lives possible. The money he made from working at Adelaide's fish stand after school was the only stable income they had.

"The rain has stopped, I think you better be off. School will be starting soon."

Looking outside the window, Theodore could see the sky brightening up. He stood and folded the blanket he'd had across his shoulders.

"Do you think my clothes are dry yet?"

"No, just wear what you have on. I'll bring your shirt to the market with me for you to take home after work."

"Thanks," Theodore smiled. "And thank you for letting me stay with you until the storm passed."

Adelaide tilted her head. "Don't be silly, you're always welcome here with me."

The walk home was pleasant. People were beginning to emerge from their homes to start the day. The sun was shining and a light mist still filled the air. The moisture entangled itself into Theodore's hair, causing the sandy blond locks atop his head to stray in any direction they chose.

His house sat at the end of Crickets Pier, the last one along the main stretch, known as Peddler's Way. The small abode sat on rickety stilts, elevating it high above the volatile waves below. Behind it sat jagged cliffs made of sedimentary rock.

Theodore walked up the crooked wooden stoop and pushed through the screen door; the wind must have knocked their poorly-made front door open during the storm. It happened often and they didn't have enough money to get a proper door installed.

Chester Finn, his father, lay passed out on the couch. His large body barely fit on the cushions and his long limbs were sprawled over every edge. He was snoring loudly and Theodore hoped to sneak in without being seen. If he could change his clothes and head to school early, he could avoid dealing with his father and his inevitable hangover.

He took off Eustice's baggy flannel and got dressed for school. He wore a t-shirt over his dingy white undershirt, his light blue jeans with holes in them, and his baggy beanie, which sat upon his head precariously. Ready to leave he crept back into the living room, hoping to depart without any conversation with his dad.

The floorboards creaked and Chester rustled. Tip-toeing delicately toward the front door, Theodore made every effort to be quiet. Another plank whined loudly as he stepped upon it, and his large father groaned. His eyes opened and immediately focused in on his son creeping out of the house.

"What are ya doing, boy?" Chester asked, his voice hoarse from a long night of heavy drinking.

"Going to school."

Chester glanced at a clock on the wall, then back to his son, "School doesn't start for another hour. Get back here. I need breakfast."

Theodore sighed and resigned to spending the next half hour with his cranky dad.

"I'll take scrambled eggs with Swiss and a side of bacon." Theodore was used to having orders barked at him, and he obeyed without complaint.

"Glass of orange juice, too?"

"Thatta boy." Chester winked at his son, then stretched loudly. His yawn came out like a growl and his enormous arms brushed the

18

ceiling as he did his best to wake up. His hairy belly showed beneath his sleeveless undershirt and remained exposed after the yawn with the garment bunched up over his torso. Chester did not care. He scratched his burly auburn beard and collapsed into a kitchen chair, restlessly awaiting his morning meal.

Theodore held his breath as he cooked because his dad smelt like stale malt liquor and dead fish. The combination was atrocious.

"You better hurry cause you ain't leaving for school till I have a plate of food in front of me."

Theodore ignored the threats and continued cooking at his own pace.

"You know, I could teach you how to cook meals like this if you let me. It's pretty simple." He offered innocently, hoping his dad would bite and learn to take care of himself, but the suggestion only angered Chester.

"You're an ungrateful little bastard, you are. Fifteen years I've had you strapped to my side, taking care of you, tied down by your childish needs, and now that you've grown a bit, you can't even make me a meal without complaining?"

"I'm not complaining. I just thought you might like to know how to cook too."

"Shut up. You have been nothing but a pain in my side since you were born. Needy, whiny, demanding. It's why your mother left, you know." Chester wore a scowl so rotten its bitterness reeked. "You're the reason she abandoned me."

Theodore said nothing and turned to face the stove so his father could not see his lip quiver. With great strength, he beat the urge to cry and swallowed the pain. He knew it wasn't true, but it didn't change the fact that it hurt him all the same.

"Has to be, right?" Chester went on. "If she left cause of me, she woulda taken you with her. Only logical explanation is that you and your incessant needs drove her away." Chester spit on the floor, adding to the grime that already coated the tiles. "Selfish bitch, she was. Leaving me with you. Like I wanted to deal with the crying and responsibility any more than she did."

Theodore took a deep breath. This rant was the usual; he'd heard it a million times before. It was especially harsh on mornings like these, when Chester woke up still drunk in his hangover.

The food was done and he turned to his father with a face of stone.

"Here you go. I hope you like it." He slid the plate across the table with force.

Chester laughed. "Stop being a sensitive little girl." He continued talking with his mouth full of bacon, "You're my family, I'm allowed to be honest with you. Doesn't mean I don't love ya, just means you annoy me sometimes. I annoy you too, don't I?"

Theodore rolled his eyes, not wanting to partake in this downward spiral of strange and toxic apologies.

"See," Chester said at Theodore's silent answer, "I do. But you love me cause I'm your dad. So quit the bullshit and the sad faces and give me a hug before you leave."

He obliged, only doing so to silence his old man, not because he forgave him for the harsh burdens he constantly placed upon him. Chester's odor was offensive so he held his breath as he leaned in for the hug.

Chester flicked his wrist, indicating that Theodore go away. "Alright. Go learn something."

He gladly obliged; any reason to leave home was a good one.

Chapter 3

Theodore grabbed his knapsack and navy pea coat. It had two rows of gold buttons down the front and was the nicest item he owned. The rain had not ceased, so he put on his blue rain boots and left in a hurry. He had fifteen minutes to get to school, which was possible but tough. He had to walk down the long stretch of Peddler's Way, past the South Market and numerous piers. Then he had to cross over Terre Bridge, which would bring him to the mainland. Triste Academy sat one mile from the bridge. Theodore hustled because he hated to be late.

The morning air was misty, making the walk unpleasant. By the time he got to school, he was barely on time and wet. He raced through the front doors, down the hall, and toward his classroom.

The starting bell rang through the hallway as classroom doors shut along the corridor. Room 107 was fourth on the left. He peered in through the door window to see his teacher already beginning the first lesson of the day. With a deep breath for composure, Theodore slowly opened the door and crept to the back of the room, wishing he was invisible. He didn't want to be an interruption.

He quickly realized he was not, in fact, an interruption, and that he might, in fact, be invisible. Ms. Courtier shot him a disapproving look but did not stop speaking to address his tardiness and none of his classmates even glanced at him. Not a single one gave him any attention at all. They ignored his walk to the back of the class, making no eye contact with him as he sat at his desk. Theodore settled in, taking off his coat and retrieving his notebook from his knapsack.

The classroom was chilly. He looked toward the windows and saw that one was left ajar, allowing the cold and stormy air to filter through. Too far from it, he shook his head, deciding he'd have to shut it himself during a break from their lessons. Before turning to face the front of the room, he noticed the normally vacant desk near the window was taken. A new student sat there. The small girl had billowing brunette curls and sat quietly in her seat, two rows to his left at the back of the room. She must be new; he'd never seen her before. Did he miss her introduction? Surely he hadn't, he was less than a minute late. Theodore scowled as he realized Ms. Courtier probably brushed over introducing her. It wouldn't surprise him; she made no attempt to help him get acquainted with this new school or the other kids. She showed very little interest in any students other than the brightest.

Theodore looked over at the new girl again but she did not look back. Just like everyone else, he was merely a blip on her radar. It didn't matter, she was very pretty, and soon enough she would be swarmed with new friends. She didn't need his empathy on her first day. She'd get through it, probably better than he had.

The teacher droned on for hours, switching from literature to arithmetic to history. Finally lunch arrived, which meant a full hour of food and recess. As the bell chimed, students poured into the hallways from each classroom and made their way to the other side of the building where the large cafeteria sat. Since the rain had started up again, everyone had to remain inside.

Theodore found a table in the back corner of the cafeteria. He forgot to pack his own lunch that morning so he resorted to eating a leftover bag of fruit chews that had been in his knapsack and buying a carton of milk. The hour passed dreadfully slow. He watched the kids from his class sit together and socialize—talking, laughing, joking with one another. He searched the large room for the new girl, thinking he could introduce himself now, but she was nowhere to be found. He wondered if she had brought her lunch into the lavatory to eat alone, as he had done on his first day when no one invited him to join them at their table.

He no longer cared that he sat alone. No one made fun of him for it, or seemed to care about anything he did, so neither did he. Over the last six months he grew accustomed to his role as their invisible peer and found a strange sense of peace within it. Nothing to live up to and no pressure to fit in. He could be whoever he wanted with no one to look harshly upon him or his choices.

The milk tasted old. Not spoiled, but old. Maybe the taste of cardboard somehow mixed into the liquid. He didn't know, but he finished it regardless. Without some nutrients, paying attention until 3 p.m. would be impossible. Halfway through the hour break, once everyone had finished their meals, kids began taking out cards and things to entertain themselves on this dreary day. Theodore watched in amusement as some students played respectable games while others resorted to pranks and trickery to pass the time. The lunch aides went into a tizzy as a small food fight broke out near the doors to the gymnasium.

Ruby Klearstone escaped the food fight, giggling and wiping crumbs off her blouse. Her bright blonde hair was wavy with sea salt and her pretty eyes gleamed as she smiled. Theodore spoke with her once; she was the only person who welcomed him on his first day. She wished him luck and offered to help him with anything he needed. He never took her up on the offer because he hadn't needed help with anything, but he never forgot her kindness. He sometimes wondered if he should pretend to need her assistance with something, but whenever he made up scenarios in his head it just left him feeling dumb and awkward. She was really popular and always surrounded by friends, so it was intimidating to try and breach the line of people she was always buried within. He hadn't spoken to her again since that day but sometimes she would flash him a small smile from across the room. It wasn't often but when it happened Theodore couldn't help but feel happy. At least someone liked him, even if it was from afar.

The bell rang to let them know the hour for freshman and sophomore lunch was over and all the 9th and 10th graders filtered through the hall back to their classrooms. At his old high school they got to switch rooms for each subject, but here on Nether Isle the population was so small that there was only one school for 5th to 12th grade and they had to stay in the same room all day. The amount of students in the tenth grade was so small, they only took up two classrooms. The whole setup made for a terribly mundane routine. He missed the way his old school operated but was doing his best to adjust to this small town lifestyle.

Ms. Courtier continued her lesson plan for the day as soon as they were back in their seats. Thunder roared outside, followed by an onslaught of heavy rain. As she droned on about the Civil War, Theodore intently watched the rain drip down the window panes. No one had shut the open window and water spritzed onto the sill next to where the new girl sat. But she left the window ajar. She didn't seem to mind the mist of rain covering her and everything on her desk. He wondered again where she disappeared to during lunch, then reminded himself it was none of his business. He wondered instead what her name was. It was so strange that their teacher went through the entire day without properly introducing her to the rest of the class. It bothered Theodore a great deal. If he got the chance, he'd do what he could to make her feel welcome, even if it was just a simple 'hello' when the timing was right.

He continued to stare out the window, longing for the school day to be over. Wishing he was drenched outside rather than trapped at his desk in this class. Time trickled away and the closing bell startled him as it sounded off without warning.

Everyone around him stood and hurried with their belongings in an attempt to get out the door first. Theodore remained in his seat and intuitively looked over toward the new girl's desk again. This time, she was looking back at him. They made eye contact and she gave him a friendly smile. Caught off guard, Theodore hesitated before smiling back. By the time the shock of being acknowledged wore off, his classmates were filtering past him, creating a human wall as they exited out the back door of the classroom. His sight of her was obstructed. A minute passed and the crowd was gone, but so was she. Only Theodore and Ms. Courtier remained in the room.

"Did you need to stay after class for help with something?" the teacher asked, her tone indicated that she hoped he didn't.

"No, Ms. Courtier. I'm good, thanks."

He gathered his belongings and left through the back door as well. The girl smiled at him. Theodore smiled now too, recalling the moment. Maybe he would finally make a friend here. Maybe this was his opportunity to find camaraderie in this lonely, forsaken sea town.

With a new determination to try again tomorrow, Theodore left Triste Academy feeling excited. He headed to the market for his after-school job with his head held high and a plan in mind.

Chapter 4

The North Market was only a ten minute walk from school. With the rain pattering off, Theodore made it to Adelaide's fish stand on time for his 3:15 p.m. shift.

The sign for *Adie's Fish & Chum* was made of old wood and weathered from its constant contact with salt air and water. The white paint was chipping and Theodore was tasked to repaint the letters once a month to prevent them from disappearing. Business was slow when he first started. Adelaide explained that without Eustice working as captain of the fishing vessel they owned, they had no product to sell. Theodore wasn't sure when he stopped acting as captain, but it was before he moved there. He entered in the midst of hard times. After a few months, she finally found a replacement captain to take over the job.

Theodore wondered why Eustice stopped working. He was old, but able. He supposed there was more to the situation than he would ever dare ask.

"Help me unload the latest catch," Adelaide called out to him as he approached the stand. She was old, in her late sixties, but she had the spirit and strength of someone half her age. She was lifting fifty pound boxes from the docked boat, carrying them across Peddler's Way, and delivering them to her stand on the other side. Without haste, she placed the large fish into the ice bins that were on display for passersby. Luckily, she was located at the front of the market and did not have to maneuver through the chaos and disorganization that ensued behind the front row of stands. Theodore tossed his knapsack through the door of his workplace, then immediately followed her back to the vessel.

"Bluefin tuna," Adelaide smirked. "Huge catch of them. We should rake in a nice sum for these beauties."

Theodore helped her carry another five crates of the heavy fish back to the stand.

"They also brought in a fresh batch of shrimp," Adelaide explained, thrusting the net of prawns at him. "Grill these up, usual prepping. I'll have to let the Baudins know we got them for sale tonight. Marcus loves his shrimp." Adelaide gave him a wink, merry with the thought of big sales, then left him to his work. Theodore updated the dry-erase signs, then tidied up the dead fish, making sure they were presented as perfectly as possible. Straight lines, all facing the same direction.

The shrimp were easy to grill. A pinch of salt and pepper and a squeeze of lemon juice was all that was needed. The grill at the back of the hut was lit and the food cooked in no time. He threw them onto a tray and set them on the front counter display.

The crowds passed by as people left work and headed home. He knew many of them would return at some point to buy whatever they needed to settle in for the night, so he waited patiently for the mad rush of sales to flow in.

Theodore watched the countless tired faces trudge along Peddler's Way: defeated, dirty, distant. Many wore expressions that looked very far away, like they were lost deep within the creases of their own minds. Life on Nether Isle was taxing. The hard work never ceased and many residents could not dig their way out from beneath the hardship life presented them while living here. Smiles were rare, good spirits were often non-existent. A rare few found enjoyment amidst the general dreariness, but that was usually only because they reveled in mischief and taking advantage of the disheartened individuals who had no spirit to bother defending themselves. Like the many handicapped elderly who retired from their lives on the sea to tend their broken minds and bodies doing simple jobs around town.

The Linville brothers ran past Theodore's stand. Rowan was in his grade, the other three were younger. Known to be troublemakers, they let out hollers and laughs as they threw handfuls of rocks into the market, hitting the vendors and causing minor damage. A stone hit Gus Yonk in the fruit stand to his left. Got him right in the eye. While Theodore wanted to chase after the boys, he knew it was better to make sure his fellow market tenant was okay.

Gus was over 70 years old and he had a bum leg from a fishing accident. He was confined to a wheelchair that had rusted spokes and took muscle to move. Though he couldn't walk well, he always kept his cane with him. It was a great weapon when anyone he didn't like came too close.

"Hey, Gus, are you alright? I saw those idiots got you right in the eye."

He groaned before answering, "Yeah. Bunch of punks. I've been working on getting a motor for Old Bessie here." He patted the side of his wheelchair. "Haven't quite figured out how to make it work, but once I do, those delinquents will be sorry they didn't learn some manners."

Theodore smiled, "Let me know if you need help. I used to help my dad fix up his boats when we lived in Alaska. I know some mechanics."

"Hmph," Gus grunted, not accepting the offer. "You've got a customer. Better get back to your stand."

Theodore looked over and saw Marcus Baudin peering over the wall of the fish stand, eyeing the cash register. He wanted to shout at him, tell him to back off, but he couldn't. They could not afford to lose business so Theodore played it cool.

"Hi, Marcus," he said, catching the man off guard and stopping him from acting upon his devious inclinations to steal. "Did

32

Adelaide tell you we caught some shrimp today? I grilled them up. They came out real nice."

Marcus's eyes shifted with guilt before he regained his composure and wrongfully determined he hadn't been caught. "Yeah, I ran into her by Ballantine Dock. She let me know. How much you charging for a pound?"

"$8.00."

"What? That's insane. These prawns look a day old." He thrust his hairy arm toward the bowl of cooked shrimp.

"They came in today. I helped take them off the boat myself."

Marcus scratched his beer belly as he scrunched his face in disapproval.

"I don't like it. Don't like you guys jacking up the prices. I bet Adelaide does it cause she knows I like 'em. Am I right? Evil old lady."

"The price of fresh shrimp has only gone up .30 cents in the past six months." Theodore was used to Marcus giving him a hard time. "It's eight dollars. Take it or leave it."

Begrudgingly, Marcus threw eight, wrinkled, single dollar bills onto the counter. Theodore packed his pound of shrimp into a Styrofoam container and handed it over.

"I'm not happy about this," Marcus complained. "I'm going to talk to the market manager about this thievery."

"Good luck with that. Mr. Carlin already approved the price increase."

"Jedd is my buddy. Watch how fast I get it switched back." Marcus gave Theodore a shifty grin before turning to walk away.

"Take a bath," Gus called out from his fruit stand at Marcus. "You smell like an ass!"

Theodore laughed but Marcus didn't hear him. He looked over to Gus and received a wink before the old man went back to pretending the world around him didn't exist.

Adelaide returned with a gallon of orange juice. Her hair was disheveled and she was out of breath. Theodore looked at her confused.

"I heard a cold was going around, so I got us some vitamin C," she explained, "Walked all the way into town. Grocery store on Main Street was closed due to a power outage, had to go to the gas station instead."

"That's really far." Theodore's eyes widened at her in concern.

"Yeah, well, when you and I don't catch this bug, you won't think I'm crazy."

She poured them both a glass without another word.

"Marcus came by. Said he was going to complain to Jedd Carlin about the new prices."

"Oh, he can shove it. What a miserable leech."

Theodore nodded as he drank his juice. As he finished his last sip, the mad rush began. The next two hours passed in a blur. Sale after sale until the ice bins were empty. No fish remained and Adelaide was elated.

It was 8:30 p.m. and he was able to head home. Adelaide tallied his hours for the day, gave him three pounds of Bluefin tuna she had set aside, and then let him leave. He took his time as he walked down Peddler's Way. There was no rush, nothing urgent to get home to. In fact, he cherished the time he wasted as he walked extra slow toward his house. He never knew what he would find when he got home and he felt no urgency to find out what was in store tonight. Whether it be an incapacitated father, any of Chester's nasty "ladyfriends" over for the night, or a small party of cruel middle-aged men, all options were unpleasant. It was rare that he ever walked into a quiet home where he could enjoy a night of peace.

He passed Tortoise Pier, then Cirripedia Pier, which were across the way from Terre Bridge and the mainland. Next came Krill Pier and Periwinkle Pier, both situated on the opposite side of the South Market. Each pier had smaller piers and docks connecting them to each other. Theodore never wandered down any of them. They were a long, crooked, and crowded maze of run-down houses, small shops, and diverging pathways. It was too easy to get lost in. He finally reached Crickets Pier, where his house sat.

Everything seemed quiet. No noise came from behind the front door, which caused him great unease. He had to assume this was a bad sign. Walking through the entrance way and into the small living space, Theodore was greeted by Chester, somewhat sober and sitting at the kitchen table with his back to him.

"Hi, Dad," Theodore said, locking the front door behind him.

"Kid, I have some good news," Chester spoke, his words slurred. Theodore sighed, realizing he wasn't as sober as he had originally thought. "I got a job. It's a three month fishing excursion up along the eastern coast of Canada." He took a swig of his beer. "So, you'll be here alone the next few months."

"Okay," Theodore said, "I can manage. I'm glad you landed a good job."

"Yeah, it's about damn time. Those assholes who got me to move us all the way out here fired me after four months for no good reason. The past two months of doing random day jobs, helping on the docks, have been brutal."

"Yeah, well, that's over now." He did not want to bring up the fact that his first employer at Nether Isle fired him with just cause after Chester showed up to work wasted one morning and fell over the side of the boat before they even had a chance to disembark.

Theodore lit the stove and prepared the fish Adelaide sent home with him. She always saved some food for him, and he always cooked it for both himself and his dad. It wasn't long before the fish

36

was decently skinned, cut up, and baked. He prepared two plates and placed them at the table.

They ate in silence at first. The fish came out delicious and he made a mental note to let Adelaide know that the quality of that day's catch was superb.

"While I'm gone, you need to be extra diligent about locking up the house and taking care of things. I don't want to return to chaos or unpaid bills."

"Yeah, I can handle it." He already did. His dad's absence would not make much of an impact. Theodore just needed to be careful how he spent his earnings so he could guarantee all the bills got paid on time. Chester only put a small amount toward the utilities and rent checks each month, but it was enough to make Theodore wonder if he'd need to dip into his own savings to make the cut until his dad came home with a big paycheck.

Cautiously, Theodore added, "Just be careful out there. This is a great opportunity for you so hopefully it goes better this time."

"What is that supposed to mean?" Chester knew what he was implying.

"I'm just saying, the last job went bad but you learned from that and I'm sure this one will go more smoothly."

"They fired me for no good reason. I slipped and fell over the side of the boat because the damn boat janitor left fish guts on the deck. It wasn't my fault, yet they claimed it was and fired me."

Chester's face was red with anger. "There was nothing for me to learn from that job except to watch where I step."

In denial, as usual. Theodore remembered that morning clearly and how intoxicated his father had been before he left for work. He shook his head, not wanting to put his dad in a bad mood before his big day.

Neither said another word and finished their plates with only the sound of waves crashing against the rocks beneath their house as ambiance. Theodore took his last bite and washed his plate.

"Goodnight, dad," he said, pausing before turning down the short hall to his bedroom.

"Yeah." Chester raised a hand but kept his back to his son.

Theodore was used to this type of nightly departure. It was too early for bed, but he'd rather be alone. He resigned to his room and lay quiet until he fell asleep.

Chapter 5

Theodore woke up to an empty house; Chester left without saying goodbye. Three months until he'd see his son again and there wasn't even a note. He tried to convince himself he'd enjoy the many peaceful days to come in his cold and quiet home, but he kept coming back to the fact that he was really alone. As much as his father proved to be mean and ungrateful, he was still company. Another person to talk to and have around. He was sure there would be many moments when his father's lack of presence proved to be quite calming, but overall he feared it might get lonesome.

Breakfast was a bowl of cold cereal. The flakes were stale and the milk was on the verge of going sour. He would have to make a point to restock sometime soon, if the funds were there.

He made the walk to school. Since he left a bit early, he did not need to hustle. Saddlebag Pier sat across from Crickets Pier and as he reached the midpoint between the two, he saw Adelaide emerging from that direction with Eustice.

She marched forward angrily and he followed close behind, sulking and ashamed. When she saw Theodore, she paused in her stride.

"Off to school, Theo?"

"Yeah, I'm a little early today. What were you guys doing at Saddlebag Pier?"

"Eustice here has begun to wander. I told him to stay in the
house but he can't oblige. Got a call from Betsy Mae saying he was
sitting in her kitchen when she woke this morning." She gave
Eustice a nasty glare. "Makes me wonder what that implies."

Sorry he asked, Theodore tried to diffuse the situation, "Maybe
he was just sleepwalking."

"What?" Adelaide blurted brashly. "How could someone who
doesn't sleep sleepwalk?" She shook her head at Theodore, always
forgetting he was still blind to these things. "Get to school. Learn
something good and tell me about it later."

"Yes, ma'am."

Adelaide continued forward with Eustice following behind.

He got to class on time and sat in his seat as the rest of his
classmates filtered in. He looked to his left and saw the new girl
sitting in the same seat she had been in the day before. He
continued looking at her for a few moments, waiting for her to look
back, but she didn't. She just sat there, staring out the open
window.

Ms. Courtier began her first lecture, painfully choosing chemistry
to start the day. Theodore paid attention the best he could but
found himself being distracted by the new girl. She was very small,
very pale, and very pretty. Every so often, he caught a glimpse of
her bright blue eyes. Her long brown curls were tied back in a
ribbon and the dress she wore was more formal than what all the

other kids wore to school. While it suited her, it also made her appear out of place. He had to assume it was why no one was befriending her right away. She was too pretty to be ignored so it must be that her appearance, while lovely, was a little odd.

Hours passed and lunch was finally drawing near. Theodore planned to catch the new girl before he lost her in the bustle of students trying to get to the cafeteria. As the bell rang, everyone rushed the exits. The new girl headed for the door at the front of the classroom so he followed her.

She dipped and ducked through the crowd, making it hard for him to keep up. Once in the hallway, they were surrounded by an even larger herd of hungry students.

He kept his gaze on her bright blue ribbon and continued to pursue her. At some point she'd slow down and the crowd would disperse, making it easier to introduce himself. The longer it took, the more he lost his nerve. He only hoped to make a friend, but he was beginning to feel too eager and the possibility of coming off as weird made him sweat. Taking a deep breath, he brushed the silly fear aside. Even if she wanted no part of him, he wouldn't be any worse off for giving it a shot.

As Theodore expected, the crowd that amassed in the cramped hallway filtered into the expansive cafeteria. Kids took to the food line while others found tables and began to dig into their lunchboxes. He still had his eyes on the blue ribbon, which was now headed toward the side exit. Confused, he ran to catch up to her.

"Hey! Where are you going?" Theodore shouted to the girl right before she made her escape outside. She spun around, eyes wide from being caught. After a moment collecting herself, she shifted back into her normal state.

"I need fresh air," she said calmly. "Why were you following me?" He was surprised to hear she spoke with a British accent.

"I wanted to introduce myself and see if you wanted to eat lunch with me. I noticed you were new here and I didn't want you to feel alone." She gave him a small smile, which he took as encouragement to continue, "My name is Theodore Finn." He extended his hand but she did not take it.

"I'm Bianca Wrey." She gave him another smile. He lowered his outstretched hand and took a step back.

"Do you want to sit with me for lunch?"

Bianca hesitated. She looked toward the door and back at Theodore.

"Yeah, I can sit with you today."

He wasn't sure why she seemed unsure about spending lunch with him, or why she appeared so eager to leave the building, but she followed him back into the cafeteria. For the first time, people noticed him. He caught the eye of many students who glared silently at him and Bianca as they walked to an empty table. He wasn't sure why they cared or why this warranted as news, but he could feel their whispers all around him.

He brushed it off. Bianca sat next to him and suddenly he could smell her damp, moldy odor. Trying not to be rude, he said nothing, but wondered if she hadn't washed her clothes in a while.

Theodore pulled out his brown bagged lunch from his knapsack, which consisted of a mushed sandwich and a bruised apple. Bianca watched him quietly.

"Didn't you bring lunch?"

"No, I forgot mine today."

"I can give you a few dollars if you want to buy something from the kitchen."

"Thank you, but I can only eat my mom's cooking. Everything else makes me sick." She fidgeted uncomfortably. "I have many allergies."

Theodore shrugged and took a bite of his PB&J. She was a little strange. Every few moments she would glance around the room nervously, as if checking to see who was looking at them. Eventually, Theodore couldn't help but do it too. What was she so nervous about?

Then he noticed a few kids at different tables were still eyeing them down. They tried to be discreet but Theodore caught them every so often. Their glances were mean and judgmental; their vibe was unkind. This was the most attention he had ever gotten and it felt horrible.

"Why does everyone keep looking at us?" he asked in a hushed voice. She sat up straight and rearranged herself with confidence.

"Maybe they're jealous."

"Of what?" Theodore asked, confused.

"It doesn't matter. Who cares what they think?"

She was right. He never cared before.

"Where are you from? You don't have the same French-American accent everyone else here has."

"I'm from Derbyshire, in England. My family just moved here for my father. He's a fisherman and he got a job at one of Nether Isle's ports." This explained why she smelt weird. Theodore often found himself wearing his father's odor if he forgot to wash his clothing on their shared coat rack. Sometimes he also smelt fishy after working a night at the fish stand, though that washed off easy with a shower.

"My dad is a fisherman, too. He shipped off this morning to a job that takes him to Canada for three months. We just moved here too, about six months ago. So I know what it's like to be the new kid."

Bianca seemed distant. She was there, but she was also someplace else. From the look on her face, her mind was a vast place.

"Do you have many friends here?" she asked, quietly.

"No," Theodore responded honestly, feeling the sting of her innocent query.

"I'll be your friend." Bianca's face lit up as she spoke.

"Okay," Theodore said, trying to retain his cool composure as he got excited. "Maybe I can take you out on my sailboat sometime. I sail it in the gulf, near Maudit Cove and the lighthouse."

Bianca flashed him a nasty look. "What's your intention?"

Confused, Theodore stumbled over his words. "I just thought it might be fun to go out on the ocean. Do you not like being on the water?"

"No, I just cannot go near Apres Monde Lighthouse."

"Why not?"

She eyed him carefully, so intensely he could not help but imagine she was scanning his thoughts. After a moment, her expression returned to its usual, pleasant state.

"It's just too far out. My parents wouldn't like me being so far from land."

"Alright, then, I'll just show you my sailboat."

"That could work."

The bell rang and Bianca bolted up from the lunch table.

"This weekend?" Theodore asked before she could run away from him.

"Yes, Saturday at noon. I will meet you by Ballantine Dock."

As he watched her walk off, he saw Ruby on the other side of the cafeteria, watching him intently. Instead of her normal friendly look, she gave him an expression of great concern. Theodore furrowed his brow in confusion but ignored it. If Ruby wanted to be his friend too, all she had to do was talk to him.

He picked up his knapsack and headed back to class. Bianca was already at her desk, sitting with rigid confidence as the students filtered in around her. Theodore tried to make eye contact with her but she was focused intently on the open book in front of her. Baffled, he took his seat. He couldn't tell if she was oblivious, socially awkward, shy, or just rude. Or maybe this was normal behavior in England and he just wasn't used to it. Either way, he was happy he made the effort and knew Adelaide would be proud of him. With time, he might have a new friend.

The rest of the day flew by and when the last bell rang for the day, so did his classmates. They rushed past him in a frenzy, giving him no time to catch Bianca to say goodbye before she left for the day. Slightly deflated, he headed to work.

The next two days passed without much excitement. Bianca wasn't in school on Wednesday or Thursday, leaving Theodore to question if she was all right. He didn't know where she lived, so he couldn't go and check with her parents to see if she was okay. Plus, he did not feel they were close enough friends to do something like that quite yet.

Work was busy and his home was quiet. The first two nights without his father's drunken presence proved to be a relief. So far, the tranquility of living alone was not bothering him. He knew it would eventually, but for now he was enjoying the hushed solitude. It wouldn't last forever, so he savored it.

As Friday morning rolled around, he woke to a cloudy sky and wet ground. The storms had been wretched the night before and from the way it sounded outside, he was grateful the roof didn't collapse on him as he slept.

He knew the storms weren't over yet, so he put on his rain boots and grabbed an umbrella before heading to school.

He was a few minutes late again. Without interrupting her own lesson, Ms. Courtier shot him a nasty look as he walked to the back of the classroom. Bianca was absent again.

The day droned on. Lunch came and Theodore ate alone. He watched Ruby laugh with her friends on the other side of the cafeteria. Her smile lit up the room, infecting his heart as he observed. He couldn't help but be fascinated with her. She wore a lovely confidence that drew others to her. She was like the lighthouse, attracting boats from every direction because her light shone so bright. Everyone adored her. She was kind yet poised, extremely certain of who she was and what she stood for. No one could shake her foundation. Not even the typical pettiness that swarmed through high schools, eating away at teenager's cores. Ruby was immune to that.

The lunch hour was almost over. Theodore finished his orange and yogurt a while ago and had been people watching ever since. He knew he would need to spend money at the market this weekend. Food was already sparse at home and he barely had enough to pack for lunch today. He didn't like the idea of spending money right before the end of the month but he didn't like the idea of starving either.

Theodore silently trudged along within the masses as they all filtered back through the skinny hallway and into their respective classrooms. This routine, day in and day out, proved to be numbing. By the end of each week, he found himself yearning for more but unable to define what else he needed. It was an empty slot within his soul that still needed to be defined. The monotony of his life echoed through his mind like a thousand screams, a cacophony so loud it tormented him that no one else could hear it. It was a loud and clear reminder of the lack of purpose in his life. The ambiguous pain always became intensified after completing another week filled with events identical to the previous week. Some days, it rang louder than the deafening school bells. Just like those, his own alarm always arrived right on schedule. Telling him this life was not enough, that he would never be fulfilled. Theodore was waiting for the day it drove him mad.

After school, Adelaide had a fresh batch of Atlantic cod ready to be sold. It wasn't the tastiest of fish but it was the start of the weekend and people would buy it anyway. The afternoon turned into night and although he was busy, he found himself wondering if Bianca was okay. It was strange that she missed three days of school and he had no way of determining the reason for his new friend's absence. He had been excited to take her sailing, but now he had to assume those plans were cancelled.

The bustle of the market did not slow down until 9 p.m. Adelaide let him go home at 9:15 p.m. even though there were still a few customers filtering through.

The walk home felt longer than usual. He was tired and his body felt heavy. Sleep was calling his name and he found his subconscious wishing he could stay asleep for a long time, skipping through these dark and lonesome days. It was foolish to desire that, but he couldn't help but feel comfort when his mind wandered to such depressing thoughts.

The house was dead silent. Without changing his clothes or eating, he collapsed onto his small, uncomfortable bed and passed out. Dreams of happiness engulfed his mind. For the next few hours, all was well.

Chapter 6

The sun rose, illuminating Theodore's closed eyelids. Angry that he had forgotten to close his blinds, he took his pillow and buried his face beneath it. But it was too late; the new day had greeted him and he could not fall back to sleep. The alarm clock read 6:45 a.m. He cursed beneath his breath.

He looked himself over in the bathroom mirror. The skin on his face had crease marks from where it weighed upon his pillow all night. His sandy blonde hair stood up in all directions and his blue eyes were blood shot. Not wanting to look at himself any longer, he brushed his teeth and headed into the kitchen.

Only one packet of oatmeal remained in the pantry. Theodore boiled water in the teakettle and took out a bowl. In a matter of minutes, breakfast was served. He cringed as he ate. The oatmeal had no flavor and felt like mud in his mouth. After forcing half the bowl down, he threw the rest away.

They had no television, so he took out a book to read. Although he had read it multiple times, he picked up his copy of *Treasure Island* and dove back into the world of pirates and adventure. While the story kept him engaged, he occasionally looked to the clock on the wall to monitor the time. He had not forgotten that Bianca said they'd go sailing at noon, and although he was fairly confident it was no longer happening, he still hoped that it might.

Halfway through a chapter, Theodore fell asleep. Tired from the dullness of the day, exhausted from the indefinable darkness that loomed over him. He had no reason to be unhappy, yet he was. Sleep brought solace and though his body didn't need it, it took the opportunity to seize it anyhow.

When he woke again, it was quarter to noon. Startled that he managed to stay asleep that long after a full night's rest, he jumped up and ran to his bedroom. With haste, he changed out of his clothes from the day before and into new, fresher garments. He ran out the door, locking it behind him, and raced to the dock.

He tried not to get his hopes up. A day spent with a friend would be nice, but there was no reason he should expect it to happen. Whatever kept her out of school for three days would most likely keep her from hanging out with him today, too.

When he arrived at Ballantine Dock, Bianca was nowhere in sight. Without letting it bother him, he walked down the dock, descended the creaky ladder, and sat in his sailboat. His model of the dinghy sailboat was on the bigger side, just enough for two people to fit. He never took anyone out with him before, but the room was there. His boat clanked lightly back and forth against the boats surrounding it. It irked him every time the vessels tapped his. The ropes became knotted together throughout the week so Theodore unraveled them, expending his patience. Once they were untangled, he unlatched his boat from the dock and let his boat float away from the clutter lining the pilings.

The air on the water was crisp and clean. It coursed through his lungs with fluidity, making a home in his body. He savored it. It was much easier to swallow than the stale air that circulated throughout the piers.

The wind was steady, allowing him to maneuver as he pleased. He headed toward Apres Monde Lighthouse. It was a nice distance away and gave him space to sail freely with no destination in mind.

The lighthouse was peculiar. It sat in the middle of the water with no apparent land holding it up. Adelaide explained that Apres Monde was sculpted from a single stone that rose from the water. It was a large dolomite, sedimentary rock that sat in the middle of the gulf and the rough, lapping waves crafted the bulk of its shape. It glowed naturally, between the moonlight and the water's reflection off its white surface, so the sailors and townspeople decided to carve it into a proper lighthouse. They carefully hollowed out the top of the white stone to house the light. The lantern room had no glass windows, only thin slits cut into the rock walls so light shone through but wind couldn't enter. It was created eons ago when there was no electricity, so fire was their only light source. Each evening, the townsfolk sailed out to the lighthouse to ignite bright flames in the lantern room, warning ships of approaching land. He never saw anyone sail to light the fire, yet it glowed with intensity every night. He assumed they must have switched to solar power once that technology was invented.

Apres Monde was a pristine beacon set dead in the middle of the water. Immaculate in the way the sun reflected between the flawless white stone and the waves surrounding it. Theodore was always fascinated by it but never had the opportunity, or the time, to venture that far out. It was a good distance from the town, set all alone in the middle of the vast ocean.

He had an entire day at his disposal, so he continued to head toward it, thinking today could be the day he examined it closer. Maybe he'd finally get close enough to see the details of its complicated design.

Sailing onward, the voice of a girl carried past him in the breeze. Theodore turned around and looked toward the town. It was a few nautical miles away, but he saw a small body standing on the docks. She shouted again, her voice somehow reaching him. He wasn't sure how he was hearing her. With a hand on his forehead to block the sun, he could see a small girl with long brown curls in a short, ruffled dress. His thoughts immediately went to Bianca.

He turned his boat around, leaving Apres Monde Lighthouse behind. Not realizing how far he had gone, or how long he had been out on the water, it took him 45 minutes to reach Ballantine Dock.

"Way to forget about hanging out with me today," Bianca called down to him from above.

"I didn't forget, I figured it wasn't happening anymore. You weren't in school the past three days. I thought you might be sick."

"No, I'm fine."

"Wanna climb down and jump on board? We can tour around a bit."

"No, you've been out long enough. Let's go on a walk instead."

Theodore didn't question her suggestion. He was ready to retire from the water anyhow.

He climbed the ladder and was met by a smiling Bianca. She appeared to be in a great mood, much better than when he first introduced himself to her in the cafeteria. Theodore's hopes were lifted and he was happy to be greeted by a friendly face.

"You were out pretty far," she stated as he climbed over the edge and got to his feet.

"Yeah, I've never seen the lighthouse up close. Since our plans seemed to be cancelled, I had a full day to explore."

"Sorry I ruined it."

"No, I wasn't implying that," he insisted, suddenly nervous he offended her. "I just saw it as a large slot of time to sail that far out. I didn't mind coming back. I was getting hungry anyway."

"The lighthouse isn't all that great. You're not missing much."

"You've been to it?"

"Yeah. It's just a big, carved rock. Pretty boring."

Theodore looked at her with skepticism, not believing that a piece of divine architecture made from nature could be described as boring. He didn't want to insult her by whole-heartedly disagreeing with her, so he changed the subject.

"Are you hungry?"

"I can only eat my mom's cooking, remember?"

"Oh yeah. Do you mind if I grab a snack from the market before we walk?"

Bianca shook her head and they walked toward the food stands. Adelaide took Saturdays off to rest, so her stand had a tarp over it. Sundays were always busiest because people bought food in bulk to prepare for the week, so she liked the extra day to relax. Gus Yonk had his fruit stand open. He approached the stand and Gus ignored him.

"Hey," Theodore said to get his attention. Gus was the worst salesman he ever met.

"What?"

"I want to buy some fruit."

"Yeah?"

Theodore rolled his eyes, "I'll take a stem of grapes."

He handed the old man a medium sized batch of purple grapes, then watched them get weighed on the ancient scale Gus liked to use.

"$2.45." He extended his wrinkly hand and Theodore placed $2.50 into it.

"Keep the change."

"Who's that?" Gus asked as his eyes narrowed in on Bianca.

"My friend from school."

"From school?" Gus asked, his tone not convinced. "She looks like a ghost."

Appalled, Theodore leaned in and whispered through gritted teeth.

"What's wrong with you? She's new here, from England. Maybe there's less sun, I don't know, but it's hard being the new kid. I should know. And the last thing she needs is a rude old man making fun of her."

"I wasn't—"

Theodore shook his head, cutting him off. "I'll see you tomorrow."

He approached his friend, cautiously trying to determine if she had heard the insult Gus paid her. Her pleasant mood appeared the same so he figured she hadn't.

They walked toward Terre Bridge. On the way, they received many nasty glares, the worst of which came from two older girls Theodore had never seen before. One looked like a celebrity: tons of make-up, long blonde curls, fancy outfit; totally out of place on

Nether Isle. The other stayed hidden beneath a hooded coat; only a long black braid and her accusatory emerald eyes were visible. The girls exchanged nasty whispers as they walked past them. Their negativity seemed aimed at Bianca, not him. He glanced over at his friend who stared straight ahead, unaware of the judgment placed upon her. If she didn't notice it, he wasn't going to point it out. Better to protect her feelings than hurt them.

They crossed Terre Bridge and to their right was the town. It had bigger grocery stores, banks, pharmacies—regular things that would be found in a town in the States. The mainland was where the richer people lived, though no one living on Nether Isle had a lot of money. They just seemed better off compared to those living along the piers. Theodore and Bianca followed a path to the left that led to a common hiking trail people walked on nice days.

"Do you live on the piers or the mainland?" Theodore asked, trying to learn more about his new friend.

"My family and I live on the mainland. On a street behind Myrtle's Deli."

"Is it just you and your parents?"

"Yeah, and my little sister. Her name is Cadence. She's 9 years old."

"I always wished I had siblings."

"She's my best friend," Bianca said, her voice drifted far away as she did so.

"Why were you out of school the last three days?" Theodore switched subjects, catching his new friend off guard.

"Oh," she stammered, "Cadence was really sick. I stayed home to help my mother take care of her." Bianca smiled. "She's better now."

"That's good. I heard a nasty virus was going around."

"Yeah, that must have been what she caught."

They rounded the hill to face the open gulf. A steep hill led toward the rough water and they could see the vast ocean in the distance. They continued to walk, talking about small matters such as the foods they liked, hobbies they each enjoyed, and the boring lessons taught at Triste Academy. The conversation remained light and happy, never diving too deep or touching upon subjects either felt uncomfortable discussing. Theodore made sure to steer clear from talking about his own family; he did not want his new friend feeling pity for him. She came from a loving home and he did not assume she'd understand the sorrow that engulfed his own.

They stopped to sit at the top of the hill. Bianca played with the long grass, running her fingers through it as they watched the sun dip toward the ocean. Time sped past them, stealing the day away. The sun was setting and they enjoyed the show in silence at the top of the trail. It was a comfortable silence; Theodore felt no need to fill it with words.

Quite a few moments passed before Bianca broke the quiet.

"Maybe we ought to head back down before the sun has completely set. I want to get home before it's too dark out."

"Okay, let's walk back."

Together they made their way down, chatting about Bianca's pet cat named Ferguson and how he could not move to America with them. Her Aunt Maude had to take him in. She was upset about it, but knew her aunt was giving him plenty of love. Theodore never had a pet, so he couldn't relate.

They reached the bottom of the trail and saw the sun sink into the ocean. Night was upon them and it was time for goodbyes.

"Thanks for spending the day with me," Theodore said.

"Yes, it was fun. We will have to do it again sometime," she smiled, her pretty blue eyes reflecting the starlight from above.

Theodore nodded; no previous day spent in Nether Isle ever felt this content. Bianca gave him a small wave as she turned and walked toward the town. He watched her go for a moment before turning and crossing Terre Bridge to get back to the piers.

It wasn't too late yet; the sun was setting earlier and earlier in preparation for winter. As the cool night air of autumn caressed his cheeks he breathed a sigh of ease. This was the best day he had in a long time.

Chapter 7

The market was always packed on Sundays. Theodore hated working on the weekend but it was essential, especially now that he had to pay all the bills on his own. His dad wouldn't have a check to put toward expenses until he returned home in three months.

During the week Adelaide would come and go, but on Sundays she stayed the entire time to help. Adie's Fish & Chum stand had a line that reached the other side of Peddler's Way. Luckily, her fishing crew hauled in a massive catch on Saturday and also came back with another early that morning. They were out on the ocean again, stocking up on whatever they could catch to fill the void that would come once all the current products were purchased. Very often they would run out of food to sell because her merchandise was in high demand. She was one of three fish stands amongst the markets and neither of the other two rivaled the food she provided. Her fish were always freshly caught and of the finest quality. If you bought and ate food from the other fish stands, it wasn't uncommon for food poisoning to follow.

The day crept by slowly as Theodore worked hard to keep up with the never-ending line of customers. At noon, Adelaide put up a sign to indicate they were taking an hour lunch break. He couldn't believe he had already been there for five hours, or that he had another six hours to go.

Adelaide pulled the drape down to block the crowds from where they ate within the stand. The curtain not only blocked out the chaotic scene of Peddler's Way and the entry way to the market, but it also blocked out the heat from the autumn sun that was unusually hot this afternoon. Adelaide always brought sandwiches on Sundays. She took them out of the small cooler stored beneath the front counter and they ate together. Out of the side of the fish stand, through the open door, they could see Gus fast asleep at his fruit stand. Now that they were on break and not focused on their own sales, they saw the Linville delinquents stealing his produce as he snored loudly in slumber.

Adelaide shouted his name, but he did not stir. She wet a washcloth in her bucket and threw it at his head. It hit him smack in the face, waking him up. As he began to yell at Adelaide, he saw her pointing toward the front of his stand and his anger shifted toward the teenagers pocketing his apples. Without any delay, he grabbed his cane and swung it hard at Rowan, the oldest of the crew, clubbing him against the side of the head. The boy groaned in pain and put the apples back, as did his younger counterparts.

"You're welcome," Adelaide shouted over to him, but all she received was a dismissive wave and a grunt. She expected nothing more.

"Gus told me you made a new friend." The conversation shifted onto Theodore.

"Yeah," he said with a mouthful of salami and provolone cheese. "Did he tell you how rude he was to her?"

"No, he left that part out."

"Thankfully she didn't hear his mean comment."

"Now what kind of friend is this? It's a girl, so do you like her? Or is it just a companion?"

Taken aback, Theodore considered this for the first time. He had never thought of her romantically, never saw her the way he saw Ruby. Bianca was beautiful too, but he had no feelings for her besides friendship.

"Just a friend. I think she's a good one. It's nice to have a friend who likes being my friend, too."

Adelaide looked at him skeptically. "Yeah, well, be careful. I'm a girl, and I know firsthand that you can't always know what we are really thinking; what our real motives are. We have lots of wires crossing inside our brains and sometimes we don't even know what we are up to until it unfolds."

Theodore gave Adelaide a blank stare.

"I'm just saying," she continued, careful with her words, "be cautious." She tightened her lips. "Gus mentioned that she didn't seem normal but you were adamant that she was. This town isn't like the rest of the world. You're not from around here so you need to be extra careful. The people here are different; both males and females. They are concerned with their own survival, first and foremost. Everything else comes second, including the wellbeing of others. I'm sure this new friend of yours is fine but Gus is a man of few words and the fact that he wasted a couple to tell me about this new friend of yours means he felt it was a worthy conversation. Something I ought to discuss with you. And I've never met an individual with as good of a radar as Gus."

"She is a normal girl with a normal family. This is ridiculous. Gus is a loony old bat. He may have a good read on people but he is clearly off his meds." He glanced over at Gus again, who was now trying to swat a fly with his cane. He swung the stick through the air haphazardly, missing the bug every time.

"Fine, I'm not doubting you. And I'm not trying to scare you. I just can't tell how aware you are of the goings on here and I mean to watch out for you in these matters." Her eyes scanned him with sincerity, trying to read him, trying to determine if he understood her. He seemed fine, his feelings unaltered by this conversation, so she took that as a sign he absorbed her intentions correctly. "You should bring her by sometime. I'd like to meet your new friend. What's her name?"

"Bianca."

"Okay, bring Bianca by sometime and we can all have a meal together. I'm glad you're making friends. It's healthy and about damn time."

Theodore assumed this is how any mother would react to their child having a new friend. Adelaide was not his mother, but she was the closest he'd ever had. He was sure Bianca wouldn't mind meeting her sometime; she'd just have to cook something his friend wasn't allergic to.

The lunch hour ended. Adelaide removed the drape that separated them from the rest of the world and business resumed. Six hours later, she let him leave. It was 7 p.m. and there were still customers, but they trickled in sporadically. It wasn't anything she couldn't handle on her own.

He passed the South Market as he walked home, which was still filled with people. This side of the market possessed a more artistic theme. The products and stands were eclectic, containing creative products and trinkets made by the vendors. The North Market held mostly food, but the South Market held home goods and novelty items. Many kids his age still roamed the cramped passageways between merchant stands, browsing the fascinating items being sold.

When he got to Crickets Pier, the world hushed. No one was outside their homes and he was far enough away from the markets that their inherent noise was significantly dimmed. He could hear the waves crashing beneath the pier and against the large rock wall it backed up to.

He cooked himself a quick dinner. The fish Adelaide let him take was delicious. It filled his belly with the nutrients he had been missing after his first week living alone. It baffled him why he had eaten more poorly this week than any other week with his father present. His dad didn't do any of the work, never picked up the groceries or cooked them meals. Theodore was just as alone as he ever was, the difference now was that he didn't have someone to please all the time. Only himself. He thought that should be enough to motivate him to keep up the hard work he did on a normal basis but perhaps he was more tired than he ever realized. Always trying to please his father was exhausting and all that effort didn't seem necessary to put forth toward himself. He'd survive just fine without a properly prepared meal every day. It made him wonder though; did he enjoy surviving with the constant pressure of perfection placed upon his shoulders? He couldn't deny that his old routine brought out a healthier and more productive side of him.

This dinner was exactly what he needed. He couldn't deny that. He felt more energized and awake than he had in the past few days. Maybe after a few weeks of his father's absence, he would feel inclined to start treating himself with the same extreme effort he felt obligated to treat his father with. He just needed this time to decompress from his old routine.

Monday morning came as soft as a whisper, coaxing Theodore out of bed without any struggle. His alarm went off at 6 a.m., giving him enough time for a quick sail around the Bay of Fundy before school. He put on a woolen cap, his nice, gold-buttoned jacket, and his boat shoes. He walked swiftly down Peddler's Way, passing Adelaide's home, which was still dark. When he reached Ballantine Dock he got into his sailboat without any trouble. The water was calm and the boats did not clank against each other like they did when the water was rough.

The morning air carried him away from the dock and out onto the open water of the bay. Its crisp chill touched all his senses, making him feel more alive than any other sensation could. He was here, in this moment, breathing in the life that circulated all around him. It moved through his body, giving him the most vibrant energy. An energy that could come from no source other than nature. Being immersed in its power always proved to be a needed reminder that he was very much alive and part of this world. These moments were invaluable to him.

He sailed on, moving further away from Nether Isle. He could see Apres Monde straight ahead in the distance. He did not have time to travel all the way to it, but he kept his sails aimed toward it anyway. He looked behind him and saw Maudit Cove to the left. It was a decent distance from the docks and often went unnoticed from the piers, but from this location he could see it perfectly. On

66

this morning, a light fog settled around it, concealing it in gray mist. Strangely enough, this haze covered the cove exclusively. It did not stray to any other sections of the isle. It was peculiar but Theodore did not question nature. There was no reasoning behind its wonders.

The lighthouse grew closer; there appeared to be a faint glow encasing the stone sculpture. The light at the top burned bright as ever, even with the sunlight slowly beginning to show as it crept toward the horizon. The wind picked up but the gusts were not that of a storm. In fact, they felt like solitary streams blowing exclusively in this area, unconnected to the rest of the air flow. They were stale, brushing across his face and clogging his pores. It made no sense; there was no smoke, no pollution that should cause such a feeling within a clean breeze. Yet he found this new set of winds to be uncomforting. They were stagnant, moving unevenly with no rhythm or flow. Their currents seemed foreign as they passed him harshly. The overall feel was unfamiliar and it caused him great concern. They crossed him like warnings, as if he had unknowingly sailed into the middle of a place he was not welcome. The behavior of his surroundings made him feel like an intruder and he could sense an unseen force willing him away.

Through the warm and sporadic breezes, he focused on the lighthouse. Its glow grew brighter, the white stone shining in a blurry haze. The winds became stronger, warmer, and even more uncomfortable. They seemed to be coming from Apres Monde and passing straight through him. He turned around again and saw Maudit Cove still covered in fog. He did not know what was happening, or why. This strangeness was new and had never occurred while he was out sailing before.

He rolled up his sails to stop his boat from moving any farther. It no longer felt right to continue toward the lighthouse. As his boat came to as much of a stop as it could upon the active water, a chill amidst the warm air pierced his body. The winds circled around him, sounding like a hundred lonely sighs. Overwhelmed with sudden despair, Theodore became frantic to escape whatever invisible nightmare he sailed into. With a paddle, he turned his boat around. He unlatched his sails, letting them drop to their open positions, but he did not move. The winds were trapping him in place. The sounds of heavy breathing grew louder until a solitary note rose above the rest, releasing a final lamented howl, then everything stopped: the noises, the warm winds. The air became stuffy and still; unnatural in its absence. He paddled, finally able to move again. After a few frantic strokes, cool air replaced the stagnant. His boat was able to catch the current and move forward.

Shaken, Theodore raced back to Ballantine Dock, sailing as fast as his boat would allow.

Chapter 8

The first hour of class was tough to get through. Theodore couldn't stop thinking about what happened on the water. Nothing bad came of it, but it was the strangest sensation he had ever experienced. All of it felt wrong and unnatural. He had to stop thinking about it.

Bianca was in attendance today and once lunchtime rolled around, his mind shifted toward other thoughts. Before he knew it, he was already forgetting about that morning's incident. She was a potent distraction.

They sat at their usual table. He ate his peanut butter and jelly sandwich while she ate nothing at all.

"You need to stop forgetting your lunch."

"I know, I'm just so sleepy in the morning, I always wind up walking out the door without it."

Theodore shook his head, aware he could not solve this recurring dilemma for her.

The room bustled. Freshmen and sophomores roamed the space, buying their lunches and settling in at their chosen tables with their chosen friends. He was envious, but he did sometimes wonder what it would be like to have a group of buddies who happily chose him as a companion. He looked over to Bianca and smiled, happy to have her friendship. And though it wasn't what he was picturing, he was perfectly content to have something similar with her. She came to lunch that day, expecting to sit with him and content to do so. Maybe one day more people would join their friendship, but for now he was happy just to have her. He glanced toward Ruby's table. Today she was with Rowan Linville and his obnoxious posse. The girls she normally sat with were scattered across the cafeteria. Marie Strehl sat with her but the rest found other people to eat with. He wondered if they had a fight, or maybe she and Rowan had started talking. His heart skipped at the thought of her dating him. He was foul and she was too good for him. He watched the scene with great concern.

Bianca noticed. She followed his gaze to the sight of Rowan playfully pushing Ruby's shoulder while shoving a chicken nugget in his mouth.

"Do you like her?" She caught Theodore off guard.

"What?"

"Ruby. You are staring at her. Do you like her?"

"I just don't know what she is doing hanging out with that asshole. He's the worst. He won't be good to her."

"Why do you care? I've never seen Ruby pay you an ounce of attention."

"She was nice to me when I first got here. You weren't around."

"Well, why'd she stop?"

"What do you mean?"

"Doesn't seem all that nice to befriend the new kid then ditch him."

"It wasn't like that. We weren't friends exactly, she just made me feel welcome when no one else did." He realized he'd never be able to describe the strange unspoken respect he and Ruby shared, "It's hard to explain."

"Yeah, because it's imaginary." Bianca said flatly. "You've built her up in your head. If she was as sweet as she pretends to be, she'd be friends with you and not that gross loser she's sitting with now."

"Who knows? High school, or whatever this school would be classified as, is a weird time. I don't read too much into it."

"You clearly do. Before I interrupted your intense stare, you were definitely overthinking it. You still have a crease between your eyebrows." Theodore scowled at her.

"You're making something out of nothing. It was a passing thought, nothing more." He ended the conversation with that. Bianca shrugged her shoulders and stopped pressing the issue. But she watched him intently as they continued to discuss other matters. Once his guard was down again, she caught him discreetly stealing glances over at Ruby, never breaking his concentration on the conversation with her, but distracted nonetheless. Bianca saw every moment in which he looked over at the other girl with intense curiosity, but she never called him out on it again. Instead, she

71

digested this knowledge and let it simmer; determining what this discovery about her new friend meant to her.

They had a nice lunch together. He learned more about her cat back in England, her great affinity toward the game of backgammon, and her deep love of jazz music. She was fascinating, but as he talked with her, Theodore found himself feeling very uncultured. Besides moving around the country, he didn't know much about anything outside of sailing and the inner workings of a fishing village. He told Bianca all about his favorite books but he was more excited to hear what she had to say. Maybe he'd even pick up new interests once she taught him how to play these new games he'd never heard of before. Though he felt uniformed, she was still very interested when it was his turn to share things about himself. Maybe it was all a matter of perspective; her interests intrigued him because they were foreign, but to her, his knowledge and hobbies were foreign too. Theodore determined that they both could learn a lot from each other.

As the bell rang and lunch ended, he stole another look at Ruby to see if there were any clues to verify his suspicions. Instead of seeing Rowan hugging her or them openly flirting with each other, he found them both staring in his direction, scrutinizing him and Bianca. They wore grim expressions. Upon catching their glares, they did not turn away hastily, embarrassed for being caught. There was no sense of urgency to look away. Why were they watching him? Why did they care? Bianca did not notice and Theodore did not mention it to her. There was no need to pass his paranoia onto her.

They walked back to class together, Bianca took her seat near the window and he took his own. Ms. Courtier droned on, teaching them lessons Theodore found no interest in. Once 3 p.m. rolled around, everyone was eager to leave.

He said goodbye to Bianca, who seemed eager to get away from school. He didn't blame her, it had been a particularly boring day. Once she was gone, he received a gentle tap on his shoulder. He turned around and saw that Ruby was the source. Her face was worried.

"Hey, Theo," she shortened his name as if they were good friends. Theodore couldn't help but enjoy this. "I need to talk to you."

"Okay, about what?"

"I wanted to apologize for not being a better friend. I know that I made a point to welcome you during your first week here but then disappeared after you settled in. That wasn't nice of me and I am realizing now how wrong it was."

"It's been six months. I've adjusted just fine. I appreciate you coming to me with this, and I'd love to be real friends, but there is no need to apologize."

"It's just that when I saw you hanging out with *her*, I came to see that what I had done was deplorable and I should have stayed with you to make sure you knew how things worked here."

Theodore only heard half of what she said. He could not get past the way Ruby had said *her* with utter disgust in her voice.

"Do you mean Bianca?"

"It has a name?"

Aware now that Ruby was being cruel, Theodore got defensive.

"What's wrong with you? She is really sweet. Just because she is foreign doesn't mean she isn't worthy of having friends."

Ruby's face scrunched as she tried to read between his words.

"Foreign? You do realize what she is, right?"

"She is a new student from England."

"No. She is unnatural, and honestly, I have a feeling that one is evil. I don't know for sure, but there are old rumors about her."

"You don't even know her." Theodore was furious. "You haven't spoken to her once." He was beginning to think Bianca was right about Ruby; maybe she wasn't as kind as she appeared.

"I don't need to talk to her to know she's up to no good."

"Enough. I'm done with this. You're being mean and I won't abandon her just because you say I should." Theodore took a deep breath. "Good bye."

As he walked away, Ruby shouted out to him.

"I'm just trying to be a friend!"

But Theodore ignored her and continued toward the piers. He never felt so angry in his life. His loyalty roared for Bianca, but his heart ached as the image of the girl he once admired dissolved into something ugly. He didn't want to believe Ruby was that cruel, but how could he pretend that conversation didn't just happen? How could he erase her mean words about his innocent friend from his memory? Maybe one day she'd find out she was mistaken. Maybe she'd come and apologize. But right now, his anger toward her was overwhelming.

He stormed over the bridge and went straight to Adie's Fish & Chum stand. Adelaide was there, organizing the catch of the day into nice displays. The ice bins were full; another busy night was ahead of him.

"What's the matter with you?" Adelaide asked, catching Theodore's icy vibes immediately.

"Just this girl at school."

"Your new friend? Bianca?"

"No, a different one. She came up to me after school and attacked Bianca behind her back. I guess she expected me to believe all the nasty things she was saying. It wasn't cool and put me in a really bad spot."

Adelaide's interest was piqued. "What did she have to say about your new friend?"

"She called her evil, for no good reason. They've never even talked to each other before."

Adelaide was deep in thought. She tried to mask the concern on her face but did a poor job of it. "Girls can be catty. Don't worry too much about it." She went back to perfecting her display. "When are you bringing Bianca over for dinner?"

Her tone gave Theodore suspicion and he knew he should've kept his mouth shut. Now Adelaide was wary about Bianca too.

"I don't know. I'll figure it out." He didn't want to talk about it anymore. He finally had a friend and everyone was trying to ruin it for him. It made no sense.

Taking the hint to drop the subject, Adelaide went silent. They prepped for the dinner crowd without talking much. Theodore tried to shake off his bad mood; he hated feeling this way. He wasn't used to having issues with other people because there never were other people who cared enough about him to have issues with. His dad didn't count because he grew up with that situation and was used to it, and Adelaide was very easy going and was more like an extended family member. In his fifteen years of moving around, he never made a solid friendship. Now, as he made an attempt to, he was already feeling stressed and it was only a few days into it. He would have to determine whether it was worth it or not to mention Ruby's comments to Bianca. He didn't like the idea of keeping secrets from his friend but he also didn't want to hurt her feelings by telling her another girl in their class hated her for no reason at all. The whole thing felt heavy and Theodore wished it had never happened. Having friends was proving to be complicated.

Theodore worked very hard that night, putting all his energy into selling fish. Before the crowd came, he cooked the scallops and oysters that were caught along with the fish. He was getting really skilled at seasoning them properly. The customers were coming back with great reviews. Adelaide mentioned that if he kept it up, she might let him prepare the fish to sell as pre-cooked meals. The idea of it made her face light up; that would be big money if people took a liking to it like they did with his prepared shellfish.

At the end of the work shift, Adelaide handed Theodore an envelope.

"There is a little extra in here for all the hard work you do. It's been half a year and you've proven to be an invaluable employee." Theodore took the stained envelope, thick with cash. "Treat yourself to something nice." She gave him a wink.

"Thank you," he said, truly shocked by the gesture. As much as he would like to treat himself to something he could enjoy, he knew the money would be going right toward the bills and groceries. He had a feeling Adelaide knew that too. She meant it when she said she valued all he did for her but he had to wonder if her intention was to subtly help him with the responsibilities his father left him with while he was gone. None of it mattered; he gratefully took the money and gave her a hug.

"Now get on," she shooed him away. "It's getting dark and you've got school tomorrow."

Theodore exited his work stand, but instead of turning right and stepping onto Peddler's Way, he went left and entered into the heart of the North Market. Adie's Fish & Chum stand was right along the entrance, so he never had to deal much with the madness that ensued between the crowded huts and narrow passageways. He had to get groceries to replenish the empty cabinets at home, so he ventured into the chaos. The dinner rush was almost over, but the market still bustled with people. Shifty characters meandered about, brushing shoulders and looking at each other with mistrust.

He saw the hooded girl with emerald eyes again. This time, she was accompanied by an angry little man. He argued with a vendor over the cost of ground beef as he walked by them. Without Bianca, the mysterious caped girl didn't notice him.

Mabel Bissette ran an egg stand toward the back of the market. The wispy old lady was aged with grace and her smile lines were etched into her face with permanence. Though quirky in nature, her aura radiated positivity. Bright and cheerful, she was part of the minority in this gloomy place.

"Theodore Finn," she exclaimed as he approached. "It's been too long."

"Had to save up."

"Well, you came on the right day." She pointed at a large brown hen in a crate on the floor. "Lady Madonna laid a fresh batch this afternoon. Look at these." She held an egg close to her face, making herself go cross-eyed. "Fit for a queen."

"They are quite nice. I'll take a dozen."

"Splendid." She collected twelve eggs and wrapped them in her special packaging. Each egg got a cushy blanket before being placed with care into a sturdy cardboard crate. Every single egg was given her full attention, as if she was saying farewell to someone she loved.

"Thank you, Mabel."

"Hope to see you again soon." She twirled to tend to Lady Madonna and the skirt of her sky blue sundress danced in the air around her.

Back into the worst of the congested market, Theodore made his way to his next stop. Swarmed by people, he wished to leave. In record time, he got his things and departed; he did not like to linger within those crowds longer than necessary.

Milk, two boxes of cereal, bread, peanut butter, jelly, eggs, ketchup. Enough to live off of. There were other items he wanted to buy, but he could not spend more money than he had.

Grocery bags in hand, he headed home. This had been a particularly rough Monday. From his highly unsettling morning sail, to the awkward confrontation with Ruby, he was ready to fall asleep and try again tomorrow.

Skipping supper, Theodore went to bed. His heavy thoughts receded as sleep took over, though they crept in the corners, shaping his dreams as they wished.

Chapter 9

Theodore woke up in a sweat. His sleep was laced with terrifying dreams. In them, Bianca could fly. With glowing red eyes, she snatched Ruby by her long, golden waves of hair and dragged her above the sea toward the lighthouse. Ruby screamed and Theodore was forced to watch helplessly. He took his sailboat and followed them out toward Apres Monde, but as he grew near, a storm rolled in and stopped his progress. He watched the traumatic scene from afar. Waves rocked his boat and frozen rain lashed his face as Bianca flew through the storm, unfazed, with Ruby in tow. He screamed for help but there was no one around to hear him. As the girls reached the lighthouse, a huge waved capsized his boat. He lost sight of them as the water drowned him. Right before his final breath, he woke up.

As he recapped the dream in his head, he was baffled. The roles each girl played in it were reversed. Bianca had done nothing wrong, she shouldn't have been the villain.

Eager to erase the awful start to this Tuesday, Theodore did his best to forget the dream so he could begin fresh. He ate his bowl of cereal slowly, then headed to school.

Bianca was already in her seat when he arrived. She always got there before everyone else. He smiled and waved at her, then took his own seat. He was barely on time, as usual, and Ms. Courtier would begin any moment.

Lunchtime came around sooner than he expected. Normally the day dragged but today it sped by. They sat at their usual spot and he ate his sandwich while she watched. She forgot her lunch again.

It was a typical mid-day break. They talked about trivial things. He learned more about her interests and hobbies. Apparently she enjoyed making crochet blankets and cooking bread with her mother. He told her more about sailing and how to command a small dinghy.

They were in the middle of discussing steering tactics when Rowan arrived and sat down across from them, uninvited.

"You don't belong here," he said, looking straight at Bianca. There was intense malice behind his eyes. Theodore went on the defensive immediately.

"Who do you think you are? No one invited you to sit with us, go away."

Rowan gave Theodore a bored look, then focused back in on Bianca.

"You know you don't."

"So long as he wants me here you have no right to say that."

"Once he learns what you are he'll be just as disgusted by you as I am."

"What are you guys talking about?" They both ignored him.

"I am just another new student. It's very unbecoming for a boy like you to attack an innocent girl."

Rowan laughed. "You're no innocent girl. I've gotten you to leave once before and I'll do it again. You're rotten and you won't be spoiling any other new kids at this school on my watch." It sounded like Rowan was sticking up for Theodore, but none of it made any sense.

"Leave her alone," Theodore tried to step in but it seemed like this was just the continuation of a previous altercation. Their faces were smug, challenging each other to something he was unaware of.

"You ought to take my advice when I say to ditch this freak," Rowan spoke to him now.

"She's not a freak."

"Are you sick? Cause only a clogged nose could block her stench."

"Didn't your mother teach you any manners?" Theodore said. He knew why Bianca smelt weird. It wasn't her fault; anyone with a fisherman in their family understood the odor that was often hard to wash away. "Your dad is a doctor. You come from a world of entitlement. If you lived one day like ours on the piers, you wouldn't be so quick to judge how we smell."

"I don't care where you live or what you do or the money your family has. That has nothing to do with this."

"It obviously does."

"Man," Rowan looked genuinely astonished, "You really don't know anything, do you? I thought Ruby filled you in yesterday."

Catching on to what was happening now, Theodore's blood pressure rose.

"Yeah, she came to me yesterday and tried to bully me into ditching Bianca as a friend. You are both jerks. Neither of you have a legitimate reason to dislike her, yet you have a thousand cruel words to throw at her."

Rowan took a deep breath. "Well, I'm not gonna be the one to tell you. I've seen what this one is capable of. I don't need her resentment aimed at me." Bianca's glare was lethal; Theodore was amazed she held it together so perfectly under such mean circumstances. "All I'll say is that I warned you. And when you realize I was right, I'll be here to help you clean up whatever mess she gets you into." Rowan stood up and left. Theodore was utterly confused.

"What the hell was that?"

"I don't know. Just a typical bully."

"But why you? It seemed like you two had it out before."

"Yeah, in the center of town. We got into a fight at the grocery store. He started picking on Cadence for no reason, so I stood up to him and told him off. Really embarrassed him in front of his brothers. Now I guess he has it out for me."

"Why didn't you mention this to me before?"

"Didn't seem important."

"Of course it's important." Theodore sighed. "Is your sister okay?"

"Yeah. She's really shy, so she was shaken up for a few days, but she's all right now."

"If it happens again, tell me. It's not cool that he thinks he can go around town harassing everyone he comes across. Just the other day he tried stealing fruit from Gus Yonk's fruit stand. And he and his brothers are constantly running past, launching rocks at us as we work. I can't even imagine how many people they have hurt by their antics."

"They aren't worth our time. Don't grant them the gift of your attention."

An uneasy feeling remained in the pit of his stomach.

"I have been adamantly defending you against all these strange accusations, but if there is any truth to it or there's something I ought to know, you can tell me. I am your friend and you can confide in me." Though he meant it kindly, Bianca took it as an insult.

"If you were my friend it wouldn't have even crossed your mind that there was any truth to their hurtful words. You've spent time with me, we have gotten to know each other pretty well, and if you are going to believe rumors over what you've learned from me first hand, then you're just as terrible as the rest of them." She stood up, looking like she was about to walk away.

"Stop, sit down. I'm sorry. Of course I don't believe any of it, but you can't blame me for wondering. You have an overwhelming amount of people questioning you. And now they're all questioning me for choosing to be your friend. It's concerning, even if I haven't found any truth or valid reasoning to warrant their suspicion."

"It's hurtful that you even asked."

"Tell me honestly that I have nothing to worry about and it'll never come up again."

"Of course you don't."

"Okay. The topic is dropped."

She looked at him with hurt in her eyes, but sat back down. They sat in silence for a few moments before Theodore began talking to her about trivial things once more. It took her a few minutes to stop feeling sad for herself, but she eventually came around and participated happily in the conversation. The rest of lunch flew by and the bell rang indicating it was over. They walked back to class, consciously staying far from where Ruby and Rowan walked ahead of them.

The school day ended and Bianca left briskly. She seemed okay, but Theodore understood why she might want to escape this place after the day she had. He headed to work, feeling very numb and unsure of all that took place around him.

The night passed, as did the next few days. Bianca was absent from school the rest of the week. Theodore was furious. He couldn't help but assume it had something to do with the confrontation with Rowan. At the end of the school day on Friday, Theodore stopped Ruby in the hallway.

"I hope you're happy."

She looked at him sympathetically. "I'm sorry she went away."

She appeared apologetic, but not for what she claimed to be sorry for. She was sorry for Theodore, not that Bianca was gone.

"This is your fault. You recruited Rowan to do your dirty work. He embarrassed her, made her feel terrible, and now she's been missing for days."

"If you recall, she only showed up to school twice last week. They tend to come and go as they please."

"She's probably mortified to come back!"

"Talk to Adelaide. I know you're close with her, she'll fill you in on everything. Rowan is right. I can't mix myself up with that girl. I've heard stories and I don't want to be on the receiving end of her vengeance."

Theodore let out an aggravated growl and stormed away from Ruby. He couldn't stand all the lies and mean spirited comments anymore. If this was how kids his age treated each other, maybe he was better off alone.

The market was busy and the constant interaction with customers helped keep his mind off everything else. Adelaide tried to cheer him up with jokes but he was feeling too glum to accept her efforts. This whole thing was new to him: the social interactions, the teenage drama, the conflict. He was having trouble adjusting. He couldn't cope with the sudden onslaught he'd received since befriending Bianca and he hoped things got easier soon.

On Saturday at noon he went to the docks, hopeful that Bianca might be there. Since he didn't know why she was absent or if she'd be returning to school, he figured it was the best shot at seeing her again. He didn't know where she lived and they had met there the previous weekend, so it seemed a logical expectation.

He waited an hour without any sign of her. The autumn afternoon sunlight beat down on him as he patiently let the time pass. The air was crisp and chilly as he watched the pier for her arrival. After another half hour passed, he finally conceded that she was not coming. He climbed down the dock's ladder and made his way to his sailboat.

It was calm on the water. He let the idea of seeing his friend go and tried to enjoy the day. Moments came and went where he thought he could hear her calling to him from the docks, like she had the last time, but it was never really happening. He was alone again. No one looking for him or wondering where he was.

He sighed as he sailed on. It was a very strange feeling knowing that he was out on these dangerous waters sailing with no one aware of his whereabouts. It was scary to think that if something went wrong, no one would know where to look. Or even worse, no one would even realize he was missing. Adelaide would when he didn't show up for work, but by then it would be too late.

Apres Monde Lighthouse was visible in the distance, but after what happened the last time he got too close, he decided not to sail any closer. He no longer had any interest. Instead of aiming toward the open sea in the direction of the lighthouse, he went west, toward the distant cove that was an uninhabited part of Nether Isle. Its rocky surface and rough waters made it impossible for people to live or hang out there, so it was always abandoned. He could see the heavy fog settled in all around Maudit Cove as he got closer. It was always masked by mist. A peculiar anomaly in the way the air, land, and water met in that exact location must have been the cause.

He could not get too close because the water was volatile near its jagged shores, but as he grew nearer the air became frosty, leaving him with an alarming chill. The scream he heard two weeks ago during his morning sail returned, echoing through the afternoon sky. Theodore looked back toward the docks, but no one there was startled or alerted to the desperate cry. Trying to find the source of this scream, he looked harder, trying to see through the smog. The horrible noise sounded off again, causing the pace of his heart to quicken. Somebody was in trouble and he did not know how to help them. The last time he heard this noise he thought it was the crossing of air currents playing tricks on his ears, but this time, how could that be the case? It was a mild day and he could pinpoint the location the scream originated from.

Unsure what else he could do, he turned his boat around and headed back to the dock as fast as possible. Upon reaching it, he hurried up the ladder and begged for help from anyone who would listen.

"There's a girl out there," he shouted, "by Maudit Cove. She's screaming and sounds to be in terrible pain. We need to help her." But the few people on the docks looked at him with critical stares and ignored him. He ran up to Oscar Dregg, the local butcher, to plead for help.

"There is a girl who needs help out there. She sounds like she is dying."

"By the cove?" Oscar growled.

"Yes. I couldn't see her, the fog was too thick, but I know her cries were coming from there. We need a bigger boat and a rescue crew."

"Nobody can get out to them rocks there, nor does anybody want to. So either it's a figment of your imagination or a phantom."

"I swear, it was real," Theodore pleaded. "She will die if we don't help her."

"Ain't nothing can help her now. If she's at Maudit Cove, she's already dead." He turned away, leaving Theodore appalled at his lack of compassion.

"What if it was your daughter out there? Or somebody you cared about?" he called out as the butcher walked away. "Then you'd be inclined to try!" His words were ignored and he was forced to find someone else to help him.

Market manager Jedd Carlin stood at the dock's edge, fishing with Marcus Baudin. Theodore pleaded his case to them but their reaction was similar to Oscar's. They laughed at him and told him to leave them alone. They were more concerned with fishing in peace.

As he continued his quest to get the girl help, everyone he encountered either ignored him or showed him the same dismissive behavior. The responses he received were harsh; they all advised him not to bother. But how could Theodore live with himself knowing he ignored the desperate cries of someone in need? That he let a person die because he did not find them help? How could all these other people be so content with letting this happen? No one felt called to action; no one took the initiative to be a Good Samaritan.

He climbed back down the ladder and took matters into his own hands. Instead of getting back on his small sailboat, he got onto a slightly larger one, figuring no one would notice if he borrowed their piece of junk for an hour. The boat was scratched and poorly taken care of, but it had a better chance of tackling those rough waves successfully than his dinghy.

He never sailed a boat as big as this one before but he did his best and made it back to Maudit Cove in good time. Upon reaching the edge of the fog, he rolled up the sails and coasted. The screaming had stopped; he had not heard it once upon reentering the water. He listened carefully now for any sign of life, but there was none. No whimpering, no soft crying, no sounds of someone breathing. He turned on the motor so he could steer the vessel and get closer to the shore without crashing into it.

There wasn't a soul in sight. He hoped to at least see the girl who sourced those awful cries, even if it was only her lifeless body, but he saw nothing. There was no closure or answer to the mysterious screams. His heart pounded as his sight shifted to the dark water. If she drowned, he would never know.

Saddened, he did one more lap to scour the unfriendly shore of the cove before heading back to the docks. Someone just died, or so it seemed, and no one was bothered by it except him. When he reached the docks, the vibe of everything being perfectly okay was unnatural. People should care, they should be outraged, but no one was affected at all. The day continued as normal. It was overwhelmingly discouraging and Theodore would have to find closure in his own way. He didn't know where to begin. He was never this close to death before.

He headed back to his home, drenched in sweat and fighting off tears of anger.

Chapter 10

The next two weeks passed in a blur. Theodore was distraught; unable to accept the lack of compassion that resided within Nether Isle. Did he do enough to save that girl? He played that afternoon over in his mind a hundred times, imagining different scenarios where the outcome was brighter. Every time he imagined saving her, his heart ached more remembering that he didn't. Everyone told him not to worry about it, that the noises could have been a product of nature, but it felt too real. He hoped it was the winds rustling together that created the sound of a human cry but he couldn't make himself believe it. And since he couldn't convince himself it was all a figment of his imagination, he subsequently couldn't help but come to the conclusion that the source of those cries had perished, all alone, at Maudit Cove. Nothing could console him.

Adelaide tried. She told him that she heard similar cries come from that direction but that they never originated from a living human being. She tried to tell him that it was one of the many peculiarities that occurred among Nether Isle and that he was just unaccustomed to this phenomenon. He considered believing her, but his gut told him there was more to it. He was there when it happened, only a mile or two offshore. It was too real, too life-like to be nature playing tricks on him. Everything felt wrong and he was having trouble coping with it.

Bianca hadn't come back, so he did not even have a friend to confide in. After the second Saturday of her not showing up at the docks, Theodore resigned to her chosen departure from their friendship. He would never understand why or what he could have done differently, but it was too much to process on top of everything else. He was used to feeling alone but lately, the solitude had become suffocating and every second he spent without a distraction was torture. He found himself trying to crawl out of his skin in the dull, quiet moments he used to enjoy. Ripping at his hair, scratching his skin where there was no itch, and digging his dirty nails into his palms. This behavior had him questioning his mental stability. He was not sure what was happening to him, but he was fully aware of his slow decline into a harrowing depression.

Nothing was wrong, yet he felt a sadness so powerful it could not be contained. It loomed over him every day, growing larger at each attempt to ignore its presence. His loneliness had never bothered him before; in fact he thrived in solitude. He had to believe that was not the issue now. Was it this place? This isle of selfishness and cruelty that had shifted his perception on life? He hoped not; he was stuck here for a while and could not have an unsolvable problem being the cause of his grief.

It must have been the glimmer of friendship he felt before it vanished without cause. It must be the fact that a person died on this isle and no one gave a damn to investigate it further. It made him realize how alone he really was. If he died, would they all dismiss it as easily as they had the unnamed individual at Maudit Cove? Would he be deemed as unworthy for love and compassion as that lost soul? Would anyone care enough to try to save him if there was still time?

Adelaide would, but she was old and barely ever knew of his whereabouts. She'd be too late. Maybe Bianca would have while they were friends, but now she was gone and it was like she never existed at all. He could only count on one person in a town full of people and the idea of this made him sick.

It was a Wednesday; half the week complete, countless others to go. Theodore was at the market working his usual shift when Marcus Baudin came up to buy some crawfish.

"What's wrong with you, boy?" He slurred his words. His French-American accent was heavier when he had a buzz going.

"Nothing. What can I get you?"

"A pound of them crawfish and a pound of the fresh catch." The man squinted his eyes, trying to see one Theodore instead of two. "Ya look pale as a ghost. You sure you ain't sick? I can't be catching nothing from ya. I've got a life to live."

"I'm not sick, I'm tired. But thanks for letting me know I look like shit."

"Adelaide's workin' you too hard, huh?" He placed a hairy elbow on the counter and leaned in closer. An onslaught of rotten breath and body odor assaulted Theodore's senses. His gag reflex triggered without pause.

"Back off," he said, shooing the middle-aged man from his counter.

"I told ya you was sick!" Marcus bellowed. "I don't want your food, it's contaminated!"

Everyone around him looked at Theodore skeptically, questioning whether or not it was safe to purchase food from here today. As Marcus ranted on, people slowly trickled away from Adie's stand.

"I'm not sick, you just smell horrid!" Frantic that he was losing a big chunk of business, Theodore called out onto the pier. "I'm not sick. Everyone come back!"

But no one listened. They all dispersed, finding other vendors to buy their dinner from and leaving Theodore with no customers at all.

"You're a foul jerk, Marcus Baudin!" Theodore shouted as loud as he could. Marcus heard him, turning around as he backed away. A devious smile crept onto the man's face.

"Shoulda kept your prices fair." He turned around and disappeared into the mayhem of the inner market.

In defeat, Theodore fell back onto his flimsy folding chair. He looked over to Gus in his neighboring fruit stand. The old man shrugged his shoulders at the whole ordeal and then tipped his bucket hat over his eyes, resuming his nap. Theodore scoffed; Gus was robbed all the time because he chose to sleep while his produce was left out in the open. It never bothered Theodore before, but suddenly, he felt enormous rage at the old man's lack of responsibility. Gus knew this town was full of dishonorable people that would take the opportunity to steal free items, yet he slept, fully aware that this took place right in front of him.

"You shouldn't be sleeping if you're the only one manning your stand," he yelled over to him. Gus lifted his hat to inspect Theodore more closely.

"All that fruit up there is close to rotten anyhow. I get a new shipment in tomorrow." He placed the hat back over his face, talking through it now. "I'm an old man. Sleep is more important than that damned fruit."

Theodore didn't say another word to him, nor did he watch his back while he slumbered. He didn't care anymore.

As the weekend arrived, Theodore skipped his usual Saturday sail. He had no motivation to get up and move. It was alarming him how little enthusiasm he now had for the few things that used to bring him joy.

The afternoon passed. He stayed in bed, staring at the ceiling all day. At 5 p.m. he forced himself to get up. There was no place to go. After pacing the small space between his kitchen and living room for a half hour, he decided to go to Adelaide's. She would welcome him in if he showed up at her doorstep.

When he did, she hurried him inside as the rain clouds swirled overhead. He hadn't even noticed them.

"You didn't even wear a raincoat," Adelaide scolded.

"I didn't know a storm was coming."

"All you had to do was look up to know one was brewing." She saw the blank look in his eyes. "Sit down, right now."

Theodore obliged and Adelaide put her hands on her hips.

"What on earth is the matter with you? Over the past two weeks, the happy-go-lucky, self-sufficient boy I once knew vanished. You hadn't a care in the world when you shoulda had a million. All of a sudden, *you're* the walking rainstorm I need to be concerned about. You need to tell me what's happened so I can help you."

"Nothing has happened. Everything just feels different."

"Is it cause of that voice you heard by Maudit Cove?"

"Maybe. I don't know. I try to believe what you told me about it not being real and those weird sounds happening all the time, but I can't."

"There's a lot going on here on this isle at all times. Too much for any one person to fully comprehend. Our rules aren't the same as regular towns; there's lots of oddities to get acquainted with. Maudit Cove is one of them. I've been trying to lay the knowledge on you slowly so I don't overwhelm you. I've seen folks go crazy when they learn certain truths."

"What else do I need to know? Until recently, I thought this was just a regular, gray fishing town. Dreary and miserable like all the rest I've lived at."

"You need to cheer up before I go telling you things you ain't ready to hear. I need my happy Theodore back. He can handle all the wild tales I'll tell you. This new boy I see in front of me now would crumble beneath my words."

Theodore did not fight her on this. He couldn't imagine she really had anything all that life changing to tell him. Her hints at there being a greater secret amongst Nether Isle slipped away from him as his sadness returned. Even in her presence, he could not shake it.

"Is it possible I miss my dad?" he suddenly said aloud, having never thought of this before.

"Of course it's possible."

"He's the worst though."

"But he's still your companion. He may not be the best one, but he's all you've ever known."

Theodore sighed. Maybe the non-stop silence was getting to him more than he ever realized it would. The absence of his father's constant complaints left a void in the space between work and school. Even if it was unpleasant communication, it was better than going an entire day without saying a word to anyone.

"You can always come here and spend time with me, like you're doing now. Anytime you want, and as often as you want."

"I know. I just don't like burdening you. This isn't your problem."

"Stop your foolishness. I never get company. Having you over for dinner is a treat."

"Well, maybe it's not you I'm worried about. I know Eustice doesn't like visitors. I don't want him disliking me any more than he already does."

"Don't worry about him. He's a grumpy old man. In time, you'll understand why I don't give a crap what he has to say. Freaking pain in my side, that man is." She continued mumbling aggravations for Eustice as she bustled about, pulling up two tray tables and a chair for herself.

"You're in luck," she said. "I made lasagna tonight. I made a whole tray, with plans to eat the leftovers throughout the week, so there's plenty to fill a plate for you." She gave him a warm smile, then disappeared into the kitchen.

Her warmth crept into him, infecting his darkness with light. The heaviness that plagued him was momentarily lifted and he embraced this moment of ease with vigor. He would hold onto this feeling of happiness for as long as it lasted.

Theodore scarfed down his lasagna. The food hit his belly hard, causing it to grumble in delight. He hadn't realized how hungry he was until eating this proper meal. Maybe that's why he was so out of it.

Adelaide served him a second plateful, which he ate every bite of. Too full to move, he leaned back in his chair and let his body digest. His mood was still lifted. This was exactly what he needed: good company and a good meal.

A strange chill took over Theodore's body. Out of instinct, he looked toward the kitchen. Eustice was standing there in the shadows, watching him with narrowed eyes.

"Come join us, Eustice," Theodore called out to him, offering an olive branch and refusing to let the old man's dislike of him ruin his mood. But Eustice said nothing and crept backwards into the darkness until Theodore could no longer see him.

Theodore sighed, unsure why Adelaide's husband held such animosity toward him.

The antique grandfather clock stationed near Adelaide's stairs began to chime. After eight bells, Theodore snapped out of his relaxation. It was already 8 p.m. and he couldn't believe how fast the time had passed.

"I have to get going. Thank you so much for the meal. I am already starting to feel a lot better."

"Good. Come over more often. We'll get you back to your normal self in no time." She gave him a smile. "Then I can start filling you in on all the secrets this little isle holds."

"Sounds like a deal." Theodore gave her a grateful hug before departing.

He walked along Peddler's Way, gazing up at the starry sky. Whatever storm had been brewing earlier was gone now. It was lifted, just like his spirits.

Chapter 11

Upon reaching the outside of his home, an uneasy feeling crossed over him. A light filtered through the front window but he did not recall leaving one on. He paused before entering, sure it was only passing paranoia. It was entirely possible he had forgotten such a small detail. He was quite distracted lately.

He walked through the front door and immediately realized his suspicions were justified. Marcus was standing in his kitchen, knife in hand, breathing heavily. While his stance and presence was a clear threat, his face remained blank and his eyes empty.

"Come here boy," he growled, waving him over with the knife in hand.

"What are you doing in my house? Get out!"

"I've got a task to complete." His head jerked upon his neck, "I gotta take care of this first."

"What are you talking about?" Theodore remained near the door, ready to bolt. Marcus let out an agonized cry. There was a strange internal battle going on. "You shouldn't drink so much," Theodore continued. "You're going to regret this in the morning."

"I'm not drunk," the fat man shouted. He was drenched in sweat and the hair on his exposed belly was matted to his skin. His face was bright red, his eyes were bloodshot, and his body spasmed in unnatural ways as he moved.

"Why are you here?" Theodore asked, not believing that Marcus was sober.

"To take what's mine."

Without a moment's warning, Marcus lunged at Theodore, catching him by the arm before he had time to run out the door.

"I don't have anything of yours," Theodore shouted, but he was already yanked to the ground and straddled.

"What I need is your life. Well, just your body." He noticed for the first time that Marcus's heavy accent was gone. "All these years, I've sacrificed everything for you. Now it's time you pay me back."

Theodore screamed and fought beneath the weight of the man. While he thrashed, trying to break free, Marcus had his knife pointed at him with one hand and used the other to turn Theodore's head to the side.

"Stop fighting me, boy. This is your obligation to me." Theodore punched Marcus hard in the groin but the man didn't seem to feel it. His eyes were vacant but his actions were calculated and forceful. He acted with intention. Something was not right.

"Why are you doing this to me? You barely know me," Theodore screamed at him, "You're going to kill me, put that knife down."

"You ain't dying, just being replaced." He took the tip of the knife and pierced the side of Theodore's neck. Suddenly, Marcus began having a conversation with himself.

"No! It has to be the back of the neck. I can't slip through the side."

"I'm trying, he won't hold still!" Marcus's accent returned momentarily.

"Choke him. When he's outta breath he'll be easier to move."

"I don't want to."

"You have to. I ain't leaving till you finish the deed."

Frantic, Theodore fought harder. Marcus grabbed his throat, squeezing the fresh wound on the side of his neck. His air passage shrunk and he gasped trying to hold onto his last breaths.

"Don't kill him. He's no use to me dead," Marcus said without his accent. Theodore's strength was weakened, he could not fight him any longer. Marcus backhanded the side of his face, then flipped his body over. Theodore could feel the knife enter into the back of his neck. The cool metal traveled in a jagged line through his skin. As the knife pulled out, blood spilled down the sides of his neck.

The front door to his home swung open, bringing with it a frigid breeze. Dizzy from the loss of blood and lack of oxygen, Theodore could not tell what was going on, but he felt Marcus's weight lift a little as a voice began to chant:

Par la puissance de l'Univers:
Quittez maintenant,

vous ne pouvez pas rester.

Votre présence est indésirable.

Être allé

au royaume de l'au-delà

où vous appartenez.

(By the power of the Universe:

Exit now,

you cannot stay.

Your presence is unwelcome.

Be gone

to the realm of the afterlife

where you belong.)

The voice was that of a female. She chanted these words multiple times, doing so with rhythm and melodic intensity. The tone of her voice was severe and the words were having an effect on Marcus. His entire body started to convulse.

"Stop it," Marcus shouted. He flailed his arms toward the girl, trying to take her down, but the words she spoke held an invisible power over him. Theodore could not see the girl; he could barely move and the loss of blood was making his vision blurry. Marcus abandoned him on the ground to stop this girl's chant, but the longer it went on, the more Marcus broke down. After a few minutes, he was on his knees, screaming in agonized pain.

"We were so close," he said to himself in the strange new voice.

"*Help me,*" Marcus's regular voice returned.

The girl finished another round of the chant and Marcus collapsed to the floor. He landed right next to Theodore, who watched him out of the corner of his eye. He still could not move, but he felt his strength slowly returning.

Marcus convulsed on the floor. His eyes rolled into the back of his head while his limbs shook uncontrollably. The sight of it was terrifying. For the first time, Theodore began to suspect the man might be possessed. Before he had time to scoff at his own imagination, his crazy suspicion proved to be true.

Marcus's mouth opened to an unnatural width and a misty vapor exited his body. Appalled, Theodore mustered up enough strength to sit up and scoot his body far away from the demon now leaving Marcus. He averted his stare from the supernatural freak show taking place before him, to the girl by the door who had saved him. It was Bianca.

She wore a crown made of herbs: sage and rosemary, and held a blood-red candle with both hands, keeping it sturdily placed before her heart. Her gaze was focused and intense. She did not look at

Theodore once; only at the spirit who was under the control of her spell.

As he refocused on the strange sight now unfolding before his eyes, he watched the phantom begin to take shape, morphing into a human. As the transformation continued, he recognized the ghost. It was his father.

Chester Finn now stood before them. Tall and foreboding, having previously been mere mist. Theodore's mouth was agape and he was at a loss for words. Stunned, he sat there immobilized. Chester ignored him and tackled the issue of Bianca first.

He quickly lunged at her, ripping a necklace holding a green crystal from her neck. At its removal, Bianca let out a pained scream, tossing the lit candle to the floor and knocking the crown of herbs from her head. The candle's fire remained, precariously rolling toward the long window curtains. Neither Chester nor Bianca attempted to squash the flame.

"Stay back, I'm stronger than you," Bianca threatened.

"Not without your crystal." Chester let the necklace dangle in front of her. "I did a little research before possessing that idiot." Chester motioned toward the ground at Marcus. "I know what you are and you can't do those kind of spells without this. I hung by them Ouijans on Salamander Pier. Did my homework. I'm not gonna let you stop me now."

"You clearly did not do enough."

"What was that enchantment you had goin? Ain't one I heard the Ouijans practicing."

"Leave, before I place it on you again."

"Like I said, you ain't got your crystal to protect yourself from its effects now. You can't do nothing to me. Nothing, and no one, can stop me."

"You don't have a body to possess," she spat back at him. "Marcus is unconscious. Useless. Not to mention, he's onto you now. He'll fight you the next time you try to enter him, making it impossible for you to succeed. You'd need a new host and I will not let you find one. I will stalk your every move, warning people of your intentions before you get an opportunity to take them by surprise."

Chester laughed at her threats.

"You can't keep up with my every move. I've been watching you, too. You're a busy little bee, with motives of your own." Chester's eyes narrowed. "Theodore is mine."

"No, he is not. You can't make the incision on your own."

"I suggest you get out of my home before I *make* you get out."

"This stopped being your home the minute you died."

"Don't test me, girl." He went at her with both hands aimed for her neck, but Bianca began her chant again:

Par la puissance de l'Univers:

110

Quittez maintenant,

vous ne pouvez pas rester.

Votre présence est indésirable.

Être allé

au royaume de l'au-delà

où vous appartenez.

As she said it this time, her face grimaced, like the words hurt as they came out. She continued through the pain. Chester stopped, appearing to be halted by an invisible force. An inexplicable breeze picked up and swirled through the room, rustling Theodore's hair as he watched this horrific scene unravel before him. It was so strong it extinguished the candle's flame before the fire reached the long curtain and set the entire house ablaze. Both his father and his friend fought the new wind as it lashed at their faces. Bianca placed her hand near the knob of the front door and it swung open. The airstream sucked Chester outside, causing him to disappear from sight between a set of blinks. Without stopping the chant, Bianca took out a black piece of chalk and scribbled symbols onto the wood floor that lined the entrance. The winds grew stronger as she continued the chant. Something flew into Theodore's eye. He rubbed it, trying to free the foreign substance. When he opened his eyes again, Bianca was gone too.

He got to his feet and hobbled to the doorway. He stuck his head into the night air. Not a soul in sight. The mysterious wind had vanished right along with Chester and Bianca.

He was enraged with questions. Blood dripped down his neck, but the pain of his flesh wound did not compare to that of his heart. He felt like a pawn in everyone else's schemes and it was too much to tolerate. Enough was enough. Without putting his shoes on, he slammed the door, locked it, and stormed into the night.

Chapter 12

"Answers, now!" Theodore barked as he barged through Adelaide's front doorway. It was near midnight and she was sleeping. The sound of his angry entrance woke her and she emerged from her bedroom in her nightgown and curlers. Normally, she wouldn't tolerate this kind of attitude from anybody, but upon seeing her young friend covered in blood, her normal defense dropped.

"What happened to you? Who did this?" she exclaimed, horrified. He stared back at her with a blank expression, realizing for the first time, he really had no clue. Ghosts? Demons? Body snatchers?

"My father, I think." Theodore tried to make sense of what just happened to him. So many things he once thought were imaginary came to life, all at once. The words to explain it felt absurd.

"Your father?" Adelaide's eyes grew wide in horror. "But why? How? I thought he'd be gone another two months."

"He's back, but he's dead." Theodore collapsed beneath the words as he said them. Saying them aloud broke the barrier between his perception of reality and actual reality. An explanation of the weird terror he just endured poured from his mouth. "Marcus Baudin attacked me, but it turned out to be my father's ghost inside him that was really doing the deed. Bianca saved me with some supernatural chant. It ripped my dad's spirit out of Marcus, revealing him to me." Theodore crumpled into a nearby chair and buried his head into his hands.

"Oh boy," Adelaide said, seeming to understand what was going on now. "This was definitely not how I wanted you to discover Nether Isle's secret." She shook her head. "Let me tend to your wound, then I'll fill you in on everything."

She returned from the kitchen with a tube of topical antibiotic ointment, a large sheet of gauze, and medical tape. She nursed his deep neck wound and then covered it, leaving him with a sizeable bandage covering the back of his neck.

"We will need to go into town to have that stitched up. It's not too deep that it can't wait. You deserve an explanation." She sat down on the couch next to him. The only light in the room was that of the fireplace, which Adelaide relit upon his arrival.

"Nether Isle is a special place," she began. "Not only is it home to us, but it is also home to the deceased. In fact, this was their land first. Nether Isle is essentially the waiting room for the waiting room. Some people pass quietly into their next life, the next world. Others go straight to the damnation they fated themselves to from living evil lives. The rest—the majority—end up in the netherworld. Not quite Hell, but just as terrifying. These spirits are at unrest, they are unhappy, they do not want to be dead and some even have unsettled scores they wish to finish. They are dangerous because they can only see what they want. They have afterlife tunnel-vision, causing them to be unaware of the damage their actions cause to those still living. Often times, they only stick around in order to complete one thing they could not finish while alive. These types of spirits, or ghosts, roam the entire globe. You've heard of them, I'm sure." Theodore nodded, he knew some people believed in ghosts. He'd heard stories about ghosts with vendettas and spirits who haunted particular places for selfish reasons. He just never believed any of it before.

"The difference is," Adelaide continued, "on Nether Isle, these ghosts can take on human form. They look real. If you don't have a trained eye to spot the signs that they are dead, you'd never realize. Nobody knows why or how, but it's the way it has always been here. As far as anyone knows, it's been this way since the beginning of time. That lighthouse in the middle of the ocean is a beacon for them. Apres Monde Lighthouse, better known as the Light to the Other World, guides them here from afar. Maudit Cove is the portal. It's where they are ripped from this world and sent to their final fate. It's why, so often, the sounds of screams will come from there. They don't want to go."

It sounded like an old wives tale, but Adelaide spoke with grave seriousness. "These spirits are so dangerous because they will do *anything* in order to stay here. Nether Isle residents have adapted to this reality by growing hard and emotionally unattached. They had to. It's the only way to survive. That's why they seem so cruel and heartless to you. The ghosts would rule this place if the humans were not always on their guard. I'm very surprised your father managed to get into Marcus."

"There are millions of people on this planet, this place should be overflowing with spooks," Theodore added, trying to make sense of it all.

"This isn't the only isle for them. There are quite a few, spread across the globe. I know of at least three others, and I'm sure there are plenty undiscovered. Plus, many spirits ignore the light summon and remain where they are. They don't want to let go and some don't even know they are dead."

"So what just happened to me then?" He needed to get back on track. His dad died and tried to take him along for the ride. Chester's selfishness stung worse than any insult he paid him while alive, and Theodore had to make sense of it all.

"Sounds like your dad died while out on the job, came back, somehow learned the ropes of being deceased around here pretty quick, possessed Marcus, and then attacked you." She pointed at Theodore's neck, "What it looks like he was trying to do was a permanent possession. For temporary ones, the spirit enters a living body through the mouth, eyes, ears, or nose. Any of those work because they are right near the brain. They then settle themselves into the body and seize control of the mind. This type of possession is temporary because they only have outside control of the body. They need to truly be inside in order for it to last. To do this, they must slit a deep gash into the back of the neck or down the center of the ribcage, right above the heart. Deep enough to slip in, but not too deep to cause lasting damage to their new body. It's rare to see the incision made on the chest, the neck tends to be much easier for them."

"Why didn't he just do it himself?" Theodore asked, hurt that his father would do this to him. "Why did he hide behind Marcus instead of owning his actions and letting me see him as the evil bastard he really is?"

"Well, your father is a terrible man, in life and death, but he had no choice but to take a host body to capture his permanent body. Even on Nether Isle, ghosts can't make true contact with us. They can only hold real-life objects for short periods of time before the object falls through their hands. And for ghosts as new as your father, I'd imagine he couldn't hold a knife longer than two seconds before it fell to the floor. With years of practice, some spirits can hold inanimate objects for a few minutes, but no ghost can touch a human. So even if they could wield their weapon long enough, they wouldn't be able to hold their victim down long enough to use it. They pass right through us."

"I'm having trouble believing you aren't just telling me far-fetched folklore."

"This is why I was waiting to tell you. I was going to ease you into it. Teach you slowly instead of dumping it all on you at once. It sounds like gibberish, trust me, I know. But it's the truth. I was going to start you off with Eustice, let you see it yourself. Never thought you'd be attacked by a ghost, your own father no less, and used as a replacement body."

"Eustice?"

"Yeah, Eustice is dead. Has been for a year and a half now. Refuses to go to Maudit Cove without me. Won't go near the lighthouse cause it sucks them in like flies to a flame, landing them right on Maudit Cove before they realize where they are. Nothing I can do about him, he's as stubborn dead as he was alive."

"So essentially, he's rushing your death, since he will only go if you go with him."

"Bingo."

"Now I get why you're always so mean to him."

"Yeah, it's a selfish game he's playing. But like I said, these spirits have tunnel-vision. Once they're dead, their goals become very focused and intense, and always revolve around their own wants."

"This is terrible. My dad will come back for me. I need to learn that chant Bianca did."

"That part confuses me. Tell me more about it."

"I'm not sure when she came, or how she knew what was happening. I haven't seen her in weeks. But as I was pinned to the ground and Marcus was slicing my neck open, she arrived. Started speaking in a different language. It was a chant of some sort, but I couldn't understand the words. Sounded like French. Anyway, she went through the chant once or twice before Marcus couldn't handle it anymore. He got off me and the magic of her words captured him. He started convulsing on the ground and I managed to garner enough strength to make it to the other side of the room. That's when my dad exited Marcus's body. The whole thing was surreal. I'm still having trouble believing it happened."

"I'm just shocked Bianca was able to cast a spell on a ghost."

"They were talking about Ouijans. Sounded like a religion, or a cult. Looked like magic to me. I've never heard of it before."

"It's a branch of the Wiccan religion. They exist here because they need to. We need them here." Adelaide's eyes were worried. "Tell me more about what Bianca did."

"She was wearing a crown made of herbs and was using a candle with her spell. Once my dad was revealed, he spoke to her and mentioned the Ouijans. That he had been studying their rituals. He didn't recognize the chant Bianca had used though. It all got weird toward the end. My dad ripped some green crystal from around her neck and she freaked out. But she kept the chant going. Its magic swept them both out of the house."

"So she cast the spell, and got swept out of the house along with your dad?"

"No, she lingered. Drew something in chalk on the floor by the door before running off. I don't know why she didn't stick around. It's really frustrating; I thought she was my friend. She could've explained what she did. I need to know how to protect myself."

"She 'ran off' because she didn't belong there. I'll get you the training you need."

"What do you mean she didn't belong there? Thank God she *was* there, otherwise I'd be lost forever."

Adelaide looked baffled. "I still have the creeping suspicion she's a ghost too. Everything everyone has told me leads me to believe I'm right. Your friend Ruby even came to me one day, expressing concern. It's why I wanted to meet Bianca, to see for myself." She inhaled deeply before continuing, rationalizing against her own claims. "But if she cast this spell herself, I don't know how she could possibly be a ghost. The Ouijans of Nether Isle purposefully crafted their spells so that ghosts could not use them."

"You, and everyone else, need to get off Bianca's case. I can see now why everyone was concerned; she was new, and weird, in a town filled with ghosts who take solid form, but I think we can safely put this case to rest now. She risked her life to save me."

Adelaide did not look so convinced. "What was this necklace you mentioned? It was a crystal?"

"A green crystal, yeah."

"And after your father ripped it from her neck, that's when she started acting peculiar? Removed her crown and started to rush the chants?"

"Yes," he answered with hesitation. "What are you getting at?"

"She's using something in addition to the Ouijan magic. Or something completely separate from it. There's no telling how old of a ghost she is, perhaps she knows more than we or the Ouijans do."

"I thought we established she wasn't a ghost."

"I need to meet her. I need to meet her without her suspecting I know, or that you now question her."

"But I don't question her."

"Well, you should."

Theodore didn't want to argue. "She ran off. I don't know where she lives or if I'll ever see her again."

"You will. They always come back. Like I told ya, they are selfish and have tunnel-vision. If she's been after you, for whatever reason, she'll be back. They can't help themselves, even if it's in their best interest to stay away. Whatever her goal is, she will do all in her power to see it through."

"You realize, you are asking me to doubt the girl who just saved my life."

"You need to stop being so naïve. You'd think after what ya just went through, you'd be feelin' a bit more cautious about everyone now."

"Yeah, well, I'm not ruling it out. First and foremost, regardless of what she may or may not be, I need to find her and thank her. Even if she is a ghost, she doesn't seem like a bad one. I'd be eternally possessed by my father right now if she hadn't intervened."

"Fine, but be careful. Don't just buy everything she tries to sell ya. Listen carefully and use your better judgment to see if she's tellin' the whole truth or not."

"Fine." Theodore didn't want to talk about it anymore.

"You stay here tonight. Marcus is gonna be confused, angry, and in a lot of pain when he wakes up. It's better not to be near him when he does. Karma is dealing him a solid for his spiteful behavior as of late."

"He really is a royal jerk."

"Universe always comes around to getcha. Always remember that. Better to be kind and well-intended today than sorry and repenting tomorrow. You'll always pay for your misconduct, one way or another."

Theodore yawned, beat up by life. He needed to sleep. He imagined he might need to sleep for a few days to feel right again. Part of him wished he could stay safe in his slumber, away from this madness for a while. He couldn't imagine the aftermath that lay in store for him when the sun rose again.

Adelaide showed him to a spare bedroom. He collapsed on the bed, awakening the dust that had settled on the untouched quilt. It scattered through the room and Adelaide swiped it away with haste.

"Sorry. It's been a while since I've had any overnight company. This room hasn't been used in years."

"Not a problem. This bed is way better than mine at home. I'll sleep just fine alongside the dust." He smiled at her, happy he wasn't alone this night. She gave him an approving nod and left the room, turning off the light and shutting the door behind her.

In a matter of seconds, Theodore forgot about the pain resonating through his neck wound or the fact that even in death, his father had it out for him. At the end of it all, Chester still prioritized his own desires over the wellbeing of his son. He let this heavy fact brush past him, letting it go before it had the chance to nest inside his head. Sleep embraced him, giving him a temporary sanctuary from reality.

Chapter 13

It was past noon when Theodore woke up on Sunday. He never slept this late but he supposed he needed it. Part of him even wished he could shut his eyes and fall back asleep until Monday, but he knew this was impractical.

Adelaide was sitting in the kitchen, sipping a cup of coffee when he emerged from the guest bedroom. She took the morning off and had her boat captain manning her fish stand for the first half of the day.

"You sleep okay?"

"The best I could. Just to verify, last night actually happened, right? It wasn't all a weird dream?"

"Nope, that's reality, kid. The ghosts, your dad's attempt at possessing you, all the secrets of Nether Isle I revealed to you. It's unfortunate, but true." She scanned him over carefully, "Now that you've had a night to digest it all, do you have any more questions for me?"

"Do you really think Bianca is a ghost?"

"I can't be sure. All I want is for you to be careful. Be aware that she *might* be."

"Are all ghosts bad?"

"No. Most of them aren't. The problem with them is that they are selfish and determined. A lot of them are resentful and bitter. They want what they want, no matter the cost. Which is why we must be careful around them, because the cost is usually our safety, and sometimes our lives."

"My dad is dead."

Adelaide let out a heavy sigh. "It seems so. I'm sorry he's still causing you pain."

"I can't even *pretend* like he was a good guy. He died and *still* has it out for me. How can I get closure when he is literally haunting me? Most people can let the pain a person caused them go after that person dies, they can find forgiveness and move on. They can focus on that person's good qualities and try to remember them in a happy light. How am I ever supposed to do that when my dad is trying to steal my life from me so he can keep on living his?"

"It's terribly unfair, I know. But we won't let that happen. I'm going to set up some time with you and my friend, Delilah Clement. She practices both ideologies of magic on the isle: Wicca, which harnesses the light, and Ouija, which controls the dark. She can teach you some ways to protect yourself from his spirit."

Theodore just nodded his head, he didn't know what to say anymore. All of this was foreign and strange to him. It still seemed like make-believe, even after seeing the truth present itself right before his eyes. He wanted to escape, wanted to leave this horrible place forever, but without his father he had no place to go. No family to live with, no money to support himself. At least on Nether

Isle he had a job and a home with minimal monthly rent. He wouldn't even know where to begin if he tried to start over someplace else.

Most importantly, he had Adelaide here. If he ever left, there wouldn't be anyone who could replace her.

"Let me take a look at that wound of yours." She stood up and met him by the kitchen. Upon peeling the gauze back, her face tightened in displeasure. "It's not gonna heal right. We need to get this stitched up so it doesn't scar, otherwise people will think you have a spirit nestled inside you. Trust me, after determining the new folks aren't ghosts, they instantly look for the scar to make sure they aren't dealing with someone unnatural. Come with me, I'll walk you to the sickbay in town." She opened the front door. "Put your hood up. No need for anyone to see the bandage and start gossiping."

He obeyed and followed her down Peddler's Way, over Terre Bridge, and into the mainland. They reached Maladey Medical Center and were lucky to have no wait time. Dr. Roger Linville, Rowan's father, brought him into an examining room and Theodore removed his hood. The doctor let out a horrified gasp.

"Don't worry, I'm still me."

Dr. Linville's eyes remained suspiciously fixated on the neck wound. He took out a small flashlight, removed the bandage, and moved the skin around the gash. He did so without concern to the additional pain he was inflicting upon Theodore. With his fingers, he stretched the skin open so he could see into the lesion. Upon seeing nothing unusual, he moved it back and forth, then squeezed it deep below the surface, like he was trying to pop a pimple. Theodore clenched his teeth to avoid howling in pain. The doctor perpetrated additional tests to determine nothing had entered the boy's body. Theodore couldn't imagine how he'd be able to tell, but assumed he dealt with situations like this before, considering the town was littered with bitter ghosts. After a few more pokes and jabs, Dr. Linville spread the skin apart once more and stuck his gloved finger inside the wound. This time, Theodore hollered in agony as the doctor moved his finger deep within the cut. In an attempt to fight the searing throb, he clenched his teeth together, accidentally chomping down on his tongue. Blood now poured from his mouth as well.

Dr. Linville concluded his examination, took a step away from the exam table, and looked at his patient with a look of fatherly concern.

"Please don't tell Rowan," was all Theodore could think to say.

"What happened?"

"I was attacked by Marcus Baudin."

"I'm sure he'll be stumbling in here sometime today. Be prepared, he'll be in a foul mood," Adelaide said from the corner of the room.

"He was possessed?"

"Yes. He was tasked to make my body ready for permanent possession, but I got away."

"Do you know whose spirit it was?" he asked. Theodore choked on the words as he tried to answer and the doctor understood he was prying too deep. "It doesn't matter. You're safe." He took a suture kit out from a drawer and readied the threaded needle. Before he started, he handed him a ratty stuffed rabbit.

"This will hurt. Do what you need to the toy to make it easier to bear. I'm going to do my best to make a stitch with minimal scarring."

He began the procedure without warning. Theodore choked the neck of the rabbit, causing the fluff inside to peek out of the holes in its head. He kept his eyes shut and mentally went as far away as possible. He was on his boat, past Apres Monde Lighthouse and headed for nowhere in particular. Europe sat on the other side of this ocean. He wondered if his sailboat could make it that far. The sails caught the breeze and he directed them onward, ignoring the debilitating pain that resonated from his neck down his spine. Sunshine filled his vision, illuminating the black space behind his eyelids.

The pain stopped and a hand rested on his shoulder. He opened his eyes and was blinded by the florescent ceiling bulbs.

Back to reality.

Dr. Linville shook his hand, told him to be wary of the spirit returning, and sent him on his way. The stitches would dissolve naturally after the wound was healed, which saved Theodore another trip back to Maladey.

Adelaide escorted him back home; she wanted to see the chalk markings Bianca made before departing. On the way they picked up Delilah Clement from her home on Cirripedia Pier. She was in her fifties and wore thick spectacles that made her eyes freakishly big. Her long frizzy red hair was bespeckled with white strands that she constantly blew out of her face with spit-filled huffs. Theodore learned not to stand too close. Her accent was the thickest he'd ever heard on Nether Isle and he had to focus intently to understand what she said during her rapid bouts of conversation. Despite her unbecoming appearance, she was very sweet. She chose not to live with the Ouijans on Salamander Pier because they often times were too consumed in darkness and it dampened her buoyant spirit. Adelaide thought it best to use Delilah's skills before going to the Ouijans because she had a healthier balance of insightful magic and wouldn't corrupt Theodore's youthful purity with nefarious philosophies.

When they arrived at Theodore's home they were thankful to find it vacant. Marcus already dispersed. He presumably traveled to Maladey to be treated, but it was also possible he was too embarrassed and decided to ride out the aftereffects in private.

Being temporarily possessed wasn't deadly, and with time he'd recover just fine. There wasn't anything a doctor could give him besides painkillers to help him through the subsequent nausea and bone-rattling aches. The worst side effect from a temporary possession was the mental trauma. He would need a therapist more than a doctor, and knowing how proud a man he was, it was likely he'd never seek professional help of that kind.

Delilah walked into the house first. As she entered, her quirky demeanor shifted into one of great gloom. Her eyes widened, shoulders slunk, and her breathing became alarmingly heavy. After taking off her shoes, she tiptoed through the room with a hand over her heart. Her head darted back and forth as she examined the aftermath of the previous night's atrocities. Deliberate movements carried her through the space. Each time her bare foot touched the floor she absorbed something new. The area to cover wasn't big, but she circled its circumference twice then crisscrossed through its center. Though Theodore tried to avoid eye contact, he found that Delilah kept staring back at him amidst her ethereal exploration of the room. Her glances of pity made him extremely uncomfortable.

Once she finally finished feeling the aura of the room, she made her way to the front door, where Adelaide and Theodore stood watching her work. With a flick of her wrist, she motioned them to step aside. She crouched like a frog in front of the messy chalk symbols and inspected them.

"Babylonian," she announced after a minute of silent scrutiny. "Ancient Mesopotamian religions had strong beliefs about the afterlife and somehow this friend of yours learned their spell for keeping spirits out of a home. She's messy though. Either she isn't well-versed in Babylonian scripture or this is a twist on the ancient way they practiced it." She motioned them to come closer. "See this symbol? It's an Assyrian protective deity called a Lamassu. Its placement indicates she intended to keep this house safe. This one looks like the normal half-man, half-winged bull, but its mirror image on the other side of the line is missing its head. Not a good sign. It means they belong to someone other than the person they were created for. This backwards **g** is actually a **B** in ancient Babylonian. Your friend's name is Bianca, right?"

"Yes."

"Well, this seems to indicate the Lamassu have an allegiance toward her, not you. She created this with her own intentions in mind and the power of the Lamassu will always favor her over you."

"If it's only for protection, maybe she felt she needed it from Chester?"

"Under no circumstance would she ever need more protection from him than you," Adelaide pointed out.

"She also included a Pazuzu," Delilah continued. "This stick figure with a crown and scorpion tail represents that. He is king of the demons in Babylonian mythology, and his inclusion is good and bad. He is the bringer of all misfortunes, but he also keeps other evil spirits away. There are rumors that sects still exist who worship Pazuzu, thinking it will let them live forever in the afterlife. Perhaps she caught wind of this and explored it."

"If she's already dead, it would make perfect sense why a religion like that would appeal to her," Adelaide said.

"Or maybe she thought it was a good way to guarantee Chester could never enter this house again. Maybe the bulls are for her, so she can find refuge here if needed, and that demon king is for me. Sure, I'm in more danger from my dad than her, but she did thwart his plan and it's possible he now has a vendetta against her too."

"You're making excuses for her."

"No I'm not. I'm just trying to keep us from automatically assuming the worst about her."

"You ought to assume the worst," Delilah spoke, pointing at the symbol directly in the middle of all the rest. "Most of these other scribblings are letters and numbers, which don't hold much meaning to me, but this is an Egyptian scarab. It represents reincarnation. Within the beetle is a Babylonian **B**. The circle of backwards **P**s around it are Babylonian **R**s."

"There is a huge **X** through it all, like she crossed it out. Does that cancel it?"

"No. That **X** is really a **T**, which I assume represents you."

"You'll be staying with me from now on," Adelaide said at the announcement of this grave news. Theodore had no words to defend Bianca now, all he could do was hope Delilah's reading of this enchantment was wrong. Delilah stood up, rose to her tippy toes, and circled her left foot, massaging the dirty floor. She did this for a few seconds with her eyes closed before breaking her concentration and walking toward the sofa. She got on her knees and reached beneath the couch. Her arm reemerged holding the arrow gem necklace Chester ripped from Bianca's neck. Delilah rolled the pendant through her fingers.

"It's a cypress opal and its magic is powerful. Opal enhances magical rituals and absorbs all energy that surrounds it, positive and negative. With it around her neck it shielded her from the spell she was casting, preventing the magic from affecting her too. It strengthened her curse while absorbing it. It kept her safe from the spell. If she is in fact dead, she never would have been able to utter the words without the protection. It also allowed her to wear the herb crown and hold the candle. The cypress has protective properties given by the power of nature that, when partnered with opal, would protect a person from harmful magic."

"And what type of magic is this?" Adelaide asked, thoroughly baffled.

"Wiccan. Well, the magical elements of these two particles come from Wiccan beliefs. I've never seen them mashed together like this before. It's almost like she made up a new magic of her own."

"Fantastic. We are dealing with a clever phantom proficient in necromancy." Adelaide seemed distraught.

"Hopefully she's not actually dead," Delilah commented. "If she's alive, then she's just messing around with the combination of beliefs. But if she is dead and capable of this, then we have a very large problem on our hands. A young, living girl I could mentor, but if a ghost did all this, then the wicked intentions are already established and I'd never be able to sway them."

Both women looked at Theodore, who was shell-shocked, unable to form a rational opinion about any of it. Was his friend really out to get him? What could she possibly want from him? She never came off as malicious before *and* she saved his life. But if Delilah was right about all she uncovered, then the state of his friendship with Bianca was looking like a lie, start to finish. There was no way to know for certain until he spoke to her again.

"I'll stay with you for a while," he conceded to his old friend. He packed a bag of clothes, some school supplies, and followed Adelaide back to her home. It would be his new temporary residence until all of this was resolved. Nobody knew what would come next. And if he lived with her, at least he wouldn't be forced to face the unknown alone.

Chapter 14

Monday rolled around and a fresh school week was upon him. He packed plenty of turtleneck shirts so he could hide his wound from his classmates. Particularly Rowan and Ruby. Rowan already gave him grief and Ruby made her concern for Theodore's safety common knowledge. He didn't want either of them making a bigger deal out of this situation than it already was. There was enough baggage that came along with the incident; having acquaintances magnify it would only make it worse. Theodore just wanted to go about his life like none of it ever happened. That was impossible, of course, but he tried anyway. He kept the crushing feelings about his father's actions at bay and let the uncertainties about Bianca slip into the recesses of his brain. None of it was in his control and he saw no point making himself sick over it. If he let the negative feelings fester, all they would give him were days upon days of nausea and a wretched case of insomnia. No answers, no explanations—just a bad case of the barfs.

He was certain of it because it already happened. When he got back to Adelaide's after Delilah's explanation of Bianca's markings, he sat alone in the bathroom for five hours straight. The emotional stress hit him all at once and caused him to be ill the remainder of the day. He suffered a cold sweat accompanied by the spins, and was bound to the toilet for fear he'd vomit if he moved at all. It was miserable. When he woke up this morning, the sickness ceased and he was determined to keep it away. Even if it meant pretending he wasn't torn apart inside.

School was dreadful. Ms. Courtier's voice came out as an excruciating whine as she talked about the solar system. The high-pitched tone of her babbling pierced Theodore's tired ears and shot directly to the back of his eyes. The migraine arrived with jubilance and made a comfy home in his skull. It physically hurt to be in school this Monday.

He did his best to champion through pain and exhaustion. He hadn't gotten enough sleep the night before. His mind raced in circles around the same thoughts, driving him to the brink of madness. At 3 a.m. he got out of bed to do pushups and jumping jacks in hopes of getting so tired that his body might overpower his brain. What time he actually fell asleep was a mystery, but the fact that he didn't get enough rest was evident all day.

Bianca wasn't there, as he suspected she wouldn't. Another annoying detail to add to the pile stacked around him. He wasn't sure how he would continue to defend her if she stayed hidden. He needed an explanation from her.

When the final bell of the day rang, Theodore flattened his face against the surface of his desk. He rested there for a moment, blinking slowly and letting the coolness of the fake wood press against his cheek. The contact pushed his skin into his eye, smushing the side of his face together. Vision blurred, just like his mind.

All his classmates hurried past him, unconcerned that he remained in his seat after they were dismissed. Somebody walked past and he could feel them stop to stare.

"Are you okay?" It was Ruby.

"I can't." Even his voice sounded blurred. Ruby sighed, aware he needed to be alone.

"Maybe tomorrow then." She walked away. No one was left in the classroom with him. Even the teacher departed, showing no concern for Theodore's state of emotional surrender. The stillness was serene, exactly what he needed. Suddenly, school didn't hurt so badly. In fact, the peaceful vacancy acted as the remedy he needed all day. The lights went out from lack of motion in the room, and Theodore's consciousness followed shortly after.

A crack of thunder woke him up, five hours later. The clock on the wall read 8 p.m. and the sky outside was black. The storm beat upon the flimsy school roof, creating a clamorous rhythm. The sound of it snapped Theodore out of his lethargic calm and back into reality. He missed his entire shift at the market.

He ran through the rain to Adie's Fish & Chum Stand. Adelaide was there, cleaning up. She didn't look angry, just exhausted. Theodore ran over to her, out of breath and soaking wet.

"I'm so sorry, I fell asleep at my desk after school ended."

"I know. Ruby came by and told me you looked dead tired when she left. She stuck around a few minutes till ya started snoring then made her way over to me to let me know. She's a good girl, that one."

"I'm really sorry."

"It was best to let you sleep."

He helped her finish cleaning, then they headed back to her house together. Theodore put on dry clothes while Adelaide got the fireplace going. To warm up, he sat in front of the roaring flames and found he had no will to move until the blaze dwindled to a flicker. The lack of light and heat snapped him out of his comatose behavior. He looked around the room for the first time in an hour to see Adelaide contently knitting on her sofa and Eustice hiding in the shadows of the kitchen, casting him a venomous stare, as usual.

"Sorry, I drifted away."

"What were ya thinkin' about?" she asked casually, not breaking stride in the stitch she was crafting.

"Nothing," he answered honestly. "Everything went blank. I saw nothing, felt nothing, and thought about nothing."

"And how'd that feel?"

Theodore wasn't sure how to answer.

"It felt like nothing."

"That sounds nice," Adelaide said, her tone genuine and understanding. Life dealt Theodore a crap hand, and continued to do so. Up until recently, he stayed brave and strong and resilient, never letting the odds deter him from moving forward with a smile. Now, those years of old and new sorrow besieged him. It happened gradually without warning, but here he was, buried beneath it all. All the time he previously defied depression caught up with him, leaving him too weak to continue doing so now.

"You probably need a few days of feeling nothing," Adelaide continued. "Enjoy it. I won't be tolerating this mopey 'tude for much longer. We both know you're not a quitter."

She was right. He was letting the misery win. He was allowing it to consume him. Maybe a few nights of quality sleep would reset his mind.

The rest of the school week passed without excitement. Ruby sat with him at lunch every day that week, which was a nice change. Rowan even joined them on Friday. He wasn't so bad when he made an effort. It occurred to Theodore that maybe he just liked to appear tough. He would hold this opinion to himself for a while though. There was no need to jump to conclusions about someone who was capable of causing him great aggravation.

Adelaide let him take the week off from work. Every day after school he went back to the house, took a nap, and then went on an evening sail. The change of pace was nice and gave him the time he needed to recollect his wits. He never realized how worn out he was from acting like an adult all these years. Being allowed to act like a teenager gave him enormous relief from the burden of responsibility he was used to carrying. It would not last forever—he'd be back to work next week—but the time away from his normal grind was the perfect medicine for this newfound depression. It was beginning to lift and he hoped this airy feeling lasted after he got back into his old routine in the coming weeks.

It was Saturday morning and Theodore didn't feel like sailing today. Instead, Adelaide let him borrow Eustice's dusty fishing rod and he spent the afternoon learning how to fish. He stood at the edge of Ballantine Dock from noon until dusk, catching and releasing Arctic char, Atlantic salmon, and rainbow trout. He even caught one eel, which turned out to be a disaster. Unhooking the long, slimy creature was difficult. It wasn't used to getting caught and fought Theodore's attempt to save its life with ferocity. Once he finally freed the eel of the hook, the stupid ocean snake slapped him hard across the face with its lengthy tail before flopping back into the water.

Theodore rubbed his red cheek and laughed. He and the eel weren't too dissimilar. No one liked to have their life threatened. Not even brainless eels.

The sun was beginning to set. Theodore packed up his lures, secured the hook to the fishing pole, and sat at the edge of the dock to enjoy the daylight's surrender to night. The blue sky faded to orange, then pink as the sun dipped below the horizon. Once the dark purple sky revealed evening stars it was time to return to Adelaide's. He gathered his fishing gear and turned to head back. When he did so, an unexpected sight startled him. There stood Bianca, watching him from afar. For the first time, he noticed the faint, smoldering luster that outlined her silhouette against the dark night backdrop.

Chapter 15

Bianca

Finally home.

The journey from Rolle, Switzerland to Derbyshire, England always felt exceedingly long after finals. A full school year away from her family was never easy. Luckily, this past year was spent with Cadence nearby. After waiting patiently for her little sister to grow up, she was finally old enough to be there with her. Cadence turned nine a month ago and completed her first year at Le Rosey boarding school with honors. As she entered the Cadet Section, Bianca was leaving it. She would turn fifteen this summer and become a Juenes Senior next year. It was quite exciting. She was moving on with top scores and would graduate in a few years amongst the best in her class. The Chateau de Rosey was enormous and palace-like. Staying there all school year wasn't bad, but it did not have the comforts of home. And living in a palace was not a novelty for the Wrey girls; they were born into one.

Mr. Beasley, their driver, steered through the gates of the Chatsworth house. It was an enormous home and held the seat to the Duke of Devonshire, her grandfather, Cornelius Cavendish. Since her mother Felicity was the only child her grandparents had, the seat had not passed on yet. It was the first time in history the title hung in limbo. Her parents tried for years to have a son, but producing two girls was a feat. The doctors told them to be grateful because her body was fragile and having two healthy babies was a miracle. The title could not pass onto their father Oliver because he was a Wrey and not of the proper bloodline. It could not pass onto their mother or the girls since they could not be Dukes of anything; they were females. Her grandmother Laurel wanted her husband to retire and pleaded that he make Felicity the first Duchess to head the house in history, but Cornelius was old fashioned and headstrong. He did not want the surname of Cavendish to disappear from the Devonshire legacy. So he stubbornly waited for Oliver and Felicity to produce a boy, who would take the last name Cavendish rather than Wrey. If they did not produce, the title would pass onto Felicity's cousin, 46-year-old Gregory Cavendish, who nobody liked. He was a classless relative who had no right to the title and would alter the state of Chatsworth for the worse. Bianca did not know if her parents were still trying to have more children but they were in their mid-30's and had time.

They pulled up to the front entrance of their manor home. Unlike previous years, their parents weren't at the front door waiting to greet them. Bianca looked at her younger sister, upset she would not be welcomed home with fanfare after finishing her first year at Le Rosey. Cadence wasn't rattled, and if she was she did not show it. They both were raised to be polite, dignified, and stoic. Their home was filled with royals and aristocrats far too often for them to behave like typical teenage girls. Giggling, silliness, and tantrums were never allowed. Alone, they could be themselves, but since they were approaching the manor, Cadence suppressed any unacceptable feelings their parents' absence caused her.

"Let me see your smile," Bianca said to her sister. Cadence whipped her head toward her sister and flashed a dazzling one. "Perfect."

"Do you think they are waiting inside for us?" Cadence asked, trying to mask her disappointment. All her life, she stood alongside her parents to greet Bianca as she returned home for the summer. Now that she was finally on the other side, it was unfair that they didn't award her with the same treatment. She wanted to feel special too.

"I'd bet on it," Bianca reassured her sister.

The car came to a stop. Mr. Beasley opened the back door for the girls to exit, and then unpacked their suitcases from the trunk.

The sisters entered the manor and walked into an empty entrance hall. No one was there to receive them. No love, no support, no nothing. They were gone for nine months, yet no one eagerly anticipated their returned arrival. This was new to Bianca; there were no balloons or flowers or people. Many times, other relatives and family friends would come over on arrival day to turn her homecoming into a celebration of sorts. This year, only the echoes of their footsteps in the spacious foyer welcomed them home.

While it hurt Bianca's feelings, she felt much worse for Cadence. She happily participated every year when they praised Bianca's accomplishments. And now that it was finally her turn, the joy and festiveness had vanished.

"I'm sure there's a valid explanation," Bianca said as she noticed her younger sister holding back tears. Cadence nodded without saying a word. Mr. Beasley entered through the doors behind him, shocked at the lack of excitement as well.

"Shall I bring your bags to your bedrooms?" he asked, aware of the tension that engulfed the vacant space.

"Yes, please," Bianca answered.

Mr. Beasley took the first set of bags toward the marble staircase. Before ascending, he paused to face the young girls once more.

"If it is any consolation, I am very proud of you both. I could never pass one year at that school. Academically, they are top notch."

"Thank you, Mr. Beasley. You're very kind."

"I watched you both grow up. Though I'm an employee here, you've never failed to treat me with the same respect you'd show a friend. That kindness goes both ways. I must say, you two have garnered safe spots in my heart." He gave them a charming wink. "Also, in regards to the state of your family, you missed a lot this past year. Based on the sad looks you're both wearing, I assume they didn't tell you much. I think once you hear them out, you'll understand the lack of enthusiasm you received this afternoon. Just be patient." He gave one last half-smile before continuing his job of delivering their bags upstairs.

The afternoon passed with no explanation. They did not even see their parents until the next day. After a silent breakfast, all was uncovered. The girls discovered they came home to a family meltdown. Their grandfather was on his deathbed, their grandmother was distraught and bringing about her own untimely demise, and their mother suffered a miscarriage one month before their homecoming. After years of staying sober, their father picked up his old habits again. He now lived at the bottom of his fancy scotch bottles. Cousin Gregory had moved in after the miscarriage and callously anticipated the obtainment of his late uncle's title of Duke of Devonshire. On top of all that, the estate took a hefty financial blow after their investments crashed, and now the penny pinching put all the adults on edge. None of them were used to living on a budget, so this frugal change flipped the entire atmosphere of the place. Everything was horrible and being home never felt worse. Everyone was angry all the time. Anything Bianca or Cadence did was often answered with hostility and annoyance. After a month of this, they found it easier to stay locked away together in one of their bedrooms. There, they could talk freely and be happy without any bitter adults squashing their joy.

Come July, the state of the Chatsworth house was in dire distress. Cornelius died on the first Monday of the month. Before his death he finally allowed Felicity to take the title as the first head Duchess of Devonshire. She accepted it, gratefully. Gregory moved out after throwing an epic fit, embarrassing himself and all who played witness to it. Things should have gotten better, but they didn't. Oliver was lost in his addiction. The alcohol had firm control of him and everyone suffered the consequences. He terminated public access to the Chatsworth House, which eliminated the tourist income. All the staff, except Mr. Beasley, one maid, and one chef, was laid off. Eight people now lived in a mansion that could house hundreds.

Their financial woes were intensified. The air conditioning and lights were kept off at all times to avoid large bills they couldn't afford. If the electric companies shut off their power, the gossip throughout England would run rampant. Felicity did all in her power to prevent this social catastrophe and the pressure kept her on edge. Oliver was insistent that the public was not allowed on the grounds, and she agreed since his constant drunken stupor was humiliating. It was a loss of income, so she tried to brainstorm other ways to garner money for the family.

Bianca began eavesdropping on her parents. When they thought she was asleep, she snuck downstairs, laid on the floor, and listened to their conversations through the crack beneath the study room door. The more she spied on them, the more she worried. They both were spiraling down a dangerous slope. Their mental states were on the fray and their high-pitched, unproductive bantering was terrifying to hear. The sound of it made her believe they were losing their minds. In her psychology course at Le Rosey, she watched a documentary covering the top mental asylums in Europe. The patients there were unstable, delusional, and dangerous. As she studied her parents increasingly devolved conversations over the next few weeks, she began to wonder if their mental states had diminished to a level that required hospitalization.

During the long, hot days of summer, she and Cadence barely saw their parents. When they did cross paths, their behavior was unpredictable and scary. So much so they often peeked around corners before going places to avoid any interaction with them. Mr. Beasley kept them company in the gardens on nice afternoons, playing games and holding meaningful conversations with the girls. Their grandmother Laurel tried to eat lunch with them whenever she had the strength to get out of bed, which wasn't often.

When August arrived, Oliver and Felicity fired Mr. Beasley, along with the other two members of the house staff. Only Oliver, Felicity, Bianca, Cadence, and senile Laurel remained.

Bianca had never been more excited to return to school. Her parents were now strangers who turned her home into a toxic place swarming with melancholy. Being there felt foreign and she was eager to leave. None of the warmth they used to share survived the wrath of their tragic year.

She and Cadence stayed close together at all times. With Mr. Beasley gone, no one was there to protect them from their parent's volatile madness. They hadn't hurt them yet, but many times arose where it felt to Bianca like they might. The mere mistake of getting in their way while crossing paths was enough to send either into a violent fit. The resentment Oliver and Felicity felt toward the girls was now tangible; it filled the rooms like a dank fog. Bianca did her best to keep herself and Cadence far away from their irrational hatred.

Only two more weeks until they returned to Le Rosey. Two more weeks until they were back in Switzerland, safe from this destruction and misery. Once there, Bianca would figure out how to stay there through break. There were summer programs and camps they could sign up for, maybe that was enough to fill the space between school years. She wanted to believe things would get better while they were away, that her parents would seek help and get healthy. That her father would quit drinking and her mother would get treatment for her stress-induced psychosis, but in her heart she knew it wouldn't. They were both too proud to admit they were drowning and too deep to realize they were running out of air. The way things were unraveling, she did not suspect her family would recover from this in such a short span of time. Safe in their bedrooms until their much anticipated departure, Bianca and Cadence drew up a calendar counting down the days until they left for school. Two weeks, starting tomorrow.

Two weeks proved too far away. That night, their gray year turned black. All remaining light was smothered by morning.

Cadence sat on Bianca's bed while her older sister lit candles around the room.

"It's going to be nice when we are allowed to use modern technology again back at Le Rosey." She blew out the match. "Living like this is depressing."

"I hope mum and dad get better while we are gone." Cadence wasn't handling the breakdown of their family very well. "I miss them."

"They will. And if not, we will stay at school over the summer. We won't be subjected to this again next summer. I won't allow it."

It was close to midnight and the girls weren't tired. They found comfort in sharing a bed at night. Nothing felt safe in the Chatsworth house anymore and having a trustworthy companion during the hours of precarious sleep helped settle their uneasiness. If they had each other, they'd be okay.

Many nights they stayed up through the wee hours of the morning, chatting and acting like normal girls. They left the heavy topics untouched as much as possible, though they still came up. With their best efforts, they kept their harrowing reality outside their locked bedroom door. These hours of solitude together, when the rest of the house slumbered, were precious to them. It was the only time the poison of their parent's breakdown didn't plague the air they breathed.

This night was no different. They sat on the floor together, drawing pictures and telling stories about their friends and crushes at school. Both girls were impeccable artists. Bianca won many awards at Le Rosey for her paintings and many of the professors encouraged her to explore this avenue as a career. While it gave her great joy, she wanted to use her smarts in a job that would pay better. They told her not to worry about money because happiness was worth more, but she wasn't sure. She had a few years left to decide and she hoped the decision became clearer as she got older.

The girls chatted and giggled, granting themselves a few hours free from worry. Bianca turned some music on at the lowest volume possible and they sang their favorite songs together in melodic whispers.

At 2 a.m. the doorknob to the bedroom jiggled. It was locked, so it did not open. Both girls went quiet. Bianca quickly turned off the music.

The doorknob moved again, this time with force.

"Why is the door locked?" their father screamed. "Open this, now!"

A moment passed before Cadence moved to open the door. Bianca grabbed her arm and stopped her. She silently shook her head and Cadence sat back down. At their lack of obedience, Oliver began slamming his fists against the door, making it shake within its frame.

"Let me in," he slurred.

"Why?" Bianca asked, doing her best to sound docile. If she gave him an attitude, his temper would flare. "You seem unwell. Maybe it's best to wait until morning."

Oliver responded with continued fist slams. They were growing in intensity and the wood was cracking. He kicked the door, splintering the wood near the handle. It only took him another minute before he broke through.

He stood in the doorway, panting and covered in sweat. His eyes were wide and crazed. Behind him stood their mother, drenched in tears. The girls sat on the floor and said nothing. The space between them and their lunatic parents was thick with uncertainty.

"Why are you crying, Mum?" Cadence broke the silence. The sound of her voice asking this innocent question made Felicity cry harder.

"We cannot explain to you what needs to be done. You'll never understand," Oliver answered. "Don't think we are acting impulsively, we've thought long and hard about this for weeks. It torments us that this is the only option, but after finding no other solution, we had to accept the hard facts."

"What on earth are you talking about?" Bianca wasn't a child anymore and she was aware this shadow of her father was up to no good. Her attempt to stay calm was no longer an option. "You and mum need to leave our bedroom, now."

"You don't make the rules around here, Bianca, I do," he responded. The glazed look in his eyes was alarming. "I determine your fate, as does your mother. You have no say." He took slow steps toward them.

"You're scaring me," Cadence whimpered. Bianca grabbed her sister and maneuvered them backward until they hit the wall. They sat arm in arm, pressed against it. Bianca frantically looked for an escape route. Before she could think of one, Oliver towered over them.

"Neither of you ought to be here," he said, his face slack and emotionless. "We made a mistake."

"Stop it, Dad, you're just drunk. Sleep it off."

Oliver hit Bianca hard across the face for calling attention to his drunken state. No one was supposed to talk about it. He made that clear the first time Felicity called him an alcoholic in June. As she uttered the words, he threw a porcelain lamp at her head. It sliced her forehead and gave her a concussion. In his mind, if the problem was not talked about, it did not exist.

"Watch your mouth." Oliver shook the sting out of his hand as Bianca cowered beneath him, protecting her face in case he struck again. "This is not how I want to remember you."

Her heart raced. What did that mean? Before she could ask, Oliver summoned Felicity over, who crouched down next to Bianca and wrapped her in an embrace. Bianca began to sob as her mother consoled her during this moment of parental betrayal. Her touch was warm and made her feel better, but only for a moment. Without warning, the harsh reality hit her. Her mom wasn't hugging her, she was restraining her.

Oliver yanked Cadence up by the forearm and dragged her to the other side of the room. Bianca put all her energy toward breaking free, but her mother's hold was too strong. Felicity wept loudly in her daughter's ear, crying profusely and soaking Bianca's brown curls with selfishness.

"*Stop!* Please stop," Bianca pleaded, her voice cracking in desperation. Her face turned red as she struggled to escape and defend her little sister. Her bright blue eyes were wet with defeat. "Anything you need from us, tell me. We can help out more, or get jobs. *Anything*! Just please don't hurt her."

"It's too late." Oliver placed his large hands around Cadence's tiny neck. She used her skinny arms to punch him, but it did not stop him. From the way he continued to move methodically, like a programmed robot, it looked like he hadn't felt her strikes at all. He choked her without mercy, like she was a faceless doll and not his beautiful, living daughter.

Bianca threw elbows into her mother's abdomen, bit her forearms, and screamed until her throat went raw, but it wasn't enough. In Cadence's last moments, Oliver laid her down on the bed because she was too weak to stand. All Bianca could see were her sister's small legs hanging over the edge and her father leaning over the body, arm muscles still engaged in a chokehold. Bianca sobbed as she watched her father strangle Cadence to death. Her tiny feet gave a final twitch before Oliver let go.

"You'll never get away with this," she wailed at the stranger she once loved.

Oliver didn't respond. He crouched down and stared blankly at her. There wasn't a trace of her father left inside the man before her now. Just an empty body controlled by his demons.

"Stop looking through me! Focus, damnit. Really look at me," Bianca demanded, but his gaze continued to travel beyond their intense eye contact. "Do you even see me at all? Or am I only a blur to you with no name or heart? I'm Bianca, your baby girl. Why are you doing this?"

Oliver's eyes shifted to Felicity. "You'll need to hold her down. She's stronger than the other."

"No," Bianca flailed, "please don't." She shifted to look into her mother's eyes now. "You don't need to do this. I love you, please stop."

Felicity's eyes were bloodshot. "Don't look at me."

She placed her frail hand over Bianca's eyes as they pinned her to the floor.

"Mum, let me go. You haven't done anything wrong. The authorities will only take dad. *He* killed Cadence, not you." While she did not believe this, it was her only angle. She couldn't see anything but heard her mother begin to sob again. A moment passed. Did her plea bargain work?

Finally, her father spoke. "You need to shut up."

Her moment of hope was only a moment spent to acquire a gag. He shoved the scarf in her mouth.

Oliver's cold hands wrapped around her neck and squeezed. Not only did he restrict the flow of oxygen, but he also broke the blood vessels in her neck. She thrashed beneath their bodily restraints and produced a muffled scream despite the gag. She did everything in her power to defeat their evil, but it was too strong. Her parents would make sure she was dead before morning.

The fighting and screaming drained her air supply fast. Her head throbbed and her eyes rolled backward as the oxygen disappeared.

She couldn't fight any longer, there was nothing left in her to try. The pace of her heartbeat slowed and her vision was gone. Not just by her mother's hand but by a new, natural veil of darkness. She no longer saw the cracks of lights spilling in between her mother's fingers. This was the end. The constricting feeling throughout her body and the black fog blinding her from the world was indication that her final moment had arrived. All she could hear was the heavy breathing of both her parents. They breathed with ease, effortlessly, while stealing the air from her. It's all she could focus on. Their continued breaths as she took her last angered her beyond compare. The exact moment she slipped into death eluded her, but the rage living in her heart remained as she entered the other side.

Chapter 16

"I'm surprised to see you again," Theodore said while keeping his distance from Bianca. He remained at the end of Ballantine Dock while she stood at the intersection of the dock and Peddler's Way.

"I'll explain everything."

It didn't elude him that this might be the only chance he got to hear her explanation. He thought she would disappear forever after what happened last week, but she was back and he needed to capitalize on the opportunity to get her side of the story. He walked toward her, scanning her new and strange appearance. In addition to the faint glow, her neck was bruised.

"What happened?" he asked alarmed. His emotions toward his friend were erratic. He was angry she kept vanishing, leaving him all alone. He was grateful she saved him from his father's trap. He was suspicious that she was not what she claimed to be. Right now, he was worried that someone tried to hurt her. "Was it Chester? Did he come back for you?"

"No, Chester didn't do this to me." Her face was somber. "Someone very similar to him did."

"Tell me who so we can report them."

"No, we can't. It doesn't work that way."

Theodore was confused why she didn't want his help. Despite all her secrecy and elusiveness, he was still choosing her over the rumors. Still choosing to help her instead of giving her the cold shoulder, like he ought to.

"If you won't be honest with me, I'm done." He began to storm off.

"Stop," she pleaded. "I will tell you everything, just not here. It's too busy and I don't want anyone to overhear us."

"Fine. Let's walk to the top of the hill."

They traveled there in silence. Theodore kept his distance. She was radiating a chill that prickled his skin every time he got too close to her. A few minutes later they sat at the top of the hill, facing the lighthouse that smoldered in the moonlight.

"Talk," he demanded.

"The bruises are from my father."

"He beats you?"

"No, never until this one time. He was my favorite person in the world, up until the night he did this to me."

"Let's go to the authorities and tell them so he doesn't do it again. If he gets away with it, it'll happen again."

"No, it'll never happen again. Don't worry." She sounded very confident.

"How can you be so sure?"

"Because I'm dead."

The blood in Theodore's face drained and he tried to remember to keep breathing. Ever since learning the possibility that she *might* be a ghost, he was desperately hoping she'd have some other explanation for all the weird coincidences of late. But Theodore's hopes were dashed and all his friends of Nether Isle were proven to be right. He was so uncomfortable he couldn't speak.

"I died the night my father gave me these bruises."

"Why haven't I ever seen them before?"

"Because you didn't believe in ghosts. You only see what your mind is trained to see. If you don't believe something is possible, your cognizance will pass over the small details that reveal what you believe to be impossible as true. I assume someone filled you in about the workings of Nether Isle after what your father did to you."

"Yeah, Adelaide did."

"That's why you can see the real me now. Ghosts weren't even a possibility before, but now that you know they are, your mind is on alert and you can see what you never saw before."

"Your glow, too?"

"Yes. That you might have seen if we ever spent time together in the dark, but I never let that happen. I didn't want to frighten you."

"I always felt the coldness that emanated from your body, and the strange odor you carry."

"Are they both worse now?"

"Yes."

"I'm sorry I didn't tell you sooner. I wanted the timing to be right."

"How could the timing ever be *right* for something like this? You've been my only friend here up until recently. Learning you were actually dead, walking around like you weren't, was never going to be easy to accept."

"A time may have come when it happened more naturally."

"You had plenty of chances. Everyone was warning me. I shooed all their doubts and gossip away, choosing to trust you over them. When you were confronted about it, you denied it with insistence. You could have told me, one-on-one, that all of it was true. I gave you the opportunity to come clean and you chose to continue the deceit. Why?"

"Because you would have chosen them over me if you knew the truth. I wanted to make sure our friendship was solid before I told you everything. I didn't want to lose you."

"You wouldn't have. I was defending you, despite people like Adelaide, who I adore, telling me I was foolish for doing so. If there was ever a time to be honest without risking our friendship, it was then. Now my whole world is exploding around me and I can't be sure who is safe to trust."

"You can still trust me. I'd never let anyone hurt you."

"Learning you're a ghost, the opal necklace makes sense. You couldn't have cast Chester away without it. But what were all those markings you left at the threshold of my house?"

"I put them there to keep Chester out forever."

"Delilah Clement came over and explained all the markings to me and Adelaide." Bianca's face tightened. "There were ancient Babylonian letters and symbols. Some of which were demons, others were protectors with their heads cut off. The whole explanation of it was appalling, honestly, and I'd like to hear your side of it before I assume you're up to terrible things."

"I am dead. The missing heads made the Lamassu allegiant to me so I was still allowed in the house. If I didn't do that, I would have been cast out forever too. The Pazuzu was just extra to ensure he couldn't slip through. With the Lamassu assigned to me, I wanted to make sure there was enough strength to keep other spirits out for you."

"The Egyptian reincarnation beetle with all the letters around and through it. That was the most concerning part."

"This is why I wanted to explain it to you under better terms."

"Then explain it to me how you would have on a different day under different circumstances."

"My life was stolen from me. My parents killed my little sister and me because they couldn't afford us anymore. They couldn't pay for our elite schooling, and instead of putting us in a common

162

school that was free, they murdered us. They didn't want the bad press speculating that there were money problems surrounding the Duchess of Devonshire. That the Chatsworth house was going bankrupt after the death of the Duke. The death of my grandfather, the fight over his title, the ruined state of their banks accounts, and my father's fall back into alcoholism—it was all too much for them. They went insane. They should have been hospitalized but they were too proud. They fired all the wait staff and my grandmother was terribly ill. Cadence and I were all alone with them. The summer between my Cadet and Juenes year was horrific. I knew they lost their minds so I tried to keep us safe from their arbitrary outbursts, but I didn't do enough. I should have run away with Cadence. If I knew what they were capable of, I would have, but I never suspected they'd hurt us more than an intoxicated beating. Two weeks before we were to return to school in Switzerland, they murdered us. Strangled us, then buried our bodies in the garden. They went on with their lives like they sent us back to school. As if the murder never happened. They ignored the letters from Le Rosey, asking why they didn't enroll us in another year of school, while all of Britain thought we were there and never questioned it. Eventually, our absence went quiet and people forgot to wonder where we were."

Theodore felt awful for Bianca. He knew what it felt like to have a parent betray your love in such a deplorable manner.

163

"No one knows you and Cadence are dead besides your parents?"

"No, and it's terribly unfair. When our next summer break came, they told everyone we stayed for summer programs."

"How long has it been since you died?"

"A while now." Bianca's eyebrows furrowed. "Time feels different when you're dead, but at least two or three years now."

"How did you learn to cast spells and create enchantments in such a short amount of time?"

"A lot of traveling and studying."

Theodore thought being dead meant everything went black, that everything came to a sudden halt and the person who died would have no awareness of their lack of existence, only those left alive knew they died. But his simple view on death was rapidly altered. Now he imagined what it would be like to have a spirit in the afterlife that was aware of the world that kept on spinning without him in it, at least not *really* in it. Being dead still meant you could never take part in human life again. Everywhere except Nether Isle, and similar portals scattered across the globe, a ghost went unseen. They could watch their loved ones and enemies live out their lives, but never participate. You'd see how they mourned, or worse, how quickly they forgot about you. The more he thought about it, the worse he felt. What if you died and no one cared at all? Then he realized, that's exactly what happened to Bianca.

"The neglect you must feel seems unimaginable, with no one mourning your life or even wondering where you went."

"It is. Every time I'm reminded that no one loves us enough to realize we are gone, I can feel my father's hands around my neck again. I see his face, but its appearance is replaced by those who I thought would have cared."

"Why not leave this place then? I'd imagine there is peace through the light."

"Because I cannot let my parents get away with this. I need retribution, if not for me, then for Cadence. I watched them kill her. My mother restrained me as my father strangled her right in front of my eyes. I saw her fight for her life against a man she adored and trusted. A man whose main job in life was to love and protect us. He betrayed us on the deepest level. It was the worst crime he could have committed against us and every time I remember that he, and my accomplice mother, are getting away with it, I feel like I'm dying all over again."

"I'm so sorry. I wish there was a way I could help."

"There is." Bianca took a deep breath. "I know a way, but you aren't going to like it."

"Tell me."

"I need Ruby's body. And I need you to help me get it."

Theodore's heart raced. His sympathy for Bianca turned into outrage.

"Like what my father tried to do to me? Absolutely not. How could you ask that of me?"

"I promise to let her go as soon as my parents have paid for what they've done. I can't temporarily possess her; she's too smart and would cast me out before I made it to England. I need to make it semi-permanent. I will enter her body through the slit you make and I won't latch on forever. You'll know I'm in there, so it won't be a secret, and as soon as I complete my task, I will come out. If I don't, you can force me out."

"This is absurd. Ruby is my friend, too."

"Please, I need your help. This is why I wanted to tell you once you got to know and trust me better. You'd see I'm not so bad, just a victim of circumstance trying to avenge my life."

"You did a really bad job letting me in, considering you disappeared for weeks at a time."

"It was because of Cadence. I had to stay with her. She is fading and slipping away from me. I'm going to lose her. If we don't enter the afterlife together, we will be separated forever. That's why it's so crucial that I turn my parents into the British police now. I can't wait much longer."

"Why Ruby?"

"Her dad owns a charter ship company stationed in Maine. I can use him to get to England."

"Why me? Why not possess someone to do it for you? I don't want you to do that, I just don't get why you need me."

"I don't want to hurt anyone. Temporary possessions screw a person up forever. Don't listen to anyone who says you can recover from it, because you can't. You become a shell of your former self after a foreign spirit has covered your soul. Wait till you run into Marcus Baudin again. You'll see."

"This is wrong," Theodore was torn. He wanted to help Bianca, he understood her dilemma, but he could not betray another person in the process. It wasn't fair.

"Please help me. I'll prove to you I'm trustworthy. I don't want to hurt Ruby any more than you do. I wish there was another way, but there isn't."

"You figured out all those spells and curses, I'm sure you can find a different way to fulfill your quest for revenge."

"I don't have enough time. Cadence is drawn to the light of Apres Monde more every day. She's all I have, I can't lose her. It took a while to learn that stuff. With all that time and research, I never saw anything about taking solid form outside portals like Nether Isle. It's not possible. I can't tell the police what happened or show them where our bodies are without possessing someone else. They won't be able to see or hear me without this step of the process. I need a living body."

"I'll go for you. You tell me every detail I need to know, and I'll go to London to turn your parents in. You can follow me there and witness the police arresting your parents. You can watch as the press shuns them for their reprehensible actions. The justice you are seeking will be settled."

Bianca's eyes were wide with undeterminable anger. Theodore thought he presented her with the most reasonable solution, but she appeared enraged at his suggestion.

"No, it has to be *me*. I need to be the one to tell them. I need to inflict the justice upon them. Even if it's not my face, it needs to be my soul and spirit resolving this travesty once and for all. I can't have someone else do it." Her expression softened. "It has to be me. It's the only way I'll find peace and the only way I'll finally be ready to leave with Cadence."

Unfortunately, Theodore understood this sentiment as well. If he ever saw his father's ghost again, he wanted to be the one to stop him rather than needing a savior again. Their situations were similar, just flipped. They both had evil parents that needed to be stopped, whether by magic or law enforcement.

"Let me think about it. This is a lot to take in. All this death and supernatural magic is overwhelming. Reality keeps slipping further away from me every day."

"This *is* reality. You just need to accept it."

"Can I let you know my decision next Saturday? I need the time to process and digest everything. Maybe by then, I'll have thought of a better way."

"There is no better way."

"Let me try. I want to help you, just not like this."

"Fine, but next Saturday is all the time we can waste. Cadence can't hold on much longer."

"Okay. I'll meet you here next Saturday at noon." She nodded and Theodore stood up. He walked down the hill, not waiting for Bianca to join. There was nothing left to say and he needed to remove himself from her presence in order to end this new discomfort.

Distraught, yet again. After a long week of remembering how to feel content, this new burden landed heavily upon him. The weight of it erased all his rediscovered happiness.

Chapter 17

Returning to Adelaide's, he went straight to the guest bedroom. If she saw him now, she'd know something was up. He had to deal with this on his own. Any passionate and biased opinions from her would only complicate it more.

Bianca put him on a tightrope separating right from wrong when she made this request of him. While he felt terrible for his friend and what she went through, helping her in the way she requested was immoral. Ruby didn't deserve to have her body kidnapped. No one did. Theodore understood how invasive if felt to have someone try and he could not justify taking part in doing it to someone else.

While he believed Bianca's motivations were legitimate and her intentions were truthful, he could not sacrifice one friendship for another. There had to be another way he could help her. He hoped to think of one in the next seven days, otherwise their meeting next Saturday could turn hostile. She was determined and he didn't imagine that denial would sit well with her. She was a powerful ghost, capable of dark magic. If they could not find a better option and he had to decline helping her, Theodore hoped she'd understand.

Sunday morning, Adelaide made a huge breakfast for them. The meal included shrimp and red pepper omelets, crab hash, a bowl of fresh fruit, and homemade orange juice. Theodore had no appetite but he ate until his plate was clean. Adelaide could not know his weeklong recovery was spoiled in a single hour last night.

He spent the day helping Adelaide clean out her attic. She had the captain of her boat cover their Sunday shift again. He didn't mind the extra hours since they counted as overtime.

Eustice stood in the dark corner of the loft the entire time. Now that he knew Eustice was dead, he looked much different. Last week, he noticed for the first time that his dark gray hair was always wet and matted across his forehead. His skin was also bloated and colored a subtle shade of blue.

"How did Eustice die?" he asked, not worried about offending the old man anymore.

"He tripped over a crate on his boat and drowned at sea. I never even saw the body. Was greeted by this version of him before the crew returned to tell me the news. It was night when it happened, so his band of dimwitted fishermen couldn't find him to save his life. They did inform me, however, that he was wasted and serenading a lovely bunch of ladies they picked up at one of their ports when it happened." She shot a nasty glare at Eustice who seethed in the corner. "When they told me that, I didn't feel as grieved about the accident."

"I'm sorry."

"Don't be. He loved me most of all, hence why he won't leave without me. Just a shame to learn the man you love was gallivanting unfaithfully while you stayed home without a doubt toward his loyalty. The longer he stays in the real world, the more transparent he gets. He's losing his afterlife wits, so to say, and has been wandering. Keep getting phone calls from the local ladies, all notoriously single, saying he's in their home, lost as a blind puppy, and too aloof to obey their commands to leave. I have to retrieve him every time, entering the homes of the women I never suspected as mistresses until his actions in death gave them away. Makes ya really start to hate people."

"Why not have Delilah cast him away? Like how Bianca did to Chester."

"First of all, whatever spell Bianca placed over your home was a dangerous mish-mash of magic. Combining different forces and beliefs is usually catastrophic. Delilah told me so while you were getting to know the toilet better last weekend."

"It worked though."

"Yes, but it only keeps Chester out so long as Bianca commands it. If she ever changed her mind, or stopped caring, he could return. The allegiance of those protective symbols lie with her."

"She wouldn't though." Theodore meant to sound confident but his voice came out unsure.

"We don't know that."

"Delilah would make a steadfast protective shield. She'd never let it waver."

"Continuing my previous thought, there's more than one reason I won't do that to him. I still love the damn fool. I hate to admit it but I'm a pathetic mush of a person when it comes to him. Too long of a love to dismiss. I should hate him for all the treachery he committed against our marriage, but I learned it after he was dead. I never had time to be rightfully mad cause I was so damn sad. He was dead, and since I didn't hate him alive, I couldn't hate him in death, even if I should. Lots of resentment harbors between us, but no hate. I've been told if we don't cross through Maudit Cove together, we may never find each other again on the other side."

Theodore also heard this via Bianca, but he wasn't going to confirm it now.

"If I knew the kind of man he was a long time ago, I woulda divorced him. No woman deserves a love like that. But the timing of its reveal was awful and trapped me in a state of confusion. I'm still tryin' to make sense of it and he's been dead over a year."

"How long can ghosts remain here before they start to fade?"

"Depends how strong their will is. Some flutter right into the light. Others hold out for months or a few years, grasping onto whatever idea won't let them go. Then there are the spirits who endure decades, and sometimes centuries. They are the ones who don't believe they should be dead, or that they have an inherent right to continued life. Those are the ones to be wary of most. They are the ones trying to steal our lives so they can continue theirs."

"So my dad has the drive to survive centuries on Nether Isle?"

"He trying to possess you permanently only a few days after his death is a bad sign. But it's possible his determination will falter as he continues to fail."

"Let's hope he keeps failing."

"I'll make sure of it."

"At the least he lost the element of surprise."

"Exactly. Gonna be an uphill battle from here on out. The whole town has eyes out for him now. Marcus came out of his seclusion yesterday while you were fishing. Told everyone who'd listen that Chester Finn was dead and possessing people."

"Great, now everyone at school will know what happened."

"Nah, Marcus is a prideful man. He didn't confess that *he* got possessed, so the details of that night were spared. He just told them all it was happening and to be on the lookout."

Theodore was relived.

"It took him a whole week to heal?"

"Yup. And that was only a temporary possession."

"How long does the permanent kind take?"

"Assuming it's even detected, months. But most spirits get away with it until the end of the host body's life. It's tough to spot, but there are ways to force them out. When I was younger, my friend's mother was possessed like this. They figured it out pretty quick because we live in a town that anticipates these types of horrors.

Also, her body was taken by the spirit of a teenage boy and her behavior after the possession was a blatant sign. The Ouijans were able to rid her of the spirit, but she remained in a coma for six months after. When she came to, she was never the same. When the ghost was pulled out of her, it took her personality along with it. Or maybe the Ouijans did that. I don't know, I just remember her being a shadow of her former self."

Theodore said nothing. He was consumed in thoughts of Ruby's vibrant personality disappearing forever. Her kindness, positive disposition, and good-hearted nature were what he admired most about her, and if he was honest with himself, they were the reasons he had an unspoken crush on her since the day they met. There was no way he'd let anyone steal that from her.

They were in the attic for two hours before the dust became unbearable. Moving the chests and boxes lifted ancient soot from every crack in the room. Theodore's eyes were watery from allergens by the time they finally stopped. He wasn't even sure what the purpose of this task was; all they did was move the forgotten artifacts from one side of the attic to the other. Maybe Adelaide just wanted to keep him busy.

When they went back downstairs, Eustice was already there, standing in his favorite kitchen shadow. Theodore still wasn't sure how real-life ghosts worked. Did they float through the walls? Could they appear anywhere they wanted at any time, like teleportation? He'd seen plenty of movies starring ghosts, but those were all make believe. This was real life and many facts still eluded him. He could've asked Adelaide but he had too many other new realities to dissect and make sense of. It was a minor detail he did not need.

"Have you seen Bianca since everything happened?"

Theodore was prepared for this question. He decided after a good night's sleep that he wasn't going to drag anyone he cared about into Bianca's scheme. He still valued her friendship and understood the desperation to stop her parents from living a happy life without any consequences. Telling Adelaide, or anyone else, what she requested of him would only make them hate her more. He'd rather keep it to himself so he could remain friends with her sans drama. His answer to Bianca would be "no" and she would need to deal with it. It would upset her but he hoped their friendship would survive this setback. And together, they could think of a new way.

"I haven't seen her. I really don't think she will show herself after what happened."

"She will." Adelaide clicked her tongue. "She better. She owes you an explanation at the least. I'd like to meet her to figure out if she's dead or alive, it's a big factor now that we know she can produce magic. Delilah needs to establish a connection with the girl either way in order to get her unruly abilities under control."

"Even if she is a ghost, she's not necessarily bad. Just lost."

"Enough with your excuses! If she's dead, she's no good for ya. Not as a friend, or a protector, or nothing. I know she was your first pal here, but ya gotta let that go if she's a ghost. You need real, living people in your life, not imaginary friends. I know she seems real, but she ain't. She's a vapor, only visible on Nether Isle."

"I get it." Theodore was in for a fight if he planned to keep Bianca around until she and Cadence left for good. Dealing with this now was illogical. There were other battles to win before tackling this one with Adelaide.

Chapter 18

Theodore was back to his normal schedule. School all day, market all night. It was nice to have his regular routine back in place after a week off. It was helpful, but ruined by the end. Bianca's request set back his progress toward happiness and staying busy now was crucial. It kept his mind off the upcoming confrontation.

During school hours, he tried to keep to himself but Ruby made that hard. She sat with him every day at lunch, like she had been since the incident with his father. He didn't suspect she knew what happened, but she seemed to have a 6th sense that Theodore was struggling. He appreciated her presence previously, but now that he was aware of Bianca's devious plan for Ruby, it made it hard to hold conversations with her. Ruby was clueless and radiant with positivity. She lifted his spirits just by being next to him. Her aura was the first type of intoxication Theodore ever felt, and imagined it was the only kind he'd ever need. He wanted to tell Ruby everything Bianca suggested, wanted to warn her in case Bianca went forth with it using someone else as her hands to make the incision, but he couldn't come clean. He didn't want to scare her. If he told anyone, the whole situation would blow up and become uncontrollable. Right now, it was between Bianca and him. No outside parties to make it worse than it was. He could handle it on his own.

He wondered if he had the strength to let Bianca take over his body temporarily in order to fulfill her need to tell the police the news herself. Maybe if they told Ruby the truth and filled her in on Bianca's tragic story, she would find a way to let them use her father's boats.

Then he remembered the terrible side effects and how he would never be the same if he sacrificed his body for a few days in order to help Bianca this way. Helping find closure in her life was not worth ruining the rest of his. He didn't want to be a walking zombie until he died. This was not an option.

He wished he could think of an alternative plan to Bianca's scheme, but nothing plausible came to him. The week went on with no new ideas. By Wednesday, he stopped trying to think up new plans. If she would not accept his offer to travel to England and tell the authorities himself with her watching it take place, unseen, then he couldn't help her at all. It was not his problem to fix. He sympathized for her but he would not ruin multiples lives for one that no longer existed.

The market was busy all week. He worked long hours every day, which was tiring but helped him sleep through the nights undisturbed. The good sleep was essential with all that weighed on his mind. If he was unrested, he'd surely have a meltdown. For now, he was maintaining his composure quite well amongst the terrors that stalked him.

On Friday, school went fast and he was manning Adie's Fish & Chum Stand before he realized more than half the day was gone. As the line of customers dwindled, he was forced to face the reality that tomorrow was Saturday and he'd be facing down an angry and powerful ghost in a few short hours. He wanted to imagine she wouldn't be furious or act out irrationally against him, but he also knew how formidable she was. Her powers were daunting and their extent were still unknown. He did not think her capable of hurting him, but the thought that she could lingered in the back of his mind. Surely their friendship would trump her displeasure with him, but what if it didn't? What if her ghostly tunnel vision was so intense, all bonds they formed dissolved the moment he refused her? What if he became faceless to her and she used her dark magic against him? It was a lot to consider going into tomorrow and he put off contemplating this possibility until now. It caused a great lump to form in his throat. He choked on the words as he spoke to the next customer.

"What can I get you?" he asked Oscar Dregg, butcher at Myrtle's Deli.

"I need some tuna. Ran outta tuna salad at my place."

"How much? We have them as wholes," he said as he stretched an arm toward the Atlantic tuna in front of the stand on display, eyeballs and scales still intact. "Those you'd have to fillet and debone. They all range between 30 to 80 pounds. If those are too big, I can chop one in half. Or we have some precut chunks in the fridge that average below 10 pounds."

"Chop the head and tail off one of those 30 pounders. I can do the cleaning at my shop."

Theodore grabbed a fresh tuna out of an ice bin, weighed it, chopped it, and then wrapped it up in parchment paper.

"The Bluefin goes for $18.00 a pound," Theodore said as he plugged the numbers into the calculator. He mumbled as he said the total price.

Oscar was used to high prices for large orders of quality fish, but to Theodore, the price seemed astronomical. He supposed he was just poor and unaware of the cost of fine items. He'd never pay that much for food, though this wasn't just a meal for Oscar. He planned to make weeks' worth of tuna salad with it for his customers. Through preservatives and the freezer, this fish would last him a while. Oscar mostly sold cold cuts at Myrtle's Deli: turkey, bologna, roast beef, salami, ham, and liverwurst. But he came to Adie's once a month for tuna, crab, and sometimes shrimp and lobster. The price made sense to Theodore the more he thought about it. It was the cost of business. Being the best deli in town, he had to spend money to make money if he wanted to keep his reputation as the best quality delicatessen. The hairy, middle-aged man laid down the cash without a flinch. He picked up the large chunk of wrapped fish, placed it between his massive body and arm, and departed. Marcus Baudin was up next.

"Can't believe Oscar pays so much for your crummy seafood."

"He serves quality meat. Of course he'd come to the only fish stand with quality fish."

"Whatever. Nice turtleneck," he smirked, knowing the secret wound Theodore hid beneath the sweater. Marcus was a hateful man.

"What do you want?"

The man leaned in close. His eyes were still horribly bloodshot from the temporary possession.

"I want to know what you're gonna do about that dead father of yours. He'll be back for ya."

"It's none of your concern."

"It is my concern. He robbed me of my dignity, so now I wanna see that ghoul burn."

"Worry about not getting possessed again, and I'll worry about avoiding my dad."

"I'ma be checkin' on you often. The second I think you ain't you, I'ma kill you with my own hands." His voice was raw and desperate. "I'll make Chester pay for what he done to me. Stupid bastard stole a piece of my soul when he did what he did. I can feel it missing." Marcus scrunched his face in pain. His hands were at his sides, palms wide open, unconsciously waiting to catch his missing piece if it ever returned. His red eyes watered in anger and his nostrils flared.

For the first time ever, Theodore felt bad for Marcus. As foul as he was, seeing him in this broken state was miserable. The man was lost and pitiful, a pathetic version of his former self.

"Stay away from me," Theodore commanded. Though he was distracted by this new, desperate version of Marcus, he hadn't missed the threat. "I have people assisting me and there's no way my dad is taking over my body. You need to concern yourself with fixing you, not waiting to kill Chester through me. It's a terrible waste of your time cause it's never gonna happen."

"We will see. Them ghosts are persistent. There ain't no real way to stop them forever, and they don't quit till they get what they want." Marcus's eyebrows raised. "I hope you're ready to fight till your death cause that's what you're in for."

"We will see." Theodore was aggravated. Marcus might be the biggest living nuisance to him on Nether Isle. "You need to go now. You've threatened my life and ordered nothing. This is a business, not a social shop."

Marcus scoffed but obeyed. He walked away, head jerking in various directions like he was on the defense, waiting for something to attack him.

Theodore took a deep breath before addressing the next customer. It was Delilah Clement. She smiled at him.

"I heard everything. Don't worry about Marcus. He was rotten before the possession took a piece of his spirit."

"Oh, I know. He's always been the worst."

"I'm going to teach you everything you need to know in order to protect yourself." Her demeanor was warm and comforting. "But not right now. All I can think about currently is that delicious lobster salad you and Adelaide serve."

"Coming right up." Theodore went to the corner with the prepared dishes and filled a small tub with the lobster salad. It was a new recipe Adelaide came up with two weeks ago and it turned out to be a huge hit amongst the locals.

They exchanged food for money and Delilah cracked the lid to smell the food inside.

"Nothing quite like this little gem." She closed the lid. "Can you meet up for a lesson soon?"

"Yeah, the sooner the better."

"Great. Have Adelaide call me when you plan to come. She'll benefit from these lessons too."

"Okay, sounds good," he said and Delilah departed with a wave.

He served the final two customers before the line for the night was gone. It was 9 p.m. so he began closing up shop. The stand was small and the cleaning was minimal. He started with the front by taking the ice bins and stacking them, unsold fish and all, into the large freezers behind the stand. Then, he tackled the front counter, which was always gross. Lots of different people and food products touched this space and he liked to wipe it clean of germs as thoroughly as possible. He scrubbed and scraped at the crud that caked on throughout the evening. One spot in particular was giving him trouble. It was a hunk of fish slime caught in one of the many dilapidated cracks of the wooden counter. It took a while to clean it out and make the counter spotless again. By the time he was finished, the market was almost vacant. All customers were gone and only a few merchants remained. The eerie quiet incentivized Theodore to hurry up.

He wiped the counter one last time before turning to clean the back half of the stand where the daily specials were prepared and stored. Another feat in regards to layered food filth. As he shifted his attention to the back of the shop, he was startled by an unexpected presence.

A girl he had never met before stood in the back corner, cowering in the only shadow she could find. Her skin appeared illuminated as she remained there, saying nothing and not moving. He immediately suspected she was not alive.

"Who are you?" His guard was up and he immediately assumed the worst since that's all he had known lately.

She answered him in a small, sad voice, "Cadence."

Chapter 19

Cadence

She watched as her mother pinned down her older sister's shoulders with her knees and covered her eyes, while her father straddled her with fingers laced around her neck. Together, they killed Bianca. Cadence was invisible to them now, but she observed them do it. With utter callousness, they ended both their daughters' lives. Tears stained her ghostly cheeks.

She waited for the moment Bianca joined her on the other side. As soon as her last breath was gone, her parents released a heavy sigh and exited the room. It took a few moments before Bianca appeared next to Cadence on the opposite side of life. They were in limbo, an eternal space where they weren't heard or seen, but could exist forever. It was cold here. The icy atmosphere that engulfed this in-between world made Cadence uncomfortable. She could feel warmth in the distance and hoped to head toward it as soon as Bianca appeared and settled. The first few moments were confusing. Cadence did not know where she was or what happened until she adjusted her blurry vision and saw her parents choking the life out of Bianca.

When Bianca arrived, it took her no time at all to adapt. She appeared with a scowl on her face and a fury so large it heated up the dead, frigid world around them.

"How could they do this to us?" she asked, appalled.

Cadence was not angry, only relieved to have her sister with her in this scary place. She buried herself in her arms, grateful they hadn't lost the ability to hug each other.

Bianca held her little sister but continued to seethe. She could not let go of her hatred.

"Where are they?"

Cadence let go. "They left the room. I was waiting for you, so I didn't follow them."

Just then, their parents reentered Bianca's bedroom. Felicity's arms were filled with sheets and her father carried two shovels. The girls watched as their parents wrapped their dead bodies up in blankets and carried them down the grand staircase, one at a time. Their dad transported the bodies and their mother followed behind, no longer crying. Her face was now blank.

It was a few hours before dawn and the world outside was hushed. The only sound was that of the summer grasshoppers. They played their woeful music in tempo with the shovels hitting dirt. Dig, throw, dig, throw; the little violins kept time. It was sunrise when they completed the second small grave. Oliver stopped digging and wiped the sweaty dirt off his face. Felicity shot a glance at the cloaked masses as the grasshoppers ended their song.

Bianca and Cadence watched as their parents placed their bodies into the freshly dug holes. They hid the girls' bodies in the middle of the most popular Chatsworth garden. Without a goodbye, they covered the holes, hiding their bodies inside, never to be seen or thought about again.

For weeks, the girls watched their parents move on with their lives. Oliver lived at the bottom of the bottle and Felicity stayed buried in pills. She picked up the habit shortly after the murders. The painkillers numbed her mind and helped her forget, temporarily, what she'd done. Whenever their effects faded, she'd remember and need to take more to dull the memory. She could not live without them. Bianca tried futilely to destroy the pills, to knock the stash in the toilet and ruin them, but she could not touch them. She could not figure out how to hold a solid object. She could touch Cadence because she lived in the same realm as her, but she could not touch her parents or any objects residing in the real world. Time after time she'd swipe at the bottles to make them fall but her hands always passed through them. It infuriated her. She wanted to take away her mother's self-induced remedy and force her to face what she'd done. With the effects of the pills, she felt no remorse: she wore no emotions on her face and seemed to move happily on with her life, socializing and pretending she hadn't buried her murdered daughters in the back garden. The pills needed to go and her mother needed to suffer. Bianca tried every day to remove the pills from their old home.

Laurel died a few months after them. She saw the girls in the afterlife but she died too doped up to understand Bianca's pleas for vengeance. She could not understand, or believe, that their parents murdered them. She insisted, repeatedly, that they were in school, getting good marks and awards for their intelligence. Bianca tried to talk reason to their grandmother, tried to gain her assistance in retaliating against her parents, but all Laurel kept responding with were questions about their courses and classmates. She wanted to know if they were learning interesting things and making new friends. Bianca gave up and Laurel departed. She accepted the light and followed its orb toward an unknown location. One that was probably much warmer than where they stayed.

Cadence desperately wanted to leave too. She wanted to go with her grandmother far away from Derbyshire, England. She wanted to feel bliss and serenity instead of enduring this endless gloom. Staying in the house she was murdered in and watching the people she once loved and trusted appear happier without her around, completely unremorseful for their crime, was unbearable. The sight of their smiling faces sent freezing daggers through her heart. She begged Bianca to leave with her on a daily basis, but her older sister refused to oblige. She was too focused on revenge and fueled by fiery hatred to feel the bitter chill of the half-world they lived in. Bianca felt cheated and her reaction was hostile. Weeks turned into years of reliving the betrayal placed upon them. Every day they saw their parents their afterlife emotions grew stronger, Cadence shivering with sorrow and Bianca embittered with venomous animosity. But nothing Cadence said or did could convince her sister to let her quest for vengeance go. Promises of peace and happiness were not enough to sway her. The warmth of the light in the distance was captivating. All Cadence wanted was to feel its heat radiate through her, to let it take her to a place where she could forget about the horrors of her human life. The light was where they needed to be, but she couldn't leave her irrational sister behind. So she waited patiently by her side, trapped in the eternal cold.

They watched their parents grow old. Over the years, Chatsworth Manor shifted from a prestigious estate into a haunted house. Oliver allowed tourists back onto the premises a few years after the girl's deaths in order to garner some income, but after one summer of visitors, the rumors that the house was spooked ran rampant. The tourists sensed the girls' spirits, but could not place a name on the eerie feeling the place gave them. It was only a few months before the public stopped coming and rumors multiplied from afar.

Her parents lost all revenue and had to hire an investor to put their remaining funds into new stocks. To Bianca's dismay, the stocks soared and their parents were richer than ever. After a few years, they brought the Chatsworth house back to its old glory, hired a brand new staff, and slowly rebuilt the reputation behind the Devonshire line. The house remained unvisited by the public due to their rightful suspicion of ghosts on the premises, but the social graces of the Wrey's were returned. They were invited to parties again, hosted many of their own, and were highly respected all across England. They never spoke of their late daughters and when people who knew them before their long break from the public eye spoke of them, they answered their questions briefly with the simple answer that both girls chose to live abroad after graduating. This socially elite crowd was so fast paced that many lost track of the girls, forgetting they existed at all.

When Oliver and Felicity died, they were in their eighties. They were blessed with long and healthy lives. They toned down their addictions to socially acceptable levels once their riches returned, but never truly quit. They couldn't, otherwise they'd be forced to deal with their sober consciences.

Bianca and Cadence stayed in that house through it all, watching their parents' lives play out perfectly without them. The pain of it was enough to kill them all over again. They never met them on the other side. Cadence waited for them, hoping to see them and ask for an explanation. She wanted to ask if they still loved her, missed her, or regretted killing her. She feared the answer might make everything worse since they died so happily, but she had to know. They died in bed, next to each other, and she stood by their dead bodies for hours, waiting to see them again after so long. She waited through the night, all the way until their nurses arrived the next morning to check on them. They never showed. Either they found a way to avoid her or their spirits were immediately ripped away to another place. Bianca was happy to think they went straight to hell.

The day they died, Bianca went to the spots in the garden where their bodies were buried and screamed for hours on end at the unjustness of their situation. She never got her vengeance, never got to see them pay the price for their crime. She wanted to watch them fall from social graces, wanted to see all their fake friends abandon them as they learned the truth of what they'd done. Bianca wanted to watch their world burn to ashes. Instead, she saw their lives end in idyllic fashion; they got everything they ever wanted. She hoped they were sent to hell and that it was worse than any vengeance she could have given them, though she doubted it. The best revenge would have been in their conscious lives; to watch them live through the rise and fall of their rebuilt empire. Everyone would have hated them if they found out they murdered their own children. To see them hit a high, thinking everything was better, and then watch them fail all over again. It was the only proper punishment. But now, no one would ever know.

Hell would never beat that type of justice, the kind one feels when the whole world turns against you. It tore Bianca up inside. While she worried about their Hell, Cadence couldn't help feeling they were stuck in a much worse Hell. Dragging out their misery all these years was torturous and the prolonged wait for peace was cruel. It was unnatural and it was all because of Bianca's absurd desire to play God and manipulate their parent's fate.

Now their parents were dead and they achieved nothing. No vengeance for Bianca and no serenity for Cadence. It was infuriating for both of them.

"Can we please leave now?" Cadence asked her older sister who laid sprawled out over their hidden graves. Bianca did not speak. She lay there comatose, expressionless, and void of purpose.

"Please," Cadence whined, sitting down on the lush grass next to her.

"What do I do now?"

"Now, we leave. We accept the light and follow its orb toward the next phase of this journey. Just like grandma did. We can be happy there. We can finally be at peace."

"How can I ever forget this? We were cheated, robbed of life. Killed by the people who brought us into the world, the people who were supposed to sacrifice their own lives to protect ours. They broke every code, every law of life. They needed to pay for their sins."

"I think they are. We didn't see them in this purgatory because they are murderers and were yanked right down to Hell. I think. There's no way they went to Heaven, so it has to be the only explanation."

"Whatever Hell deals them, it won't be enough. Fire and torture are mere physical pains that cause no real harm to a dead person. I wanted to watch them burn alive. I wanted to watch them die in agony, *then* be sent to eternal damnation. I wanted to see the perfect life they built after killing us disintegrate around them, see them shunned from society, and watch as they rotted in jail until their natural deaths. Punishment in death isn't enough. It doesn't erase the long, picture-perfect life they look back upon. The memories they can recall when their new Hell hurts too much. While they are burning in Hell, they can find solace in the recollection of their impeccable lives before death."

"You don't know that. Maybe in Hell, you forget where you came from. Maybe the only thing they'll be allowed to remember is the night they killed us."

Bianca looked at her sister skeptically, then back at the sky without saying a word. She didn't know the answer. All she could be sure of was that she failed in her mission. Failed at accomplishing the one task she remained all these terrible years to complete.

"I'm sorry I wasted your time just to fail. I know you've been suffering the cold for me, but I really thought I'd find a way. I thought I could enact vengeance on both our parts. You may not have understood, and still might not, but once you saw them shackled and locked away, you would have felt great relief, too."

"Maybe, but it's over now. All I want is for us to leave this awful place together."

Bianca sat up and took a deep breath. She had to surrender, there was no reason left for her to fight. Her purpose was gone and her resentment was put on hold.

"Thanks for waiting for me." She took Cadence's hand and squeezed it. "Let's go."

With relief, Cadence shut her eyes and allowed the distant warmth into her being. When she opened her eyes, the orb of light floated in front of them. Simultaneously, the girls placed a hand into the glowing sphere and their vision became saturated with light. They saw nothing but felt their bodies flying at high speeds toward someplace unknown. The air smelled salty and they traveled through a thick mist for most of the trip. When they slowed down, the light disappeared from their eyes. They were suspended above the ocean facing a very enchanting lighthouse. Cadence drifted toward it without a second thought but Bianca paused. She grabbed her sister's arm and stopped her progression.

"Listen," she said. Cadence snapped out of her revelry and paid closer attention. In the distance, beyond the radiating lighthouse, came onsets of weeping and yelling. Some desperate and sorrowful, others blood curtailing and angry. If they hadn't stopped they'd have been pulled straight past the lighthouse and into the mysterious horror taking place beyond it.

"We don't want to go that way," Bianca continued.

"But that's the light. It's the warmth I've felt tugging at me all these years." Cadence looked distraught. "This is where we need to go. I'm positive of it."

"Toward the sounds of agonized screaming is not where we are meant to go."

"Maybe the spirits there are just confused. I'm sure once you pass through, it all makes sense and isn't as terrifying. Maybe they just weren't ready to go."

"I'm not going until I'm sure of what it holds. I can't see anything past the illuminated haze of that lighthouse. Let's go west, toward that little town, and investigate the situation first. If it looks safe, I'll stop fighting you. But I won't let us enter a worse fate than this, not if I can prevent it."

Cadence wanted to cry. She was tired and exhausted, fed up with waiting. All she wanted was her soul to finally rest.

Bianca pulled her toward the fishing town. This little village was made up of rickety docks and piers that were attached to the mainland and covered with precariously placed homes. All of which were just as run down as the maze of wooden beams they sat upon. It smelt of spoiled fish and sea mist, and the summer heat on the water created a thick fog around the town. They floated to the nearest dock and landed. An old man sat on the edge with a fishing rod in hand. He sensed their arrival.

"Best to fish this early in the morning; the fish ain't expectin' ya yet." His line tugged and with great zeal he reeled his catch in. On the end of his hook was a sizable salmon. The old man tossed it into his cooler and cast his line back into the sea. He turned his head to look at the girls now. His eyes narrowed at the sight of them.

"You both ought to be followin' the light that brought you here. Your journey ain't done yet."

"Where are we?"

"Nether Isle," he said, then spat into ocean below.

"You can see us?" Bianca's eyes filled with newfound passion. Cadence cringed as she saw the twinkle of stubborn determination return to her sister's eyes.

"Yep. Wish I couldn't but I can. Terrible curse this place holds. Lets you spirits walk around like you're one of us. You can't stay here though, y'ain't welcome." His eyes were serious. "You don't belong here. I promise you, there will be eternal peace once you pass through Maudit Cove."

"Doesn't sound like it, with all the crying and hollering."

"That's part of the course, them ghosts are just scared cause they don't know what happens next. It ain't bad, you just gotta be brave."

"Let's go," Cadence tugged on her sister's dress, pleading they end this half-life misery.

"Listen to the little one," the old man advised, but Bianca heard neither of them. Her full attention was focused on the town of Nether Isle ahead of them. This was a place where she would be seen and heard again. Her mind spun with possibilities and the fire in her angry heart reignited.

Chapter 20

"Cadence," Theodore asked, "Bianca's little sister?"

"Yes." Her ghostly appearance was blue and the markings from her death were much more pronounced than Bianca's. She was fading, like Bianca explained.

"Are you okay?"

"No, I've come here to warn you about my sister. You cannot trust her." Her teeth clattered together from the violent shiver that entrapped her.

"What do you mean?"

"She told me everything she told you, and it's all a lie. She is delusional. Her mind is warped from our extended time spent in limbo. She was crazy in England, and when we came here, her psychotic tunnel vision became even worse. I wanted to leave her behind years ago but she found a way to trap me here with her."

"Years ago? She said you guys have only been dead for two or three years."

"No, we died over a hundred years ago."

"But she wanted Ruby's body as a vessel to rat your parents out. If it was over a hundred years ago—"

"They're long dead too."

Theodore's heart was racing. "Then what is her real motivation?"

"She wants Ruby's body to live in, forever. She doesn't think she should be dead. She thinks she was cheated and deserves a second chance. Once she has Ruby's body, she was going to find one for me. I don't want one; I never did. All I want is peace. I want to stop feeling so damn cold." Vapor steamed from her eyes, "I just want this to be over." Cadence wore her sorrow like a veil, it covered every inch of her. She was suffering terribly and her years of pain filled the space between them. Theodore caught a chill as he felt it too.

"How long have you been on Nether Isle?"

"I'm not sure exactly, but at least twenty years."

"Why now? Why me? All that time passed and she's only acting out this horrible agenda now?"

"Most of that time she traveled. She learned the magic of the Ouijans here, then scoured the globe for additional spells and rituals. She wanted to be the most powerful ghost in existence. It became an obsession and it took over her. We were only here a year before I expressed my desire to enter the light, with or without her. My declaration enraged her so thoroughly, she cast a spell on the basement we hid in and trapped me there. I was only allowed to leave when she accompanied me."

"How'd you get out this time?"

"I stopped trying to break free years ago and she subsequently stopped strengthening the enchantments as they grew weak. It's been years since she's updated them. I never had a reason to try and leave until now. She confessed everything to me and I had to take action, so I approached my barrier to find it broken. I love my sister, but she has grown evil in death. She is consumed with negative energy and these new motives have absorbed her completely."

"Does she know you're here?"

"No. She journeyed to Egypt to double check the hex she placed over your house. It's a good thing you stopped living there. You'd be putty in her hands by now if you had. What she cast there was an unbreakable curse meant to sway your loyalty toward her. Once it grabbed hold of you she would make all your future decisions. You'd have no say in anything anymore."

"Again, why me?"

"Timing, I guess. She is stronger than ever and she likes you. She said you fancied Ruby, so if she took that body and eventually convinced you that she exited it and it was the living girl you liked again, then you'd fall in love with her while she was inside Ruby's body. She was trying to set herself up for the perfect second life."

"I'd have known. I saw what it looked like when my father left Marcus's body, and I'd know she hadn't left Ruby's."

"She planned to tell you she went straight to the light after her mission was complete. The whole ordeal would look different if she did it that way."

"This is horrible." Theodore was appalled that his judgment of Bianca was so wrong. While her request was cruel and selfish, he thought the story behind it justified her reasons. But that was a lie too: her parents were dead, there was no vengeance to seek, and her real intention was to steal someone's life.

"I know. I had to warn you. I don't know what your answer would have been to Bianca, but you must refuse her. She is tarnishing her soul with these nasty deeds and dark magic. I fear we will never rest peacefully together on the other side if she keeps it up." Her expression was troubled. "I'd imagine you could still earn yourself a seat in Hell if you behaved poorly enough in purgatory. I don't want to lose her, but she's lost all capacity for reason."

"I always planned to say no. I was told what happens to a person's spirit after they've been possessed. They are never the same again. I'd never let that happen to Ruby."

"Good. You can't let Bianca win this one."

"What will happen when I refuse her?"

Cadence's face tightened. "I'm not sure. Make sure you aren't alone. Bring a Ouijan with you, or something. Bianca likes you a lot, so much so that she wants to live out her second life with you in it. I doubt she'd hurt you but she's violently unstable. If she thinks she can't have you, she might find a way to make it so no one can."

"Fantastic." Theodore's worst fears were materializing. Everyone's suspicions of Bianca were correct: she was evil and dangerous. Now he was learning her afterlife tunnel-vision was possessively linked to him and he couldn't escape it without one of them being eliminated for good.

"I'm supposed to tell her my decision tomorrow. I don't have enough time to plan a good defense."

"Lie to her until you figure it out. Warn everyone you can, especially Ruby, and build up an army. You'll need one against Bianca."

"Can you help at all?"

"There's nothing I can do that I haven't already tried. She has never listened to me in death. She's always been too focused on what she wants to hear and doesn't care how her actions affect me."

"I'm sorry."

"It's fine, I just need closure. I hope you can end this for all of us. I cannot stay in this half-life hell much longer. If you can't stop her evil plans and convince her to depart with me, I'm going to have to leave her behind."

"I'll do my best." Theodore shook his head. "I really thought she was my friend. I believed she had a good heart despite everyone warning me to keep my distance from her."

"In life, she had a good heart. When she died, she entered the afterlife with an intense hostility that she cannot let go of. It's engrained into her core and she won't be free of it until she chooses to be. She needs to enter the light to rid herself of that curse. The longer she stays here, the worse it gets."

"Thanks for the warning."

"I'm hoping you can save us all."

She gave Theodore a sad grin then disappeared. Suddenly, he had multiple fates resting upon his actions: his life, Ruby's life, Cadence's sovereignty, and Bianca's salvation from Hell.

Chapter 21

Saturday came too fast. Theodore wasn't sure what he was going to do. Lying to buy more time seemed like the best approach but he worried his nerves would give him away. He didn't know if he could pretend to be cool while being aware of the dastardly truth behind Bianca's request. He was scared, but also very angry. She lied to him with conviction. He wanted to shout at her and call her awful names and make her aware of how betrayed he felt, but he couldn't. Until he figured out a way to protect himself and those around him he needed to remain calm, like nothing changed over their week apart. He would have to decide how to handle things as they unfolded.

He walked up the hill toward his meeting spot with Bianca. She was sitting there, waiting for him as he rounded the last corner five minutes after noon.

"You're late," she said.

"Barely."

"Have you made up your mind?"

"No," he answered, "I need more time."

"You can't have more time. Cadence is fading, my parents are growing old, and all will be lost if we do not act now."

"Another week or two won't change anything. I've been very patient and understanding with you, now you need to do the same for me. I learned only one week ago that my closest friend was actually dead. How can you expect me to digest that ghosts are real, along with my father's death and your crazy request in such a short amount of time?"

Bianca only heard one part of his statement: *closest friend*.

"How much more time do you need?"

"I can't be sure, but not much longer. Just give me space. I'll come back to this exact spot when I'm ready."

She looked at him suspiciously but didn't voice any concerns.

"Fine. I'll check back here for you on Saturdays at noon," she paused. Her voice went up in pitch, "Please don't make me wait too long, there isn't much time."

"I won't." He gave her the best smile he could before turning to leave. He exhaled deeply as he reached the bottom of the hill and temporary freedom from her grasp. He escaped unscathed and now he needed to come up with a brilliant plan to stop Bianca before she figured out his loyalty wasn't hers anymore.

He went straight to Adelaide to fill her in on everything. After he explained the whole situation, she called up Delilah Clement, who rushed over. They repeated the long story once more. Next they called Ruby, who came over with her mother, Dorothea. Again, going through every detail. They sat in Adelaide's living room with the fireplace blazing as they contemplated what to do next.

"I can make you both protective crystals to wear. Bracelets or necklaces work best," Delilah offered.

"Will that be enough if she strikes first?" Theodore asked.

"No," she was deep in thought. "There is a blood curse I can perform. It would save you both from possession if she ever tried."

"Do that," Adelaide said, as if the decision was obvious.

"This curse will be painful for them and will require someone to take their place. If the ghost tries to enter either of them while they are protected by this curse, the ghost will think they are entering them but will be immediately redirected to the person it's linked to. For example, if I linked them to you, Adelaide, Bianca would be sent into your body instead of theirs."

"Oh geez," Adelaide's certain tone changed.

"Right. I think it's best they link to me if we do it. I am the strongest, magically, and I can fight her off if she enters me. I know the spells to make her transition very difficult. It would probably buy me enough time to remove her before she took full hold of me."

"Are you sure you're willing to do that for us? That's an awfully large sacrifice," Ruby asked.

"Absolutely. I have a much better chance at surviving her attack than either of you. And there's a good chance we will get her through the light before she gets the chance to try. I'm going to work with the Ouijans on a hoodoo sachet powder. It's called the wall of confusion. It'll protect you from her while confusing her beyond comprehension. She won't know where she is, what she is, or who anyone is, not even herself. Hopefully, during the duration of this spell, Cadence can drag her through the light. We just need to make sure she doesn't catch onto this plan before it is executed. It'll be much easier for Theodore to blow the powder into her face while her guard is down. If she's onto us, she'll use magic to prevent us from succeeding."

"Then we stay hush hush until the powder is ready. All that was discussed in this room stays here," Adelaide said with grave urgency. "Do not tell a soul what we have going on. Only Delilah's most trusted friends amongst the Ouijans will have any clue what we are up against."

Everyone nodded in agreement. Before going their separate ways, Delilah performed the blood curse on Theodore and Ruby. It was painful, like she warned. With a needlepoint, she linked the two teenagers to her by carving a nearly invisible symbol on the back of their necks. She promised to have their protective crystals ready in a few days.

Theodore wasn't sure what he'd do in the time between now and seeing Bianca again. He hoped she didn't pop up unexpectedly; he was certain he'd blow their cover if she pried too deeply. Secrecy was never his strong suit.

Chapter 22

"What have you done?" Bianca seethed as she entered the abandoned warehouse behind Myrtle's Deli. Cadence sat in her corner of the basement, silent and shivering.

Bianca stormed toward her younger sister, who sat in the chalk confinement put in place to keep her from straying. The white dust was messy and displaced. The intricate cage of charms were no longer the original work of Bianca. Finger trails gave Cadence away.

"Answer me." Without thinking, Bianca crossed the barrier and grabbed Cadence by the throat. Since they were both actively living in the spirit world, the contact between them was as real as life. She pushed her little sister up against the black concrete wall and bore into her with an evil glare.

"I know you spoke to Theodore. Tell me what you said." Her fingers, still small in their 15-year-old form, tightened around the bruises forever present on the fair skin of Cadence's neck. Her hands fit perfectly into the marks already there, the ones given to her by their father.

Cadence's eyes shut. A small gasp escaped as she choked on her despair. The memories of her death resurfaced as Bianca reenacted it. The night of her murder reemerged at the forefront of her mind and a trickle of gray vapor escaped from the corners of her bright blue eyes. Upon realizing what she was unintentionally doing,

Bianca let go and stepped away. She buried her face in her hands and Cadence fell to the floor: silent, shivering, and crying.

"I'm sorry," Bianca expressed, "I'm so sorry."

"I don't know who you are anymore. Please let me leave."

"I love you."

"No, you don't."

"Yes, I do. Everything I'm doing is for your benefit as well. We will live again, we will get a second chance at life."

"You've gone mad."

Bianca scowled at her sister. "And you've gone soft. You're a mere wisp of a soul and I am trying to save you before you disappear forever."

"I *want* to disappear forever. Our time here ran out over a century ago. I don't want to be here anymore!"

"You don't know what you are saying. Your brain is poisoned by the murky air of this purgatory we are stuck in."

"The only one with a poisoned mind is you. You've gone insane with selfish desires. Pretending your actions are on behalf of me too, when you know damn well I want the opposite of what you're after. I have been begging you for years to enter the light with me. We will find peace on the other side of it. You must believe me."

"It's not that I don't believe you. I'm sure it's quite peaceful over there. Why? *Because everyone over there is dead*. They are silenced, forever. Here, we have a chance to live again. Right now it's only a half-life, but I've done my research and I can make it a full existence again."

"I don't want that! I want silence, I want tranquility. I have spent the last century waiting for you to want those things too, but you only get worse as time goes on."

"You mean smarter."

"No, greedier and more selfish. You are willing to steal another's life in order to get a second chance in that world. As someone who had their life stolen, I'd think you'd understand the pain and would never want to inflict it upon another living person."

"You don't get it."

"What if the life you steal holds a soul more powerful than you give it credit for and they haunt you the remainder of your second life? Tormenting you in each breath you take? Reminding you that they still live alongside you in your new body?"

"I know too much; I am too informed and too well practiced for a fate like that. Living or dead, I can execute my powers to protect myself from unfriendly spirits or souls."

"You're missing the point. Your karma is tarnished, your energy is black, and you will attract negativity for the remainder of your existence no matter where you are if you don't make a change now." Cadence took a deep breath and expressed her deep-rooted fear. "I worry you've already done so much harm against the natural balance of life that we won't be allowed to stay together once we reach the other side."

"All the more reason to stay here." Bianca wasn't entertaining this argument any longer. It was the same fight every time. Cadence tried to make her out to be evil when really she was fighting for both of their mortal rights. They were robbed of a happy childhood, they never experienced adulthood, and Bianca believed she wasn't doing anything wrong by fighting for their right to live one complete life.

"Then let me go alone. I never wanted to be a part of your devious obsession. I want to be free."

"You are free."

"I want to be free of *you*."

Bianca grabbed a piece of chalk off the ground and kneeled. She began scribbling on the floor, strengthening the invisible cage keeping Cadence in her possession. "One day you will thank me."

Cadence sank back to the ground, numb to the abuse. She once loved and idolized Bianca, but now, she loathed her. She tried to remind herself that death changed her. That maybe, through the light, she'd return to her old self. But the more time that went on, the less Cadence believed Bianca was capable of being saved.

"How did you break out anyhow?" she asked as she traced over each symbol three times.

"I don't know what you are talking about."

212

Bianca gave her a look of suspicion but did not push it any farther. "It's my fault. I was away too long. I grew lazy and presumptuous, always assuming you weren't strong enough in this half-life to think beyond your stubborn and self-inflicted suffering. But I know better now. Your love for me is clouded and I must keep better watch over you." She gave her little sister a smile. "I can't have you slipping away from me."

Cadence said nothing. Bianca could never be informed of her meeting with Theodore. He was her only hope. She needed Theodore to pull through with some solution that would help her get Bianca to cross through Apres Monde with her. She didn't know how he would manage this, but she had no other option than to put her faith in him. For his sake, and hers, he needed to succeed.

Chapter 23

Bianca raced to Theodore's recently abandoned home. He hadn't returned since the day Chester tried to possess him. She returned there often, hiding in the shadows to see if he'd take residence again, but he was set on staying with Adelaide. Perhaps finding out she was a ghost unsettled him more than he let show.

The loyalty enchantments she placed along the threshold never took effect, which frustrated her. Chester ruined everything. He scared Theodore, gave him a terrible outlook on the afterlife, and destroyed the slow foundation Bianca had been building. She spent weeks establishing a friendship, hoping to break the news to him gently in a controlled environment, and all of it was ruined in one night. Chester's actions forced the entire process to move much faster than she ever anticipated. She had Theodore's trust and friendship, but instead of revealing her true identity and plan on her own terms, she had to tell him on Chester's. If she could kill Chester, she would. Now that Theodore knew firsthand what it felt like to have someone try and steal his body, he was less likely to help her steal Ruby's. He understood the whole process far too well, better than she would have ever explained it to him, and he now had many more aspects to consider before agreeing to help with her task.

She needed him on board. In all her years spent in the afterlife, and the considerable amount of time spent on Nether Isle, she never met anyone she wanted to spend her living life with besides Theodore. She wanted him in her second life, she wanted to build her new world with him in it. This was why she needed Ruby's body. He liked that girl very much and if she took on that form, it was guaranteed he'd eventually learn to love her. Once he thought Bianca completed her task and released Ruby's body back to its original owner, he'd allow himself to fall in love with her. He might not know it was still Bianca in there, but that was something she could live with. She and Ruby would be one in the same at that point, so it wasn't really a lie.

Her many stakeouts at the Finn household only revealed that Chester lurked around the home on a regular basis. Despite what she told him, and Delilah's incorrect reading of her symbols, the enchantment was never intended to keep Chester out. It was only meant to harness Theodore's loyalty. That didn't work out; after deeming the house safe, Chester reclaimed residence.

Up until now, she avoided all contact with him. He was a leech, a classless shell of a spirit, devoid of any real intelligence or worth. She was shocked someone as hollow as he managed to give a solid attempt at a full possession only a few days into death. At first she wondered if she hadn't given him enough credit, but then after further observation, after seeing the countless hours he spent talking to himself and wandering aimlessly, forgetting his purpose, she determined her first judgments were correct. He was merely an infant in the spirit world and his momentary stroke of genius was a fluke fueled by the shock of death, his inherent rage, and his soul's determination. Clearly, his desire to take Theodore's life was his final objective in the afterlife. It would be the ultimate force keeping him in purgatory rather than entering the light. Perhaps he felt Theodore owed him, or that it was unfair his son got to live while he did not. Either way, Bianca had time to shape Chester into the soldier she needed while his wits and motives in this very confusing middle world developed.

She remembered what it was like in limbo the first few years. Everything was foggy, she had to fight to stay focused on the things happening around her. It was easy to slip into a coma-like state and miss weeks at a time. Cadence disappeared mentally all the time the first few months after they died. It took years of practice and extensive willpower to exist with complete awareness in the murkiness of purgatory. Except for the few moments when his abrasive attitude and self-righteous arrogance surfaced, Chester would be putty in her hands.

Theodore acted peculiar at their last meeting. It made her worried that she was losing his loyalty. If Cadence's encasement markings hadn't been ruined, she never would have suspected her, but since they were, she couldn't help but be paranoid that Cadence revealed the entire truth to him. If he found out she lied about her quest for retribution and her need to see her parents face justice, he would not only be furious but also deceived. Their friendship would be over and her plans would be ruined. That part of the lie was the only thread keeping him attached to her; he needed to continue believing the virtue of her intentions. Without it, she would need to re-strategize.

Her instinct told her to plan for the worst. Cadence was unreliable and no longer trustworthy. Where her loyalties lied were undeterminable and Bianca feared her betrayal already occurred. If Theodore knew the truth, he would tell Adelaide, who would then recruit any combination of Wiccan and Ouijan magic to fight her off. If they had a defense prepared for her, then she would need one of her own as well.

Not wanting to be hasty, Bianca only planned the beginning stages of her defense. She already had the spells and knowledge she needed, but lacked a solid support system. If they had numbers, then she needed a band of spirit soldiers doing her bidding. She would not divulge too much information to any of them yet, nor would she let them know they were unknowingly joining her army, but she had to begin the process. She needed to build relationships and secure their loyalty in case the day arrived that she needed them to act on her behalf. Chester would be her first recruit.

The electricity at the Finn home went out weeks ago, which made it easy for Bianca to hide. The choice of shadows to lurk in was abundant. She waited in the living room, watching the front window Chester always crawled through. She had no clue why he did this, but he always entered his abandoned home like a teenager sneaking in after a night of secretive partying.

Without fail, he climbed through the permanently open window and fell to the ground like a pathetic human. It was ridiculous. He was a ghost, he could pass *through* the window if he chose to, but he was stuck in his ways. His tall, cumbersome body landed without grace to the floor. He scratched his rust-colored beard and stood up. He tip-toed toward his bedroom. No one was there to hear him—no one had entered that house in weeks and he wasn't really alive to make noise anyway—yet he still behaved as if his unnoticed return home was essential. Bianca wondered what past life experience he currently thought he was in. He obviously was not living in the present, which meant he was reliving an old memory.

His head snapped to the left and a look of fury crossed his face.

"Shut up, you stupid baby," he hissed at nothing, plastering his enormous body flat against the wall. His eyes grew wide and his face went slack with defeat. It looked like he was being yelled at, but there was no one there to yell at him.

"I'm sorry. I'm so sorry. It's nothing," he wiped his mouth with the back of his hand, "I love you, babe." He was talking to a figment of his recollection. His wife, perhaps. He was being reprimanded in whatever alternate world he thought he was in.

"No, don't leave! It was a mistake, it won't happen again." His head jerked as if it had been slapped. With force, he scraped at his lips, trying to remove a stain that was no longer there. "The alcohol made me do it. I'll stop, I swear. I don't love nobody like I love you."

His eyes followed his recollection to the front door. Bianca watched in amazement. This happened to her and Cadence many times, all of these occasions she was either in the moment or knew what memory Cadence was going through. This time, it was like receiving a ticket to someone's real-life nightmare. A story she never would have heard from the mouth of Chester in a mentally present state. Something buried so deep, it only came out when he wasn't alert enough to guard its return.

He flinched as the door in his memory slammed shut.

"*Stop crying,*" he pleaded, but the long-gone infant wails did not cease. With his outstretched fingers ready to kill, Bianca's stone-heart fluttered as this moment resembled her own suppressed nightmare.

"It's not real," she called out, revealing herself. "It's only a memory. You aren't really there."

Chester's head whipped toward her, his eyes bloodshot with malice and depression. A whimpered growl escaped his lips as he returned to the present and let go of the hurt he was reliving. He looked down at his hands, then back at Bianca.

"I didn't kill him that night," he said in his own defense, not realizing that he was stating the obvious.

"But you almost did."

"I only hurt him a bit. It made him stronger."

"Right, well, it's not my place to judge. I don't really care much about your personal demons."

"Even when they involve my son, the boy you fancy?" He was back to his regular, defiant self. His words were a test of her patience, pushing to see what triggered her anger.

"You saw what I'm capable of. I suggest you keep your behavior in check around me. I have no reservations toward destroying you."

"Why are you here? You're in my home, acting like you're my boss. Well, you ain't. Get out, yer trespassin'."

"I didn't come here to fight, or to see you relive any delicate instances in your life. Trust me, not my intention." She shook her head, trying to forget seeing Chester looking pathetic during his weakest moment. "I came to offer you friendship. While I am very fond of Theodore, I know what it is like to be new in the spirit world, and after seeing your botched attempt at possessing him, I thought you could use a friend like me."

"It woulda worked if you hadn't intervened. You just wanna be my friend so you can convince me that brat doesn't owe me his life.

Well I'll tell you right now, you ain't gonna change my mind. Everything that went wrong in my life was cause of him. Everything went down the shitter the second that little bastard was born."

"I'm not here to change your mind about anything, or to convince you to leave Theodore alone. I'm here to be a friend. Maybe if you have someone explaining how all of this works, you'll be less angry all the time. Your aura has smothered this house. It's visible from miles away to those with the gift of sight, and I'm sure all the neighbors feel it."

"I don't care about none of them. I hope it makes them feel as rotten as I do. I didn't deserve to die. I was doing right by society: got a job, worked hard day and night, followed the rules. Then I die. Don't even recall how it happened. I just came to and saw my shipmates throwing my dead body overboard. Can you believe it? All for that dumb son of mine. Shoulda sent him away years ago. Got stuck in dead-end jobs for 15 years cause of him. All the responsibility to keep two people alive instead of just myself ended up being the death of me."

"I'm sorry Theodore instilled a sense of accountability within you and motivated you to be a functioning human being rather than a wasteful sack of bones, drowning in alcohol every night and breathing air you don't deserve."

Chester's eyes narrowed. "I thought you said you were trying to be my friend?"

"What good is a friend that lies to you? I'm not going to baby you. I may look young, but I have decades on you. I will be brutally honest with you in order to help you."

"I don't need any help, ya know. Been doing just fine."

"I can help you stop the memories from haunting you. I can teach you how to prevent them from taking over your consciousness. You won't have to relive them in real time anymore."

"Is that right?"

"Yes," Bianca clenched her teeth and tried to prevent her annoyance from showing. His righteousness was overbearing.

"Then maybe there is a friendship that can form between us. I suppose you want something in return?"

"No. I just want you to stop filling the atmosphere with your black energy. It's affecting the entire pier. I have to live here too, you know." Her lie was believable. Asking for nothing in return would be suspicious and she had a close enough eye on Theodore to make sure he didn't try to possess him again anytime soon.

"Alright then, we'll see how good a teacher you are."

"Another time. I am busy today. I'll come back and then we can begin."

Chester scowled but Bianca maintained control over the situation and him. It would all occur on her timeline, not his. Today, she needed to create other brief connections similar to this one. She needed to establish the first phases of friendship with the multitude of spirits living on and around Nether Isle. These bonds were crucial. With the proper timing and strategy, these new friends would turn into her devout followers, ready to fight on her behalf if such a need arose. They'd become dependent on her, feeding off her knowledge and cowering beneath her power. Once they saw her full strength, they'd never do anything that landed them on the other side of her kindness. Her promises to them would be empty and only fulfilled if she had the time or desire to do so. In all cases, they would need to assist her first before she ever used her magic to grant whatever wishes she swore to deliver. She was positive they'd ask for human bodies of their own to possess, or possibly assistance in completing their own personal afterlife vengeance. After she established connections with them all, showed them her powers, and slowly built these alliances, the requests would filter in. It was human nature to abuse advantageous relationships; if they thought they could use her, they would try, and she'd let them think they were gaining something for nothing. She'd never ask for a single favor until it counted. When that moment arrived, her army would materialize out of obligation and she'd be impossible to defeat. They wouldn't realize her power over them until they were already slaves to her command.

Chester was minion number one. He was already savvy to her capabilities; he saw them in action the day he tried to steal Theodore's life. Bianca watched him consider the ways in which he'd benefit from her friendship. He surely believed he would learn how to become as powerful as she was through this new acquaintance, or perhaps he assumed that after she taught him how to stop the memories, she would also help him complete his larger task: possessing Theodore. Either way, the greed in his eyes was abundant as he saw the opportunistic possibilities that might come to him by befriending her. She had him locked in tight. Her manipulative and self-serving offer of friendship was insincere but he bought it with zest, signing his allegiance over to her without even realizing it.

He slumped back to the floor and his eyes glazed over. A memory had hold of him again. Bianca left him where he sat and exited the Finn household. Today would be a day of great beginnings. She traveled the extensive maze of piers, introducing herself to every spirit she could find. Many were eager for a companion, someone to talk to and spend some time with during the endless days and nights that accompanied death. There was no sleep in the half-world they existed in, no purpose except that which you created for yourself. Many were lonely souls, desperate for a friend. Desperate to find meaning in their afterlife, even if it was Bianca's agenda they'd find their purpose in.

Others were angry and resistant to receive her. It did not matter, she would take her time with those individuals. They'd join her cause in time. She would massage the loyalty out of them, using various methods of mental trickery to persuade them, unknowingly, onto her side.

Chapter 24

Ruby met Theodore at Adelaide's house and they walked to Triste Academy together. For the past week, they accompanied each other to and from school. It was safer this way.

Friday morning felt just as daunting as Monday's. No promise of a weekend break could alleviate the pressure Theodore felt to protect Ruby and himself from the malevolent ghost he once called his friend. Now that he knew and had accepted the truth about the supernatural nature of Nether Isle, he couldn't believe he hadn't noticed sooner that Bianca was a ghost. All the signs were there: the smell, the appearance, the suspicious behavior. She even had the markings from her death displayed with prominence upon her neck. Now that it was so clear, he felt dumb for resisting everyone who tried to warn him. And for giving her the benefit of the doubt after she confessed. He wanted so badly to believe in her, to show allegiance toward the first friend he had in years, but in the end, his loyalty only made him blind. It cast a shadow over reality and landed him in this mess.

"I'm sorry I was so stubborn when you tried to warn me. I was trying to be a good friend to her. I had no clue it would cause all of this," he confessed out loud for the first time.

"Don't beat yourself up. It's not your fault. She set her sights on you and played on your ignorance. She knew you were unfamiliar with the way things work here. She used you; the blame is all hers."

"Still feels crappy."

"You didn't even know ghosts were a real thing until your dad came back to possess you. I wanted to tell you, but it's hard to explain it to someone who didn't grow up with it like I did. You always end up looking crazy."

"Yeah, I don't think I would have believed it if anyone told me previous to my dad's attack."

"It's really frustrating to explain to people outside of Nether Isle. I've tried and failed many times. People raised in the states are conditioned to believe that ghosts are imaginary, and they are not able to see them for what they are when they encounter them in real life. Many tourists come to Nether Isle and carry on with the ghosts like they are talking to the locals. Oblivious and unable to see the death blows still present on the spirit they converse with."

"Why does that happen? I couldn't see Bianca's strangle marks until she confessed she was dead."

"When a person doesn't believe something is possible, doesn't believe it can exist in real life, their mind will gloss over it, even if it stands before them in plain sight. To protect their grasp of the world and reality, their consciousness will erase certain details or replace them with something more socially acceptable. This prevents them from questioning their own sanity. Often times, people will create logical excuses for the nonsensical encounters, explaining it in a way they can rationalize internally and accept as normal."

"So it's our minds protecting us from ourselves."

"Yeah. When your eyes betray your hardened beliefs, your mind goes on the defensive. It will alter the perceived reality in order to protect a person's psyche. It does this to prevent the possibility of a mental breakdown, or worse. Basically, if you don't believe it, you won't see it. It's how we are hardwired."

"Crazy how that works."

"I wish we told you sooner, though. Rowan and I plotted ways to tell you that wouldn't freak you out, but by the time we thought out an explanation and got up the nerve, you and Bianca were already really close and you were too protective over her to listen."

"I should have listened. Everyone was hinting that I needed to pay closer attention to who she really was. I never would have guessed ghost on my own, but I might have seen she had devious intentions."

"That was another reason it took us so long to agree to tell you. Bianca's been around for a while. I remember seeing her hovering around the high school kids when I was little. She would do magic and taunt them, finding ways to hurt them from afar with her powers. One time, she lit a girl's hair on fire. She's haunted the school for a long time and her reputation precedes her. When you moved here, she started showing up again."

"She never entered our class until a few weeks ago."

"Yes, but she was lurking about, always hovering in the shadows near you. You didn't know to look for her, so you didn't notice her, but the rest of us did. And when she began sitting in our classroom and acting sweet in order to befriend you, everyone got scared. It's why everyone stayed so far removed from you. No one knew what she was up to and didn't want to get in the way for fear she'd take it out on them."

"I've got great luck, I'll tell ya." Theodore rolled his eyes.

"Yeah, sorry if you felt ostracized, or like we were all super unwelcoming. We've just grown up with her presence, and honestly we are terrified of her. There are rumors she possessed a girl once, without any help from a living person. No one knows for sure, it happened when I was little and was a very hushed situation. But the story goes that Bianca possessed her on her own, the Ouijans intervened, saved the girl, and then she was pulled out of school. If it's true, she is not the ghost you wanna mess with. She can do things no other ghosts can."

"Yikes," Theodore felt sick to his stomach. He never realized he was such a bad judge of character.

"I felt terrible cause I knew you felt alone. I tried in small ways to let you know you could talk to me whenever. The smiles and quick hellos. But every time I did, I saw Bianca lurking somewhere out of sight, casting evil glares my way."

"I always wondered why you'd smile at me so often but never say much."

"It just would have been easier if you approached me rather than the other way around. Bianca couldn't take it out on me if you initiated the conversation."

"I see," Theodore sighed.

"Eventually Rowan and I knew we had to do something. In case Bianca was going to hurt you, or, like we later found out, use you to hurt someone else. I went to Adelaide one day after school, cause I knew you worked for her, and expressed my concerns. She said I had to tell you and gave me this necklace." She held up the long chain with a golden stone attached by wire. "It's pyrite. It's a protective stone that would weaken any attempts of retaliation. If she tried to hurt me for speaking out against her, this stone would *hopefully* stop, or lessen, the blow."

"All this magic crap is weird. Spells, charms, symbols, crystals, powders, candles. It's overwhelming. I want to learn ways to protect myself, but it's hard to believe I'll ever get the hang of this stuff. Or remember what any of it means."

"If you stick around here long enough, it'll become second nature."

"I really hope that doesn't happen. This is all too weird to become normal."

"You're long past normal, buddy. I hate to break it to ya, but with all that's going on, I have a feeling you'll be a pro in no time." Ruby gave him a playful wink. The teasing manner in which she spoke enhanced her peculiar French-American accent. She was the most fascinating person he had ever met.

At school, they sat in desks adjacent to each other. Rowan adopted Theodore as a new pal too and was much less abrasive toward him. Everyone was friendlier now that he knew the truth and Bianca no longer came around. The contrast was black and white. Complete solitude had morphed into constant interaction. He felt ostracized before because of circumstances out of his control, but now everything made sense. This newfound validation that he was a worthy friend was liberating. While this sudden acceptance cheered him up, it did not diminish all that vexed him. It would take time to get over the betrayal his father cast upon him. It hurt, even though he expected nothing better from him. He also still had to deal with Bianca. The loss of that friendship would be tolerable, once it was truly settled. Right now, everything felt unsafe and each step he took had to be calculated. Any wrong move could result in devastating consequences. The cautious nature in which he was forced to exist was tiring. It was a terrible way to live.

Luckily, Ruby and Adelaide were on his side, as were the lot of Wiccans and Ouijans. Having this great force of light and dark magic at his back helped ease his worry. He had no clue how to beat a wicked ghost, so having them on his side was crucial. He had an appointment with the Ouijans after school that day and hoped they could teach him some skills that would make him useful in the battle against Bianca. It was cruddy to feel helpless. He wanted to save the day; he wanted to save the girl.

Ruby was all smiles during lunch. She told him and Rowan about the adventures she had with her one-eyed cat named Uno. All the rides on her bicycle with Uno in the front basket and the outfits she crocheted for the cat, which she swore he loved wearing. As she spoke of the feline with loving tenderness in her voice, Rowan spat out in protest every time she referred to Uno in a positive light.

"That cat is the devil," he proclaimed. "I swear its sole purpose in life is to scratch out eyeballs. It's a bitter rat, that cat. Reggie still has a scar on his neck from when it attacked his face."

"Reggie was a toddler when it happened and he was taunting Uno. Of course he was going to defend himself as his fur was being pulled out."

"Reggie is 10 now. The scar is still there."

"You'll have to meet my cat sometime, Theodore," she said. "You can be the judge if he's evil or not." She gave Rowan an angry glare.

"Sure thing. Though, with what I'm hearing, and the fact that I work at a fish market, I'm a bit nervous he'll try to eat me. I always stink like fish."

"He'll turn you into a Cyclops like him. Watch out," Rowan warned.

"Oh, stop it. Everyone loves him except you."

"And Reggie."

"Now that I think about it, I have seen a brown-speckled cat in an orange sweater before," Theodore remembered. "He sits there and hisses at people until they give him food. He bit Gus Yonk once."

"And Gus." Rowan added to the list.

"It must be a different cat. Uno would never bite someone."

"Yours is the only cat strolling around town in people clothes," Rowan reminded her.

"I love my cat. I don't care what either of you think."

"Between the costumes you put him in and the missing eye, no wonder the little jerk is so nasty," Rowan concluded.

"The outfits keep him warm."

"They do look quite cozy, actually," Theodore commented, recalling the fuzzy, sweater-wearing cat at the market.

"I use mohair yarn. It's the softest."

"You're out of control," Rowan laughed. He liked to tease her. Theodore thought her unshakable love for a creature so contentious was endearing.

"The most unlovable among us are the ones who need our love most."

"Okay, Shakespeare."

"Shakespeare was a playwright," Theodore corrected him.

"Better than calling her Dr. Seuss."

"I didn't even craft a rhyme."

"Whatever, a philosopher, alright? Geez, you guys are too cool for me."

Ruby rolled her eyes but let it go. He was sensitive when he was called out on his wits, so she dropped it and was glad Theodore did too. Rowan was rough on the outside but mush at his core.

"Have you seen that ghost again recently?" he asked Theodore.

"No."

Rowan didn't know about Bianca's plan to use Theodore to borrow Ruby's body. They couldn't tell him because they could not control his reaction. The Linville brothers had terrible tempers. If he found out Ruby's life was threatened, he'd freak out. He'd ruin their plans to stop Bianca in a peaceful manner and then potentially initiate a supernatural war. This was what they were trying to prevent by going about this plan with secrecy.

"It's weird that she just vanished. If she had some reason to befriend you, she wouldn't just abandon it. She never tried anything weird or explained what her deal was?"

"No, she just stopped showing up. I saw her once after my dad attacked me. She admitted then that she was a ghost and then never sought me out again."

"Maybe part of her plan required you *not* to know she was a ghost and your dad ruined that for her by giving you a front row seat to their evil ways. Maybe him trying to kill you actually ended up saving you."

"That's one way to look at it."

"Well, we don't know what she wanted with you, but I can only imagine her plans were way worse and would be more successful than your dad's had any chance to be. She's ancient. She can do things most ghosts are not capable of. Most of them are reserved and spacey. They are barely here and can't cause real harm because they can't stay mentally present for more than a few minutes. But not her. She's a wildcard."

"I'm just glad she's gone," Ruby offered, hoping to end the conversation before Rowan made Theodore's opponent sound any more daunting than she was.

"Let's hope she stays gone." Rowan took a big bite of his salami and mustard sandwich.

The lunch bell rang and they returned to class. The day sped by and Theodore was on his way to Salamander Pier before he realized it. It was a daunting walk but necessary. If he wanted this saga to end, he would need their help.

Chapter 25

He had no clue what to expect when he got there, but Adelaide and Delilah would act as buffers if things got too strange. The Ouijans were a mystery to him. He had never met or even seen one before. They lived in solitude on Salamander Pier, only speaking to their neighbors when their neighbors sought them out.

Ruby could not attend this introduction because she had to help her father with some paperwork at his company. They had a busy weekend and all his charter boats would be in use, taking travelers to and from locations across the ocean. Ruby was skipping school tomorrow to help him, so she'd be on the mainland all weekend, helping him out at his port in Maine. As much as Theodore would have liked a friend to be there when he met the Ouijans, it was good that she would be away for a few days. Being far from Nether Isle was the safest bet right now. Plus, she already knew everything he'd be learning this evening. Though her family didn't practice Wicca or Ouija, they were well versed in the rituals since they'd lived on this isle for generations. Ruby said she always found it fascinating and practiced the small spells in her backyard. Earlier that week, during one of their walks to school, she showed him how she could make sea pebbles glow. It was beautiful. He didn't know how that would ever be useful while fighting a malevolent ghost, but she had the gift within her. He was sure she could pick up harder spells with ease if she was taught. And she would be a great mentor as he took the knowledge he learned at the meeting and studied it in the upcoming days.

As he turned left onto Salamander Pier, he could see his sailboat rocking in the bay by Ballantine Dock. An early morning sail was long overdue. He had to remember to make time for it soon. It was the only sure way to set his nerves to rest.

Adelaide greeted him at the entrance to the pier. It was even more run-down than the others, which was impressive considering the entire isle looked long overdue for a renovation. The wooden planks were rotted, and many were missing, leaving gaping holes scattered along their walk. If you weren't careful, you could step right into one, sending your leg toward the rocky coastline below and leaving you injured and stuck. The houses built on this pier were ancient. While the houses along the other piers were shabby, they were still updated occasionally in an attempt to maintain their functionality. Though these construction makeovers were hastily applied and parts were ordered that never matched the colors already in place, leaving each house looking like spotty patchwork, at least an attempt was made. The houses on Salamander Pier were untouched. It was clear by their single colored sidings, chipped paint, and decaying wood. There was a spooky quality to the atmosphere here. It felt haunted. This was the first place on Nether Isle that actually looked to hold supernatural secrets. If he had come here previous to learning the truth, he may have suspected ghosts were an actual possibility. The air was thick with history and he could taste the forgotten lives that lingered here in every breath he took.

"Why don't I see any ghosts? I can feel them."

"You don't feel the ghosts, you feel the Ouijan magic. It's very potent."

"It feels like death."

"That's because they extract the power surrounding death to produce their magic. It's why they are so strong. Nothing compares to the energy found in life and death. Except love and fear, which is also used when available. The Ouijan magic feeds off death and fear while the Wiccan's is absorbed through life and love. Dark and light; opposing forces. Naturally, they despise each other as they cannot see eye to eye on the proper acquisition of magic. But together, the combination of their power is unstoppable. Delilah and I are hoping they will see this situation you are in logically and offer to help alongside the Wiccans. With a spirit like Bianca, light magic won't be enough. We need their darkness to battle hers."

Theodore exhaled, still amazed that all of this weirdness was his new reality. Just a few weeks ago, he had one friend, an abusive father, and a soul-crushing routine of boredom. Now he lived in a world where ghosts walked around, in plain sight, as if they were still alive. He had an army of classmates, neighbors, and sorcerers rallying to defend him and their home from the one friend he thought he had. His father was dead, but still remained a viable threat to his safety, and his routine was no longer predictable or mundane; it was unpredictable and petrifying. All the things that used to be bad were fixed and replaced by new terrible things. He tried to focus on the positive changes that came along with the bad, but it was hard not to feel overwhelmed by the death, and threat of death, that encased his existence. Maybe the Ouijans would prove to be a product of rumors. Maybe their ominous reputation would be nothing more than years of built-up gossip. He hoped they were friendlier than they sounded because they were the key to ending this nightmare.

At the end of Salamander Pier, which jetted off the mainland side of Peddler's way and backed up to a cliff, stood a creaky, dark manor. Delilah Clement waited for them there, vibrant with positive energy. She greeted them and escorted them into the crooked mansion. They ascended the stoop, which moaned beneath their weight, and rang the doorbell. An eerie melody chimed into the spacious home. They could hear its muffled tune echo through the cracks in the walls.

Not much time passed before the front door was opened, ever so slightly, chain lock still intact. A man with crazy eyes peeked through the gap.

"Hello, Delilah." His voice was low and his conduct awkward.

"Hi there, Poe. Are you ready for our meeting?"

"I wasn't told about any meeting."

"I spoke with Percival last week, and again this morning to confirm we were still on for today. It is urgent, you must let us in."

Poe's face twitched as Delilah got stern with him and it appeared he was exercising great patience. Poe's natural demeanor was not a nice one and it took great energy out of him to fake social pleasantries. Theodore remembered seeing him at the market with the emerald-eyed girl. He was nasty then as well.

"Wait here."

The door slammed.

Delilah looked back at Adelaide and Theodore and mouthed an apology. Behind the door they could hear yelling.

"Nobody warned me!" Poe shouted.

"You need to learn how to be more adaptable."

"I cannot have these types of surprises thrown at me. I need to plan and prepare for social engagements."

"It's not a freaking party, it's a casual meeting with our neighbors. There is nothing to prepare for."

The door opened again, this time without the chain lock fastened.

"Sorry about Poe." A tall man with an illuminated smile greeted them. "He has trouble with strangers."

"Quite alright, Percival," Delilah answered. "I know he is inclined toward rage. Didn't mean to throw off his routine."

"Come in, please. I have set up the great hall for our meeting."

They followed the man into his home, which was probably quite beautiful once upon a time. The rich architecture and design was there, but barely visible beneath decades of dust and decay. The grand hall was majestic. Its ceilings were twenty feet high and the long mahogany table could seat fifty people. If it weren't so run down, Theodore imagined the Ouijan manor would look like a castle. Instead, it looked like a haunted mansion.

Percival sat at the head seat; Adelaide to his left, Delilah to his right. Theodore took the seat next to Adelaide.

"Will no one else be joining us?"

"They will. I just wanted a quick briefing before I invited the others in. Many of them don't take to surprises well."

"Then why didn't you prepare them for our arrival?" Adelaide asked the obvious.

"Because I wasn't sure if your intentions were worth our energy yet." He spoke these harsh words so casually it appeared he did not see them as cruel.

"My name is Percival Archambault." He extended a hand to Theodore, who accepted and shook it.

"I'm Theodore Finn."

"Yes. Every time I hear your name I know a ludicrous story is sure to follow. Word travels faster than storm clouds around here. Quite bothersome, you are. Let's hope you don't live up to this reputation of yours." He smiled at Theodore like they were on the same page contextually, then continued, "While I'd love to start us all off as one big, happy group, I can't. My people are rather delicate, for lack of a better word. Since we don't get out much, a few peculiar social anxieties have made homes in them." Theodore wanted to let him know he suffered from one as well, but kept his mouth shut. "I need to know what you're here for so I can present it to them in a manner they can receive without freaking out." He grimaced. "You saw Poe. A few of the others take to routine interruptions as poorly as he."

"We've come because there is a spirit on Nether Isle that is a threat to us all. She is unlike any others. She can produce magic, a type of magic that is of her own creation. Nothing I've ever seen or heard of before."

"Bianca?"

"You know her?" Delilah's voice grew in volume, as did her alarm. She wore her newfound suspicion of the Ouijans all across her face.

"No. But we've seen her around. She's been here, snooping on our séances and taking notes. She thought we did not see her, but of course we did. We've been keeping a watchful eye on her since."

"Not watchful enough if you do not know why we are here now."

"I have an inkling." He shot an annoyed glance at Theodore, then returned to his charming self. "The boy befriended her. Thought she was a real, living girl."

"I didn't know ghosts were an actual *thing*." Theodore didn't like Percival. Adelaide jumped in before Theodore's impatience triggered the wrong reaction from Percival.

"The boy just moved here from Alaska. Had no clue of the workings of Nether Isle till it was too late."

"I assume you are referring to his dead father's botched possession attempt."

"No, I'm referring to Bianca's obsession with him."

Percival's interest peaked. "Obsession?"

Theodore was taken aback too. It was the first time he heard that word used to describe it.

"Yes," Delilah stepped in to explain. "She's been around for years, as you know. Always tormented the living kids, but never acted further upon it."

"Untrue."

Delilah paused, then recalled the instance Percival referred to. "You're right, my mistake. But this time it's much different. She *befriended* her victim. Instead of a surprise attack, she made a real connection with him in order to persuade his loyalty. The reason we came to you is because we finally found out her motives and need to stop her before she tries to carry out her plan."

"And what *is* this plan of hers?"

"Originally, it was to have Theodore slice an entrance point into Ruby Klearstone's neck. A place Bianca could enter for the planned possession. Long story short, Theodore learned the truth about everything after his father's attempt to possess him, before Bianca could give him her twisted version of it all. He was aware how it all worked so any lies she planned to tell him to convince him he should help her were no longer plausible. Instead, she told him some sob story to try and guilt him into helping her. Theodore would never hurt Ruby for Bianca, but still felt bad for her until her little sister Cadence, also dead, found him and told him the *real* story. Still tragic, but missing all the fabricated parts Bianca added in with hopes to sway Theodore's decision. She is determined to get Ruby's body, and if Theodore turns his back on her, we fear her obsession with him could turn lethal. As in, if she can't join him in the real world, she will make *him* join her in the afterlife."

"Ludicrous, as usual."

"Will you help us stop her?"

"I don't *want* to," Percival sighed. "Why can't the Wiccans use their sunshine and rainbows to conquer this little battle?"

"Because Bianca practices dark magic. Like yours." Delilah's tolerance was waning. "Our powers will only hold her off temporarily. We have no permanent fix besides tricking her into the light of Apres Monde."

"I see. How powerful is this spirit exactly?"

"She stopped the possession Chester Finn attempted to perform on Theodore. She thwarted him with spells and enchantments. She utilized charmed artifacts to keep her safe from the incantations she spoke that should have debilitated her as well. Not only does she combine Wiccan and Ouijan magic, but also that which she has learned by traveling the globe: Egyptian, Mayan, Babylonian, who knows what else."

Percival sighed and rested his head onto his hands as he thought out loud, a mistake by all social accounts. He stared at the table as he spoke.

"I have no interest in helping the boy. Or the Wiccans. Or the old fish lady. But this spirit does sound formidable. I don't like having uncontrollable variables present in my realm of existence. It causes drama, like that which I am handed now. If I squash this current drama, it will be over and I will never have to hear of it again. Or risk it escalating into something much larger." He looked up at his three visitors with disdain, then back down at the table. Theodore now wondered if the man was aware he spoke out loud for all to hear. "Help from the Ouijans is needed. You can be the hero. You can show them there is good in the dark."

He sat back up. "Alright. Let me get my fellow Ouijans on board. Give me a moment."

He exited the room, leaving them alone to ponder what just happened. Adelaide gave a sideways glance to Theodore, indicating with her big-eyed expression that she too thought Percival was cuckoo. He returned with a crowd of strange looking individuals. As they entered and took their seats, he introduced them.

Cynthia Monette sat next to Delilah. She was rail-thin, six feet, and sported a wispy bun of sun-lightened brown hair. Her face was sullen and serious, and her eyes darted around the room in surveillance. The way in which she moved was deliberate and Theodore did not suspect her wits were frayed from lack of social interaction. In fact, she seemed wildly aware of herself and her surroundings. Every breath she took was calculated.

Caspian Voclain entered behind her. He was of a similar build, but his facial features were softer and less intense. He was young with a fresh face. His brunette hair was slicked back against his scalp and his appearance was thoroughly thought out. Even his eyebrows were groomed. He looked like a big-shot businessman from New York City. Absolutely out of place here.

Tabitha Beauchene sat next to Theodore. She was younger than the rest of them, maybe only 23 years old. Long blonde curls fell over her shoulders and her bright eyes bore into everything she looked at, including Theodore. She gave him a smirk as she sat beside him. It instantly filled him with unease. Her intentions were unclear and it seemed like she was flirting. Obviously she wasn't, but Theodore wondered why she pretended to. It was mischievous. He remembered seeing her once; the day she and the hooded girl stared Bianca down on Peddler's Way. It all made sense now.

Morgana Roux walked in holding Morton Guillory's hand. She was shaking and muttering to herself. Her dark, shoulder-length red hair was chopped unevenly, and the thick bangs almost covered her eyes. Morton sat her next to Caspian. She was far too unstable for a woman in her young thirties, causing Theodore to wonder what tragedy reduced her to this. She rocked back and forth, eyeing Delilah as she did so.

Morton sat next to her, an arm wrapped beneath one of hers for support. He was an enormous man, the tallest one there. His wide shoulders prevented him from fitting in his seat properly and his jawline twitched as he tried to find a comfortable position. His dark skin matched his short black hair and emphasized the brightness of his blue eyes. The contrast was petrifying. He looked like he held devious magic within him. Though he behaved in a kind manner, his appearance was sinister.

Poe Lesauvage came in next, as perturbed as before. He huffed and sat next to Tabitha. He was a short man made of pure muscle. The rage he carried in his tiny frame was immense. It was tangible and the room soaked it up like a sponge. His tension came out through his fingers, which tapped the table loudly.

Last in was Gretchen Chaput. Her head was shadowed by the large hood of her jacket. All that could be seen was a long black braid and her piercing green eyes. The girl with the emerald glare; he'd seen her many times in passing. She sat down next to Poe and removed her hood. Doing so immediately changed her from mysterious to vulnerable. It revealed her youth—late twenties—and her gentle aura. She looked around the room nervously. After a moment of reconsideration, she placed the hood back over her head.

"Thank you all for sitting in on this meeting. I already gave you a brief summary of what is needed from us. Do you have any questions for our visitors?" Percival asked.

There was a long pause.

"Is she onto you?" Gretchen finally said from beneath her hood. The words came out in a tone indicating she already knew the answer.

"I don't think so," Theodore responded. "I can tell she sees a difference in our friendship now versus how it used to be, but she has no clue we are trying to send her through the light. Or that I am consulting with Wiccans and Ouijans to do so."

Gretchen did not say another word.

"We can do it without the Wiccans help," Poe muttered.

"No, they will offset our dark magic nicely," Cynthia said, her lips tight as she spoke. "If anything goes awry, they'll be there to mend it."

"Regardless of the beliefs behind light magic versus dark, it cannot be denied that both our groups are stronger with the help of the other. Together, we are invincible," Caspian said. "From a logical standpoint, it's stupid that we fight amongst ourselves so relentlessly. The fact that we've grown to despise one another is foolish. So counterproductive."

"We know your thoughts on this matter," Percival said, "but your opinion doesn't erase hundreds of years of dislike and clashes between the groups. Only twenty years ago, we almost went to war with one another. That can't be so easily forgotten."

"War?" Adelaide spat out in shock.

"You plain folk woulda been in for a nasty treat if it happened." Morgana's eyes lit up as she imagined the casualties amongst the innocent. "Might've stopped judging us once you saw what we were capable of."

"Or they would have judged us more," Morton said to hush her. "If innocents died during that time, we would have turned from misunderstood neighbors into malevolent outcasts. We would have proven everything we stand against. We don't believe in murder or war, we just happen to use the darkness caused by such tragedies to harness our magic. It's the most potent, therefore it gives us the most natural energy to work with."

Morgana twitched in her seat.

"Personally," Gretchen chimed in, "I hate it when we try to justify our darkness. It is not our job to make them understand. If they cannot see the beauty in it, then oh well. We know what we stand for and we know what we believe in. Why are we always trying to prove we aren't the bad guys? We've never done a single harmful thing to an innocent, ever. In fact, I can shout out numerous occasions where we've *saved* their lives. It's infuriating that we still have to live in the shadow of everyone's misperceived opinions."

Poe slammed his fist on the table in agreement and Morgana clapped in a rapid-fire applause.

"Congrats," Tabitha spoke in a soft voice. Her French-American accent suited her. It was the first one he ever heard that sounded pretty. "You've got the loony toons on your side."

From beneath her hood, Gretchen shot Tabitha a glare filled with fire. Maybe it was Theodore's imagination, but it looked to illuminate the shadows of her hiding place. For a second, since apparently anything was possible here, he truly believed a laser beam of lava was going to erupt through her pupils and set Gretchen's beautiful hair aflame.

"You care too much what other's think. Stop letting their unimportant thoughts rule your world."

"They call us creepy. Do I look creepy to you?" Tabitha batted her pretty eyelashes and threw a strand of curls over her shoulder.

"You look ridiculous."

"Really, though, we need to recruit more people who look normal like me," Tabitha continued her narcissistic thought process. "Scanning the room, I get it. It's a ragged crew. But if we got more recruits who were beautiful, then we would be envied, not ostracized. Pretty people attract followers; they trust us, want to be like us. We get what we want."

"You should stop talking," Percival said, nonchalantly, unaware he spoke on behalf of everyone.

"So what's the plan of action?" Cynthia was frazzled. The conversation went rogue and she did not appreciate it.

"The Wiccans are crafting up Hoodoo Sachet powder that Theodore will blow through her head. Once this is done, she will be disoriented and Cadence can drag her through the light."

"It won't work," Gretchen said without looking up.

"Why not?" Delilah demanded.

"Because she *is* onto you. I've been watching her, in my free time. She'll never let you get that close to her. She doesn't trust your blind obedience anymore."

"Does Cadence even know to be ready? She'll need to pull her through the light immediately, the powder's effect does not last long," Cynthia asked.

"She knows I'm trying to help her stop Bianca, so I'm hoping she'll be waiting nearby. She got out once, I'm banking on the fact she can do it again," Theodore answered.

"That sounds like a very unreliable plan," Percival groaned. "Gretchen, you said you've been observing the ghost. Do you know where she keeps her sister hidden?"

"No, I've never followed her to her dwelling."

"Then there needs to be a backup plan," Cynthia insisted.

"I say we give them tranq salt," Caspian offered. "Unlike the confusion powder, which needs to be blown into the target at close range, the tranq salt can be thrown from afar. If the confusion powder is a failure, this is the next best option. It will paralyze the spirit from attacking him while he makes a getaway."

"If he ends up needing to use the salt, then she'll absolutely be onto us," Morton added. "We can alter her memory after the confusion powder, but the tranq salt won't blur her mind. She'll remain lucid and remember everything. If fate takes us down that path, and she is as powerful and conniving as you claim, we will need to prepare all the Ouijans for battle."

"One step at a time, folks." Percival stopped the melodrama train before it left the station, carrying all the Ouijans imaginations along with it. "Maybe the powder will work. Let's get this kid some salt as a precaution, and then send him on his way."

"Worth a try," Cynthia agreed.

"Yes, but if the Wiccan's plan fails and we use the salt, we need your word you will stand by our side," Delilah added. "Though the salt is helpful, using it will put us all in danger."

"Got it." Percival was having trouble maintaining his friendly smile. "Who has some salt to give Theodore?"

"I do," Gretchen announced, "I'll go get it." Then she swept out of the room like she hoped to disappear in the process.

"What a crackpot," Tabitha muttered beneath her breath. Only Theodore heard her.

"Lovely gathering. You can leave now," Percival smiled, directing his comment directly at Delilah, Adelaide, and Theodore.

"Gretchen will deliver the tranq salt to you in the foyer, by the front door," Cynthia added. She shot Percival a look.

"My apologies, didn't mean to sound like I was rushing you out. Just have many items to cross off my agenda today."

This was a lie, but the three outsiders obliged without confronting his rude nature.

"Thank you all for your time. It's very much appreciated," Delilah said as they stood up. "We hope the powder works, but knowing you're on board in case it doesn't gives us great relief. Despite our differences, we do respect your abilities and value them as a great strength."

"Thank you," Caspian answered for all the Ouijans. His smile of appreciation looked genuine. A few others nodded in acknowledgment.

What an unreadable group, Theodore thought as they exited. One minute they were supportive, the next they were full of hate. No matter what they did or how kind they were, their reaction was unpredictable. It made for a very awkward and tense encounter. He understood why their reputation was so rotten; the fault was all their own.

Chapter 26

They left the room with minimal goodbyes and waited in the entrance hall for Gretchen. Theodore looked around at the decorations for the first time. There were skulls on corner tables and a few stuffed ravens hanging from the ceiling. Cobwebs littered the once beautiful mansion and covered the classic gothic paintings decorating the high walls. Gretchen returned, hood overhead, and pulled Theodore into an attached den without saying a word. He was separated from his older companions without explanation and dragged into the adjacent room.

The den's walls were made up of shelves, which were covered ceiling to floor in weathered books. The room smelt musty and unused. There were no windows, therefore minimal circulation filtered through and the air was clammy. Gretchen removed her hood; her wispy bangs and soft face were revealed from beneath the shadows.

"Here is the salt." She handed him a glass vile with a cork tightly in place. Inside the tube was copper salt. "Keep it uncorked in your pocket next time you meet with her. If at any moment you think she is onto you, chuck it at her head. It'll pass through and leave her paralyzed temporarily. Run back here if this happens."

"Alright." He took the vile and held it up to the light coming from the foyer. The copper salt reflected off it and came alive for a moment. The tiny particles danced with light as he moved the vile around.

"I have one more thing for you," she said. Theodore placed the sealed vile of salt into his pocket and returned his attention to the mysterious female helping him. Her vivid emerald eyes scanned his innocent face.

She pulled a large stone from her cloak-like jacket. "This is a pellucid onyx. It can absorb the powers of one and transfer them into another."

Theodore raised his eyebrows and looked at the rock. The transparent black onyx was exquisite. Just like the reflective salt, it caught the distant light of the foyer and refracted it like art upon Gretchen's forearms.

"Would you like the ability to *really* defend yourself?" she asked, touching on the deep-rooted nerve that had bothered Theodore ever since he discovered Bianca's true plan. His whole life he had taken care of himself. Now, with all that happened, he felt very needy. It was infuriating. He wanted to be able to count on himself. He didn't want his life to be dependent upon the magical people who surrounded him here. He wanted to feel self-sufficient again, capable of taking care of himself with simple assistance rather than complete reliance on strangers.

"Yes."

"I thought so. I could sense it." She began massaging the stone between her palms in a deliberate pattern. "I'd feel the same way."

She muttered a fast chant in French and continued moving the magical vessel in her hands. As she spoke, her eyes rolled into the back of her head and the pellucid onyx heated up. It glowed faintly, growing stronger in appearance the more she spoke. Her words came out with ferocity; her intent was strong and clear. The longer she went on, the more it sounded like a song.

After a minute, her emerald eyes returned and refocused on him. She cradled the stone and held it out to him.

"It's your turn."

Caught off guard, he stumbled, "I don't know what to say. I don't speak French, I have no clue what you just recited."

"Your part is easy. All you need to say is *libérez en moi*. It means *release into me.*"

"Am I stealing your magic?" Theodore asked, concerned for the first time about the gravity of this spell.

"Of course not. You really think I'd ever agree to that? This is more like a copy and paste."

"Will it change me?"

"Yes. Deep in your soul. You'll have the same mind, same heart, same beliefs, but your entire being will rearrange. The platform on which you were built will be shifted. For the better, I think. It will make you more engaged with nature and the workings of this world."

"Is this why you brought me in here? So Delilah and Adelaide would not object to this?"

"Obviously. The normie wouldn't understand and the Wiccan would try to convince you it would blacken your soul. Which it won't," she explained. "Everything we do is misconceived. Our depth is confused with darkness. Because we sense the richness of death so profoundly, they forget that we also, inevitably, pull from life too. We have to; life and death are impossibly intertwined. We could not harness one without believing in the other. If you accept this gift I am offering you, you will not *turn dark*. You will merely become more aware. And the purpose of it, which is the only reason I am offering it to you, is because it will help you fight off this hostile spirit if her friendship with you turns sour. I wouldn't want to be defenseless and I could tell you didn't want to hide in a corner."

"I don't," he confessed out loud, "but how will I know how to use these new powers you're giving me? I can't speak French, and even if I could, I don't know any of the spells or understand how any of this works."

"You won't need to. It will be coursing through your entire being. I'll teach you the workings of it all if you'd like to come by once in a while to receive lessons, but in the meantime, the ability will become inherent. Anytime you experience fear, or emotions of equal intensity, the magic will come out of you naturally. Your body will know what to do, even if your mind doesn't yet."

He nodded, taking it all in. Being such a novice, he still had no clue what the full range of implications would be if he allowed a part of her to enter him. He liked who he was and he did not want to change the core of who he was as a person. But he also needed to be able to defend himself and his friends against Bianca in case their first plan failed. If she decided to attack them, he wanted to be able to fight. It was a risk he had to take.

"Alright. What do I need to do?"

"Cup your hands and place them over mine. The magic I placed in the stone will radiate into you." He did as she directed. "Now shut your eyes, relax, and say *libérez en moi* until you can't anymore."

"Until I can't?"

"You'll know."

He trusted her and began.

Libérez en moi.
Libérez en moi.
Libérez en moi.

The heat from the pellucid onyx took over his hands. It was hot, and the more he spoke the more it hurt. He kept his eyes shut, but wanted to open them in question. The stone was on fire.

Libérez en moi.
Libérez en moi.
Libérez en moi.

His heart was pounding and he could feel the bones of his ribcage fighting to contain it. His chest pulsed violently, in and out, with each irregular heartbeat. A cold sweat sent goose bumps down his arms, contrasting drastically with the scorching transmission that engulfed his hands.

Libérez en moi.
Libérez en moi.
Libérez en moi.

The words were whispers now as his breathing became shallow. His entire consciousness was engulfed in black space. He was no longer in the den with Gretchen, he no longer heard the words he was saying, he could only feel the energy shooting up his arms and into his brain. Its transfer was an electric current, never ceasing, only striking his brain then tearing down his spine. He could feel it dart in no particular order through every cell of his body. It was filtering into him with utter completeness.

Libérez en moi.

Libérez en –

The final surge struck his skull. His eyes shot open; they were covered in blood. Everything was red. Their hands, still cupped around the stone, were engulfed in raging flames. He was on fire. His eyes rolled back as the last charge from the onyx dispersed through his body. Gretchen took the stone in one hand and grabbed Theodore's forearm with the other, catching him before he collapsed to the ground. She held him upright as he convulsed in agony.

"I should have warned you it might hurt."

She sounded miles away.

"What's taking so long?" Adelaide's raspy voice shouted from the foyer. Gretchen sat him in a chair and gave him a moment to come back around.

"Just teaching him how to use the tranq salt," she replied. She knelt down in front of Theodore and gave him a light tap on the side of his face.

"Come to," she demanded.

His head rocked back and forth. He heard her distant voice and tried his best to escape the blackout he was in. She tilted his head back and opened his eyes wide. Cooling drops dripped onto his eyeballs, one at a time. The blood ran down his cheeks like tears.

"It felt like I died for a minute," he gasped.

"You didn't, but you felt the power of death. It's in my magic. Now it's in you."

"When will I feel normal again?"

"Before you leave this room. Eat this." She handed him a piece of chocolate. "It will set you right." She leaned to the side to look into the foyer as he ate the candy. With one bite, he felt rejuvenated. It was amazing. The sugar snapped him back, as if none of the terror he felt ever happened. She knelt before him and dabbed the blood out of the corners of his eyes with a tissue.

"I would suggest you don't tell them what we just did. It will only worry them. I'm here anytime you have a question, or if something ever happens and you need an explanation. It doesn't need to be a secret forever, but until you get a handle on it, it's best you learn from me. They will only frighten you because they don't understand it."

"Got it."

"Will you come for lessons?" Her voice was full of concern. She now spoke to him like he was an old friend.

"Yeah, whenever I can find the time. If I'm going to have this new energy living inside me, I better understand it."

"Good. Things may happen before you learn how to control it, but at least you'll be safer now. You can defend yourself. The magic will emerge in dire situations. It will exit through you and act as a shield, or possibly as a weapon."

"It won't hurt people I don't intend to hurt, right?"

"No. It's still controlled by your intentions, even if you don't realize you're doing it. It will only aim at those you intend it to."

"Okay, good."

"Now head out. Live your life as usual and feel better knowing you now have the best protection possible."

"Thanks." He stood and extended a hand. She shook it.

"Anytime. The salt suggestion was a joke, absolute minimal effort on behalf of my people. I'm sorry that's all they offered. I've got your back, and they will too if things unfold for the worse."

"I really appreciate it."

"I know Bianca, so I know how scary she is when you're blindsided by her. No one should face that alone."

"How do you know her?"

"I'm the girl she possessed."

Chapter 27

"But you seem so normal. I was told a permanent possession destroyed a person forever."

"Usually it does, but the Ouijans helped me out a lot. I left school and moved here. They rehabilitated me. I'll never feel the same again, but I'm a lot better off than most victims of a full possession."

"I'm sorry she did that to you."

"Yeah, well, my uncle owned a fishing boat. Apparently she wanted it to get back to England as a living person. My uncle suspected something was up when he caught her lingering around our house too often. I never noticed her until she attacked me. Total surprise. Never tried to befriend me or anything. I learned her motives once she was inside my head. She couldn't exact vengeance on her dead parents, but she wanted to dig up her and Cadence's bodies to reveal the truth, then live out a second life in my body. While I get her story is tragic, she turned evil during her time spent in the afterlife. To this day, I get chills whenever I recall the way in which her demonic spirit encased my entire essence. There is no feeling comparable to that of having your life stolen from you."

"I can only imagine. Thank you for understanding and helping me the best you can. It all makes sense now."

"Yeah," she muttered. Her attention was pulled away from their conversation, back to a place she had suppressed successfully until now.

"I'm sorry if I reminded you of a bad time."

"No, I brought it up. I'll be okay. Always am." She picked up her hood and placed it back over her head. "Let's go."

They reentered the foyer to two skeptical faces.

"What on Earth did you have to tell him that took so long?" Adelaide was suspicious and Theodore knew he'd face an assault of questioning once they were back at her home.

"I just wanted to make sure he understood how to use it. Despite what you may think, I do care that he survives this spirit's intentions."

"He will. He has plenty of support," Delilah answered. "Thanks for your help, we will be going now."

Gretchen nodded, gave Theodore one last look, and departed.

"You okay?" Adelaide asked, concerned.

"I'll be fine." He held up the vile of copper salt. "Let's go."

They left Salamander Pier without any further delay. Though Theodore felt fine, he could not shake his paranoia. He felt *too* fine. A moment ago he felt like death and now it was as if that never happened. Like it was a terrible memory he fabricated. It happened, he was sure of it, and he wondered what strange aftereffects were on their way.

Upon returning to Adelaide's home, Delilah departed and Theodore relaxed. Adelaide cooked up some soup and they ate together in her kitchen.

"Do you have any idea when you might see Bianca next?" she asked.

"No. I told her I'd return to the spot on the hill when I was ready. She said she'd check back every Saturday at noon for me."

"Do you think you're ready to finish this?"

"I think I need another week."

"Probably not a bad idea. Gives everyone a bit more time to digest the situation and prepare in case things go awry."

"I need to learn magic. It's terrible feeling like I can't defend myself."

"You've got a good team backing you up. Don't sweat it. We are going to take things one day at a time."

"Let's hope plan number one works out. That'll save us all a headache."

"Agreed."

They ate in silence. Eustice was absent. He did not hover in the corners like usual and Theodore wondered where he was. Normally he lingered, attempting to make Theodore uncomfortable so he'd leave. He supposed he ought to take this pleasant absence as a gift, since he was sure to be back soon.

He contemplated all that happened at the Ouijans abode: the conversation, the salt, the pellucid onyx. It seemed like the right choice to let Gretchen share her magic with him and so far, no unwelcome side effects had emerged. As he sipped on his soup it was clear that no amount of second guessing himself would help determine the result of that decision. Only time would tell if he made the right choice.

Chapter 28

Saturday came and went with no sign of Theodore. Bianca's anger multiplied. Her plan was rapidly unraveling around her and she could not stop its collapse. She was losing Theodore; she could sense it. Though he did not express his shift in their friendship, she was astute enough to notice. No verbal cues were needed to know he was no longer loyal to her. It was time to reevaluate her strategy.

Her attempt to recruit soldiers was slow but fruitful. Building friendships took time, but she was doing her best to speed the process up without forcing it. To obtain loyal followers, she needed to appear genuine in her approach. She did not want any of them to suspect she truly did not care for them at all. A few days had passed and she was already in touch with the majority of spirits on Nether Isle. Now she just needed to enhance those relationships into bonds she could control.

She left the meeting spot on the hill, frustrated but not deterred. She wanted Theodore in her human life, but maybe that part of the plan would need to change. Or maybe she could possess Ruby with the help of others and Theodore would never be the wiser. With an army behind her, the possibilities were endless. To determine his role in the next phase, she'd spy on him. She had to know what he was up to.

269

A ghost gathering was set for that evening. The spirits she made contact with so far were instructed to meet her in the cellar of the warehouse she resided in. She described it as a social gathering, a way to make new friends, but really it was another manipulative attempt to seize their allegiance.

When she returned to the warehouse, Cadence was curled up in the corner, shivering. Her protective encasement was intact—no attempted getaways today. They exchanged no words. Bianca mentally prepared herself for the oncoming "party" she was hosting.

At 8 p.m. the spirits began to arrive. Chester was first. He had shaped up nicely since she caught him trapped in a memory. Perhaps he was embarrassed she saw that, or maybe he really believed she would help him. Or better yet, maybe he was so lost in the haze of death that he could not define his newfound desire to be part of Bianca's world.

Eustice followed him. He was the only spirit Bianca felt inclined to use her powers to help. He wanted Adelaide to die and enter the light of Apres Monde with her by his side. When the time was right, Bianca would take great delight in eliminating her from the equation.

Elsa Mordid and Sadie Helf came together. Both died in their mid-thirties during childbirth and wished to have another chance at motherhood. Though they died during different time periods, they

270

maintained their lovely mid-life appearances, still radiant with the long-gone glow of pregnancy.

"Hello, ladies," Bianca greeted them, "Come join us."

The women entered the room and mingled. Amos Burndell arrived next. He was an old man, like Eustice, and stubborn as a mule. He died in a knife fight in the 1920s and he wore the scars to prove it. A long gash went down the right side of his wrinkled face, somehow leaving his eyeball intact. Bianca still had no clue what he wanted from her. It was possible he just wanted a reason to fight. If so, she could easily provide that. He grunted as he joined the bustle.

"Thanks for coming, Amos," Bianca said.

"I don't like parties."

"You'll like this one."

Davy Grey and Marjorie Cadev also arrived together. In death, they formed a strange romantic connection, one that was more spiritual than physical. Both died as nineteen-year-olds while serving in World War II. Davy was an American soldier and Marjorie was a French nurse. They never met in real life, but when they learned of each other's stories while lingering in death on Nether Isle, they instantly clung to the other. There was a comfort they found by having similar pasts. Each hated the government and wanted a second chance at life during a time when they wouldn't be enlisted, by force, into any wars.

Otis Redd, a burly man in his forties, came in with a huff. Like Chester, he died while working at sea. A former fisherman, he was tough and direct. He wore a knitted beanie, waders, and a t-shirt that showed off his tattoo sleeves. His thick brown facial hair hid his expression as his looming stature sauntered toward the rest of the group.

"We're ghosts. Can't drink alcohol, can't do drugs. What kinda party is this? Are we just gonna stand around and look at each other?" Otis asked, addressing the awkward tension in the room.

"It's meant to introduce everyone. Rather than hiding in our own secluded shadows, we ought to get acquainted. Learn who else lives in this realm on Nether Isle," Bianca answered.

"Why?"

"Maybe we can help each other. Or maybe it'd just be nice to have some friends."

Otis rolled his eyes, but remained. He was intrigued to see how the night would unfold. Many other spirits came in after him. By 9 p.m., the room was full.

"Thank you all for coming," Bianca addressed the crowd. The chatter hushed as their host spoke. "Though we all have different reasons for staying in the afterlife, we have death in common. In some cases it was unfair, for others it happened at the wrong time. Some of us even had it forced upon us. In any case, I think it's right that we band together. If not for company, then for help. Whether it be mental or tangible assistance we need, we can all use each other. We can make each other better, we can make the afterlife more bearable. I think rallying together and building friendships is much more productive than hiding out, alone in the shadows, letting our half-awake minds consume our awareness. We cannot function at full capacity when we live in solitude. The lack of interaction makes us dull. It muddies our wits. It keeps us trapped in the past. If we help each other, we can feel alive in death. We can wake up our minds and have a mentally sharp existence on Nether Isle."

"What is it *you* want?" Amos Burndell asked. While many of the spirits only wanted company so they didn't feel so alone, others didn't care about friendship. Amos was one of the latter. He was suspicious of Bianca's motives, as were many others who knew of her reputation.

"I want my life back," she answered honestly.

"You ain't tryin' to use your voodoo on us, are ya?" Chester called out.

"Yeah, we heard you practice magic. Is that true?" Elsa's eyes lit up with wonder.

"Yes, I have powers. I am a very old spirit. I've had lots of time to study. And no, I'm not going to use my 'voodoo' on any of you. Unless you wrong me, of course."

"Can we see it?" Davy Gray inquired.

"Yes, please show us!" Marjorie Cadev pleaded.

"That's not the purpose of this gathering. I just wanted us to socialize."

"You promised me vengeance," Otis spoke up, "and after talking to everyone else here, it sounds like you made lots of promises. You've gone to a lot of trouble to earn our attention, so obviously, you want something from us in return." Otis narrowed in on Bianca's small and fragile outward appearance. "If you want us to help you, it's time to prove you can deliver all you've promised."

Bianca did not like being challenged. Her anger was rising, but she could not let it show. His request was not out of line, but it certainly was an attempt to test her in front of everyone. She had to maintain control. Not only must they be in awe of her, they also had to fear her.

Without warning, she extended her left arm toward Otis and began chanting in ancient Egyptian. Her British accent came out in a deep tone, one unlike her usual voice and the nature of the chant was menacing. Everyone in the room froze with anticipation, waiting to see the result. Otis steadied his stance, skeptical of the unknown and ready to fight the ancient ghost in her 15-year-old form.

Amenti, eine pef-ba.
Herep pef-em moou.

(Realm of the Dead, fetch his soul.

Submerge him in water.)

Otis began to cough. His defensive stance crumbled as he gagged on nothing. He placed his large hands around his neck, trying to determine what choked him. The source was invisible, but his throat swelled with water.

Amenti, eine pef-ba.

Herep pef-em moou.

Bianca's concentration was unbreakable. Her eyes were glazed over with evil intent as she summoned the Realm of the Dead to drown his spirit. Otis's eyes were wide with fear; he was reliving his death. Somehow, she was killing him a second time in the afterlife.

"Is he choking?" Elsa asked, appalled.

"That's not possible. He doesn't need oxygen, how could she possibly strangle him?" Sadie rationalized.

"Looks like he's choking to me," Amos offered.

Amenti, eine pef-ba.

Herep pef-em moou.

Otis fell to his knees, gasping for air he did not need. He tried to speak but only managed a gurgle.

"We can't die twice, right?" Marjorie asked. The idea of suffering the pain of death twice was petrifying.

"I didn't think so," her afterlife love responded, "I don't know what she's doing to him." Davy gave Marjorie a skeptical look.

Bianca repeated the chant until Otis began to glow. Light shone through every orifice on his body. He squirmed on the ground, his big tattooed body convulsed as the light grew brighter. It came out of his fingertips and appeared to be cracking the skin on his arms. When it looked like his body might combust, Bianca released her hold of him. Otis's previously tensed muscles loosened and his body went slack. He appeared as nothing more than a puddle of a man on the floor.

"What did you do to him?" Elsa asked in a whisper.

"It's ancient Egyptian. I showed him what death within death felt like."

"Is he still in there?"

"Yes, he'll be fine. I did not complete the ritual so he'll come to in a few hours."

"Were you choking him?" Davy asked.

"I was drowning him, so yes. I summoned the power of the Realm of the Dead to submerge his soul in water."

"How? We don't require oxygen to exist," Marjorie added.

"We are dead. We do not live by earthly rules, nor are we confined by them. That being said, we are *very* real in this realm, the nether. Elements created in and executed in this space can affect us in very real ways. It's uncommon to come across anything of substance in the nether, which is why this phenomenon seems so impossible, but tangible components *do* exist here. They just need to be found, or summoned. The Realm of the Dead is where these lively parts of the afterworld thrive."

"Why did he glow?"

"That was the light of Apres Monde."

An audible gasp came from the crowd of spirits. Bianca continued, "If I kept going, he would have been sent through the light."

"You can do that?" Amos scowled, angry that any force could push him through the light against his will.

"Yes, but I didn't. He's still here. I stopped the chant in time."

Everyone was silent, suddenly petrified of Bianca. At any moment, she could decide to send them away forever. If they did anything to anger her, she could cast them into the unknown.

"Will you teach us how to do that?" Chester asked, testing to see the nature of her magic. Was it generous and kind? Or malicious and self-serving?

The entire group understood the weight of this question and waited eagerly for her response. Bianca hesitated, knowing the answer was *never*. But she couldn't push them any further away. She needed to give them a reason to stay, despite their newfound fear of her.

"I will try," she began, "but it will not be easy and I cannot promise that you will be able to do it."

The high tension that filled the warehouse basement lessened slightly.

"When?" Amos demanded. He wanted to learn now.

"Be patient. We've got an eternity." He looked skeptical but everyone else was appeased for now. "Enjoy each other's company. This is meant to be a party."

The crowd of ghosts returned to their previous scattered murmuring. Bianca left them to it and slipped out without being seen. She did not need to establish further bonds with them. They were right where she wanted them.

Chapter 29

Ruby came home from her father's port in Maine on Sunday night. She joined Theodore and Adelaide for dinner to catch up on all that she missed.

"You ought to go to your father's every weekend until this is sorted out," Theodore advised.

"I appreciate you trying to protect me but I'll be just fine. We are already linked to Delilah, so she can't possess us."

"I just have a bad feeling."

"Don't be so negative," Adelaide entered the room with a large bowl of clams. "It could be over the moment you toss that powder at her. Manifest the outcome you desire and you just might get it."

Theodore slumped further into his chair. It could be that simple, but it could also turn into a wild disaster. Gretchen's magic was nowhere to be seen or felt. It was living inside him but there hadn't been one sign of it yet. It angered him. If he felt it, he might not feel so uneasy; so defenseless.

"I meant to introduce you to the coven of Wiccans before today, but the weekend escaped us. They'll be watching over you two this week." Adelaide slurped on a clam.

"What do you mean?"

"Delilah and I assigned a few of them as your spiritual guards. Since you waited a week to confront Bianca, we think it's best you have a little extra protection when you're at school. No telling how that girl has interpreted your absence. You used to be best friends."

"She's probably even more suspicious now," Ruby added.

"Probably." Adelaide shoved the bowl of clams toward Theodore. "Eat up. You're gettin' too skinny."

He filled his plate.

"Who's on watch tomorrow?" Ruby asked as she drizzled marinara over her shellfish.

"Clementine LeClair and Leon Joubert. It'll be interesting to see how they remain inconspicuous. They have the brightest demeanor on Nether Isle. Not only do they both sport blinding white hair and skin, but they also have a taste for neon clothing. I doubt they'll make it the whole day without you, and everyone else, spotting them."

"What's the point of them being our guards then?"

"They are two of the strongest Wiccans here. All individuals assigned to protect you this week are among the best. And I figure, if Bianca sees them, it'll be more reason to stay away."

Theodore shrugged; it made sense. They finished their unconventional family-styled meal, and Ruby went home.

They met Monday morning on Terre Bridge and finished the walk to school together.

"I already spotted the dude," Theodore said.

"Leon?"

"Yes. 4 o'clock."

Ruby turned to her right and looked behind them. The lanky man was dressed in an electric orange track suit and crouched behind shrubbery a third his size. Ruby giggled and turned back around.

"I think I might have seen Clementine when I left my house. If she's dressed in a similar purple outfit, then it was her."

As they entered Triste Academy, a purple blur passed them on the left. Through a school window, Theodore could see Clementine peering from behind a nearby tree. He pointed her out to Ruby.

"Yup, that's her."

"At least they are on our side."

"Absolutely," she agreed.

They entered their classroom, sat next to Rowan, and Ms. Courtier began the day's lesson sans enthusiasm.

The day flew by without any ghostly incidents. After the last bell, Ruby went home and Theodore made his way to the market.

Gus was sleeping at his fruit stand. As usual, people were robbing him.

"Stop!" Theodore shouted at a middle-aged woman filling her purse with apples. At the sound of being caught, she scurried away.

"Gus, wake up." he gave the old man a shove. "People are stealing from you again."

"What'd they take?" he yawned.

"Some raggedy lady siphoned half your stock of apples."

"Them apples were rotten anyways. They'll probably give her diarrhea."

Theodore shook his head and entered Adie's Fish & Chum stand. It wasn't shocking that Gus sold spoiled produce; he only worked the stand to get out of his house each day. The old man was snoring again by the time Theodore had the grill started.

He prepared crab bisque and shrimp coleslaw as that night's pre-cooked options. He was sure people would complain they weren't full meals, but he wasn't in the mood to appease the masses. Besides the whole fish out front, all the other chopped fish were deboned, scaled, and ready for sale; Adelaide's fishermen did this as part of their job requirement. All the customers needed to do was cook it. Their laziness baffled him.

Once the food was done, he took a seat and waited for the rush to filter through. The first customer to arrive was small and wrapped in a hooded cloak that shadowed their face. It was Gretchen. She removed the hood and her emerald eyes shone with intensity beneath the wisps of black around her face.

"How are you doing?" she asked with grave seriousness.

"Fine," he answered, caught off guard.

"Has the magic settled within you?"

"I have no clue. It feels like it hasn't. Nothing particularly special has happened since you sent your death into me."

Gretchen ignored his tone. "It might not surface until you need it."

"Can you teach me how to draw it out? I'd rather practice using it than let it come out of me in any manner it pleases."

"I can." She looked around. "Don't talk about it anymore. Just meet me at our manor before school on Thursday."

Tabitha sauntered up from behind, her voluminous blonde curls bouncing.

"What are you creeps talking about?" Her eyelashes fluttered as she insulted them.

"Nothing. Just deciding which fish to bring back to the house," Gretchen answered.

"Gross, I hate fish."

"You're living in the wrong place if you don't like seafood," Theodore said.

"Tell me about it." Tabitha rolled her eyes. "I prefer natural vegetation. I'll be at the fruit stand next door if you need me." She was gone.

A vision of pretty Tabitha suffering the aftereffects of Gus's rotten fruit made Theodore laugh.

"What's funny?" Gretchen asked.

"Don't expect to see much of Tabitha later, I expect she'll be living on the porcelain throne all night."

"Seems like a more suitable throne than the one she thinks she sits on now." Gretchen did not question why he made this comment, or make any attempt to save her fellow Ouijan from whatever unpleasantries he implied. Perhaps she believed Tabitha needed a good dose of humbling reality.

"Can you give me a quart of the crab bisque and two pounds of salmon?" Gretchen continued. Theodore put together her order and collected the money owed.

"Thanks." She put the food in her satchel and secured the strap over her shoulder.

"I'll see you Thursday morning," he said, eager to determine what the ordeal she put him through was worth.

"See you then." She covered her face with her hood and disembarked to find Tabitha.

The dinner crowd came shortly after and Theodore tackled the influx of orders like a pro. It was hectic, but he made it to 9 p.m. without any issues. As the rush died down, he had a moment to breathe and notice his surroundings again. The night air was chillier than he realized. He threw on his jacket before beginning the cleanup process. As he swept, disinfected, and scrubbed, he couldn't help but feel like he was being watched. Only a few stragglers remained in the market and all the other merchants were preoccupied cleaning their own stands. Maybe it was Clementine and Leon, still acting as guard until he returned to Adelaide's, but the eyes on him now did not feel kind.

He hurried to finish his chores, locked up the stand, and sped back to Adelaide's. Once inside, the paranoid feeling vanished. He could not wait for all of this to be over. He was beginning to regret not meeting with Bianca last Saturday. He now had to wait out the remainder of the week before attempting to put this drama to rest.

Tuesday passed in a blur. Virgil Bonhomme was on duty to watch over Theodore and Ruby during school hours and he was much more discreet than Clementine or Leon. Theodore only saw him once. He accidentally stood in front of the cafeteria window too long during lunch, revealing himself to them. He was a stout man with a thick moustache. He didn't look very fast, so it was surprising he was quick enough to avoid being seen all day.

By Wednesday, trying to spot their guardians became a fun game. Mabel Bissette, the egg merchant, was their mid-week protector. She was very slow and dainty. They spotted her so many times throughout the day they suspected she wasn't even trying to stay hidden. She wore a white linen dress and fluttered around the school like a fairy. She was so old that those who did not know her assumed she escaped from her nursing home for the day.

"Why is the egg lady dancing around the schoolyard?" Rowan asked, but Theodore and Ruby just shrugged. He had no clue what was going on and they thought it best to leave it that way.

Thursday morning came much faster than Theodore anticipated. His meeting with Gretchen was a secret kept from everyone. He thought to tell Ruby, but decided against it. He wanted to give Gretchen a chance to help him master it before outside opinions flooded him with negativity. They'd all disapprove of what he let her do to him, so it was best to follow through on this decision without them. There was no going back now and no amount of discontentment would reverse the spell.

Chapter 30

Gretchen stood on the stoop of the Ouijan manor as he approached. It was 4 a.m. and the rest of Nether Isle still slept. The sun wasn't even awake yet. He yawned as he reached her, wishing to still be in bed.

"We cannot practice here. They cannot know I've given you some of my power."

"Then where do we go?"

"There is a house a few lots down that is abandoned and stable enough to hold us. Follow me."

Reluctantly, Theodore followed her back down the pier, skipping over missing boards as they went. The roaring ocean below was so violent, its mist came up through the cracks as it crashed against the rocks. Theodore's shoes were damp by the time they reached their training house.

It was in shambles. Half the roof was missing and the windows were all broken.

"Are you sure this place won't collapse beneath our weight?"

"Positive. The foundation is still strong. I come here whenever I need a break from the group."

He followed her in, taking very light steps as he did so. The vacant old home smelt of mothballs and mold. There were spiders everywhere and he did his best not to walk face first into any of their webs. Gretchen swatted the bugs and spider silk away as she led them into a large living space.

"Look at me." She wasted no time. "What are you most afraid of?"

"Excuse me?"

"What's your greatest fear?"

Theodore was unsure. His palms began to sweat as she asked him to reveal a personal detail he didn't even know the answer to.

"I've never thought much about that."

"Of course you have. Our fears live inside us every moment we are alive. It's on your mind at all times, even if it's buried deep."

"I really don't know."

"When you have nightmares, what are they about?"

He pursed his lips as he tried to remember his last restless sleep. In his dream he was in a crowded room, bleeding to death, but no one could see or hear him. They walked right past as he bled to death.

He must have gone silent for a while because Gretchen spoke again.

"Well?"

"Being alone."

Her nose scrunched. "Solitude?"

"No. I like having time to myself. Alone on a bigger scale." He released the breath he held. "Being so alone no one knows, or cares, that I'm alive. That if I disappeared, it wouldn't affect anyone significantly."

"I see." Gretchen's approach shifted. "What if I told you that we all are desperately lonesome? No matter how many friends or loved ones we have, there is still an insatiable thirst that it's not enough. A void with a hole at the bottom that drains empty every time we try to fill it. And when we question why, the answer lies in the simple fact that no matter how much company you keep, you will still die alone."

"Then I'd tell you you're misinterpreting me. It's not about having a ton of friends, it's about having a few who care so much for me they'd be heartbroken if I ever left. Someone who smiles because I am smiling. Someone who cries for me when I am sad. Someone whose heart lives in mine, and mine in theirs. I never had that with my parents, and I've moved around too much to ever establish a friend like that. I am not afraid to die alone, I am afraid to die having never mattered to anyone."

"Then I have some bad news for you. You're living your greatest fear."

"I already know that."

"You have no one that cares. Not that deeply, anyway."

Theodore furrowed his brow, now she was just being mean.

"Did you ask me my greatest fear in order to make me feel *worse* about it?"

"No, I'm just being realistic. You're wildly alone. So alone that I feel quite bad for you."

"Stop."

"If Bianca kills you, how many people do you think will show up to your funeral?" Her eyes narrowed. "Would they cry?"

"What is wrong with you?"

"You're right. I *am* wrong. There probably wouldn't be a funeral at all. Those cost a lot of money. Who would possibly spend that kind of cash on your behalf?"

"Stop!" Theodore shouted and the wall nearest the ocean split in half. He gasped. He felt the energy leave his body; *he* caused the wall to crack.

"Whew," Gretchen sighed. "It was taking you so long, I started to fear you might direct it at me."

"I'm surprised I didn't. You were being a bitch."

"Just trying to pull the magic out of you. Obviously didn't mean a word of it, so calm down." Theodore still huffed with rage. "Hold onto that feeling though. It's one way to summon your powers."

"Anger?"

"In this case, it took anger. I was trying to make you think of your greatest fear to pull it out. But you wouldn't go that deep, so I had to make you mad."

"I thought about it."

"But you didn't *feel* it. Just because you say it out loud and admit it doesn't mean you're experiencing it. You have to feel the fear in order to evoke the magic."

"Anger and fear. Got it." Theodore's heart still raced. He did his best to calm it.

"Or sorrow. That works too."

"So you walk around feeling all those horrible things at all times?"

"Of course not, I'm just very in tune with those emotions in myself. I can recall them in mere seconds."

"This is miserable."

"But it works. And honestly, it makes you wiser. Instead of burying the worst of your feelings, you embrace them. Once you let them make a safe home inside you, everything is less foreboding. If you can handle the scariest parts living inside you, then the rest of the world becomes much less terrifying."

"I want to go home."

"Stop it. I don't actually believe any of the things I said. I was just provoking you. Stop sulking. You know damn well Adelaide adores you like a son."

Theodore hoped so, he certainly considered her to be his family now.

"Fine. What's next?"

"Now that you know how to pull the power out, you can practice that on your own time. Just make sure no one is nearby. Don't want to accidentally hurt a bystander."

"I thought you said it would never hurt anyone I didn't intend it to?"

"I did. It will always go toward your intended target, but that doesn't rule out accidents. Sometimes, the innocent just get in the way."

"I see."

"Next best thing I can teach you is direction. The magic is manifested in our core and released in whichever manner we choose. If you don't control it, it will come out of you however it likes: mouth, fingers, eyes. The best way to guarantee it comes out of your hands and shoots in the direction you intend is to learn our basic stance. Mirror me."

She stood facing Theodore with her feet wide and body sturdy. She tucked her elbows into her sides and kept her forearms outstretched in front of her.

"It's not always the most conducive position in certain situations, but it's a guaranteed way to hit your target. If you keep your palms facing inward, toward each other, and direct your fingers in the direction you intend, you'll never miss."

Theodore mimicked her. It was an easy move to learn and remember.

"Good," she continued. "You've got it."

"Now I just need to practice harnessing the worst emotions imaginable."

"I promise, once you learn to control them, they'll never affect you the same again. You don't realize it, but they weigh upon you every day. Just cause you don't think about them, doesn't mean they aren't there. They shape your moods and guide your days. This unseen force molds every occurrence in your life. Once you get a mental handle on the negatives, the positives will grow stronger."

"If you say so."

"I do. You'll see."

"What time is it?"

"Not sure, we've been here a while. Maybe 6 a.m.?"

"I need to leave. I'm gonna need the downtime before heading to school. Thanks for this lesson."

"Make sure you practice in your free time."

"I will."

"When will you be seeing Bianca again?"

"Hopefully this Saturday. I plan to go to the hill to try the confusion powder on her."

"That's soon. Practice every day until then. If plan A doesn't work out, you have the tranq salt. And if that fails, you'll have your magic."

Theodore's heart beat harder in anticipation. Each pulse hurt. Gretchen gave him a curious look, like she could hear the new rhythm his heart played.

"You'll be fine either way," she continued. "You've got an impressive team backing you: Ouijans, Wiccans, friends. Don't worry. Best to be calm when you meet her so she suspects nothing. She'll sense your unease if you don't play it cool."

"I know. I think she already suspects I've abandoned her. Our friendship has changed drastically in the past few weeks. She's not stupid. She must notice it."

"She does."

"What?"

"I spy on her occasionally. She visits your old house a lot. I go once in a while to see what she's up to."

"Why haven't you said this before?"

"Because I've never seen anything worth reporting. She just camps out at your house, waiting for you to come back, I think. She's definitely suspicious of your friendship, and she's made nice with your dead dad, which is a bad sign. But otherwise, she seems to be holding out hope that you're still loyal to her. That you two are still friends. I've seen nothing to indicate otherwise. You still have a chance to end this peacefully."

"I hope so."

"She's dangerous, I know firsthand the nature of her wrath." Gretchen's emerald eyes went black in momentary memory before returning to normal. "So it's crucial we end this forever. No one else need suffer because of her. She doesn't belong here, and the longer she stays, the stronger she gets."

"Why didn't the Ouijans get rid of her after she possessed you?"

"They underestimated her power. They thought thwarting her attempt would scare her from ever trying again. Plus, they had to deal with me. It took years to get me back. I was a shell of a person for a long time. They had to coax me back to the living."

"You seem so normal."

"I'm lucky I had the Ouijans on my side. They took me in like I was family and did not quit until I was right again. Well, as close to right as I could get."

"I was told most people never recover after being saved from a full possession. That they walk around, like a ghost, until they die."

"Yup. Most regular folks can't drag the life back up from the victim's depths. They usually lack the knowledge and patience required to do so. Doesn't matter how much they love the person, it takes something special to fix a person that damaged. I think I was saved because the Ouijans understood the darkness I was trapped in. They could relate and go there with me. Many times, they met me in my shadows, held my hand, and walked me slowly toward the light of the real world. The light outside the shell I hid in. Small steps, always, but over time, they got me out."

"That's amazing."

"Yeah. They have a bad reputation around here. I'll be honest, I thought they were creepy before my incident, but they are, by far, the best people on this isle. They don't display it outwardly, they don't put on a show to prove it to others, but at their core, they are the truest and kindest souls. Better than you, Adelaide, Ruby, or the Wiccans, who are a manifest of light and virtue. You're all beautiful souls, I'm not dismissing that, but the Ouijans are just a different breed of good. And I believe the good that does not ask for recognition, the good that understands evil because it has touched it, is the most well-rounded kind."

"You may be right. I find I am learning a whole new version of life exists every moment I spend on Nether Isle."

"Whether you stay forever or visit for a day, this place is bound to change you. And if you let it, it'll change you for the better."

"I already feel one thousand times wider than I did when I lived in Alaska."

"Wider?"

"Like my ribcage extends for miles in every direction. Like everything I come in contact with causes me to *feel* something. I am touched by every little nuance, and at first I thought it was annoying and that I was becoming weak. That the weight of sorrow in my life up to this point was finally wearing me down. I thought that maybe I was losing my mind. But I see now that what I am experiencing is strength."

"Often times our strongest moments feel like our weakest. When we want to collapse and give up, when emotions cripple us, or when we feel paralyzed with no explanation why, we feel weak but we continue on. We keep moving forward, and that is the strongest thing you can do."

Theodore nodded. He felt like a wimp the past few weeks, like a big baby drowning in self-pity. Like he had no right to be sad or confused. He felt weak for letting those feelings get the best of him, but here he was, working through it the best he could. He wasn't weak, he was brave. He was allowed to feel all those terrible things and more. He was human. And it was true—only someone with great strength can make it to the other side of their darkest moments.

"Thanks for everything." He smiled at Gretchen. What a wild ride these Ouijans sent him on. Every other moment he was feeling brand new things.

"You got it. We are on the same team. If you want to meet again before Saturday, let me know. Otherwise, I'll be waiting with the others at my manor Saturday evening, waiting for your report on how things went."

"Let's hope I have good news."

They both walked out the front of the abandoned home and went their separate ways; Gretchen back toward the end of Salamander Pier where the Ouijan manor sat, and Theodore toward Peddler's Way. He had plenty of time to get to school before the first bell rang, so he took his time.

He stopped at Ballantine Dock to check on his sailboat. It floated there, bobbing back and forth between the bigger boats on both sides of it. He'd need to take an afternoon to repaint the sidings since the paint was chipping from the rough and unruly conditions the boats were stored in. He also needed to make time for a sail. He missed it terribly. Part of him imagined his nerves were on edge because he'd been away from the ocean for so long. There was no time to sail with all that was going on, but he had to start remembering to *make* time for it. It was important to him and he had to remember to take care of himself amidst the chaos. He had to remember that his happiness was a priority, too.

Chapter 31

Thursday's Wiccan guard was Wilhelmina Gardinier. Theodore and Ruby saw her a few times, mostly between classes. She was young and beautiful, a captivating sight for all their classmates.

"She looks like an angel," Ruby commented as their Wiccan protector sat at a table nearby during their lunch period.

"Who does?" Rowan asked with a mouthful of bologna and cheese.

"The new girl, the 12th grader." Ruby quickly covered up her slip. She kept forgetting Rowan was clueless to all that was happening.

"Where is she? Maybe she's into younger guys." Rowan scanned the room, looking for this beautiful older female Ruby referred to. He spotted Wilhelmina.

"Wow, she's a looker." Rowan squinted to examine the faraway beauty. "I feel like I've seen her before though. Are you sure she's a twelfth grader and not a student teacher?"

"Not really sure." Ruby took a bite of her sandwich, hoping Rowan would drop it.

"I bet she'd be into me." His chest puffed as he said this.

"You look ridiculous," Ruby giggled.

"What do you mean?" Rowan's words came out as a whisper as he tried to maintain his beefy façade by holding his breath.

"You've totally got this," Theodore chimed in. "Just try not to pass out while hitting on her."

"Yeah, it's a real turn off when a guy faints."

"But keep holding your breath. Girls love a guy with a breathy voice."

Rowan let his breath go and returned to normal size. "You're just hating cause you know she'd be all about it." He motioned to himself with a confident neck jerk, causing Ruby and Theodore to roar with laughter, simultaneously spitting up food all over the table.

"Ew, gross guys," Rowan scowled at them. "Clean that up, you're nasty."

"Do it again," Ruby pleaded. "The neck thing."

Rowan was getting mad. He looked back at the mysterious older girl, who now watched as their table regressed into complete disorder. "You guys are embarrassing me, stop."

"Sorry." Theodore wiped his face and Ruby rubbed the tears of laughter off her cheeks.

"It's not this funny. Why wouldn't she be into me?"

"It's not that, it's just how ridiculous you looked trying to be bigger and talking with a squeak. Then the neck-jerk as you said she'd be all about it." Ruby began to lose it again. Tears welled in her eyes as she recalled the moment.

"You guys are real assholes, you know?"

"Don't sweat it. Go talk to her if you want," Theodore suggested, knowing very well he wouldn't dare attempt it now. "Just leave the chest puff here with us."

Ruby snorted again and Rowan clicked his tongue with disapproval as he took another bite of his sandwich.

"I'll talk to her when I damn well feel like it," he said with a full mouth, "when you two idiots aren't around to embarrass me."

"Good idea," Theodore nodded with a smile, then ate the rest of his lunch. Even if Rowan got up the courage to talk to Wilhelmina, she'd never engage. She was here for work. Plus, even though she looked like a twelfth grader, she must be a bit older than that, otherwise she *would* be a student here.

Friday came too soon. Theodore woke up with dread. Only one more day until his encounter with Bianca. He had practiced channeling his new power every evening since his lesson with Gretchen, but found it wasn't easy. Fear never worked, and it was hard to go all the way with sadness or anger. He could get halfway, but never enough to evoke the magic. It was frustrating because he needed to practice controlling it. He also wanted to get so good at bringing it forth that he could ask Gretchen to teach him specific spells. Things he could send out with intention. But it was Friday and he did not imagine he'd master cultivating the power that evening.

Friday's Wiccan guard was much more intense than the rest of the week's. Perhaps they assumed they'd need more protection today since tomorrow was the meeting. Alastair Durant and Rupert Chevalier were on duty. Both men were large and solemn. They stood at the front doors to Triste Academy that morning and acknowledged them with a nod as they entered.

"Who are they?" Rowan asked, running up from behind to walk into class with them.

"No clue," Theodore said with a shrug. Rowan dropped it.

They sat in their seats and Ms. Courtier began their science lesson. As Ruby's favorite subject, she was too engaged to notice that Alastair and Rupert stood at the classroom's back door, watching them through its small window. For some reason, unlike the other Wiccans, their presence caused great unease in Theodore. They were intimidating and reminded him of the oncoming feat he was tasked to pull off. Seeing them and feeling their forceful aura reminded him he really was no match for what he was up against.

Adelaide gave him the night off from the market. She covered his post and he used the free time to practice his magic. With the house to himself, he went out on her back porch and trained in private. The porch overlooked the ocean. While he could see Ballantine Dock to his left, and the many house-covered piers that jetted out to the right, he knew no one was watching him. Adelaide's home was one of the few that sat on Peddler's way and was set a bit higher than those built along the countless piers.

He could see Apres Monde Lighthouse in the distance. Its ethereal glow was as bright as ever. He imagined Bianca's spirit being pushed through it and felt intense relief. As the sensation coursed through him, his fingers tingled. Could joy evoke his powers too?

He shut his eyes and concentrated on the feeling. When he opened them again, his body was floating a foot above the wooden porch. Shocked, his concentration vanished and he thudded back to solid ground.

Well, that's something, Theodore thought. Probably not what he needed to fight off evil ghosts, but better than no progress at all.

He tried again, this time focusing on his greatest fear, letting it bring out the sadness it caused him. He felt the overwhelming despair of dying and no one giving a damn. He let it seep into the corners of his mind, he let it create heartbreaking scenarios in his imagination, and just as the sorrow swelled in his soul, threatening to combust, an icy chill engulfed him, causing him to shiver and lose the feeling.

He opened his eyes and looked around. It was late autumn; cold, but certainly not cold enough to produce a chill that frigid. The evening sky was a deep orange as the sun sunk into the horizon, drowning in the ocean. Just like he had all week, he felt the sensation that someone was spying on him. At school it was the Wiccans, but after school? There was no one around. All that surrounded him was ocean, rocks, and the outskirts of Nether Isle.

He dipped back inside and locked the door behind him. Alone in the house, he felt a bit better. Eustice was absent for at least two weeks now, so he did not have to worry about his creepy presence hovering over him as he decompressed and mentally prepared for tomorrow afternoon. He could try to practice his magic inside, but feared he'd accidentally destroy her home with a blast too big, similar to what he did to the abandoned home on Salamander Pier. It wasn't worth the risk.

Adelaide came home a little after 9 p.m. with a basket full of food. She whipped together a delicious meal consisting of lightly seasoned arctic char, honey-glazed carrots, and buttered potatoes.

"Are you ready for tomorrow?" Adelaide asked in-between bites.

"As ready as I can be."

"Just be calm. Pretend you don't know she's an evil ghost out to steal Ruby's life. Pretend she's just the living friend you knew a few weeks ago."

"I'll try, but she really screwed things up. Between the lies and devious schemes, I hate her. She let me look like a fool for weeks while I defended her against everyone who knew better, everyone with spot on intuition. Every time I think about that short frame of time, I get furious."

"Don't. We already talked about this. It's not your fault, nor could you have ever even imagined the situation to have turned out like it did. You entered into a whole new realm of crazy and you can't blame yourself for not suspecting the seemingly impossible."

"I know," Theodore grunted, still unsatisfied with his foolishness. "Once I end this, I'll feel better."

"Exactly the motivation you need. The end is in sight."

Chapter 32

Scrambled eggs with crab meat, hash browns, and a glass of orange juice. Theodore filled up in preparation for the oncoming encounter. It was 11 a.m. and time to head out. Adelaide gave him a hug and expressed her unyielding confidence in him. He appreciated the sentiment and wished he felt as sure about himself as she did. He was out of his league and hoped it did not prevent him from succeeding.

The walk toward the mainland felt longer than usual. He saw many of the Wiccans pass him as he made the trek. Rupert Chevalier was arm in arm with Clementine LeClair, both of whom gave him enthusiastic waves as they passed. Mabel Bissette even wished him good luck when she twirled past him a few moments later. They were all heading to Salamander Pier where they would wait with the Ouijans for Theodore's return. If it went well, Bianca would be sent into a stupor and Cadence could drag her through Apres Monde. If Cadence did not, or could not show for some reason, they determined they would send her through the light via magic. Step one of this plan depended solely upon Theodore.

He walked up the path that circled around the hill. When he reached the top, Bianca was there waiting.

"Took you long enough," she said as he approached.

"Sorry, you're asking a lot of me. You want me to ruin a person's life so you can have a second one. Doesn't seem very fair."

"Does that mean your answer is no?"

"No."

"So then it's a yes?"

"No, it's not a yes either."

"Why did you come back if you haven't made up your mind?"

"I wanted to talk to you. I still want to help you. I want us to be friends, just not under these conditions. If you force me to do this, I will end up resenting you."

"I don't want that to happen."

"Neither do I. So I came here today to talk to you, to see what other options there are."

Bianca took a few steps closer. "The problem is, there aren't any other options. I already told you that." Her voice was low and menacing.

"You're being stubborn and unreasonable. Let's just talk it out."

"There's nothing left to talk about."

"Yes there is. I want us to solve this together."

"I don't believe you."

Theodore took a step back. "Why not? I've been nothing but a good friend to you."

"You *were* a good friend to me."

Theodore reached into his pocket and began uncorking the tranq salt.

"I still am."

"Liar!"

Bianca lunged at him and before he could toss the salt through her, she dove into his skull.

Theodore crumpled to the ground, his entire being heavy with her spirit.

"It's much darker in here than I imagined it would be," she spoke, her voice echoed through his head.

"Have you possessed me?"

"No, I'm just inside your mind. I need to know what treachery you're planning."

"You lied to me about everything. Cadence told me the truth."

"I knew she escaped," she hissed. "I can't believe she betrayed me. What I'm doing is for her, too."

"She doesn't want any of this. She just wants to be at peace."

"We will be at peace in our new bodies and new lives."

"Get out of my head!"

"If you don't reveal your secrets to me, I'll just keep spying on you," she threatened, "We both know how much you didn't like the constant paranoia."

"Now that I know it's only you, it won't bother me as much. Thanks for easing my mind."

"Tell me what you're up to."

"Never." Theodore focused on lighter topics: sailing his boat, the math lesson Ms. Courtier taught on Friday, the saltiness in his crab flavored eggs at breakfast. Bianca dug through his thoughts but he kept the important ones buried. It hurt as she siphoned through his brain. He had to use every ounce of energy to keep his mind in frivolous places.

"Stop thinking about stupid stuff! Who are you plotting with? Why have you turned against me? What is your plan to try and stop me?"

No matter how many questions she asked, he kept his mind on the image of the marvelous setting sun he witnessed from Adelaide's porch last night. Bianca screamed.

Blood trickled from Theodore's ear as her earth-shattering screech echoed through his skull. She stopped talking and stopped digging through his thoughts. After a moment of calm, Bianca spoke again.

"Look over there," she helped direct his eyes toward a tree at the bottom of the hill. "Your dad is patiently waiting for me to let him have a go at you."

"I was warned you took residence at my old home. I should have assumed you aligned with my asshole father."

"Well, you left me little choice. I had to make new friends since you turned out to be a lousy one."

"You're one to talk. You betrayed me first."

"How?"

"Everything you ever told me was a lie. When you had the chance to come clean, you continued to lie. It was never about friendship, it was about manipulating and using me to get what you want."

"Believe what you will, none of it matters now. I have new friends. Many actually, all of whom fear me."

"Sounds like real cruddy friendships, if you ask me."

"I didn't. And they are wildly beneficial. More so than yours ever would have been. You never feared me like you needed to. My mistake, not yours."

"You're sick."

"I'm smart. Fear is the only way to guarantee loyalty. If they know the pain you can cause them, they'll never waver. I am far more powerful than the lot combined. If they serve me, they know I can reward them with just as much impact as I could harm them."

"My answer is no. Always has been. I thought maybe I could chat it out with you, but you are far too evil to be saved."

"Fascinating." She began to dig again.

"Get out of my head!" Theodore channeled his anger and summoned the black magic Gretchen gave him. Bianca could feel the surge detach her tentacles from his mind.

"How are you doing that?"

Before she could see his answer, he ejected her from his skull. Her spirit flew across the field and landed in a heap on the ground. She was disoriented. He sprinted toward her, tranq salt in hand, but he was too late. She was up and gone as he tossed the salt. The copper particles scattered through the spot she just vacated and landed on the dirt ground.

Theodore watched as her spirit shot into the sky and flew away. His head throbbed, but he needed to get to Salamander Pier to let the Wiccans and Ouijans know what happened.

He was unsuccessful, but not defeated. He felt proud. He managed to harness his new power and beat Bianca, all on his own. He was not helpless, he was a force to take seriously. With a newfound gusto, he ran to Salamander Pier to relay the news.

Chapter 33

With a strategic sprint, dodging the gaping holes along Salamander Pier, Theodore raced toward the Ouijan manor. Gretchen was waiting outside with Delilah on her right and Percival Archambault on her left. They watched him approach with curious stares.

"Didn't work," Theodore gasped as he reached the stoop.

Percival huffed in annoyance and walked inside.

"What happened?" Delilah's faced was lined with worry. Her frizzy red hair was tucked behind her ears as she waited eagerly for an explanation.

"Before I could throw the salt, she entered my head."

Gretchen's brow furrowed. "She possessed you?"

"No," he tried to explain, "she was suspicious of me before I even arrived, she's been spying on me all week, so she dove into my mind to dig for answers."

"Did she say what she wanted answers to?" Delilah's voice shook with worry.

"Yeah. She wanted to know what kind of 'treachery' I was planning. Who I was working with and how we planned to stop her. I kept my thoughts blocked though. She saw nothing."

"How can you be sure?"

"Well, she screeched with annoyance as I pictured the breakfast I ate this morning. So loud, my ears bled." He pointed at the trickle of blood down both his cheeks that the women hadn't noticed yet.

"Are you alright?" Delilah raced to his side.

"I'm impressed." Gretchen nodded proudly. "Most folks wouldn't even think to keep their wandering thoughts protected. Good job."

"Let's get you inside and clean you up." With an arm around his shoulder, Delilah guided him into the manor.

"Dear boy," Adelaide shouted as she hurried to his side. She noticed the blood right away. "You're bleeding. What happened?"

"Bianca got away."

"Damnit. Least you're back, and relatively unharmed." She spit on her sleeve and wiped some of the drying blood off his skin. "How'd she do this to you?"

"Her spirit entered my brain."

"What?"

"Did you say she entered your brain?" Cynthia Monette stood up from a chair hidden in the shadow of a nearby corner.

"Yeah."

Poe Lesauvage emerged from a door at the end of the foyer, scraping two kitchen knives together. They were covered in chopped meat.

"Are we ready for this gathering yet?" he asked, his voice tense with impatience.

"Looks like it," Cynthia answered. "Inform the others. Percival is already in the great hall with the Wiccans. Gretchen," she said, focusing on the young girl who stood behind Theodore and his protectors. "You're in charge of Morgana. She's having a particularly hard day. Morton gave up a few hours ago after she tried to hex him."

"Great," Gretchen moaned, ascending the enormous staircase.

"Follow me," Cynthia said, motioning to Theodore, Adelaide, and Delilah. They followed her into the grand hall and took the empty seats next to the situated Wiccans.

"Hi there." Mabel Bissette gave Theodore a wrinkled smile as he sat beside her.

"Hey, Mabel. You put on quite a show the other day. Your afternoon dance in our courtyard caught all my classmates' attention. I think my whole school knows you now."

Mabel smiled with delight. "I love young people. So bright." She circled the space around his head with her hand, gliding it through his aura. "Warm as fresh cookies."

With no comment, Theodore faced forward. Wilhelmina Gardinier sat before him, radiant as ever.

"Take this." She pushed a lacy handkerchief across the table to him.

"I'll ruin it."

"I have tons. You need to clean up." He took it and thanked her.

A pitcher of water slid at full speed down the long table. Theodore caught it just before the force with which it was passed knocked it over. He looked to see where it came from. Percival sat at the end seat, unsure why everyone looked at him with shocked expressions.

"If he plans to clean up, he'll need water to do so. The blood is dry."

"Thanks," Theodore mumbled and began wiping his face.

Rupert Chevalier and Alastair Durant sat next to Wilhelmina. They were also young, but built with bulk and sturdiness. They didn't speak much, and they didn't need to. Their power and intention seeped through their pores. Again, Theodore found himself slightly intimidated by their presence. Though this time it was in awe rather than fear.

Clementine, Leon, and Virgil were in attendance. They sat on the other side of Adelaide, yapping her ear off. She indulged their enthusiasm as kindly as she could. When the rest of the Ouijans entered the hall, she was happy to have an excuse to focus on something new.

Gretchen came in first with Morgana Roux in tow. They held hands and sat in the seats furthest from everyone else. Theodore wanted to tell Gretchen how he summoned the power she gave him to ward off Bianca's spirit, but couldn't until they were alone. His excitement to share it with her was overbearing.

Poe, Cynthia, and Tabitha entered next, each taking an empty seat. Morton Guillory came in wearing a nasty scowl. His forehead had a fresh gash along it, no longer bleeding, but raw. He sat in a seat as far from Morgana as possible. His bright eyes bore into her with anger and she cowered behind Gretchen.

"It's your own fault," Theodore heard Gretchen whisper to the fidgety woman clinging to her back. "He was only trying to help you and you tried to slice his head open."

Morgana let out a nervous laugh, one laced with barely contained hysteria. Everyone in the room became tense as the Ouijans brought with them their usual, uncomfortable energy. They were so unaware of the awkwardness they carried that the feeling shifted by default onto the outsiders witnessing it.

Caspian Voclain entered last. His perfect appearance was unruffled, though his demeanor seemed frazzled. He scribbled furiously into a notebook as he took his seat without making eye contact with anyone.

"Theodore," Percival said with an outstretched hand in his direction, "you're up."

"Ok, so the tranq salt didn't work. Well, it's not that it didn't work, I never got the chance to try. She was in my head before I even had the vile out of my pocket."

316

"In your head?" Percival asked. "What does that mean?"

"She was in my thoughts."

"Can they do that?" Virgil asked. "I never heard of that before."

"I've never heard of a *ghost* doing that before," Morton answered, "but I have heard of other sources of magic with those capabilities."

"So, she's not only learning and executing *our* magic, but also that of origins we know not." Cynthia shook her head.

"We suspected that. After seeing her markings in Theodore's home, I knew she found access to other magic," Delilah commented. "Her symbols were ancient; both Egyptian and Babylonian. She must have spent quite a few years traveling the globe to acquire that knowledge."

"Do we know where this mind-raiding deal originates from?" Tabitha asked, twirling her hand in the air with boredom.

"I suspect she got it from the Atharvaveda," Caspian announced without looking up from his notebook.

Blank stares followed his response. He looked up at the countless expressions begging for more of an explanation.

"It's the fourth Veda of Hinduism. These sacred texts originated in Ancient India. Common use is solely for positive gain, but if she dug in ancient archives, or warped the mantras she learned, it's very possible she turned the magic dark."

317

"What makes you think Hinduism is its origin?" Clementine asked.

"The marking her spell left on his forehead."

Everyone turned to look at him. Theodore touched his brow, but felt nothing. Adelaide grabbed him by the cheeks and turned his head so she could look closer.

"There's nothing on his forehead," she insisted.

"Turn out the lights," Caspian requested. Poe stood up and flicked the switch. As soon as the room went dark, everyone gasped in unison.

"What?" Theodore insisted. "What is it?"

"It's the Om symbol. Similar to the cross in Christianity, the Om is the most important symbol in Hinduism. Those three Xs you see in the bends? They aren't supposed to be there." Caspian motioned to Poe, who took his cue to flip the lights back on.

"How do you know all of this?" Wilhelmina asked, bewildered.

"I minored in religion at Notre Dame. Took a course on ancient India in college and they taught us all about the Vedas. Beautiful culture and religion. This spirit we are dealing with has sullied the proper teachings and manipulated its powers to suit her own needs."

Theodore wiped his forehead, wondering if he'd be stuck with this glow-in-the-dark marking for the rest of his life. Caspian sensed his question.

"It will be gone by tomorrow. It's just residue."

"We already knew she was a menace, but now that we confirmed she is a true threat to our world, how do we destroy her?" Rupert asked, voice deep with determination. For a Wiccan, his intent was quite dark.

The room went silent as everyone contemplated their new predicament.

"The element of surprise is gone," Tabitha offered.

"Not completely," Alastair added. "We can still surprise her with *when* we strike. If she doesn't know it's coming, or how, she will not be able to prepare."

"Yes, it's crucial she does not know how to ready her defenses. Our best shot is forcing her to wing it," Wilhelmina agreed.

"Did she say anything else of use while you were with her?" Gretchen directed the conversation back to Theodore.

"Yes. She implied she has 'friends' now, spirit allies." Theodore recalled the conversation. "First, my father, who she pointed out was hiding in the distance watching us, waiting for his chance to try and take my life again. The way she said it implied he was waiting for *her* to allow him to attack me."

"So he's under her command?" Caspian asked.

"Yes, but I didn't get the impression it was due to any spells she cast on him. It seemed natural, like he chooses to obey her."

"And he's not the only one?" Clementine asked, bright eyes concerned.

"So she said."

"Why would they follow her?" Poe inquired, disgust in his voice.

"She said they fear her. That she learned her lesson with me. I didn't fear her and my loyalty strayed." Theodore shook his head, "She's wrong though. It had nothing to do with loyalty, it had to do with the truth. My loyalty changed once I saw who she really was."

"But the ghosts already know who she really is. If they are following her now, they are fully aware of the choice they are making," Gretchen rationalized. "It's quite possible fear is how she is cementing their loyalty."

"There must be more," Poe seethed. "She must have made promises."

"A promise to fulfill the desires these ghosts remain in the nether to obtain," Caspian hypothesized out loud. "She's powerful enough to perform them, and they know it. I'd believe her if she presented me with an offer like that."

"And fear that if they don't obey her, she won't grant them their wish?" Wilhelmina suggested as the opposing side of that thought.

"That seems logical."

"Or maybe, they fear she can do worse. That their betrayal would not only lose them their deal, but also garner some kind of punishment." Cynthia offered as additional reasoning.

"It's possible," Caspian agreed. "She is very powerful. We don't know the extent of her capabilities, so maybe they don't either."

"Or maybe they do." Morgana said for the first time, silencing the room with her grim prediction.

"And that's why they choose to be on her side, the winning side," Caspian finished her thought.

"We are in for a bigger fight than imagined," Percival sighed. "First order of business is determining how we will force her through the light. Second is finding a way to implement it as soon as possible. We cannot waste any more time. The more we give her, the stronger her defense becomes."

"I might be able to get her little sister to help," Theodore offered.

"Her little sister?" Percival scoffed at him, "Did she even show up today?"

"I don't think so, but it's probably because she couldn't."

"I don't like it. She's of relation to the monster. I don't want her lurking about, taking part in our plan. She'll ruin it."

"Cadence isn't like that. She wants to go through the light and find peace, but Bianca won't let her. She keeps her locked away in a basement somewhere, forcing her to remain in the afterlife until she finds two bodies for them to inhabit for a second chance at life."

"And the second spirit does not agree with this plan?" Cynthia asked with skepticism.

"No, I already told you she escaped once to warn me of Bianca's true intentions. She begged me to stop her. Cadence just wants to end the suffering. I believe her."

"That's great and all, but if she couldn't break free this afternoon, how on earth will she be of use to us?"

"We can determine where she's being kept," Theodore continued. "Then we can visit her and she can act as our spy. With so many of us on board, we can easily have eyes on Bianca and Cadence simultaneously. Shouldn't be too hard to manage this."

"Can Cadence keep a secret? Does she seem trustworthy?" Poe asked.

"When it involves the fate of her desired serenity, yes."

"Do you know where she is imprisoned?" Morton jumped in.

"No. All Bianca ever mentioned about her home was that it was located somewhere near Myrtle's Deli on the mainland of the isle."

"I can find her," he continued, "locating secrets is my specialty. You'll need to come with me the first time I go," Morton said to Theodore. "She will need to see your face so she knows we are all on the same side."

"Okay. We also need to consider Ruby's safety. That's the body Bianca wants. If she gets it, then we've lost."

"She's still connected to me," Delilah chimed in, "as are you, Theodore. If any attempt at a possession is made, I'll feel it. And if she succeeds, she'll enter my body instead."

"This spirit will be in for a rude awakening if she goes that route," Leon spoke up. "Delilah is the best spirit fighter I know."

"Unless she has some strange self-concocted incantation to do a possession. She seems like a spell masher, and if she uses one of her own creation, there's no telling the way it'll affect us, our defenses, or our intended outcome." Everyone nodded as Gretchen said this. It was a good reminder. They needed to be on the offense, making the first move, because defending against this new and unstable magic was too dangerous.

"Meanwhile, we will practice and perfect the banishment spell," Percival said, sounding tired. "We have not had to use it much, so we will make sure we have it working properly before we try it on her. Can't afford any mistakes. She's too strong."

"Between our combined magic and the help of her sister, maybe we can catch her off guard and succeed without much of a fight." Delilah was hopeful but the sentiment was not unanimous. This was new territory for all of them.

"Let's just tackle this one day at a time. Morton and Tabitha, you are in charge of locating the sister."

"I can help with that," Rupert chimed in, "I have a knack at locator spells."

"Lovely," Percival's tone was unenthusiastic. "The oversized Wiccan will be joining you. Poe, you will spy on this Bianca character. You're small and shifty and always manage to be in the same room with me for countless minutes before I even notice you're there. You excel at sneaking about like an invisible rat."

Theodore was ready for a fight to break out, but somehow, Poe took this as a compliment. Percival continued.

"From what I witnessed of the Wiccan guard over the juveniles at school, your people are terrible at espionage. Absolutely dreadful. So I will assign Gretchen to assist Poe in this endeavor. Plus, you will all need to be here with us, learning the banishment spell, or am I mistaken?"

"No, you're right. We don't know that one," Delilah answered begrudgingly. Percival was acting self-righteous and all the Wiccans barely contained their annoyance.

"Cynthia, Caspian, and I will teach you. In the meantime we will *all* act as watchful eyes over Nether Isle: surveying the behavior of the spirits lurking about, reporting regularly to one another so we are always on the same page, making sure we teach each other all we know." He took a meditative breath before continuing, "That means you learn our ways and we learn yours." He almost choked on his tongue as he said this.

"Beautiful," Mabel said wistfully, either not acknowledging or unaware of the contempt with which he expressed this notion.

"We are all on guard over every nook and cranny of Nether Isle until this drama has been resolved." He shifted his gaze to the end of the table. "Except you, Morgana. You stay here until I say we need you."

Her nose scrunched up like a defiant 5-year-old's and her head plopped onto the table. Skin squished against the wood and eyes glazed over. She officially checked out.

"She took that well." Percival stood up and straightened his overcoat. "That's all." He left the room.

Cynthia took over, "Any questions?"

"Once we learn and perfect the banishment spell, we will be in charge of the streets." Delilah said with authority on behalf of the Wiccans. "We are much more sociable than the lot of you, which I doubt you'd argue, and we already have established friendships amongst the general public. Having an ear there might help also. Many times the gossip in the streets is much more telling than people give it credit. If you read the rumors carefully, you'll often find the truth."

"Fine," Cynthia conceded. "It can't hurt and I surely have no interest in hanging out at the market to listen in on mundane conversations. So by all means."

"I'm starving, let's wrap this up so we can all eat," Alastair said from the edge of his seat.

"Go on, scatter," Cynthia said, not realizing how haughty she sounded. The room dispersed. Gretchen stayed behind to talk with Theodore and Adelaide before they left.

"No one really addressed keeping Ruby safe," he said to Gretchen as she took a seat next to them.

"Poe and I will have a constant eye on Bianca. If she gets too close, we'll know."

"What about the other ghosts? Would she be safer on the mainland with her father?"

"Possibly. Maybe once the Wiccans learn the spell, we can assign a few of them to be her guard."

"Alright. Until then, I'll let her know it's best to be away from here on the weekends."

"If you think that's best." She wanted to ask him if his magic came out during the encounter with Bianca, but Adelaide was there.

"I wonder if Eustice is part of Bianca's little crew now," Adelaide thought aloud. "He's been suspiciously absent lately."

"I noticed that, too."

"If so, we need to be alert at home. Who knows what deals he made with her." Adelaide clicked her tongue, feeling terrible frustration toward her late husband.

Theodore was exhausted, "I need a break."

Adelaide put an arm around his shoulder and they exited the grand hall. Gretchen followed them out.

"Come back soon," she implored, mainly meaning Theodore. He could sense her desire to chat with him in more depth. He wanted that too, but now was a bad time.

"I'll be back tomorrow to see how Morton's progress on locating Cadence is going."

"Okay, see you then."

Adelaide and Theodore took their time along the rundown pier. There was no rush and he was savoring every moment he felt safe beneath her arm. She was the only family he ever had, and even if his life felt like a wreck, he was grateful that finding her was a result of moving here. Having her as his adoptive family was worth all the trouble.

Chapter 34

Bianca stormed into the warehouse and let out a blood-curdling scream. Cadence remained in her corner, unaffected by her sister's outburst. Chester followed close behind, trailing her like a comically large puppy.

"Did you get the answers you needed?" he asked.

"Does it look like I got the answers I needed?" Bianca paced the room. "He must be working with the Wiccans, they trailed him all week. Unless they did that on their own accord and he knew nothing of it. They might be on to me. Even so, their magic doesn't come close to matching mine." She was talking to herself now. "I've seen no signs of the Ouijans, but I haven't been able to trail Theodore close enough to observe his every move. Their involvement is not out of the question. If they are on board, the situation is drastically intensified. I am a walking target. They know I am the enemy now. I need spies."

"Want me to gather the crew?" Chester asked.

"Yes. Call them here, now."

Chester left. It wouldn't take long. Spirits could get around quite fast, popping in and out of locations without the hassle or time wasted by walking. Many chose not to do this, as it made them feel more like ghosts than they wished to be, but it was always an option. Slowly, her set of followers began emerging. Some appearing upstairs, others materializing into the basement. Once a large crowd was present, she spoke.

"We have a problem. The living are trying to stop me. If they succeed, they also stop the lot of you from receiving the promises I made. Many of which are your sole purpose for being here in the afterlife. If they defeat me, they defeat your chances at fulfilling your greatest desires."

"They ain't tryin' to get rid of us. I'll get my revenge some other way," Amos spat.

"You do realize your murderer is long dead."

"Maybe, but he ain't *gone*. I'll find him on my own."

"Let's say you do manage to find him, how do you plan to exact revenge? Lots of mean words and evil glares? You have no leverage over him; you're both dead. I know how to inflict pain upon the deceased." She shifted her focus to Elsa and Sadie. "And you two. How do you plan on having children of your own without my help? In order for the baby to recognize you as its mother, you need to possess a woman already pregnant. Otherwise, you'll never have that bond with the child."

"We don't want to steal another woman's chance at motherhood," Sadie explained, "we just want babies in this realm to satisfy the void of what we lost."

"Then you need me more than you realize. The innocent go straight into the light. Pure and untainted souls do not stick around.

If you want a baby in the afterlife, you'll need my magic to snatch one before it enters Apres Monde."

Both women slouched in defeat. Bianca continued on.

"Davy and Marjorie, you want a life without war? Well, there will always be conflicts here and there, but your countries no longer force enlistment. Now is the time. I can help you get the bodies you need." She had their attention. "Most of you want revenge or bodies to inhabit, both of which require my expertise to accomplish. We all saw how Chester's attempt to possess his son on his own ended in terrible failure. I suspect the rest of you would have similar outcomes. With the help of magic, you do not need a living host to make the incision on the body, which takes out the middleman and presents a fail-proof possession. Doing it this way also latches you to the host more closely. Much harder for outsiders to notice you've taken over."

"Fine then. What do you need from us?" Amos spat back at her.

"I need you to act as my spies. They are onto me, so I need to stay out of sight. I need your eyes and ears on the Wiccans, the Ouijans, Adelaide McClaine, Theodore Finn, and Ruby Klearstone. You need to determine what they are up to and how they plan to attack me."

"Does this mean you'll help fulfill our wishes once we get this information for you?" Elsa asked.

"No, that comes after I am safely inside Ruby's body. I already told you this. My magic will intensify once I have a living host."

"I'm on board," Davy said, addressing the crowd. "I was raised to fight for my freedom. We have rights too, and I plan to see to it that I am given a fair chance to try again."

"I bet if the living knew this place existed after they died, they'd have a different outlook on death. I bet the majority would want second chances too. Some might even sacrifice their mortal lives to give a loved one, or a person worthy enough, a second shot," Marjorie said, thinking of the brave men and women who died unjustly while thousands of others stayed safe in their homes, far from war.

"These desires we have are not unnatural. We aren't monsters; we're human," Davy added. "And Marjorie is right. I bet hundreds would have lined up to donate their bodies to geniuses like Albert Einstein, Leonardo Da Vinci, and Galileo if it meant they'd get a few extra decades to apply their brains to the advancement of the human race."

"You ain't wrong, kid," Amos chimed in.

"I'm in," Otis shook as he spoke. The large man stood at the back of the crowd. After acting as the example for Bianca's power, his tough exterior shifted into weakness. He was still enormous, but his confidence was shattered. Any resolve or assuredness he had previous to the attack was stolen from him.

"I'm glad you all see this from a reasonable perspective. We are friends, after all. And friends help each other, no matter what."

"Anything particular you need us looking out for?" Amos asked.

"Everything: who they interact with, what they talk about, and most importantly, anything involving me. I also need a team to travel beyond Nether Isle to recruit outsiders. We have a solid seventy-five here, but we need more. We need to grow. Recruit them however you see fit. Just get them on board, solidify their loyalty, and bring them here. Who wants to tackle this part of the plan?"

"I will," Chester volunteered.

"Count us in," Lazlo Deceal spoke on behalf of himself and Matilda von Wittelsbach. They were new to the group. He was a former vizeadmiral for the Deutsche Marine; classier than a fisherman but just as rugged. As a leader of the German Navy, his poise commingled with his ability to coexist amongst typical, unrefined sailors. Though his beard was full, it barely covered the scars of his previous life. They ran across his face like artwork.

Matilda was the oldest ghost there. As a German princess from the European Renaissance, she outdated them all. From the House of Wittelsbach, and as daughter of the Holy Roman Empire; King of Germany, Louis IV, Matilda's expertise was in social politics. When she looked at Bianca her gaze was filled with contempt. Matilda was smart, smarter than the rest of the spirits there, and very used to living in the afterlife. She had no spells of haziness or haunted memories that plagued her. She conquered those side effects of death a long time ago. Though she was a strong ghost, she did not have the magical abilities that Bianca possessed, or the foresight to pursue that avenue in all the years she spent trapped in her half-life. She was jealous. Her gray eyes gleamed at Bianca and it looked like she was trying to rip the magic straight out of her. Her loyalty stemmed from the promise that Bianca swore to teach her how to conjure supernatural powers of her own. Hell would be raised if that promise was broken.

"Fantastic. The three of you can travel about, recruiting an army. I'm sure many spirits will be eager to learn of this place. Existing, and being seen, is a great delight after living invisibly for an extended period of time. Use that to your advantage."

"Of course," Lazlo replied, "I planned on it. If Matilda had not traveled back to Germany in 1998, I never would have learned of this place. I'm grateful every day to be seen."

"Don't worry about us," Matilda scoffed, "I am royalty and Lazlo was in the Deutsche Marine. I think we can handle enlisting soldiers." Her voice was condescending. Bianca took it in stride, aware that the former princess had a superiority complex and wished to be in her place of rule. She would keep a close eye on Matilda's behavior to ensure she had no plans to backstab her, but in the meantime, she thoroughly enjoyed the power trip. She reveled in the princess's jealousy.

"I trust you have it under control." Bianca played to their egos. "But I do suggest you head out now. There is no time to waste."

The men obliged without a second thought, but Matilda wore a scowl. Though she did not like being told what to do, she followed the men up and out of the warehouse basement.

"The rest of you, get to spying. I need information." Bianca was blind with determination. "I need to know how to defeat them."

The spirits in the room dispersed, leaving only Bianca and Cadence. Cadence had her eyes shut as she cradled her legs to her chest in the corner. She listened to the meeting, but did not partake. She had no assignment but to wait. Wait for Bianca to force her into a living body she did not want.

"It would be best if I could find a female body your age in Ruby's life. She only has a little brother, which won't do. Perhaps a younger female cousin. I need to do some digging." Bianca was talking to Cadence but they both knew Cadence was no longer listening.

"Go away," Cadence whispered.

"Excuse me?"

"Leave! I am tired, freezing, and I don't want to hear your voice anymore." Her small declaration was filled with spite. "*I* would leave, but I can't."

"That's because I cannot trust you in your current state. You'll either blab or head off into the light without me. You haven't a loyal thread left holding you together."

"You've tortured me enough; I don't need to hear your nasty and incorrect thoughts about me. Just go away."

"You're still my sister. I love you more than I love myself." Cadence rolled her eyes, but Bianca continued, "I don't want to leave you alone."

"Your company only intensifies the loneliness." Cadence's eyes grew bright as the glimmer of shadowed tears covered them. "You are a stranger living in my sister's body, and having you near makes me feel more alone than I ever dreamed possible."

Bianca's expression did a slow shift from compassion to rage. "You are such a little brat. The fog of death has altered your mind. When we are in our new bodies, you'll see clearly again and you will be at my feet, begging for forgiveness, thanking me for my patience. You will see the crap you put me through and will be humbled that despite your resistance, I never gave up on you."

"I wish you would give up on me." Cadence curled back into her nook in the corner.

Her hurtful words stung Bianca's hardened heart, cracking its shielded exterior slightly. The notion that her sister would rather be alone in death than accompanied by her any longer silenced her anger. She stormed out of the room without another word.

Chapter 35

"This will be easy," Matilda scoffed. "Most ghosts never shake the haze; their minds will be putty in our hands."

She, Lazlo, and Chester stood at the edge of Ballantine Dock. Apres Monde shone in the distance.

"Where to first?" Chester asked, excited to be traveling with well-versed spirits. Being newly deceased, he hoped their company rubbed off on him and taught him how to cope more effectively.

"I say we go west, into the southern states of America. Mississippi or Louisiana, that region. Many angry ghosts from oppressed time periods linger there, hoping for justice," Lazlo suggested.

"Fine. Then we travel to Eastern Europe. I go there often. The spirits there know me and hold me in high esteem," Matilda added.

"I'm gonna need you guys to show me how to just appear someplace. I died off the coast of Nether Isle barely a month ago and never traveled anyplace but here."

"Oh, you're just a baby," Matilda cooed, excited to have one of Bianca's fresh souls under her supervision. By the end of this trip, Chester would belong to her. "I'll teach you how to thrive in the afterlife. Take my hand."

"Let's go to Courtland, Alabama," Lazlo suggested. "Rocky Hill Castle is a historic plantation with tons of ghosts looking for retribution. All kinds: tortured slaves, Civil War soldiers, and the Lady in Blue. We can probably add an entire leg to our army from that one location."

"To Courtland it is," Matilda conceded, dragging Chester along with her as she followed Lazlo there. They moved in a blur. The world around them smeared as they relocated from Nether Isle to Courtland, Alabama. Within seconds, they were at their destination and Chester was none the wiser on how they got there.

"How did we do that?" he asked.

"With our minds. We don't exist in the real world, therefore, we do not abide by their rules. We are vapors. We can move in a similar fashion to air; we are shadows, mere mists, and if you accept that, you can travel as such."

"Even if I want to go to a place I can't picture because I've never been there before?"

"Yes. It'll take time, but you can direct your course. It's just like walking to your destination, but a lot faster. We will practice, don't worry."

"In we go," Lazlo instructed as he led them onto the property. The 640 acres of land looked very different than it did in the mid-1800s. Rocky Hill Castle was demolished in the 1960s due to its ruinous state. The ghosts spooked its last inhabitants out and by the time new owners bought the land to farm on, the home needed to be condemned. Though the structure was long gone, the ghosts remained. They scattered the field, walking around aimlessly, waiting for something to happen. Many were in a state of disorientation, caught up in their ancient memories and reliving the horrors of their old lives. Others were encased in rage, aware that they were dead and searching desperately for the place and people that once existed there. In all cases, the ghosts residing here were hopelessly lost. Despite being dead for over a century, none of them had successfully transitioned into their hollowed existence.

Lazlo whispered as they walked through the field, "This plantation was known to be one of the cruelest in the South. The owners built a guard tower and locked the slaves in at night so they could not run away in the dark. The master would sit on top of the prison during the day to watch the slaves as they worked his vast domain of fields, then trapped them beneath his tower throne while they slept at night. Terribly inhumane."

"No wonder they look so angry and sad," Chester commented.

"How do you know all this?" Matilda asked, her German accent just as thick as Lazlo's.

"I've always been fascinated with the Civil War and the slavery that existed in America. Just like the Holocaust in Germany, this time period in America was home to its own breed of evil. It would be foolish to let its memory fade."

They walked in silence for a few minutes, digesting the tragic vibe that lived on.

"They aren't all slaves," Matilda noted.

"No, many are soldiers. The mansion was used as a hospital during the American Civil War. I assume many of these ghosts are soldiers who died and were buried here." Lazlo went on, "It was also used as a weapon factory and a spot for illegal slave trade. This place is home to a lot of tense history."

"They've been invisible in an abandoned field for over a century. Do they even know they are dead?" Chester asked.

"They most likely knew they were dead at some point. People used to live in the house, and someone came later on to demolish it. But that was years ago, so it's possible time wiped their memory of that. Living memories are always stronger than the ones you make in death," Matilda answered.

They walked further onto the property. The road was far out of sight, no living bodies for miles. The way these spirits lingered was desperate, like they were ensnared by time. Though they haunted this property into desolate ruins, these spirits were clearly haunted as well. They may have scared off any living person from inhabiting this place ever again, but looking at their faces, their terrifying nature was caused by something much greater than them. They could not control the demons that haunted their afterlife existence.

"Who should we approach first?" Chester asked.

"Someone less lost than the few we've passed." Lazlo scanned the field as he spoke.

"Is that a woman up there?"

Lazlo and Matilda looked in the direction Chester pointed. A lady in blue floated in the sky, appearing to be sitting on something that was no longer there. She was calm, so they walked toward her.

"What are you doing up there, ma'am?" Lazlo asked.

The lady turned her head to look down at them, then returned her gaze outward.

"My children have gone missing. This tower is the only place high enough to look for them." Her voice was soft as she spoke. Not only was her 1920's draped dress colored in blue, but her skin, even in death, appeared a cold and wet hue of blue-gray.

"Perhaps we can help you," Matilda offered. "What were their names?"

"John and Louise. They are eight and six years old. I just saw them yesterday at the river. On the bridge. We were together." Her voice faded and her expression grew numb.

"And what's your name?" Lazlo asked to keep her attention. The lady sat up straight and recalled this information from the recesses of her mind.

"Irene Saunders."

"Alright, Irene. If you help us rally the other spirits that remain here, we can help you find your children."

"Spirits?" Her delicate skin creased in confusion. "What do you mean?"

340

"All around you," Matilda replied. "Can't you see them?"

"I reckon you mean ghosts?" Irene shot them a playful grin. "I may look naïve but I promise you, I am anything but."

"So you don't see them?" Chester asked as he scanned the area himself. There were hundreds scattered all over the fields. It was impossible *not* to see them.

"Ghosts aren't real!" She let out a dainty southern laugh. "I appreciate you offerin' to help me find my babies, but I can't be bothered with this tomfoolery. Not while my little ones are still out there, missing."

"Our apologies then. The offer still stands if you decide you want some help locating them."

"Do you live in the area? I've never seen you before." Irene's eyes narrowed as she scanned her three new acquaintances.

"We are just passing through," Matilda answered. "We will be around for the next hour or so. You ought to come down and observe what we have going on."

"I'm fine up here. Just don't cause any trouble or I'll have to fetch the police and report ya'll for trespassing. This is my property you're on." Her pleasant demeanor grew agitated with no provocation. "If I weren't so preoccupied with locating my children, I'd have already shooed you away."

"We understand. We will be gone in an hour. It will be like we were never here," Lazlo said, knowing she'd forget about them as soon as they left.

Irene huffed and looked back out over the vast stretch of land.

"That was a terrible misjudgment," Matilda said beneath her breath as they walked away. "Onto the next."

A man in uniform sat beneath a lush weeping willow. He fiddled with his musket, performing the act of loading it with ammunition, though the rifle was merely a figment brought into the afterlife with him. It would never fire anything solid. The man aimed it anyway, in the direction of the lady in blue. He focused on her, sitting on nothing in the middle of the sky. Once he had her locked in sight, he fired. The blast was audible, the smoke was visible, but only the shadow of a bullet left the barrel.

Irene turned in shock at the strange noise, but returned to her oblivious state shortly after seeing no source to the noise. It only took a few seconds before she appeared to forget it happened at all. The man groaned and dropped the gun to his side.

"Why are you trying to shoot that lady?" Matilda asked as she approached the solider.

"I'm not. Just trying to get her attention."

"Why?"

"Cause lookin' at her up there, every day, makes me sad."

"Where did her children go?"

"Into the light."

"I see," Matilda shook her head, realizing just how much of a lost cause Irene was.

"They haven't been back in decades. They left their mom here a few years after the three of them drowned in that river. I barely remember meeting them, it was so long ago. Not sure who's worse: the kids for abandoning her, or her for letting them go into the unknown alone."

"Either way, she appears quite hopeless."

"I'm working on it." He grabbed his rifle and reloaded it. They watched him as he aimed it at Irene again and fired. The noise captured her attention, but like last time, it only lasted a few seconds before she forgot about it. There was no easy answer to the sound, therefore she could not hold onto its memory.

"I know she sees me. I got her to talk to me once, a long time ago. Tried to tell her she was dead, that her kids were dead, and that she needed to accept it, but I got her so mad, she retreated up there and hasn't come down since."

"What's your name?"

"Lieutenant General Joseph Wheeler. Fought and led in the Civil War, the Spanish-American War, and the Philippine-American War." His voice was proud as he spoke.

"You sound like a well-traveled and educated man. Why on earth did you come back here?" Matilda wanted to know.

"I've been dead a long time, and I was aware of it from the moment it happened. I wandered for a while, saw how the world was reshaping itself. People have changed so much since I was alive. I learned a lot in death, and I came back here to make peace with my former self. This was where I have the most vivid memories of the horrors I committed. I thought if I came back, I'd be able to forgive myself, but instead, I find myself obsessed with saving that woman."

"Did you know her?" Lazlo asked.

"No, she lived here long after I was dead. Discovered her when I came back to this plantation, which was around the time she moved in. I watched her live and die here. And now I am watching her waste away."

"Is that why you stay?"

"I guess so. I found peace with myself a long time ago. Can't change the past, or who I was in it. Now I stay for her."

"What if I told you we can help you?"

Joseph looked at them quizzically. "How? If she won't believe me, why would she believe you?"

"There's a place we can take her where she will have no choice but to accept it," Lazlo continued. As a member of a military branch, he knew Joseph was a perfect recruit. The Lieutenant wore a skeptical expression, so Lazlo explained more, "It's a place where ghosts can be seen by the living. We materialize, we are visible, and we can converse with them. It's right by one of the light portals. If we take her there, she will need to come to terms with her death."

"How will we get her there?"

"I can make her follow. In the meantime, we need your assistance in a different matter."

"What do you need from me?"

"We need you to gather all the roaming spirits of Rocky Hill Castle. We need them to come with us too."

"Why?" Joseph asked Lazlo.

"You and I are building a new army."

"For what cause?"

"The realm we live in, the afterlife, is very real. Though many might say we stay by our own choosing, that we aren't *supposed* to exist here, it cannot be denied that we do. We live very real lives in the nether and we ought to have similar rights in this world as we did in the living world. Just like all pivotal points in human history, if we want rights, we need to fight for them."

"I see your logic," Joseph said, deep in thought. "But who are we fighting against? This sounds like an internal structural problem. Sounds like we need to establish some form of government in this realm."

"Perhaps, but that will come later. Right now, we need to defend ourselves."

"Again, against *whom*?" The lieutenant was losing his patience.

"The living on Nether Isle, our home. The place I mentioned where ghosts can be seen. They want us gone. More specifically, they want one powerful spirit eradicated. She is old and knows magic. They are trying to force her through the light because she scares them. They fear her, so they want to get rid of her. Sounds quite like many other moments in history when the innocent minority was persecuted without justifiable cause. If we don't stand up for ourselves, who will? If they defeat her, which of us is next?"

Lieutenant Wheeler looked around at the spirits wandering the fields.

"Many of these ghosts were victims of circumstance just like this. I am not sure how they will react. Will they be offended that after all they were put through, we are asking them to fight again? Or will they see themselves as the equal parties they are in this battle? Or will it boil down to the fact that this situation hits too close to home to partake in it. Some might want to keep that feeling buried."

"We cannot guess their reaction, we can only try. They would be fighting for their own rights too. Every ghost has equal claim to the benefits of this war."

"Right. Let's gather them."

The four spirits walked the circumference of the property, talking to spirits and directing them toward the large willow tree. Most listened and obeyed, interested to see what they had to say.

Others were resistant and skeptical, fearful to leave their spot of land they clung to. Overall, the majority waited under the tree.

Irene stayed high in the sky, occasionally looking over her shoulder at them below.

"Who are all these people on my property?" she called down to Matilda. "I didn't invite them here."

"You can see them now?" Matilda asked, bewildered. Irene's willpower to remain naïve and block them from her sight all these years was cracking. When all the spirits stood together, the sight was too overwhelming to ignore.

"Has my grandfather organized this? I told him to inform me when the yard would be used for gatherings. It's terribly off-putting to have such crowds thrust upon you unexpectedly."

"Why don't you come down and listen? You might like to hear what we have to say."

"No, I'm fine up here. Perhaps the wind will carry your voices to me." She ended the conversation and turned away from the crowd as Lazlo began to speak.

He explained their cause in the same manner he told Joseph. After giving a riveting speech, the crowd rustled with whispered conversations. It took a few moments before a man spoke up.

"I didn't get a chance to fight for my rights in my last life, I'd like a shot at it now." The man still wore a dirty cotton shirt from his days as a slave.

"What's your name?" Lazlo asked him.

"Henry Washington, free man," he answered proudly.

"I think you've made a great choice, Henry. A lot of time has passed since that terrible time and many things have changed. We are all equals here and the cause we fight for belongs to each of us."

"Good man," Joseph Wheeler commented, which incited a look of contempt from Henry.

"You best believe I ain't fightin' for you, or any of these damn soldiers who walk around here like they welcome. I be doin' this for me. For my brothers and sisters. We got shafted bein' born when we did. We deserve a chance at equal rights and freedom, at a life where we is looked at like people, not something lesser than. We may be dead, but that man is right. Wherever we is, it's real, and we ought to make our existence here known and respected. I ain't gonna hold no more grudges, I got forgiveness in my heart. I have to, otherwise I'd be drowned in anger. But I have not forgotten, so don't go acting like we friends. Cause we ain't. We may be fighting for the same thing now, but don't confuse that with no camaraderie. I'll fight by your side, but this time it's by my own choice. I do it for me, not you."

"I understand and respect your feelings toward me. I don't deserve your friendship after all I played accomplice to."

Henry exhaled with gumption. He stood tall and confident as Lieutenant Joseph Wheeler conceded to being a lesser man than he.

Though some soldier's outlooks did not evolve in death, many others did. Countless apologies had been given over the years they all spent together on the plantation as ghosts, but the roots of the evils committed were too grim to see past. What happened would never be okay, no matter how many genuine apologies were dispensed.

"I think it'll be good for *all* of you to get off this damn plantation," Matilda spoke. "There's so much more to this world than old resentment and guilt. So many places to go besides the one preventing you from finding happiness. I'm not saying forget, or even forgive if you don't want to, but get out of here and find contentment again. Let time heal you."

"You ain't wrong, Ms. Matilda." Henry had no animosity toward the ancient German Princess. "We will be followin' you and your friends onto something new."

After Henry said he was on board and laid the grounds of why they'd even consider working alongside their former enslavers, many others settled on the same sentiment. The ghosts of the former slaves and Civil War soldiers, both Confederate and Union, came to the same conclusion. It was time to fight for a new, common cause: their freedom in death.

Chapter 36

One hundred and fifty spirits followed them back from Alabama. There was no room to house so many new spirits in Bianca's warehouse, so she directed the lot to Cross Island, one of Maine's National Wildlife Refuges. It was maintained by minimal staff and was home to trees and small animals. The recruits would remain there, existing invisibly until a solid plan was finalized.

Lazlo, Matilda, and Chester continued on, heading to Europe this time. Up first was the Ancient Ram Inn, built in 1145 in Gloucestershire, England. The run-down home was constructed atop two ley lines, both of which trace all the way to the center of Stonehenge. Being placed on top of this intersection and linked to the greatest source for feeding supernatural occurrences, the Inn was riddled with death. The Ram Inn was also built over the site of a 5,000 year-old pagan burial site. Needless to say, when they arrived, they had plenty of spirits to recruit.

Katherine Sutton, a "witch" burnt at the stake in the 1500s, was the first to join their cause. She was young and swore in monotonous repetition that she was not a witch. Matilda could not wait to see her reaction when she saw first-hand the magic living at Nether Isle.

Alice and Walter Langley, children sacrificed to the Pagan Gods during the devil worshipping of an ancient cult, were next. They were the angriest children Matilda ever laid eyes upon. Their eyelids were heavy with malice and their words lined with aggression. With one look, their intent was clear: revenge.

Two monks and two nuns agreed to go to Nether Isle with them. They were not holy ghosts, they were quite the opposite. All four wore black auras. The darkness draped their silhouettes like cloaks.

Mathias Abell was an unwelcome sight, sitting cross-legged in the fireplace when they approached him. His head was charred and blistered, completely disfigured, while the rest of his body remained unscorched. The way he was murdered was apparent, and tragically brutal. Death by fire, and he did nothing to hide it.

Elizabeth Shawe, former housekeeper at the Rams Inn, was an easy recruit. Strangled and buried in the cellar of the Inn, left unfound for centuries, she was eager to leave.

In total, they collected twenty spirits from the Rams Inn, including Bernard Gilbert and his border collie, Sawyer. It was a good sweep, so they moved on.

Back in Germany, Matilda and Lazlo made a few strategic stops. Between Auschwitz and Dachau, both former concentration camps during World War II, they recruited another two hundred ghosts.

"Such a disgraceful time in our history," Matilda scoffed. "I am ashamed of this stain on our country's name."

"As am I," Lazlo agreed before leading the new recruits back to Cross Island. He went alone while Matilda and Chester continued onward from Germany. By the time they got to Rajasthan, India, Chester was getting the hang of their method of traveling.

Bhangarh Fort was an abandoned fortress haunted by the many spirits murdered there in the 17th century. After meeting Princess Ratnavati, they learned the legends of the location were true. She rejected the love of the black magic wizard Singiya, turning his love potion against him by pouring it on a boulder that crushed him. Before dying he cursed her palace, sentencing all dwelling inside it to death. Not long after, the Mughals attacked Bhangarh Fort and the 10,000 inhabitants living inside were killed. This included the princess.

"I hate that tantrik with all my being," Princess Ratnavati rambled on.

"Has he remained in the afterlife?" Chester asked.

"Singuya was a wizard, capable of dangerous dark magic. I am certain he found a way to cheat death."

"Perhaps, if you help us, we can help you. We can find him, living in a new body or dead, and help you defeat him."

"If your leader can teach me her magic, I would scour the ends of this earth to enact my wrath upon him."

Matilda cringed at the word leader. She did not like these new spirits seeing Bianca in that light.

"She is not our leader, just a ghost we are trying to save from expulsion into the light. But perhaps if we save her, she will teach you what she knows."

"Count me in, along with my people. Most of the ten thousand killed left here long ago, but those who remain will follow me."

"How many are you?"

"One thousand."

"Fantastic, let's go." Matilda and Chester escorted the large group back to Cross Island, then headed back out. Lazlo rejoined them.

At Chibichiri Cave in Okinawa, Japan, they recruited fifty Japanese soldiers who committed mass suicide rather than be captured by American soldiers at the end of WWII. These spirits were sleepwalkers. No leader, they just followed.

Next they visited Tat Tak School in the village of Ping Shan, Hong Kong, China. This led to an acquisition of thirty-five very hostile ghosts. After a failed uprising against the British in the 19th century, they were ready to fight anyone for any cause. They wanted blood and no longer cared who it came from. The lady in red, a former teacher who committed suicide in the girl's lavatory, led this branch of the ghost army. Her name was Ming Fai and she was a beautiful demon. Black was her color: hair, eyes, and heart.

Last stop was Chile's Atacama Desert where the town of La Noria sat, desolated. By the late 1800s, the once booming mining town entered its downward spiral. As their economy took hits, so did the mines and many were shut down. People fled the failing town and the remaining inhabitants were forced to live in poverty. Working conditions became brutal and bordered on slavery. By the early 1900s, everyone in the town either died or fled.

The recruits hovered by the coastline as Matilda, Lazlo, and Chester ventured inland. They traveled through La Noria cemetery, which was filled with shallow, open graves. Half-dressed skeletons were visible in their cheap coffins. These bodies belonged to former slaves, the types of tombs a grave robber wouldn't go near, so the fact that the graves were dug up led them to believe the spirits in La Noria were strong in death.

As the sun began to set, the sprits came out in droves. Appearing from the open graves and other hidden corners throughout the town. Their first encounter was with Patricio Cortez, a miner killed during an underground gas explosion.

"If you want to rally the spirits here, you'll need to speak with Camila. I died before the tough times. No one cares much for my opinion because I didn't live through the same hardship as them."

"Where can we find her?" Lazlo asked.

"Follow me."

Patricio led them to an open grave at the back end of the cemetery. There, a strong, middle aged woman sat, spirit children surrounding her in every direction.

"Don't interrupt her story," Patricio whispered as they got closer, "it will upset the children."

They listened from a safe distance as Camila told the children tales of a brave Chilean knight who fought on behalf of the poor, a man who came into towns to vanquish the monsters who treated humans as slaves. The children listened to her with hopeful fascination.

"Why didn't he come to save us while we were alive?" a small boy asked.

"The monsters here were very good at keeping our existence secret. What we must learn from this story is that good people exist. And we must practice forgiveness in order to be good people too. You cannot be a hero if you let hatred take home in your heart."

"I'm a hero, Miss Fuentes," a little girl smiled. "I led a living dog to water this afternoon. He might've died if he kept wandering without my guidance."

"That's beautiful, Francesca." Camila noticed Patricio standing there with visitors. "Everyone, go on now. Enjoy the night."

The children scattered, skipping along as they headed into town.

"What is this?" Camila's nurturing demeanor shifted in a blink. She stared at them with hostility. They did not belong there: Matilda in her ancient German gown, Lazlo in his proper Deutsche Marine attire, and Chester looking like a grimy, ignorant American.

355

"They wanted to talk to someone with authority here, so I brought them to you."

"We have no leader here. We exist individually, in peace."

"That's fine. We just wanted to talk and see if you and your friends here may be interested in helping us with a noble cause."

They went on to explain the matter in a similar manner in which they presented it at Rocky Hill Castle in Alabama. The issue intrigued Camila and it didn't take much convincing before she was eagerly persuading her ghostly companions to follow her. Many obliged. In all, one hundred spirits left La Noria to fight alongside the ghosts of Nether Isle.

Cross Island was abuzz. The animals scattered, abandoning their home for one with less spiritual activity. After a few days of observation, Bianca received the reports she needed. There was an alliance of humans forming against her on Nether Isle. She did not know all the details, but enough to determine that she no longer needed spies, just an army. There would be war and she would be ready. All ghosts were required to remain at Cross Island until the first attack. While they waited, they quietly prepared for battle.

"How many we got?" Chester asked as they left the island behind and headed back to Nether Isle.

"A little over fifteen hundred," Lazlo replied.

"Bianca will be pleased."

"Stop caring so much about her approval," Matilda spat, "this is bigger than her now. Don't let her think she rules us."

"She is the one with the powers though," Chester said, "and she's the only one who can give us what we want."

"Don't put too much faith in her yet." Matilda was ripe with resentment. "I won't believe a word of her promises until she starts fulfilling them."

"And if she doesn't," Lazlo jumped in, "we have an army to take her down."

"You better not let her know you have any thoughts of betrayal. She'll cast you right into the light like she almost did to Otis," Chester warned them.

"Then you better keep your mouth shut. Trust me, you'll want to be on our side if things turn against her." Matilda spoke with such confidence, Chester had no choice but to believe her. She may not have magical powers, but she was certainly a force to take seriously.

Chapter 37

A week passed in eerie silence. The ghosts that normally roamed the piers of Nether Isle were gone, vanished with no explanation why. The people in town didn't seem to notice, and those who did rejoiced, happy for the unexplained disappearance of their unwelcome neighbors. Theodore knew better than to celebrate, as did the Wiccans and Ouijans. The sudden lack of spiritual presence was a warning that things were about to unravel.

Poe and Gretchen had not been able to spy on Bianca as she was nowhere to be found. Similarly, Morton, Tabitha, and Rupert could not find Cadence. No progress was made on either front.

The Wiccans successfully learned the banishment spell from Percival, Caspian, and Cynthia. They now manned the busy piers and streets on the mainland, looking for any indicators of what was to come.

When Theodore wasn't spending time with Gretchen, Ruby, or Adelaide, he spent a lot of time alone. It seemed safer that way. He tended to attract danger, and with Bianca's plans unknown, he didn't want anyone getting hurt because she was gunning for him. From afar, he kept watch over Ruby. Always making sure she had a guard in place, or was far from Nether Isle on weekends. After a week of this distance, Ruby grew agitated and yelled at him. Friday afternoon ended in a fight before she got on her father's boat and headed to her aunt's house in Maine. He would apologize on Monday, but it had to stay this way for now. Once this was all over, they could have a normal friendship.

Adelaide didn't like to give him much space, so he retreated into her attic whenever he needed a moment of peace. While he appreciated her concern, her worrying only made him more anxious. She feared for him, when what he needed was her confidence. He supposed she had faith in him too, but her constant distress overshadowed it. It was a very lonely time for him, but he carried on. It would be over soon.

On Saturday afternoon, he finally made a trip out to sea. Far too much time passed without a good sail on his boat. The salt air encased him as it pushed him through the breezy autumn afternoon. The water was rough but navigable. He headed in the opposite direction of Maudit Cove and Apres Monde. Those locations were no longer of interest to him now that he was aware of the darkness they attracted. The trip was short but efficient. By the time he returned to Ballantine Dock, he felt rejuvenated. It probably wouldn't last long with all the terror on the brink of unfolding, but he planned to hold onto the pleasant feeling for as long as possible. He headed back to Adelaide's for lunch with Delilah and Percival.

When he walked through the front door, the three adults were already deep into serious conversation. He took his seat at the table where an untouched plate of hot lobster macaroni waited for him. Steam rose from the meal and its scent filled his nostrils. Without trying to garner where they were in the conversation, he dug in.

"They found her last night."

Percival's words caught Theodore's attention.

"Where was she?" Delilah asked.

"In the basement of the old paint factory."

"Did they talk to her?"

"No, they never even went inside. Bianca was there. They spotted them both through a little window that led from the basement to the street."

"Well, at least we know where they are. Should make it easier for Poe and Gretchen to get some useful information."

"Cadence?" Theodore asked, words muffled by cheesy pasta.

"Yes," Percival answered, "they located her and Bianca late last night. No sign of others staying there with them."

"Well, they are staying somewhere cause they aren't here anymore." He shoved another mouthful of lobster macaroni into his mouth.

"Poe will find out. Now that he knows where she is, he can stalk her every move. She'll reveal her secrets soon enough."

"How is Ruby doing?" Adelaide asked Theodore.

"Alright, I guess. She's mad at me right now."

"Why?"

"Because I don't want to be near her. Not right now. Being around me will only get her hurt."

"You're half right. It's probably better you guys stay apart until we get rid of Bianca, but you shouldn't act like you're a disease."

"But he is," Percival said casually.

"He is not," Delilah chimed in. "Don't listen to him. Keeping your distance is valiant, but don't go overboard. No need to be a martyr."

"I'm not trying to be, it just seems logical."

"Fine. But fix it next time you see her," Adelaide demanded.

"Or after this is all over."

"No. As soon as possible. You should never let stupid anger linger. Life is too wacky to risk it. You should always keep the people you care for in good graces."

She was right. What if something tragic happened before they mended their friendship? It would only make everything worse. Plus, he missed having her around. It just scared him to let her get too close with so much danger in the air around him. He cared too much about her to risk her safety.

Percival ate his last bite. "I've had enough for one day. Until tomorrow."

Adelaide gave him a wave as he hurried out the door.

"She's right, you know," Delilah said, continuing Adelaide's thoughts about Ruby.

"Yeah, I get it." Theodore picked up his plate and stood. "I think I'm done for today, too." He realized he was being rude, like Percival, but he needed to be alone. "Thanks for lunch, Adelaide. It was really good." He gave her a half smile, took his plate, and departed for the attic. He could hear the concerned whispers of the older women as he left, but did not care to know what they said.

In the attic, he finished his meal then began practicing his powers. He was able to open and close the many trunks scattered throughout the space without touching them. He hadn't mastered producing and directing his energy without the basic stance, but at least he could muster up something on command, even if he had to stand a certain way to do so. Gretchen tried to get him to use his powers for more significant things than messing with boxes and tidying a room, but he was hesitant. The power scared him.

Today, he was feeling agitated. Despite his therapeutic sail in the bay, coming home to the reminder that Bianca was up to no good and Ruby was mad at him caused his foul mood to return.

A spider hung from the ceiling by its silk thread, dangling and slowly inching downward. Theodore watched as it meticulously dropped toward the floor. Before it reached the wooden planks, he zapped it with a blast of magic. The medium-sized spider caught aflame and fell to the floor as a mini fireball. Theodore's senses were heightened and his brain buzzed with electricity as he watched the living creature he murdered get eaten alive by the flame. Vision fuzzy, ears ringing, he swore he could hear the microscopic cry of a dying life. He stumbled backward as the spider fizzled out. A tiny pile of ash lay in its resting place.

He wasn't sure why killing a bug caused him such distress; he'd stepped on thousands throughout his life, but this time it felt wrong and malicious, like he destroyed the bug with murderous intent. The worst part was that he enjoyed it. His mind twirled around the fact that he could encase a human in similar fire. He pushed these thoughts away. It terrified him and he feared if he let the thought remain, he'd begin to enjoy that, too.

Racing down the attic steps, he searched for Adelaide's company. Not in the kitchen, not in the living room. He walked out to the back porch and she was there, sitting on an old rocking chair.

"What happened?" She sat up, alarmed, examining Theodore's discomposure.

"Nothing," he stalled, instantly relieved just by the sight of her. "Just one of those days."

"Sit down and relax. Your brain needs a day off."

He sat down in a chair next to her and they watched the serene ocean in front of them.

"I'm sorry if I was rude at lunch. Or just in general lately. I don't mean to be."

"I know. You're goin' through a lot." She smiled at him. "I appreciate the apology, but it's unnecessary. I ain't goin' nowhere, no matter how insufferable you get. You're part of my family now, which means you're stuck with me. Good times, hard times, boring times: I'm by your side."

Theodore sighed in heavy relief. There were no words to explain the significance of her statement.

"Thank you." His entire body relaxed. He smiled at her, eyes gleaming with sincere appreciation. She knew he felt the same for her, he didn't need to say it.

"I was thinking of making shrimp parmigiana for dinner. How ya feel about that?"

"Sounds delicious," he answered.

"Good. No more talking about the crap goin' on around here either. Not until there's some solid progress. The constant chatter and whispering is starting to get to me, too." She shut her eyes and tilted her head back against the chair's pillow. "I've been spending too much time with Delilah and her chatty nature is wearing off on me. I'm not built for it. It drains me."

"Yeah, same here. I think the uninformed speculation is making everything harder. We don't know anything, yet we go on and on guessing. It stresses me out."

"This home is now decreed a safe-zone," Adelaide announced with a playful tone. "Mindless conjecture is no longer welcome here."

"Aye, aye," Theodore played along.

"Then it's done. Meetings related to these issues will take place elsewhere and you will attend only those of importance."

"Sounds good to me. I can prepare on my own. I don't need unhelpful reminders every second of every day."

"Right on."

"I suppose tomorrow's meeting will be a significant one."

"Yes, you'll need to be there for that one."

Theodore nodded in understanding. "I'm going to go back out on the water before dinner."

"Enjoy yourself."

Theodore left and headed for the dock. Two sails in one day *had* to set him right.

Chapter 38

Day was shifting into evening as Theodore drifted far away from Nether Isle in his sailboat. Once a decent distance from land, he furled the sails, eliminating the wind factor. He let his boat waft at the water's will. The steady rocking motion was soothing as he watched twilight smother the sky.

It was peaceful and he was grateful. The ocean had a way of reminding him who he really was. No dark magic or mortal danger could define him here. The sea brought his purest soul to the surface, it dragged the memory of his true being to the front of his mind. If he could hold onto this feeling, this knowledge, then life on land would be more manageable. The little nuances of everyday life would not drown him anymore because his grasp on his own reality was too strong. He wasn't sure why it was so hard to keep this feeling on land, but it was. Or maybe it was just Nether Isle; he never had this issue while living in Alaska. Something about the air here clouded his senses and dragged him into despair. It muddied what he knew to be true and replaced it with fear and anxiety. No matter how often he fought through his own thoughts, denying those produced by land and repeating those he believed by sea, he could never win. In the end, he always succumbed to the mysterious power of Nether Isle. The only cure he found so far was the ocean. Breathing it in was the only remedy.

He laid back in his boat and shut his eyes. The wind whistled as it danced around him. The music it made eased him into a brief nap. The sounds of whimpering woke him up.

He sat up to see where the noise came from. Nothing. Maudit Cove was very far away. He had intentionally sailed in the opposite direction of the creepy inlet because he didn't want to hear any ghostly sorrows. He was so far from it that he had trouble believing the wind could carry a cry that far.

There was no sign of its origin but the noise remained. He peered into the dark distance of the open ocean ahead of him. As the sun disappeared, the moonlight illuminated a far off figure. It came from Nether Isle and approached him with speed, gliding above the water with haste. Prepared to defend himself, Theodore carefully stood in his small boat and took his stance.

"Cross, cross, cross," the little voice cried, "cross, cross, cross."

The voice was frantic and sad. Theodore instinctively lowered his guard as the wind carried the ghost to him.

It was Cadence. Her cheeks were bright with vaporized tears.

"It's at the cross," she screamed.

"What are you talking about?"

"They are coming," she sobbed, "you were supposed to stop her."

"Cadence, calm down. Start from the beginning."

"There's no time. She knows."

A gale of wind materialized, pushing them hard to the east. In it was Bianca, eyes red with fury. She grabbed Cadence by her hair. She gave Theodore a mischievous glare before flying away toward Nether Isle, Cadence in tow, leaving behind an unnatural silence.

He rigged his sails back in place then hurried toward the dock. After tethering his boat, he ran to Adelaide's. As he reached her front door, he realized something wasn't right.

Inside, he was greeted by his greatest fear: Adelaide in Bianca's grasp. She paralyzed the old woman with magic. Adelaide was a puppet in her hands.

"Stop it," he screamed, charging toward them.

"I suggest you stop where you are," Bianca said calmly. She flicked her wrist and Adelaide's body twisted, causing her to holler in agony. Theodore halted his progression and Bianca ended the pain she was inflicting.

"Why are you doing this?" Theodore's blood boiled. He could feel it heat up as his fury grew.

"All you had to do was be a good friend. But you couldn't, and now everyone is suffering."

"You're dead. Nobody wants you here."

"Untrue."

"Go to hell. We both know it's where you belong."

"That's not nice." With her free hand, Bianca sent a blast at Theodore, which tossed him so hard into the wall, his body left a dent in the sheetrock.

As he stood up and shook off the pain, Bianca twisted her hands, choking Adelaide from afar. The old woman gagged on the air she was losing.

"I intended to wait on this moment. I really wanted to plan this out and enjoy it, but Cadence foiled my plans, yet again." She seethed at her little sister, who sat trapped in an enchantment in the corner. The young girl screamed and pounded at the air, but made no noise. She was encased behind an invisible and soundproof glass wall.

Theodore took his stance, blinded by rage. Without any thought, he shot a stream of his wrath at Bianca. The force punched her hard in the gut, knocking her to her knees. Her grip on Adelaide released.

Bianca let out a savage roar, but before she could strike back, Theodore hit her with another round of power. On her hands and knees, she screamed in frustration.

"This isn't possible."

"I have enough anger in me to destroy you tonight." He struck her again with another crippling blow.

She looked up at him with an expression of bewilderment and betrayal. Any remnants of their old, false friendship were shredded.

Bianca no longer looked at him like she wanted him in her next life, she looked at him like he was another target on her murder list. Scorned and aware she needed to depart before he finished her off, she broke the enchantment holding Cadence, then used her supernatural speed to grab her sister and disappear.

"How did you do that?" Adelaide said between coughs. She was still trying to get her breath back.

"Don't worry about that right now. Let's get you healed." He helped her up and assisted her to the sofa. "Cadence found me while I was sailing. She kept saying the word 'cross' but never explained what it meant."

"We need to tell the others," Adelaide said in a hoarse whisper.

"Tomorrow. I think I bought us a little time."

Adelaide squinted at him, suspicious of his sudden acquisition of powers.

"You better not be messing with things you don't fully understand."

"Stop, I'm fine. I just saved your life. Don't stress over me."

"This conversation ain't over." She coughed again.

The secret was out. Adelaide would get to the bottom of it now that she saw firsthand what he could do. He got a quilt to cover her with. As he placed it over her, she grabbed his hand.

"Thank you." She squeezed his fingers and stared at him with mortal gravity. "I owe you."

"No, you don't. We are family now." He was overcome with an emotion he never felt before. "This is what family does. We protect each other. We take care of those we love."

Chapter 39

Sunday's afternoon meeting with the Wiccans and Ouijans flew; Theodore and Adelaide had more to report than they did. Poe, Gretchen, Morton, Tabitha, and Rupert had no news despite holding a night-long stake out at the abandoned paint factory because Bianca and Cadence were busy roaming and causing drama at the McClaine household.

Adelaide woke up with a headache but was otherwise unscathed. For a lady in her late 60s, she was quite resilient. Upon finishing the meeting, Cynthia Monette fixed her a special Ouijan concoction to soothe her head.

Nobody knew what Cadence meant by the word *cross*, or why she kept repeating it, but they all agreed it was a warning. The spy team was going to look into it.

Everyone was about to disperse from the meeting when a series of loud bangs came from the front door.

"Open the door," a girl's voice screeched. "It's an emergency!"

Theodore's eyes grew big as Caspian rose to address their visitor.

"Hey," he shouted after opening the door, "what do you think you're doing? I didn't invite you in!"

Ruby burst into the grand hall, out of breath.

"Why aren't you at your aunt's?" Theodore asked, instantly fearful that his friend was back in harm's way.

"They are coming!"

"What does that mean?" Percival was frustrated.

"I was at the Linville house, at the end of Cirripedia Pier, and we saw them. Rowan and I. They are a wall hovering over the ocean."

"Who?" Alastair Durant asked with concern.

"Bianca's army."

"How many?" Rupert was ready to fight.

"Too many to count. Like I said, they cover the whole horizon."

"Leave now, girl. Start warning the locals. Direct them inland," Percival instructed Ruby. "Everyone else, prepare to line Nether Isle's borders. We need to create a shield."

Ruby exited, but Theodore chased her down.

"Ruby, wait!"

"What?" she turned around with a huff.

"I'm sorry."

"For?"

"Being so distant and pushing you away. I just had a feeling things were going to get worse and I wouldn't have been able to forgive myself if you got hurt because of me."

"We were dealing with this together just fine until you suddenly decided I was safer without you around. That's not what *I* wanted. Despite your magnetism for trouble, I actually feel *safer* with you nearby. With you, at least I'm not alone."

"You're never alone. You have a loving family and friends."

"You and I are the only main targets in this debacle. You're the only one who really gets the fear I'm feeling. And though we don't talk about it, your presence calms me. You're strong and you don't show how scared you are, even though I know you're petrified. You abandoning me does me no good. I want to be by your side. I want to feel safe."

"I'm sorry. I didn't know you felt that way."

"Now you do. So stop pushing me away." She let out a frustrated breath, then threw her arms around him in a tight hug. When she let go, she was smiling again. "I'll see you later." And she continued running out the door on her mission to get the townspeople to safer ground.

"Sure am glad *that's* resolved," Poe said sarcastically. He was leaning against the railing of the staircase, snooping in on their moment. Nothing was private around here.

"Mind your own business."

Poe cackled as he departed. Gretchen rounded the corner.

"I'm really proud of you. You saved Adelaide's life."

"Thanks again for giving me this gift."

"Sure thing. Seems you're ready just in time. We've got our first battle approaching."

"Any tips?"

"Nope. Just stay with me and do what feels right. The shielding spell will come naturally. You'll feed off my energy."

"So this is how ya did it?" Adelaide entered the hall from the kitchen. She was looking much brighter after drinking Cynthia's remedy.

"Don't be mad. I needed to be able to defend myself and protect others."

"What're the side effects?" Adelaide barked at Gretchen. "He gonna turn dark? Will he get all weird like the lot of you? Get a taste for death?"

Gretchen kept her composure. "I understand your protective nature over him, but I promise, I've done nothing to harm him or cause permanent damage. I only gave him the ability to protect himself in dire situations. He's the same person he was before the transfer."

"Yeah, but in the long run, this is gonna shift his personality, won't it?"

"No, he will always be exactly who he wants to be."

"I'll be the judge of that."

"You didn't notice anything off with me before you knew," Theodore chimed in.

"I sure did! Had no clue what it was, but I reckoned something was different."

"Oh, stop. I wasn't any different than I was on other occasions when I was dealing with heavy stuff."

"Can you undo it? After all this is over?" Adelaide spoke to Gretchen again.

"No. It's permanent."

"Did you know this before you agreed to let her warp your soul?" The volume of Adelaide's voice rose as she spoke to Theodore.

"I did."

"You're both fools." Adelaide stormed out the front door, fuming.

"One relationship mended, another on the fritz."

"She doesn't care for you any less because of this. In fact, she's only this mad because she loves you."

"I just don't like having the people that matter most mad with me when unpredictable tragedy is lurking overhead."

"She'll get over it," Gretchen said, "sooner than you'd think. Once she sees it has no world-shattering effect on who you are as a person, she'll stop being close-minded. Just give it time."

"Is everyone ready?" Percival called out to the herd of Ouijans and Wiccans gathered by the front door.

As a collective force, they marched down Salamander Pier. Intimidating in nature and ready to take on the darkest of evils.

Chapter 40

Rowan and Reggie ran down Peddler's Way, knocking on every door and warning all inhabitants to vacate onto the mainland. Their younger brothers, Ryder and Reese, went up and down the many piers, doing the same thing. Ruby stood at Terre Bridge, instructing people where to go and answering as many questions as she could. For the most part people weren't scared, they were annoyed. The disgruntled town folk bitched and complained as they were directed away from their homes and into town against their will.

"Goddamn ghosts, running this place like they have any right," Oscar Dregg complained, stopping to talk to Ruby. "Good thing I got my deli. I dunno where you think all these people are gonna go. Streets are gonna be littered. The wealthier inlanders ain't going to be happy bout this."

"They'll just have to deal with it for a bit. You saw what was coming, they'll understand."

The burly butcher shivered remembering the ghoulish sight along the horizon. The threat was real and foreboding. He continued on his way.

"Everyone, out," Rowan shouted as he ran along the main strip.

"Unless you wanna die," Reggie added. They rang bells and blew cylinder whistles.

Ryder and Reese met up with their older brothers and tagged along.

"You get everyone on the extended piers?"

"No," Ryder grumbled, "they ignored us."

"Some even yelled at us," Reese added.

"Did you tell them to look out at the ocean?" Reggie asked.

"Yup, they didn't seem to care."

Rowan shook his head and led his band of brothers down Tortoise Pier to double-back on the work already done.

As they traveled in a light jog, many people sat on their front porches, unconcerned.

"Get inland," he shouted at the first couple he saw.

"Don't go tellin' us what to do. Already told your brothers to scram."

"Then don't be surprised if ya don't survive the evening."

The man shooed them off with a wave of his hand.

"Buncha punks," he muttered as the brothers continued on.

So many people ignored the warnings that the Linville boys knew no other way to reprimand them than declare them dead. As they ran past the homes, they made tons of noise and pointed at those refusing to heed caution.

"Dead!"

"Donezo."

"Tried ta warn ya!"

"Dumb dog, get to land," Reese hollered at a mangy mutt with matted fur. Instead of obeying orders it couldn't understand, the dog joined the boys in their sprint up and down the piers. He added to their noise with loud barks.

They crossed over a causeway to Cirripedia Pier, ran down the stretch, and did a similar zigzag path through Krill Pier, Periwinkle Pier, and Crickets Pier. Back on Peddler's Way, they went to the opposite side to hit Saddlebag Pier, which had the smartest inhabitants since they were already vacated.

The South and North Market were barren and had no need for their service. Upon reaching Salamander Pier, the boys came to a dead stop. Halfway down the long wooden pier was a herd of odd and menacing looking people. Some they recognized as the Wiccans, the others were less familiar.

"Who are the Wiccans with?" Ryder asked.

"I've seen a few of them before," Rowan answered, "I think it's the Ouijans."

Reggie gulped, "Are they on our side?"

"Must be, they're with the good guys."

"Is that your friend?" Reese asked, recognizing the tall, sandy haired boy in front. Rowan squinted to see better. Upon recognizing him, Rowan's skepticism vanished and he sprinted toward the frightening progression of magical people.

"Theo," he called out, dodging missing planks as he ran toward his buddy. "You got a plan?" He turned and walked next to his friend, merging in with the group.

"We do," he answered, sensing the unease of the Ouijans around him at the appearance of a stranger. "But it's best you and your brothers get to land. I don't want you getting hurt."

"We couldn't get everyone out of their homes. Many wouldn't listen."

"You did the best you could. Can't win with some of these people, too stubborn for their own good."

"You ain't kiddin'." It took a few moments, but Rowan finally sensed the unwelcoming vibes the Ouijans were casting at him. "I'll go. Gotta get my brothers to my dad's office. We will wait it out there."

"See you later, Rowan."

They exchanged waves of farewell before he darted ahead of the group, met up with his brothers, and left for the mainland of the isle.

Morgana exhaled loudly behind him, like she had been holding her breath the entire time Rowan was with them.

"Annoying fellow," Percival commented. Theodore shot him a look of disbelief.

"He didn't do anything to you."

"His energy was chaotic. Swallowed the entire space we're in."

Theodore shook his head and refused to engage in Percival's nasty commentary.

"It's going to rain," Morgana muttered. As soon as the words left her mouth, large droplets fell from the sky.

"It wasn't even cloudy a moment ago," Theodore said, baffled. Black clouds cruised overhead, situating themselves directly above Nether Isle. They swirled with menace, indicating a downpour was on its way.

"We ought not dawdle." Mabel Bissette glided seamlessly to the front of the crowd and skipped ahead of them. Her flowing, yellow sundress cascaded behind her as she strolled to the end of Tortoise Pier. She stood at the edge, facing the wide ocean. The wind increased, blowing her aged white hair in the same fashion as her long dress. It was a sight to remember. Her silhouette was like the sun against the onslaught of untimely night.

Chapter 41

Rupert and Alastair ran toward the group from Terre Bridge, both wildly out of breath. Their massive bodies heaved as they tried to minimize their adrenaline.

"What have you discovered?" Delilah asked, curious to learn the result of their last-minute assignment.

"No signs of the ghosts on any other coastline," Alastair panted.

"They seem to have congregated here only," Rupert added. He wiped the sweat from his brow with the back of his hand. "If we cover half the isle's circumference, we should be able to make the magic connect full circle.

"Two people at the end of each pier; one Ouijan, one Wiccan," Percival instructed. "Everyone else, space yourself out accordingly."

Caspian joined Mabel where she stood, ready to fight. Alastair and Tabitha manned Cirripedia Pier; she flirted with him shamelessly, as if they were in no danger at all. Rupert went with Morgana to Krill Pier, so Morton went with Clementine LeClair to neighboring Periwinkle Pier in order to keep an eye on erratic Morgana. Theodore followed Gretchen and Virgil Bonhomme to Crickets Pier, his old home. They passed his house, which was vacant and unkempt. The weeks of abandonment showed. The front door was open and one of its hinges was broken, leaving the weak, wooden door hanging lopsided.

Once standing at the end of Crickets Pier, Theodore looked to his left and saw the rest of the crew at the edges of their own assigned piers. Percival was with Wilhelmina at the end of Ballantine Dock, so Cynthia, Poe, Delilah, and Leon covered the land, out of sight along the coastline and keeping the magic spread as far as possible. There were other Wiccans and Ouijans who surfaced once the threat of war was real, but Theodore didn't catch any of their names. They were surely on land too, ready to reinforce the shield that was about to go up.

The quick and drastic change in temperature caused a layer of fog to appear. It slithered along the piers and covered the surface of the ocean. The light drizzle was growing heavier at a rapid pace. The thick beads of rain hit Theodore's face with steady progression leaving him momentarily blind. He wiped his face and cupped his hand over his forehead.

"I can't see anything," he yelled through the blustering winds.

Gretchen took her hand and gently swiped it in front of his eyes. Then she did the same to herself and Virgil, who was spitting out the rainwater that filtered from his thick moustache into his mouth.

The short, stout man paused in awe. "What have you done?"

"Just a water repellant charm. Should block the rain for a while."

"Thanks," he said, impressed she was capable of magic so raw. Theodore wondered if Virgil was considering his light magic was now lacking something. The look of wonder he examined Gretchen with implied he did.

Now that their vision was cleared, they could see their enemy trekking through the fog toward them. There were thousands of them. They glided above the water, approaching at a deliberate and meticulous pace. If their slow advance was meant to induce a level of intimidation, it was working. Theodore caught a chill that came from elsewhere, from something much colder than the freezing rain that drenched him.

Percival spoke, but they could not hear him all the way at Crickets Pier. One by one, the message was passed across the way.

"Arms out and begin," Clementine shouted over the roaring waves that separated her from Theodore, Gretchen, and Virgil. They both looked to Gretchen, who stood between them. She grabbed their hands.

"Extend your free hand. Virgil, toward Morton. Theodore, aim yours up so your energy shoots above the cliff wall. Someone will be up there to connect to it."

"What if I can't do it?"

"Are you scared?"

Theodore looked at her like she was crazy, not needing to answer the question because it was written all over his face.

"Then you'll excel."

"What if I do something other than a shield? I still don't know how to control it."

"You're connected to me. Just feel what I'm sending you and replicate it." He looked at her skeptically. "It'll make more sense once we start."

He hoped she was right.

Gretchen tilted her head downward and gazed at the horizon. As she watched the spirits approach, her emerald eyes turned lethal. She spat out the enchantment with venomous conviction.

Nous protéger du mal.

Nous protéger de la mort.

Nous sommes la barrière entre cette vie et la prochaine.

(Shield us from evil.

Shield us from death.

We are the barrier between this life and the next.)

Gretchen repeated the melodic hymn a few times before Virgil caught on and joined. It took Theodore a few more tries to remember the foreign mantra, but he managed a few rounds later. Along the other piers, the duos held hands and chanted the same words. As the momentum built, so did their volume, and by magic, the voices of all were heard and the words were delivered in unison. Upon finishing the first round of the chant in synchronicity, the heads of all who participated were thrown backward. Their chests pulsed with luminosity as a white vapor exited their bodies and rose into the sky. The mist formed a wall between Nether Isle and the ocean. Its top curved and extended overhead, concealing the rest of the isle behind them.

The ghosts still approached, unaware of the barricade put in place; it was invisible on their side. Theodore opened his eyes and watched as the spirits grew closer.

The front line consisted of ghosts he'd never seen before. Some wore traditional Indian saris, others wore old military uniforms, and many were in tattered clothing; some sported yellow stars cut from fabric and others wore the remnants of whiplashes. All were emaciated and covered in bloodstains. It was not hard to determine where these ghosts came from: they were slaves from different time periods, cultures, and religions. Caucasian, African-American, Indian, Latin, Jewish; Theodore could place them all in history. Infuriated further that she enlisted the help of those who deserved peace more than any others, Theodore scanned the herd for the evil enchantress. Bianca hovered at the back of the crowd with two regal looking women on both sides of her. One was a Hindu princess; radiant and draped in colorful garbs, the other was pale and cold with blonde curls wrapped around her crown. She wore a beautiful scowl that was visible from miles away.

Determined to stop her, he focused back on the task. His connection streamed up and over the cliff, where he could feel someone else latched on. This person gripped tight to his energy and though they were far apart, it felt as though they held hands.

Nous protéger du mal.

Nous protéger de la mort.

Nous sommes la barrière entre cette vie et la prochaine.

The shield was strong. It coursed with high voltage magic, and with a close enough eye, the mist was visibly electric. The wall was alive and ready to defend against the death approaching it.

The first row of ghosts were upon them, only a few feet from the barricade. Heads tilted upward with jaws agape, Percival spoke and his words echoed through all their mouths.

"Come closer. I dare you."

The closest ghosts rustled with hesitation, eager and unsure all at once. Many glanced back toward the three females seemingly in charge.

"Go on. Matilda, Ratnavati, and I will protect you from here," Bianca commanded, coaxing her ghost army forward with a minimal arm movement. The breeze she crafted pushed her minions closer, propelling a few of the furthest right into the wall. Their dead spirits sizzled, catching fire that only existed in their realm.

Screams of pain echoed through the night sky, louder than the thunderstorm that roared around them. Frantic, the ghosts went into a tizzy. Some touched those nearby, setting them aflame also. Others dove into the ocean, hoping to put out flames that did not exist in the living world. No matter how many times they submerged themselves into the icy water, they always reemerged on fire.

Cries for help were shrieked in numerous languages, filling the atmosphere with desperation.

"Will they die a second time?" Theodore whispered. Gretchen took a momentary break from the chant to answer him, still holding her section of the shield strong.

"No. If they remain here, they will burn for eternity. Nothing on earth can put out flames in the nether."

Terror filled Theodore's heart. "But surely they don't deserve that. Many look like they suffered enough during their living lives."

"They brought the fight to us, not the other way around." She could sense her friend's deep concern. "Be patient." Their heads tilted back and mouths opened as Percival's voice boomed through them.

"The only way to stop the pain is to enter the light. Find peace and the blaze will cease."

Sobs resonated from the masses on fire. Their cries were filled with centuries of pain. A few darted for Apres Monde without a second thought while others were deafened by the horrific inferno that engulfed them.

"Stop," Bianca cried at the few who fled. Her expression became intense as she tried to think of a spell to douse the fire. She was unraveling and the pressure created cracks in her phantom appearance.

"Bujhānā," Princess Ratnavati suggested in a serene whisper. "Try that. It means extinguish."

Bianca spoke the word while simultaneously channeling the mystic energies of ancient Hinduism she absorbed through intense study.

Bujhānā.

Bujhānā.

Bujhānā.

The third time she said it, the word carried weight. The flames were smothered and the burning ghosts were granted relief. Another reason to stay loyal to their newly adopted leader, Bianca.

They retreated behind Bianca and her leading henchwomen, hiding behind their protection.

"What have you done here?" Bianca shrieked as she glided closer, but not too close. She could not determine where the cursed wall began.

"We've shielded you from this place. You are no longer welcome here."

A guttural scream escaped her. She began throwing orbs of magic at the wall, which all shattered unsuccessfully upon impact. When her final blast bounced back and catapulted an unsuspecting member of her army into the light, she finally stopped.

"You can't keep me out forever," she seethed, "I always find a way."

She then zoomed to hover in front of the wall where Theodore stood. She pointed at him and spoke, her voice soft beneath a sinister smile.

"You're mine."

Chapter 42

Nous protéger du mal.

Nous protéger de la mort.

Nous sommes la barrière entre cette vie et la prochaine.

At the end of the third repetition of the shield chant, Percival added a new line:

Pour vingt-quatre heures, c'est supporter.

(For twenty-four hours, this shall endure.)

He clenched his fingers into fists, crushing the connection binding the group together. He could no longer speak through them, but as he left his pier, so did everyone else. They met again in front of Adelaide's house near Ballantine Dock.

"The shield will last twenty-four hours. We need to come back here every night before sundown in order to regenerate it." Percival wore purple circles beneath his eyes.

"In the meantime, we must restrategize and find a way to be rid of that demon once and for all," Delilah said.

"Afternoons will be dedicated to brainstorming and idea implementation," Cynthia added. "Until we solve this predicament, this is our new day-to-day routine."

Everyone mumbled in agreement.

"The town is on lock-down until then," Caspian added. "No one is allowed to leave. If anyone exits the shield from the inside, it will break. Delilah and I will inform the townsfolk of this."

"They aren't going to be happy," Morgana muttered to herself.

"That's too bad," Rupert said. "If they revolt, Mabel will calm them down. Many are customers of hers. They trust her."

"We will meet again tomorrow at 9 a.m. sharp. Ouijan home, as per usual," Percival instructed, then marched off without another word.

Everyone followed suit. The Ouijans trailed behind him on Salamander Pier while the Wiccans scattered in different directions toward their separate dwellings. Theodore grabbed Gretchen's arm and pulled her to the side before she departed.

"We need to use the pellucid stone on Ruby."

Gretchen's expression shifted uncomfortably. "That's tricky."

"Why?"

"Well, I can't use it again. I already gave you half of myself. It would be a few years before I could use it again on someone else."

"I thought you said it was a copy and paste? That you didn't actually lose any of your own powers."

"I didn't, but it still drained me. If I used it again so soon, I *could* lose my magic. The more you expose and share yourself, the more faded you become. Too much exposure would turn me into a shadow, a mere wisp of my former self."

"Then we cannot use you as the base."

"I hope you aren't thinking what I think you are."

"Would no one else volunteer?"

"Absolutely not. I don't even want them to know I used the stone on *you*. If I asked one of them to act as tribute for a second outsider, after finding out I already used it on you, they'd freak out. Quite possibly disown me."

"Even though they'd be saving an innocent life?"

"To be perfectly honest, I'm not even sure what Bianca's intentions are anymore. She looked quite cozy in her new position of power. If she left the realm of the dead, all of that goes away."

"So you don't think she wants Ruby's body anymore?"

"Not sure. Maybe, eventually. Seems like right now, she's after you."

Theodore slouched from the weight of Bianca's distant wrath. "What do you think she wants with me now?"

"I'd put good money on the fact that her intentions have shifted from a friendly obsession to complete and utter hatred."

"Yeah," Theodore sighed, "I would, too."

"I have a feeling Ruby has slipped off her radar for the time being. Learning that you developed powers, then used them against her, was enough to blind and redirect her afterlife tunnel-vision."

"Better me than her," Theodore shrugged, surprisingly relieved to have Bianca's evil plans transferred to him. It put the burden of protecting Ruby on the backburner.

"Plus, like I said, she's looking high and mighty with her army of minions beneath her. I wouldn't be surprised if after she's quenched her vengeance with you, she planned to act as queen in her weird little afterlife kingdom. It would be completely delusional on her part, but if she has the followers she could certainly play make-believe for a while."

"She'll never get that far. I won't let her beat me. She'll be gone before she gets the chance to reign over any fake empire."

"I like where your head's at." She squeezed his shoulder. "You did a great job today." Her emerald eyes glowed with kindness.

"Thanks. I think I'm starting to get the hang of it."

"You'll be a pro in no time." With a parting smile, Gretchen left to follow her people back home.

Theodore raced into town to find Caspian and Delilah addressing the masses. They stood on the balcony of the courthouse and spoke down to the riled crowd. It looked as though most of the arguing was done, though many still looked dissident.

"We will be back to let you know when the issue is resolved."

They went back into the building then exited out the front door. As they walked back toward Terre Bridge they received many nasty glares.

"They are a lot angrier than I thought they'd be," Theodore panted as he ran to catch up with them before they left the mainland.

"Yeah, well, people don't like being told they aren't allowed in their own homes. We banned them from the piers until we fix this ghost issue."

"Where will they all stay?" he asked.

"With friends, family," Caspian answered. "If the town officials and hotel owners have any decency, they'll abolish room rates until things go back to normal."

"What about all the people who refused to leave and are still in their houses on the piers?"

"We just needed the majority out," Caspian explained, "but if those stragglers become a problem, we have ways of making them think it's their choice to vacate."

Theodore wondered what spell would induce that reaction, but chose not to ask.

"Adelaide is with Ruby and her mom. Over by Marcy's Pet Shoppe." Delilah pointed, then left with Caspian.

Ruby was holding Uno in her arms as Theodore approached. The cat hissed at him upon arrival.

"How could you?" Ruby demanded, face red with frustration.

"What?" He was caught off guard, unsure why he was being scolded.

"The dark magic! Adelaide told us everything."

He shot his old friend an annoyed look, which was returned by a defiant one.

"It's for my protection, and each of yours. I don't understand why you're both so angry about it. Adelaide would be dead right now without it."

"While I appreciate you savin' my life, I'd have never let you do it if I knew the cost was your soul. I'd rather die than see you harmed."

"I'm fine—" Theodore began to argue but Ruby cut him off.

"No, you're not! You'll never be the same again."

"You're acting crazy."

"Don't call me crazy! You let darkness enter your soul. It will ruin you."

"You both are blinded by your prejudices toward the Ouijans." Theodore was growing impatient. "I'll be just fine. I'm not going to change for the worse. You both need to stop with the negativity. I trust Gretchen. Not a bone in my body tells me I made the wrong choice."

"Yeah, well, we all know how reliable your gut-instincts are," Ruby hissed with cruel sarcasm. "It *is* what landed us in this mess in the first place. Your fantastic intuition about people has almost gotten us all killed."

"Low blow. Thanks, *friend*. Maybe I'm wrong about you, too," Theodore spat back. "You'll all feel like fools when this gift of magic saves your lives." He paused, then looked at Adelaide, alive and well thanks to him. "Or maybe you won't."

Overwhelming defeat crushed his heart. He saved her life and this one choice, one she viewed as a mistake, was deemed unforgivable, no matter how noble his intentions were or if he used the gift for valiant deeds. They were not family. They did not have an unbreakable bond, and for the first time, it was devastatingly apparent. She could choose to never forgive him, mark him as tainted, see all they've built as ruined, and her life would be none the worse for it.

Conquered by his greatest fear, Theodore's magic brimmed to the surface. An icy wind filtered around them, freezing the rain and producing hail. The wet fur on Uno's body froze instantly, as did the hair on everyone's heads. Ruby screamed as her wild, wet curls of dirty blonde hair turned into spiraled icicles. Realizing he was the cause of this horrific phenomenon, he ran, carrying his ice storm with him. Once a safe distance, he turned around to see them shivering, but no longer icing over. Just wet and scared. Adelaide hurriedly brushed the slushed ice off Dorothea's shoulders, but Ruby remained motionless. Frozen in place as the ice melted off her. She watched him run from them, away from her, leaving her alone again. She didn't understand.

His sadness left a trail of ice as he fled. As fast as he could, he tried to escape the rejection cast upon him by those he risked himself to protect. Another giant let down; his greatest fear come to life. He wished to disappear, but the steady flow of hail and snow reminded him he couldn't. No matter how far he ran, he could never outrun what lived inside him.

Chapter 43

He didn't know where to go. He couldn't face Adelaide, not like this. Not while encased in a self-brewed snowstorm. The air around him was frigid, but he remained warm with emotion. The intensity of this new sorrow boiled his blood, leaving him in a cold sweat. Was he overreacting? Were his fears coming true? He wanted to escape, wanted to start over someplace new, but he couldn't. He needed to stop running away. Doing so was pointless; he could not outrun the fear, he could only learn to conquer it. He needed to be strong and face this situation head on. No hiding, no crumbling beneath the pressure. It was time to take charge, regardless who still stood by his side when it all came to pass. Alone or not, he had to be confident in every choice he made. He had to live with the repercussions and own it, for better or worse.

He did not regret the choice to trust Gretchen or accept her magic, *they* did. That was something they needed to deal with, not him. He was fine. In fact, when he pushed his grief aside and really thought about it, he felt better than ever. This new strength not only gave him protection, but also clarity. Everything made more sense; he no longer felt like he was drowning in questions or confusion. Even the bad stuff was more easily digested. Perhaps his reactions were more extreme, but instead of wallowing for days, he bounced back in mere hours. The balance of dark and light *was* wisdom. It allowed his heart to break down complex situations with eloquent precision. Until now, he never realized how often he struggled beneath the simplest of matters. He wouldn't trade this new-found peace for the world.

Of course he wished his friends saw the good in this gift, that they could recognize how it was affecting him in a positive light, but he could not force them to open their minds. He could only hope with time, they learned to understand.

He chose to stay at his old home on Cricket Pier. It was abandoned and there was no need to fear his father or Bianca making an appearance since they were trapped outside the shield.

The enchanted markings were still etched into the first floorboard beyond the threshold. With a bit of work, Theodore managed to loosen the board and rip it from the ground. He walked back outside, broke the slab of wood over his knee and threw its pieces over the edge of the pier. They hit the jagged rocks and disappeared into the violent water.

He went back into his home and began cleaning. Anything to keep busy. The house was a wreck from abandonment and neglect. Water stains lined the floors where windows were left open, spider webs covered every corner, and mold was beginning to grow along the walls from the damp air. After cleaning the brunt of the mess, he got his father's toolbox out of the attic and began fixing the hinge on the front door. It needed a new piece, but with some finagling, he was able to get the door to close without coming undone and cracking open.

With no heat in the house, he took all the blankets he could find and layered them on top of his bed. Beneath them, his body heat filled the space, keeping him snug as he slept.

He was awoken by loud knocks on the front door. When he rolled to look at the clock it read 5 a.m. Far too early to be bothered, so he ducked beneath his covers once more. A few more bangs followed his lack of response. As he continued to ignore it, the knocks became fiercer, eventually breaking the hinge he spent the majority of the night fixing. Through the broken door, the visitor pushed their way into the home.

"Are you kidding me?" Adelaide's frustrated voice rang through the house. She barged into Theodore's bedroom to find him buried beneath a mountain of blankets. "You had me worried sick. Spent the whole night lookin' for ya."

"You seemed pretty done with me. Didn't think I needed to check in with you anymore."

"Stop your nonsense, boy. Just cause I'm mad at ya doesn't mean I'm *done* with ya. I already told you we are family now. Thanks a lot for thinking I quit so easily."

"I don't know how these things work."

"Clearly." She sat on the end of his bed. "I'm gonna get furious with you, as you will with me. It happens. We're human. But at the end of the day, when you care for someone, your anger never wins. That's the difference between family and everybody else. The love you feel always triumphs, even if it takes some time."

"I'm mad at you, too."

"Alright, what for?"

"For making me feel like I messed up so bad I couldn't be forgiven. And for being too damn stubborn to see the good this darkness has given me."

"What kind of good?"

"It's hard to describe, but instead of carrying the heavy stuff like it's a load, I now see it as temporary obstacles. Fluffy stuff I can get through. Things I will learn and grow from. I just get it now."

"Sounds like you're maturing."

"It's the balance of dark and light. I would've gotten here one day, with all I've been through, this just sped it up."

"Okay. So I'm not just changing my mind about this magic nonsense or the fact that I think it's absurd you let a stranger infect you with death, but I'm letting it go. What's dumber than what you did is me holding a grudge over it. It's over, it's permanent, now we move forward and deal with whatever comes next."

"It's all going to turn out good. I can sense it."

"I hope you're right. I'm just not as certain."

"Is Ruby still mad at me?"

"Your little icescapade scared her proper. Sent her into a tizzy, like we lost you to the Devil forever. But she'll come around. She doesn't want to lose you."

"The whole ice storm was an accident. When I'm pushed to extreme fear, sorrow, or anger, I can't control what happens."

"You were pretty angry last night."

"I wasn't angry, I was sad."

A look of remorse crossed Adelaide's face. "Sorry 'bout that. Never meant to make you feel that way. I know you did all this with good intentions. I just can't believe you put your life on the line to save an old bag like me."

"You're family," he reminded her. "Looks like you don't really get how it works either."

"Don't use that against me. You know damn well how I prioritize me versus those I care about."

"I do. But that's you. I have my own ways."

"You're turning more like me every day, ya stubborn ass." She tussled the top of his hair before standing up and shivering. "Let's go. This house feels like it's still caught up in your ice storm. I'll get my fireplace going. Come on."

He followed her, still in clothes from the day before which stunk of dried sweat. All his clothes were at her house, so he changed as soon as they got there. She started a fire, cooked up breakfast, and they relaxed in peaceful quiet until 8:30 a.m.

They headed to Salamander Pier for the 9 a.m. meeting. No one had any useful suggestions on how to get rid of Bianca for good. With the shield up, they'd need to wait for her to approach again. If anyone from inside exited, the barrier would be broken. The one good thing about the shield being in place was that they could now fight Bianca when she returned instead of having to put forth all their power into the creation of the wall. Now it was a waiting game. A few Wiccans were assigned to bridge and border patrol. They could not risk a local exiting the shield via boat and disabling it.

Morton was assigned to Cadence again, in case she was still inside the shield, separated from her sister, and able to help them brainstorm Bianca's weaknesses. The last Theodore saw of her was the morning he saved Adelaide from Bianca's wrath. Bianca dragged her little sister along with her as she left, but there was no guarantee where she took her. They hoped she locked her back up in that warehouse before assembling her ghost army elsewhere.

After the last attack, the group deduced that Cadence's warning meant Cross Island, a National Wildlife Refuge. It was an island off the coast of Maine that was inhabited by wildlife and only checked on occasionally by park rangers. It was a perfect spot; they were invisible there and had an entire island at their disposal.

No one knew what the ghosts were planning, but they were all ready to fight. Theodore was becoming antsy, wanting to defend his new home and defeat the girl that caused him so much trouble. He wanted to help banish her for good. He wanted to end the suffering she caused them all.

After the meeting, Theodore walked over to Ruby's house. Dorothea answered the door and greeted him half-heartedly. She was typically a quiet woman, but never cold. Today she felt frigid, like she still hadn't defrosted from the previous night's ice storm. Theodore felt bad, but had to assume her mood was a reflection of her daughter's.

"Ruby," Dorothea called upstairs, "Theo is here to see you." She turned to him, "Would you like some tea?"

"No, thank you."

"She'll be down in a moment." Dorothea exited the small hallway and went to the kitchen. Theodore waited a few moments before Ruby appeared at the top of the stairs. Uno stood by her side, rubbing his body against her ankles and never breaking his gaze on Theodore. The cat's yellow eyes gleamed with suspicion as it weaved in and out through her legs. Ruby peered down at him, too.

"Are you really mad at me over this? I did it for you."

"I'm not mad. I'm scared," she explained. "I've lived here longer than you. I've seen people turn dark."

"I'm not going to turn any darker than I would have naturally. I've been through a lot of crap, so I never would have turned out normal. This gift isn't going to make me any worse off than I would have been without it."

"It might enhance the pain."

"So far it's only clarified it. I can finally digest and swallow the years of pain. The dark counterbalances my naiveté; I can finally understand it all and let it go."

Ruby was skeptical. It showed on her face. She walked down the stairs, stopping on a step that allowed her to be eye level with Theodore.

"Come closer," she said. He did so and she grabbed his face. His heart jumped and he found his mind wandering to desires he always hoped for. Ruby's beautiful eyes gazed into his and her lips were inches away. He willed her to kiss him.

As he waited for the moment to happen, she took two fingers and stretched his eyelid open.

"Look up," she commanded. Startled, he did so, all while trying to slow the pace of his heart. The crushing disappointment helped speed this up.

"What are you doing?"

"Trying to see the darkness."

"It's not hidden in my eyes."

"For some people it is. My aunt was batshit crazy. Her irises turned jet black over time." She moved onto his other eye. "She lives in a nut house now."

"Any signs of it in there?" Theodore asked, aware the answer was no.

"Not yet." She leaned back with a watchful eye, like she planned to examine him every day. All he could think was how he wanted her to examine him in non-motherly ways.

He sighed, resigning to the fact that timing, and circumstance, wasn't on his side right now.

"So are we cool again?"

"We always were. I just needed a minute to be mad at you."

"I knew you were mad!"

"That was yesterday. Today, I was scared."

"Sure," Theodore smirked.

"Don't test me. I can be furious with you all over again if you like."

"Nah, I'm good." He put an arm around her shoulder. "I prefer us when you like me." He guided her toward the door.

"Where are we going?"

"Out on my boat, if you're up for it."

Her eyes lit up as she nodded.

"Great. A decent portion of the bay is within the confines of the shield. We can sail there."

They headed out. This new day was a stark contrast from the previous. Sunshine filtered onto Nether Isle, erasing its shadows. The light was nourishing to the mind and body. Theodore soaked it in as they walked, all while trying to forget about the gloom that lurked in the outskirts, waiting for a chance to strike again.

Chapter 44

The old paint factory smelt of mildew and expired chemicals as they searched for Cadence. Morton led Poe and Rupert through the expansive warehouse, looking for the door to the basement. It was proving quite difficult to find.

"This place reeks," Rupert said with his hand over his mouth and nose. Poe breathed in deeply, then exhaled slowly.

"Tastes like poison."

Rupert shot him a disgusted look before hurrying to walk closer to Morton.

"It has to be here somewhere," Morton mumbled. "Though ghosts can pass through walls, the humans that used to work here couldn't. There must be a door."

They scoured the large space, lifting up overturned tables, pushing aside mountains of old paint cans, hoping to find a door somewhere. After an exhaustive search, Rupert called to the others from his side of the warehouse.

"I think I've found it." His words were muffled as he kept his mouth covered and protected from the chemicals floating around. Morton and Poe made their way to him and saw the hole he uncovered. Beneath a stack of cardboard boxes was a wooden door in the floor. When lifted, it revealed a staircase.

"Looks right," Morton concluded, "let's go."

The three men made their way down the steps. There was no light, so Poe manifested fire in his palm to illuminate the way. Once they reached the bottom, Morton did the same. Rupert could not perform such magic as Wiccans only practiced in energy and vibes. They did not create tangible magic. To do so required a certain level of darkness, even when the intent was perfectly innocent.

"She's in the corner over there," Poe whispered and pointed to the far left crevice of the room, which was blanketed in shadow. "I can smell her."

Rupert squinted, but still could not see her. Morton walked closer to see if Poe was right. As he reached the spot, there sat Cadence, curled up in a ball and shaking with violent shivers. A thick line of white chalk encircled her, keeping her trapped in place. Morton knelt down and attempted to brush the enchanted dust away with his free hand, but the moment he made contact, it zapped him with a pinch of electricity. He cursed beneath his breath and stood up.

"Its powers reside on both sides of the line." He clenched his fist and put out the fire in his hand. The room turned a darker shade of black. "I need to break the curse."

Dissoudre et la libérez.

(Dissolve and free her.)

Dissoudre et la libérez.

Morton repeated the spell multiple times. His deep and thick accent intensified the more he said it. On the tenth repetition, the chalk line blasted apart, separating like two magnets of equal polarity. Cadence inhaled with drama, as if she'd been submerged beneath water for hours. She did not need air, but the curse she remained locked in drowned her in its own unique way.

She stood up shell-shocked, eyes wide and darting around. Adrenaline drove her actions and the desperation behind her eyes was worrying.

"Calm down," Morton said in the kindest voice he was capable of, "we are here to help you." He extended a hand and took a step toward her, but Cadence screeched. The noise was disturbing. It did not sound human.

"Don't touch me," she spat, panic-stricken and full of despair.

"We want to help you," he repeated, taking a step backward this time.

"You're lying. You want to use me. It's all so selfish. This world, humans, and all their desires. The lot of you, acting like you care a smidgen for me." Her body shook with fear and fury. "All I've ever wanted was peace. I just want to die forever. No more of this half-life torture. I never dreamed I'd suffer such misery in death."

"We will help you obtain the peace you crave."

"At what cost?" she hissed back. Her eyes narrowed in on him.

"There is always a price. You want me to help you stop my sister?"

Her nostrils flared and eyes filled with vapor tears as she waited for the inevitable answer.

"We would be forever grateful if you could."

The mist rolled from her eyes and floated away from her. "No, I'm done with her. I'm done with all her evilness. I tried to warn Theodore, I tried to help. There's nothing more I can do."

"You're our only leverage. You're the only one left she cares about."

"She doesn't care about me!" Cadence was losing it. Her voice rang with hysteria. "She is forcing her selfish desires upon me. She is using me as a means to justify her evilness, pretending she acts how she does for both of us. If she loved me, if she cared, she'd let me go. She'd let me have the ending *I* desire."

"I understand that, but it still holds true that you are part of her end goal. She will protect you in order to keep you with her."

"I don't want to be part of this anymore!" Her hysteria settled as she paused. "*I am done.*" Her last words came out as a revelation she only just realized. Confident and sure, her entire demeanor relaxed. With final certainty, she broke free and sped past the men who begged her to join their cause. She raced through them and out the basement door, leaving them shocked, alone, and rejected in their quest.

This was her death, it belonged to her, and now that she took back control, the final ending was hers to write.

Chapter 45

Cadence soared through town. Blurred, she made it to the edge of the piers in no time. Pausing for a moment to look at Apres Monde from the end of Ballantine Dock, she noticed the faint wall in front of her. Following its border, she saw it encased the entire isle. She did not know its purpose, nor did she care to speculate. Ideas floated to the back of her mind but all she cared about now was making it to Apres Monde. Without a second thought, she continued her trek onward, passing through the benign side of the shield. It disintegrated behind her, falling like shattered glass into the ocean as her departure broke the spell, but she did not notice. She had one destination in mind and nothing else mattered.

The ocean mist mixed into that of her pixilated state. Its coolness entered the depths of her being, passing through her like they were one in the same. Soon, she would be no more. Soon, she would be one with the earth. Meshed into nature, just as she wished to be. At least she hoped so. No one knew what lay on the other side of the light, but Cadence believed it was Mother Earth, welcoming them home. That where they originated from, they returned to, and the souls of the dead acted as a nutrient for the planet, helping it live on as long as it has. That this was the human race's way of giving back to the place that allowed them life in this world. And in this state, true peace and connection to the universe was found.

She raced on, smiling with joy at finally finding the courage to enter the light alone. In her heart, she always knew it would end this way, but the hope that her sister might revert back to her old self constantly held her back. Now that it was clear Bianca would never be saved, she was able to let her go for good. She could leave her behind without feeling guilt.

The lighthouse was a few miles away. Cadence could feel its energy pulling her in faster. She let it take her. The light grew stronger as she grew nearer and the sensation was intoxicating. It further validated this was the right choice. A few feet from the final exodus, a vehement force yanked her back. It dragged her away from the light and out of its serene grip.

Cadence cried out, trying but failing to fight the strength of whatever stopped her forward progress. She was ripped from the light in mere moments, facing the source that thwarted her.

"You were going to leave me behind?" Bianca asked, appalled. "How could you do this to me?"

"With ease," Cadence replied. The peace she felt was stripped away with haste. All that remained was hate.

Bianca's wrath crushed Cadence. With an easy swipe, she knocked her little sister into the ocean below and held her underwater as punishment. It would not kill her, but the feeling was uncomfortable, even for the dead. Though she wasn't choking, being forced into an unpleasant place against her will infuriated her further. She struggled beneath Bianca's force, seeing the light of the sky but remaining trapped in the shade of the dark ocean.

After a few minutes, she pulled her sister up from the depths of the sea.

"Don't you ever disobey me again," she screamed with madness. "Until you have a living body, I make all decisions for you. You're too dumb in death to be trusted. For now, I own you."

"Let me go." Cadence fought back. "You say my mind is fogged over by death, but you're wrong. I've never seen more clearly, in life or death. The only one with skewed vision is you. You're blind with rage. Blind by power. It's turned you into a monster."

Bianca shoved her sister beneath the water once more. From afar, she held her down, forcing her to suffer further under her watch. Her means of providing protection were cruel and she could no longer see the damage she inflicted.

Upon resurfacing, Cadence was fueled by anger. Her strength was no match for her sister's magic but she planned to stand against her anyhow. There was nothing worse she could do to her; the brunt of the damage was already committed. She lost her sister years ago, she'd grown used to being trapped for weeks in dark corners, and she could not be killed a second time. Bianca's best form of punishment was banishing spirits into the light, which was exactly what Cadence wanted. Nothing fazed her anymore. She could not be beaten for she had nothing left to lose.

"You need to stop," Cadence sputtered, shaken from the coldness of the sea. "You need to let me go."

"Never," Bianca roared. She tried to tighten her grip, but Cadence broke free. She swiped her arm again, but her little sister dodged her magic.

"I'm done with you," Cadence sobbed, her body shaking as she spoke. "If the day ever comes and you decide to enter the light, don't try to find me on the other side. I have no space left for you in my heart."

Cadence turned her back on Bianca and flew back into the light. This time, Bianca let her go. Dazed by the hurt such simple words caused, she missed her opportunity to seize Cadence and drag her back.

As the final portal approached, she could hear Bianca cry out in horror. A mixture of fury and heartbreak lined her voice as Cadence became too far to reach. With confidence, Cadence entered the light, happily leaving her sister behind forever.

Chapter 46

Engulfed in a range of intense emotions, Bianca soared to the piers of Nether Isle. From afar, she could see the Ouijans and Wiccans scrambling. Though the shield was invisible from her side of it, she assumed it was down. Their frantic behavior gave their momentary weakness away. Without further delay, she used this as a distraction from Cadence's heart-wrenching departure. Her intensity was refocused on the war she planned to wage. No longer wanting Ruby's body, she just wanted to rule the realm of the dead. To do so, they needed land, and Nether Isle was essential to obtain. It was the only place they held any leverage against the living world. It was the only place they could visibly exist.

Bianca was out for blood. She wanted them all dead. With her new motives clear, she headed back to Cross Island to inform her followers the opportunity to strike was now.

The lot of ghosts were scattered along the north coast of Cross Island. Though they were spread out, they never wandered far from one another. They stayed rather confined, considering they had an entire island at their disposal. There was comfort in pursuing the unknown together, and despite being complete strangers, these spirits clung to each other during these unpredictable times.

"Gather everyone on the shore," Bianca instructed Ming Fai of Tat Tak School in Hong Kong. The lady in red bowed her head and did as commanded. She was one of Bianca's co-leaders. After the recruit was complete, she chose the five strongest-willed females to act as deputies. Princess Matilda von Wittlesbach of Germany, Princess Ratnavati of India, Camila Fuentes of Chile, Ming Fai of Hong Kong, and Irene Saunders of the United States. Irene was a last minute addition. When she arrived, she explained she was only observing, that she was curious to see what they were doing. With extensive coaxing and the eventual accepted friendship of Lt. General Joseph Wheeler, she finally accepted the fact that she was dead. Bianca did not want her in a position of power but after seeing how quickly she adapted and thrived as a ghost, she changed her mind. Irene was ruthless. Years of chosen ignorance proved to be a great motivator for wrath: she was mad at her children, mad at herself, mad at the world. With these women by her side, Bianca had a very desirable empire ready to take shape.

Ming directed the crowd onto the beach. Bianca hovered above so she could address them all at once.

"As I look down at all of you, I see many different types of people from many different walks of life, and although we may not come from the same places, we are family now. We are a community with similar needs and desires. We have found one another and vowed to unite as a society. With devout loyalty, we will prevail and find great happiness in the afterlife. We will make a home here, one we can all flourish in."

"Here, on Cross Island?" Henry Washington asked.

"No. On Nether Isle. It is there we can exist in plain sight and act as a force to be reckoned with against the living. There, we can thrive. The fact that we materialize there is a clear indicator that we belong there. It is our home, not theirs. It was made for us, not them. They stole it from spirits similar to us years ago and it's time we took it back. In honor of the spirits they cast away and in defense of what is rightfully ours."

The Japanese soldiers from Chibichiri Cave in Okinawa began slapping the sides of their thighs. The rhythmic beating grew as others joined in. Those who came from the Ram Inn let out eerie hollers, echoing their support for the cause into the damp air. The ghosts of the German concentration camps nodded their heads to the beat, eyes remaining blank as the intent of the mission sunk in. The former slaves and soldiers from Alabama began a chant of inaudible words to coincide with the Japanese beat. The Indian citizens of Bhangarh Fort shook their arms and legs, causing the bangles they wore to jingle loudly. The spirits were riled up and ready to fight.

Bianca waved her arms and cast a spell over her ghost army, granting them temporary ability to touch the living.

"The shield is down. We attack now. You know who to leave for me," she instructed as the ghosts absorbed her magic and examined their own extremities in awe, completely understanding the gift she just gave them. Theodore belonged to her. So did Ruby and Adelaide, as leverage against the boy. The peculiar war chant continued as Bianca sent them to battle.

"Kill the rest."

Chapter 47

Theodore and Ruby were in the bay when the shield broke. They raced back to the docks to warn the others but it was not fast enough. Barely ten minutes passed before the ghosts were soaring toward Nether Isle, ready to attack. A loud whistle accompanied their flight as they rocketed into battle.

Bianca was ready to use the Hindi extinguish spell in case she was wrong about the shield, but her army breeched its borders with no trouble at all. They scattered, ready to take on the humans that lined the isle's perimeters.

The Ouijans and Wiccans were as prepared as possible. There was no time to reinstall the shield so their best defense was the banishment spell. Everyone knew it and they hoped it was enough to beat their enemies. The number of ghosts charging toward them was intimidating. They were outnumbered greatly, but with the use of magic, they stood a chance.

Theodore stood with Gretchen, hoping his powers would emit from him naturally. He still wasn't sure how to control them, but after saving Adelaide's life and helping build the shield, he felt more confident his new strengths would appear as needed.

It started to rain as the Ouijans and Wiccans took their final stance, readying for the first wave of impact. Though the rain was steady, it did not distract from the terrifying ordeal that was moments away. Theodore wiped his face as his first opponent approached.

Bernard Gilbert and his dog rushed him. The dead canine bared its teeth and the ghostly shepherd swung his herding staff at Theodore's head. With a blast from his core, Theodore pushed them back, but they fought through.

"Sawyer, herd," Bernard commanded the dog. Sawyer rounded Theodore, trapping him between the two opponents. Theodore widened his stance, hoping to emit magic from both sides of his body. A steady gush of red light poured from his palms, keeping his attackers at bay. Though it worked, it wasn't getting rid of them for good.

Gretchen fought a different opponent next to him. She growled and a surge of white light blasted from her emerald eyes. The power hit the monk she was fighting in the chest, filling him with the light and causing his spiritual figure to crack into a thousand tiny pieces. Having defeated him, she turned to help Theodore.

With both hands, she pushed her magic at his aggressors. Similar to the monk, they filled with white light and exploded.

"You need to use the banishment spell," she reminded him, "While other defenses are great, that is the only way to get rid of them for good. Everything else they can come back from."

The battle was an utter debacle. The numbers were so disproportionate, each Ouijan and Wiccan was forced to take on multiple opponents at a time. Tabitha fought two nuns and another monk to their left. The former religious figures were cloaked in black with only the glow of red eyes visible. In quick procession, she blasted them one at a time. Three seconds later, her attackers vanished.

"One second each," Tabitha panted. "That's how you do it."

"Let's team up. Maybe we can hit them with a wall," Gretchen suggested.

With Theodore in the middle, they took their stances and linked arms with outward palms. A mass of Latin ghosts covered in dirt advanced toward them. Buried then unburied then buried again, the zombie ghosts of La Noria charged. Tabitha counted to three and they combined their powers to strike the group with a single blow. It was so strong, it took out half of them.

"Again," Tabitha shouted over the rain and wind. They recharged and sent a second blast at the crowd. This time, it eliminated the remainder of the Chilean ghosts. The lot cracked along their surfaces and combusted one by one into nothingness.

From afar, Camila screeched with horror as her people perished with finality. She turned her attention to attack those who slaughtered them, but Bianca held her back. With a simple shake of her head, Camila obeyed and took her fury out on the man she currently fought. Virgil Bonhomme made his best attempt at the banishment spell, but Camila fought better. With her new ability to touch the living, she dove for his throat. Her fingers electric with revenge, she ridded him of breath. Eyes wide with shock, Virgil choked on his last gasp of life. He died before getting the chance to warn the others that the ghosts could somehow touch them.

A set of fifty WWII Japanese soldiers crept toward Percival and Delilah. The suicide ghosts crowded behind them as they took down a small group of Civil War soldiers. Wanting a fight, they waited patiently for them to finish. These scorned Japanese soldiers wanted to see the blood of their enemies on their fingertips once more.

Delilah sensed the crowd of shadows forming at her back. She turned and then lunged in for the kill. They pounced on her and Percival, overwhelming them at fifty to two. Pummeling them with brute force, they stood no chance. Their arms were bound and the shock of what was happening prevented them from producing magic. Like a swarm of bees, these ghosts teemed their prey. Rupert and Alastair, the strongest of the lot and the Wiccans most in tune with the dark magic they were taught, raced to their aid. Together, they sent a strong surge of the banishment spell at the throng of spirits. Blast by blast, they slowly chipped away at the pile covering their comrades. As the last ghost disappeared into the light, Rupert and Alastair ran to their fallen friends.

"They can touch us," Percival muttered, weak from the beating. Though he held the strongest magic, he was no match in physical combat. "Warn the others. They cannot let them get close enough to make contact."

Percival sat up, hovered his hands around the crown of his skull, and mumbled beneath his breath. After healing himself, he did the same for Delilah. Rupert and Alastair made their rounds, warning the others that the ghosts were more dangerous than anticipated.

Morgana stood alone at the edge of Tortoise Pier. Silent but raging, a whirlwind circled above her head. As the rest of her crew fought the dead minions on land, she faced Bianca's tribe of powerful females unaided. They cruised toward her without their leader, reveling in the idea that this crazy little human thought she could take them on by herself. Ratnavati led the pack. Her almond eyes narrowed on the red-haired lunatic standing before her. Ming Fai rounded the right side while Irene Saunders covered the left. Camila Fuentes floated overhead and Matilda von Wittlesbach stood behind Ratnavati, acting as backup. Morgana was hopelessly surrounded, but she did not appear to notice the dire situation. The females circled her like sharks, jeering and taunting their prey. Enjoying playing with their food before devouring it. Morgana was too insane to indulge their games; she only stood there, staring blankly ahead. Her face held no emotion, but a war raged inside. Ming Fai was her first victim. She leaned in to touch Morgana, which only caused the Ouijan to unravel. Morgana shrieked into the sky and blasted Ming into the light. The ghost disappeared in a flash.

The other women no longer bided their time. All at once they infiltrated, closing in on Morgana. Unaware of Morgana's quiet insanity, they went after her with recklessness, unprepared for her strength. With no words, only lunacy-filled stares, Morgana cast them off with ease. Whipping her head to the left, she shot Camila a powerful glare that caused her to disintegrate into the light. Two down, three to go. The remaining women were now alarmed and aware they picked a battle better suited for Bianca. Irene Saunders was inches from being struck by Morgana's third blow, but dodged it at the last second. They fled Morgana's wrath, barely escaping in time.

The original crew of Nether Isle ghosts fought together on Periwinkle Pier. Elsa Mordid and Sadie Helf took on Leon Joubert. He fought valiantly, but the women could not be stopped. Not only were they well prepped on the type of magic he'd be using against them, they also now had the ability to make contact with him. The ability to touch changed everything. They could cause him physical harm, and although he could return the contact, he could not kill them again. No amount of punches, chokeholds, or kicks dented their progress. They pummeled him to his knees. Sadie dove in, fists out, and delivered the final blow. Leon's head spun and his body fell off the pier, hitting the rocky shoreline before disappearing into the ocean.

Clementine raced to the scene a moment too late. She watched her friend fall into his grave. Enraged, she mustered up all the darkness hidden inside her and blasted it at the female ghosts. The women absorbed the hit, becoming filled with light as it filtered through their innards. Having died in childbirth, the light collected in their abdomens, recreating the pain from the day they died. The women screamed, both in pain and remembered horror. They cracked apart, slow and deliberately, as the banishment spell cast them away.

Mabel hurried toward Clementine, her white hair bright despite the rain.

"They killed Leon."

"Virgil is dead, too," Mabel added. "With them being able to touch us, our magic isn't enough. We need more bodies. People who can do the fighting so we can focus on the magic."

"The townspeople," Clementine muttered, "I'll have Wilhelmina help me gather them. Turns out they *can* be of assistance." Clementine ran off, helping Wilhelmina defeat a ghost with a scorched head before heading to town.

Mabel went back to Peddler's Way to determine where to help. The scene was chaotic. Two of her comrades were dead. Looking at the fight from afar, she could see the Ouijans were struggling to stay a few steps ahead of the murderous ghosts too. They all were relying on their magical strength to win, not their physical prowess, which paled in comparison. She hoped Clementine and Wilhelmina returned soon with able-bodied soldiers. They needed brute force, people who could stall the ghosts and give them time to work their magic. Currently they were struggling just to stay alive. With help, they could focus on their magic instead of mere survival. Without help, they were sure to lose.

Chapter 48

Lazlo, Lt. Joseph Wheeler, and Matilda stayed close to Bianca's side. From afar, they watched the slaughter. Chester and Eustice, though not of ancient ranking, remained in their elite crew, far from the massacre.

"Are we winning?" Bianca asked Ratnavati and Irene as they returned from a brief scouting trip.

"I think so," Ratnavati answered. "They can't perform their magic while they are fighting to stay alive."

"The townspeople were huddled inland and those on their piers were getting picked off one by one," Irene added.

"Good. We will wait a bit longer before heading in to claim our prize." Bianca's eyes flashed with greed. Land, power, devotion: all of it would be hers by nightfall.

Theodore sat on his heels: left eye swollen shut and a knife wound in his right shoulder. Amos Burndell stood above him. Rain ran like rivers down the scars on his face. He twisted the silver blade in his hand, turning it over methodically between his fingers. It wasn't hard to see he killed many before this same way. He stared at Theodore with no mercy. He sat as easy prey at the old man's feet, but he did not kill him. He waited. Debating how to kill him, or perhaps having some form of an internal dilemma. The old man owed him nothing, so he wasn't sure why he'd feel any pity toward him. Still, he let his life linger on. As the seconds passed in gradual torture, Theodore stopped trying to justify why he was still alive.

"Goddamnit!" Amos shouted and shoved his knife back in its belt holster. "You'd be dead, easily, if I didn't feel obligated to keep ya alive."

Theodore breathed again for the first time after holding it in anticipation of death. Blood spewed onto the ground as he hunched over, trying to regulate the pattern in which this new air left him. It was panicked; he needed it to be calm.

"Lucky, you are," Amos spat, "or maybe not. Probably woulda been a justice had I just killed you now."

"What does that mean?"

"You're being saved for someone else's hand. You'll be dead by the end of the night, just not by me." He knelt down next to Theodore and whispered, his voice taunting, "But if you beg, I'll kill you now and spare you a worse fate."

With a bit of strength back, Theodore hit Amos with a burst of magic. The energy smacked the old man across the face, tossing him backward.

"Goddamn, I wanna kill you," he seethed. "If it was anyone other than that witch commanding I don't, I woulda already."

"How shocking, Bianca wants to kill me."

"Enjoy your last few minutes of life. Your end is on its way." Then he soared off to find another person to kill.

Gretchen and Tabitha were off fighting elsewhere; they left before they knew the ghosts could touch them. Theodore was doing fine on his own, so they went to help Morgana fight the female powerhouses. Looking now, he saw the three Ouijan females conquering a new set of ghosts together.

He needed to be healed so he could fight again. The only magic he knew was that which came from him during intense situations. Simple remedies and menial spells were still foreign. He wasn't sure how to channel the energy that did not stem from desperation.

He trekked to the center of Peddler's Way. After the revelation from Amos, he realized none of the ghosts were going to pick a fight with him. As he walked through the chaos, they avoided him like a plague. Killing him meant disobeying Bianca, which was suicide. They'd be sent straight into the light for stealing her revenge.

Seeing the ghosts look at him with blood in their eyes but unable to attack provided him with a strange peace. He trudged down the boardwalk surrounded by danger, but safe from it. Though the tension in the air was murderous, his assailants remained behind their invisible cages. Some ignored him completely, others wore their devious desires plainly, but all chose not to engage him. The repercussions were not worth it. This backward form of protection was temporary, but he reveled in it nonetheless.

Rowan ran over Terre Bridge first, leading the way for the crowd behind him.

"What are you doing here?" Theodore asked, shocked to see the townspeople approaching the battle.

"We are here to fight," he explained. Reggie, Ryder, and Reese stood at his back. The Linville brothers were wild but steadfast; the only people allowed to cause havoc in their territory was them. "That pretty Wiccan girl came to let us know you guys needed help."

"Wilhelmina?"

"Yeah. We've got the brawn, you've got the fairy dust. Teamwork, buddy." Rowan slapped Theodore on the shoulder before running off to join the quarrel. He shook his head at his friend's insulting joke before watching the rest of his neighbors return to the piers in defense of their home. He was happy to have the assistance. It would surely shift the tides in their favor.

He found Percival standing near Ballantine Dock with Delilah, Caspian, Mabel, and Cynthia. Upon seeing him in his injured state, Mabel fluttered to his side. She guided him to the others, her warm, wrinkled arms around his back.

"How did you procure those wounds?" Percival asked, no sympathy in his voice.

"Amos Burndell."

"Ah, the ghost that lurks behind Nether Inn Tavern."

"Which one is that?" Cynthia's face was scrunched with scrutiny.

"The knife fighter: scars all over his face, always smells like fish and booze. You know him."

"*I* know him," Mabel cut in. "He flirts with me whenever I'm there." The old lady sounded half flattered, half creeped out.

"Yeah, well, he could've finished me off but didn't. Had orders from Bianca to leave me for her."

"So you've dropped to the bottom of the priority list," Percival concluded. A collection of shocked and abashed expressions greeted him, so he added, "for now, at least."

"You really ought to watch your words, Percival," Cynthia clicked her tongue as she scolded him.

"What? The witch ghost hasn't shown up for battle yet. She's still hiding out, waiting till they're winning to strike. When she comes, the kid goes back to the top of the list."

Caspian rolled his eyes then grabbed Theodore's arm. He whispered a Ouijan incantation in French and the laceration on Theodore's shoulder slowly sealed. A few moments later, all that remained of his injury was the wet blood on his shirt and minimal bruising around his eye.

"Thanks, Caspian."

"No problem."

"What are all the locals doing here?" Cynthia asked, lips pursed tight with concerned dislike.

"Wilhelmina and Clementine rallied them," Theodore explained. "They are going to fight while we perform the magic. That way, we aren't doing both. It'll give us the time and space to do what we need to."

"Right on," Caspian said in approval of this executive decision made by the Wiccans.

"Let's get to it then," Percival conceded, unable to diminish the brilliance behind this new strategy.

They rounded all the Wiccans and Ouijans nearby, told them the new plan, and got to work. Theodore ran on his own to the spot where the Linville brothers fought. Their father was there too. Theodore was shocked at the brute force the doctor brawled with. Stripped of his white coat and medical gear, Dr. Roger Linville looked like the scrappy men living along the piers. The sleeveless undershirt he wore revealed the muscles he hid and his veins bulged as he held Davy Gray back. The ghost dressed in American WWII military garb came back at Roger time and time again, never going down or running off. French nurse Marjorie Cadev, another 1950's WWII ghost, took on the Linville boys. They had her circled, but she had no fear. Every attack they made at her, she rebounded without effort, returning a blow of her own, which *did* hurt the boys. Though she was slowing them down, she was not defeating them. They held their ground, keeping her encased and away from Davy and Roger's fight.

Theodore took his stance and channeled his energy. The banishment spell was complicated and required special focus. He did not want to hit his friends, but it needed to be strong enough to cast these evil spirits into the light. Having never performed it alone or on an actual subject before, he gave it his best shot.

Être allé,
dans la lumière.
Toujours loin de la vie.

(Be gone,
into the light.
Forever away from the living.)

A blast of white light fired from his palms and struck Marjorie in the head. In beautiful fashion, she combusted into pieces, crumbling as the light broke her apart.

The Linville boys took a collective gasp, then shared a moment of recuperation. Rowan ran to Theodore's side first.

"Incredible," he panted, "had no clue you were a wizard."

"I'm not." Theodore rolled his eyes. "Go help your dad."

Rowan gathered Reggie, Ryder, and Reese, then led them to their dad's fight. They infiltrated from all sides, catching Davy off guard and giving their father a break. Bombarded by scrappy body slams, Davy faltered. He could not be defeated, but the young boys were certainly winning at holding him back. Theodore recharged and shouted out to his friends after another take down.

"Step away!"

Reggie heard him and relayed the message to his brothers. They all backed up, leaving Davy exposed on the ground. Before he could recover, Theodore launched a second dose of the banishment spell his way. The white light struck Davy in the chest and splintered across his body. A pained expression crossed the ghost's face before the spell consumed him. He was gone.

"Where's Ruby?" Theodore panted.

"She stayed inland with her mom and Adelaide. Only those equipped to fight came," Rowan answered, still out of breath.

"Okay," Theodore said with relief. "Onto the next fight then."

Theodore took a deep breath before they headed onward. Ahead of them was chaos: the piers were littered with wins and defeats. Between the many fights lay the dead, reminding them this night was far from over.

Chapter 49

He ran with the Linvilles toward the largest brawl. Two hundred ghosts with shaved heads, gaunt skeletal bodies, and matching cotton uniforms fought the bulk of the townspeople. Though they looked weak, they were not. Their strength was proven repeatedly as the large living men went easy on them and were tossed back like ragdolls. The ghosts chanted angry words at them in German and Polish.

Roger Linville gasped as he realized who they were about to fight.

"Get them into the light fast," he instructed Theodore, "set them free."

The Linville's ran into the quarrel and Theodore stood back with Tabitha, Alastair, Poe, and Wilhelmina.

"Replace the last line of the chant with, *vous pouvez y trouvez la paix*. It will grant them peace as they depart." Wilhelmina had tears in her eyes as she watched the tortured ghosts fight. Blind by death's grip, they continued the suffering they faced in life rather than departing and finding serenity in a new one.

The Wiccans and Ouijans held hands. The chant echoed despite the rain and carried into the fight. The white light cascading from the spell was soft this time. It filtered through the crowd with delicacy, embracing the ghosts it passed. One by one, the holocaust victims were raveled in light. As it hugged them, their angry faces relaxed and vaporized tears of relief escaped from their eyes. With ease, they dissolved into the light.

Unlike the other banishments so far, this one felt noble. Though it was difficult to witness the continued suffering of those specific ghosts, it felt right to banish them. In this case, the banishment was a gift, not a curse.

"That won't be the last tough one," Tabitha spoke. "There's a group of slaves from the Civil War over there. They deserve the peaceful departure as well."

"Absolutely."

"This whole thing is atrocious," Poe spat. "I can't wait to get my hands on that little witch and destroy her. It's bad enough these ghosts couldn't find peace after their ill-fated lives, but to drag them into this? Pure evil." The veins in Poe's neck spasmed.

"Let's help them first, then deal with the others," Wilhelmina instructed in agreement. They headed to the fight between the Rocky Hill castle ghosts and the townspeople. They joined Rupert, Gretchen, Morton, and Morgana at the edge of the fight to perform the spell. Morton had tears in his eyes as he watched the ghosts fight with short-term awareness. His great-great-grandmother lived during those times and suffered similar fates as theirs. He wanted nothing more than to grant them the peace he gave his own beloved relative when she found him on Nether Isle as a young man.

Être allé,

dans la lumière.

Vous pouvez y trouver la paix.

(Be gone,

into the light.

May you find peace there.)

With so many performing the spell, it entwined around the ghosts much faster. In moments, the spirits of the Civil War slaves left the afterlife with the same serenity as those from the Holocaust. Henry Washington was among them, and as the light cradled him, his muscles relaxed and the weight of his human burden was lifted. He sobbed with rapture as the spell cleared his sight and released him from this continued form of slavery. With a beaming smile, he let the light take him. Peace was on the other side and he was finally ready for it.

"No more niceties," Poe commanded. "The rest don't deserve it."

"You can't assume that. You don't know what battles they fought in their living lives," Wilhelmina corrected him. Poe grunted and stormed away. "Use whichever version of the spell you deem fit," she declared to those remaining.

They broke apart and found new fights to assist in.

Theodore followed Morgana to assist Oscar Dregg in a fight against Amos Burndell, Otis Redd, and Katherine Sutton, the "witch" of the Ancient Ram Inn. Gretchen was the only one there trying to perform the banishment spell so they hurried to help her.

"The butcher is fighting hard," she explained as they approached, "but these ghosts are onto us. They keep dodging my spells."

"They can't dodge all of us," Morgana said as her gaze shifted downward menacingly. Without any prep work, she cast a powerful stream of white light at Katherine Sutton. It was a direct hit and the ghost spouted light out of every orifice before rupturing. Her pieces scattered like ashes into the light.

"One down, two to go." Gretchen and Theodore's mouths were agape as Morgana went on merrily. Oscar paused in his fight, astounded by the disappearance of his opponent. In his moment of halt, enormous fisherman Otis came pummeling through. One elbow to the jaw and Oscar was out cold. Otis and Amos turned toward their easy adversaries standing a few feet away. Morgana, Gretchen, and Theodore readied themselves to produce the spell.

Être allé,
dans la lumière.
Toujours loin de la vie.

The enchantment soared toward the vile ghosts. It would have been the final blow, but they dodged the large, singular blast. It passed between them, hit a reflective mirror on one of the piers directional poles, and came hurtling back at its conjurers.

Theodore and Gretchen ducked in time, but Morgana didn't see the light rebound until it was too late. The spell hit her between the eyes, killing her instantly. Gretchen caught her frail, middle-aged body as it crumpled. Morton saw it happen from afar. With a flick of his wrist, he banished the demon children of Gloucestershire who were in his way and stormed toward the scene of the murder.

He charged forward, nostrils flared and eyes wide in fury. Amos and Otis did not see him yet; they were too focused on killing Gretchen and capturing Theodore to notice their oncoming opponent.

"She was my friend," Morton bellowed with an outstretched hand. Without slowing his pace, he daggered Amos through the back of his heart with a shard of light. The old knife-fighter fell to his knees in shock as his body fractured and glowed through the crevices. Otis took a step away from him as his spirit broke into pieces and vanished into the light.

"You're next," Morton seethed, aiming his open palm toward the oversized fisherman. Otis turned to run but was not fast enough. The banishment spell hit the side of his face, and the multi-world components of the magic caught his beard on fire. Otis shrieked in a high-pitched voice, flailing about in an attempt to extinguish the intangible flames. The white fire crept into his mouth and slithered down his throat, silencing his screams. The light ran its course through his body until it consumed him. They watched him melt into nothing.

Morton ran to Morgana's side and knelt with her in his arms.

"She was my friend. I was supposed to protect her," he said solemnly, "and I failed."

"It's not your fault." Gretchen put a hand on his shoulder. "She was strong. What happened was an accident. It could have happened to any of us."

Morton shook his head and stood up, carrying Morgana's lifeless body in his large arms. "I am going to take her back to the house. There is only one large group left to fight. You two and the others should be able to handle them with ease."

"Okay, take her home. We will mourn her together once this battle is won," Gretchen said. Morton nodded and departed.

In the middle of Peddler's Way, Percival led the repetition of the enchantment as the majority of the locals fought valiantly against the ghosts of Bhangarh Fort. Princess Ratnavati was nowhere to be found, but her people attacked the living with ruthless force.

"Once we defeat this batch, all that's left is Bianca and whoever she keeps closest," Delilah said during a brief break in the chant. They needed a breather to rejuvenate their energy. Theodore and

Gretchen joined in once they began again. The power coming from them was strong, but there were so many ghosts below, it took a while for the magic to find and latch onto them. Many times, the light fizzled out before it reached its target. The Wiccans and Ouijans kept firm grips on each other's hands as they continued their effort. They observed the fight as they chanted, watching the locals scuffle with opponents that could not be defeated. They dished out brute force, calculated blows, and all the power they could muster, but it was never enough. It never would be. In death, they could only be defeated by magic. A power capable of reaching them in their realm and affecting them there.

The ghosts of Bhangarh Fort fought with pretentious entitlement, as if their cause was valiant. The vigor with which they defended themselves led Theodore to believe they truly thought their actions were just. That they had a right to this land and killing its current inhabitants. Bianca did a number on these souls to convince them they had any claim over living land, that they were justified in taking something that was not theirs. Completely brainwashed, the spirits fought on, slaughtering innocent townsfolk as they pushed forward.

Être allé,
dans la lumière.
Toujours loin de la vie.

The banishment spell was gaining intensity and its power filtered through the crowd, latching onto the intended targets. The ghosts fell victim to the spell, one by one breaking apart into the light. It took some time, but by nightfall, they were all gone.

After the last enemy spirit vanished, the Ouijans and Wiccans collectively gasped and released their concentration. The chant ceased abruptly and the individuals dispersed to catch their breath. Some fell to their knees, others sat on the ground, and many walked away in order to be alone. Theodore remained, observing the casualties that lay before him as he calmed the pace of his heart.

Everyone around him drifted apart, wandering off in their own direction as they dealt with the shock. Death surrounded them quite literally: the dead they had just banished and the newly deceased scattered along the pier. Theodore hoped his fallen neighbors chose to enter the light rather than linger here.

Their fight was far from over. The instigator of this bloodshed still roamed free. Hatred for his former friend silenced his distress. The only way to avenge the fallen and prevent further suffering was to eliminate the cause.

Chapter 50

The moon was rising and the battle was won, Bianca was sure of it. Enough time had passed and she was certain her ghosts prevailed. She soared beneath the starry sky toward Nether Isle, her crew following close behind.

The scene she arrived to was far from what she expected. Dead humans were a given, but no ghosts? None of her army remained.

"Where did they go?" she demanded, confused why they did not stay after defeating the living.

"They would not have left," Ratnavati proclaimed. "My people would have waited."

"So would ours," Matilda added defensively. "Those we recruited were loyal. This must be some form of miscommunication."

"Maybe they went back to Cross Island," Eustice suggested in a whisper. "If I was done fightin' and had no clue what to do next, I'd have gone back to the home base. To look for further instruction from you."

Bianca huffed, "That's honorable, but we would have seen them. That's where we came from. Either on the island or on our journey here, we would have crossed paths."

"Too many still remain," Chester said as he observed the chaos below. "Look how many are still alive."

445

Bianca's breathing quickened, heavy in its false existence. She scanned the pier, noticing that Chester was correct. They should all be dead, but they weren't. They walked about with air in their lungs and relief on their faces. It only took a moment before she realized she was defeated. Somehow, they won. Though she could rally and come back stronger, the instant this loss became reality, her mind went haywire. Splintered vision frayed her sight, letting her see mere fragments of the world before her. Her army was vanquished, her plans were delayed, and the certainty she armed and armored herself with was destroyed. It didn't make sense.

She charged forward, leaving the others behind. With no purpose, no set path, she flew. Trying to ascertain any incoherent slivers of reality she could grab. Her fury ruined all chance of rational thinking; no plausible alternatives to remedy this mess would grace her now. Only anger fueled her. Within the bits of land she saw through rage-stricken vision were humans walking free. Living people on her land. Breathing, taunting her existence in death. For every breath they took, her wrath intensified. They mocked her.

Everything turned red, a hue reflecting her madness. With only a streak of reality in sight, she plummeted toward the ground, grabbing the only neck she saw. As she crushed its airway, a foreign roar emerged from her gut. Panting from the overwhelming anger she felt, she raised the nameless body and scanned its face. It wasn't who she hoped it would be.

Theodore.

She tossed the unidentified corpse to the floor.

Theodore.

It was the only word she could think of and it repeatedly rang through her mind.

Theodore.

The day would not end without a victory.

Chapter 51

Theodore searched the skies, searched the space around him for Bianca. He searched for her ghost but she was nowhere to be found. Desperate to end this once and for all, he ran, frantic and determined. No one else should suffer because of her.

Adelaide returned to Peddler's Way from the mainland. She stood, unafraid, by her home.

"You shouldn't be here. It's not over yet," Theodore expressed as he paused his sprint to address her.

"Looks over to me."

"Well, it's not. Bianca is still out there somewhere. And now, all the Ouijans and Wiccans are separated. This is quite possibly the *most* dangerous moment to be here."

"I'll stay inside, don't fret about me, kid." But as the words left her mouth, a frigid breeze crossed them. A shiver halted his guard and Adelaide was gone. Panicked, Theodore looked all around him. It happened so fast it was as though she vanished with the wind. If he didn't believe in magic, he'd assume it impossible, but with all that shifted in his perception of reality, it was plausible. So he ran in the direction of the breeze.

At the end of Ballantine Dock, he saw her. She stood trapped in the arms of a ghost. He could see the glowing shape behind her but was too far away to make out the face. He raced toward them until a voice shouted that he stop.

"Stay where you are!"

It was Bianca. Close enough now, he could see her evil eyes peering over Adelaide's shoulder. His old friend acted as her shield, no magic he cast would hit its intended target.

"I wanted to kill you, but the more I thought about it, the more I realized it wasn't sufficient enough. Death wasn't the right punishment. I want to watch you suffer." She took a step closer to the edge of the dock, a step closer to falling with Adelaide into the raging tide.

"What do you want from me?" Theodore pleaded. "I'll do anything, just let her go."

"There's nothing I want from you, not anymore. You ruined those plans."

"Take my body. I'll surrender it to you."

Bianca laughed, "I don't want your body. I don't want any body. Though you thwarted my plans, your disloyalty directed me toward a greater cause, my true calling. Now, I want land and followers. I want power. I want to reign over the afterlife."

"Then do it, just leave us out of it."

"Impossible. You dwell where I want to reside." She took another step closer to the ocean. "And you refuse to leave."

"Release her and we will go. We will let you have this place."

"If that were true, you all would have vacated the moment my army arrived. Instead, you fought back. You even won," she snickered, "but this little victory is minor. It is temporary. I will conquer Nether Isle and all its living inhabitants. But before I do, I want to watch you suffer. I want to crush your spirit, break your heart. Make you so alone on this planet that you'll beg for death."

Theodore was appalled. He did not know what to say, did not know how to reason with a lunatic. He had to save Adelaide. He had to save his family. She was right: he would slip into lifeless despair if he lost the only person who loved him back. But she couldn't know this. She had to believe her assumptions were wrong.

"This old woman does not hold such power over me. She's my boss. Yeah, she helped me out a lot. Yeah, I want her alive and would be sad if she died, but I would never beg for death just because you killed her. That's crazy."

Bianca's sureness faltered. "And what about Ruby?"

"Ruby? I haven't even known her a full year. Do you think I'm that desperate? I don't cling to people. You should know how good I am at being alone. We were friends once, if you don't recall. I told you all about it."

Bianca's nostrils flared. Her eyes darted back and forth as she tried to determine her next move. She doubted herself, doubted her assumptions about the boy she used to care for. As Theodore began to believe he fooled her, Bianca's expression shifted again.

"I suppose one only knows if they try." Then she shoved Adelaide over the side of the dock. His old friend screamed as she plunged into the storm waves below.

"The choice is yours: save her or fight me."

"I choose both." Theodore could no longer contain his fear. With a blast of furious energy, he struck Bianca in the stomach. She soared backward with a laugh.

"You'll never beat me. You aren't strong enough. And let's say you do," she jeered, "the old hag will be dead before you figure out how." Bianca sent a stream of magic at Theodore, swiping the side of his head. His sandy hair fizzled as its edges burned. Death blows; Bianca wasn't holding back.

He could hear Adelaide's drowning screams, choked by water as she tried to stay afloat. Her agony fueled him, the time ticking away acted as brilliant motivation. He would save her, he had no doubt. The love he felt for his adopted family member meshed with his hatred for Bianca. The combination proved lethal as he concentrated and aimed his stance toward his enemy. Accompanied by a guttural howl, Theodore directed his best shot at her. The white light poured from his palms, stronger than any stream he'd sent all day. The powerful emotions that coursed through it were volatile, enhancing the intensity of the spell. Bianca saw it coming toward her, but did not move. She planned to block it, but underestimated his strength. The light pierced her heart.

Eyes wide as the painful light coursed through her spirit veins, Bianca gave him her old look of utter betrayal. He walked toward her and watched as the white glow cracked her skin apart.

"I owe you nothing." He breathed heavy.

She tried to speak but only light exited her mouth. Her last words were lost as her body erupted into a thousand tiny light particles. The storm carried her away without grace or mercy. A forever goodbye: one Theodore was quite content with.

Without further delay, he ran to the edge of the dock, grabbed a life preserver from a nearby pole, and dove in. A great swimmer, he made it to Adelaide fast. She was almost under, but she held on a few moments longer so he could reach her and share the floatation device with her. She was hooked on and sturdily above water. She was going to be okay.

Theodore swam, pulling them both toward the dock. The personal buoy was still attached to a rope tied to the dock, which helped in his fight against the sea. His young muscles ached as he fought nature to save his friend. When he reached the nearest ladder he dragged her to safety. Together, they fought the violent waves and latched onto the wooden beams of the dock. Theodore climbed up, remaining knee deep in ocean water, and grabbed her hand. Yanking her toward him, they embraced briefly before he helped her onto the ladder and assisted her up. He climbed close behind, making sure she did not fall.

It was over. The fight was won. They could breathe easy again. As he climbed toward a good night's sleep, Adelaide ascended the last few rungs with unnatural speed. She disappeared before his eyes. Alarmed, he sped up, afraid what new horror he was about to encounter.

Chapter 52

When his eyes crossed the edge of the pier, he saw Adelaide locked firmly in Chester's grasp.

"Dad," he screamed, "what are you doing?"

"You don't get to be happy," his father scoffed back. His dead eyes narrowed in on his son. "You don't get to have a family."

Without a blink, Chester snapped Adelaide's neck.

Theodore's voice cracked and his shouts came out as sobs. He fell to his knees next to Adelaide's dead body. He didn't get to say goodbye. His fingers laced behind the nape of her neck and he gently lifted her head. Gone. Cold and departed. Tears streamed down his cheeks but he couldn't feel them, they blended with the rain.

He shifted his bloodshot gaze back to his father, who looked on with a grin. A rage he never felt before rose from the pit of his gut. He shook, hands trembling and vision blurred.

"You." The words barely came out. "I hate you."

"Shoulda killed you when you was a baby, when you couldn't fight back. Missed opportunity on my part."

Years of suppressed anger blasted from his palms. The red surge of energy lassoed Chester's neck, choking him in his realm. Theodore tightened its grip with unyielding confidence. His father would haunt him no more.

"The worst part about you is that I loved you through it all. Despite your abuse, despite the foul way you treated me, despite the fact that you never loved me back. I spent my entire childhood trying to find a way to make you value me. Hoping that one day, if I worked hard enough for your affection, you'd eventually learn to love me." A chilled current shot up his spine. "Wasted time."

"Can't love a little leech like you," Chester whispered, his voice hoarse from the intangible rope strangling him. "You ruined my life. Stole all my freedom. This old bag woulda seen it one day too. She woulda let you down. Gone away. Left you once she realized you ain't blood and she owed you nothin'. You can't be loved."

"You're wrong. We might not have been blood, but she was the best family I'd ever known. She was all I had left, and you stole her from me. Your reign of terror over me is through."

He held his father up with his left hand and with his right, he aimed a cannon blast of the banishment spell at his father's face. He merely thought of the chant, felt its repetition ripple through his veins, and the magic arrived in abundance. It mutilated his father, ripping him apart limb by limb. The light sliced him to pieces, devouring him within seconds. Chester's screams of pain echoed as it tore him apart. The light ate him, chewing viciously before swallowing.

He was gone.

Overwhelming grief consumed Theodore, leaving his body in a howl. The noise coming from him was unfamiliar. His sobs were feral, as if coming from a wild animal rather than a boy of fifteen.

He fell to his knees and cradled Adelaide in his arms. A forever goodbye: one he was not content with.

Eustice stood behind them, staring intently at his wife's corpse. After a moment, Theodore noticed him there.

"Go away!"

But Eustice remained. Rocking back and forth on his heels, waiting for something beyond Theodore's comprehension.

"Come to me, come to me," the old ghost whispered in repetition. He hovered nearby as Theodore tried to find closure. He kept a safe distance, knowing the boy's emotions were unstable and lethal, but he would not leave them be. He had his own desires in mind and he'd wait with patience for deliverance.

An hour passed. Theodore could not, would not, leave Adelaide's side. It felt wrong to leave her there, to leave her at all. She shouldn't be dead, she should be there with him. This wasn't right and there was nothing he could do to fix it. His insides were stripped bare, tissue exposed and raw. The smallest flicker of more bad news would slaughter him. There wasn't an ounce of self-preservation left in his body, no strength left to protect him. The weight felt so heavy he was surprised it hadn't pushed him below sea-level, drowning him with finality rather than making him bear the burden with full lungs.

"What are you doing?" a raspy voice shouted to him from behind. Theodore looked up, face swollen and eyes red. He turned to see Adelaide hovering a few feet away. Dead, but there.

"I'm sorry," he pleaded, "I'm so sorry."

"Stop it," she demanded, "stop it this instant. I'm only dead."

Theodore looked at her confused. "It's my fault. I thought I saved you, I forgot I had other ghosts out there that resented me as much as Bianca did. I should have thought it through."

"It's not your fault. This is war, crap like this happens. And if it didn't happen today, it woulda happened in the near future. I was old, in case you forgot. Probably only had a few good years left anyway."

"But we should have spent them together, as family. This is wrong. It shouldn't have happened like this."

"Maybe not, but there's no changing it now. I'm glad you care for me so much, but it's time you get up and move on. You've got a long life ahead of you, you can't carry on if you don't let go of the sadness."

"You're going to leave now, aren't you?"

"Yes."

"Please stay here with me."

"No." Firm but kind, her expression was soft.

"Why?" Though Theodore had grown into a man at a very young age, his youth poured from his eyes as he pleaded with her.

"After all this time you must have learned the living world is no place for the dead."

"I need you," he tried to hold back the tears. "Everyone goes away. I need you to stay. I don't think I can handle being alone again. Not after you. Not after the warmth and kindness you showed me."

"Now you know it exists, you just have to look for it elsewhere. Train your eye to find it. Look in the right places. It's all around you."

"It's not about finding new people, it's about losing you."

"I get it. I really do. I just can't find peace unless I know you're going to be okay. You're the strongest little man I know, far too weathered for your age but all the wiser for it. You're special. Your soul exists on a different level than the rest. I need to know you'll be okay, that this won't break you. Because it shouldn't. Miss me, love me, remember me always, but do not mourn me daily. We are family and I'll see you again one day. Let me find peace until we meet again."

Though it was difficult, he nodded, "I want you to find peace. I'll be okay."

"Thank you."

"Save a place for me on the other side."

"You're among the best people I've ever known. I'm saving you a seat right next to me."

Theodore smiled. Neither could guarantee they'd meet again because no one knew what happened after you crossed into the light, but the idea that they might helped Theodore let go.

"Leave my body. Seeing it there after I go won't help you any. Someone else can collect it and bring it into town. That's not your job."

Theodore cringed, looking at her human body laying lifeless on the boardwalk. He soaked in the reality one last time.

"Follow me," she said with gentle resolve, "I'll help you walk away."

Together they walked back to Peddler's Way. A crowd of people were gathered: those who fought and those who returned from the mainland now that the battle was won. Ruby and her mother stood with the Linville family. Her wild, blonde hair whipped as she snapped her head in his direction, sensing Theodore's presence.

"This is good," he said with a faint smile at Ruby, "She'll want to say good-bye, too." He spoke to Adelaide, but when he turned to look at her, she was already gone. His chest tightened. He searched the sky, hoping to see her light as she departed. Instead, a folded note fluttered toward him. He caught it, opened it, and read its contents.

This is my goodbye. It's not the forever kind. I expect great stories when I see you again.

Love,

Adie

He didn't know how she did it, but he was grateful. The note would stay with him forever.

Ruby called out to him, quickening her pace to reach him. "You look like a mess."

He looked at the parts of himself he could see for the first time. His clothes were covered in blood, his own and others. His hands still shook and he could only imagine the gross state of his swollen and bruised face.

"It's been a rough day."

Ruby paused before speaking again with hushed empathy, "Have you been crying?"

He wanted to deny it, on any other day he would have, but today it seemed warranted.

"Adelaide is dead."

"What?" Ruby gasped, eyes filling with tears. "How? She was on the mainland during the whole fight."

"She came back before it was over. Bianca wasn't banished yet. She tried to kill her to get back at me. Lots happened, but in the end, I stopped and banished her. Then I let my guard down, thinking we were finally safe, and my dad got Adelaide. He snapped her neck. Said I wasn't allowed to have a family."

"I'm so sorry," Ruby stammered through the tears. She threw her arms around Theodore and buried her tears in his shoulder. They stayed like this for a few moments, safe in each other's arms. When she let go, her face was puffy from crying. "I don't know how you stay so strong. Life keeps slamming you. I'd be exhausted."

"I am exhausted. I was in a fetal position, ready to give up an hour ago. But that's not who I am. Adelaide came to me before entering the light and reminded me of that. Reminded me I'm programmed to survive."

"She's right." She wiped the tears from her cheeks. "I'm glad she knocked some sense into you. I can sympathize with moments of weakness, but not with giving up. I'd never forgive you if you did."

"Well, you don't need to worry about that. I'm here to stay."

"Good." Ruby was a mess as she collected her emotions. "I need you."

She stormed back toward the crowd.

Theodore followed her, taking in the scene as he approached.

461

"Welcome back, buddy," Rowan said, throwing an arm around his friend. "Been a rough one. Glad you're not a comatose sack of organs."

"You really have a way with words." Theodore shook his head, aware that for a few minutes there, he was no better than comatose. Seeing the faces that greeted him now, he realized Adelaide was right. There was plenty of kindness hidden in this dim and rotten town. He just needed to find it.

Gretchen smiled and waved at him from afar, surrounded by her fellow Ouijans. The Wiccans stood amongst them, chatting and socializing with their old foe. He wondered if their elongated hatred for one another might simmer after this collective victory. Based on their behavior now, there was hope it might.

He looked toward the sea. Ghosts with allegiance to Bianca still lingered outside the borders of Nether Isle, but with their magical leader gone, the threat of them seemed minimal. Time would tell if that was true, but for now, the fight was over.

The town rejoiced at the conclusion of battle. For the first time since he lived there, the majority of the people wore smiles. Everyone was in a good mood, no one was acting shifty or underhanded in order to survive the day. This time, they survived it together. Survived it through teamwork. Though it may not last, Theodore was happy his neighbors got a taste of how good camaraderie tasted. They were sure to go back to their selfish ways by the time the tides turned, but at least they saw it was possible to band together. In the direst of times, they realized that other people were a source to turn to, that neighbors would help neighbors, and that they didn't always have to go it alone.

Thank you for reading Nether Isle – I hope you enjoyed it! If you have a moment, please consider rating and reviewing it on Amazon and sharing your thoughts with me via social media. All feedback is greatly appreciated!

Amazon Author Account:
www.amazon.com/author/nicolineevans

Facebook:
www.facebook.com/nicoline.eva

Twitter:
www.twitter.com/nicolineevans

Goodreads:
www.goodreads.com/author/show/7814308.Nicoline_Evans

Instagram:
www.instagram.com/nicolinenovels

To learn more about my other novels, please visit my official author website:
www.nicolineevans.com

Made in the USA
Columbia, SC
10 November 2018